THE WINNER

A Ballroom Dance Novel

ERIN BOMBOY

Curtain Call Press

Published by Curtain Call Press

Publisher's Note: This is a work of fiction. Names, characters, places, and incidents are a product of the author's imagination. Locales and public names are sometimes used for atmospheric purposes. Any resemblance to actual people, living or dead, or to businesses, companies, events, institutions, or locales is completely coincidental.

The Winner/ Erin Bomboy. -- 1st ed.

Print ISBN 978-0-9984830-3-0

Ebook ISBN 978-0-9984830-4-7

For my husband, who hasn't read this nor most of the other words I've written, yet remains my most ardent supporter. Thank you for the rosé wine, the daddy daycare, and for believing me when I told you it was important that I write this and that I write it now.

Chapter 1

NINA: THE RUSSIAN INVASION

LAST YEAR, we won.

It wasn't even a big deal, a small ballroom competition, located in downtown Baltimore at a Hyatt and attended by a few local couples. We sailed in on a sweet May breeze, husband-and-wife Oleg and Nina from New York, former Rising Star champions and current US bronze medalists. We collected everything that came with being a winner: money, medals, accolades.

This year, we weren't recalled to the final.

We stood by the side of the dance floor, a pond of golden parquet, as six couples strode past us with fixed, determined smiles. The men, dapper in tail suits, and the women, glittering in rhinestone-encrusted dresses, stationed themselves around the floor. Judges, dressed up (but not to kill, their quick-swiping pencils were for that), lifted their clipboards.

"Competitors," said the Master of Ceremonies in a stately tone. "Your first dance is Waltz."

An airy melody anchored by a slow, distinctive 3/4 rhythm filled the ballroom. The six couples took dance position, an embrace of authority for the man, one of capitulation for the woman. Because it was Standard, the oldest and most conservative of the ballroom dance styles, couples' arms would stay clasped as feet braided themselves in intricate patterns.

On the floor, the duos swept into languorous pivots, right thighs pressed together as their left legs traced semi-circles. It was beautiful in the way geometry was: resolved, rational, flesh evenly distributed between points and lines. Equation on the bottom, solution on top.

"There's been a mistake," I hissed to Oleg.

"No mistake," he said.

"I'm going to ask Papa."

Papa (born Constantine Papadopoulos, known to the world as Papa, save his wife, Maxine, who called him Stan) was the Chairman of the Judges. He was sitting in front of a calculator, shredding the score sheets from the semifinal. Once he saw me, he'd realize that he'd miscalculated the judges' recall marks.

Oleg roped his arm around my waist. "No."

"Yes."

The Waltz music drifted to a close. Applause greeted the six couples as they bowed.

"Your next dance is Tango," intoned the Master of Ceremonies.

A strident march boomed through the ballroom. A couple—eyes narrowed, lips snarling—executed a thorny chain of stamps and points a dozen feet away from us. They were good, and that was the problem.

Maxine, our coach, found us. "Let's get out of here," she said.

Oleg placed his hand on the small of my back and pushed me out of the ballroom. I kept my chin high and willed my bottom lip still, but I couldn't ignore the sympathetic smiles being thrown our way by those who remembered our win last year.

Maxine led us to a quiet sofa in the lobby. Guests in dark suits and harried expressions eyeballed us as they walked by, their brows arched in wonder. They'd checked into this hotel expecting sober industry and profitable enterprise. Instead, they'd stumbled upon a ballroom dance competition, and they didn't know what to make of all the sparkles and liveliness.

"The jig is up," Maxine said. "You need to retire. Immediately."

It'd been happening for years, couples emigrating from Eastern Europe, seeking the American dream in the form of Foxtrots and Cha Chas. In the last year, the floodgates had opened. Millennial carpetbaggers, carrying dresses made by their babushkas and flaunting talents honed since before they could walk, invaded Standard and Latin, the two divisions practiced around the world. The American style—Smooth—stayed safe, too theatrical and homegrown to be of interest.

The Russian invasion wasn't worrisome at first. A few marks here, a dance there. But now we were in a death spiral. Small backwater competitions that used to have barely enough competitors to fill a six-couple final swelled to semifinals and quarterfinals of Russian names.

Oleg and I, the original *Russkis,* had started in our teens. We were gifted and hardworking enough to rise high in the United States where Standard, with its emphasis on picky technique and old-fashioned formality, failed to excite.

But confronted with these Eastern European youths who'd started as tots, chipping away at bad habits to arrive in young adulthood ready to soar, Oleg and I foundered.

“But it's our year to win Nationals," I said and then stomped my right foot, which caused my knee to moan. The arthritis had been acting up for a while although it hadn’t gotten bad enough for me to worry about.

The previous Nationals, we’d placed third in the Open Standard division and could call ourselves second as the current second-place couple had quit due to the female partner’s anorexia.

Judges didn't like that sort of thing. Ballroom wasn't ballet, and a stick in a glittery dress caused revulsion rather than reverence. Rumor held the current champions were retiring, which left first place wide open. I could practically feel the gold medal swing around my neck, a decade’s worth of sweat and sacrifices rewarded.

Oleg ran an exasperated hand through his dark hair "Nina will not listen to reason.”

“There’s no reason to listen to,” I said. “Winners retire. Everyone else quits.”

We’d been arguing for months over retiring. Our marriage, a tranquil decade spent dancing and living with our hearts turned toward each other, had smashed upon the rocks of thwarted ambition.

"You’re not winning Nationals,” Maxine said.

"What if we took a year off to practice?" I asked.

I was finding it hard to face the truth. I'd devoted the last ten years of my life to winning Nationals. Third place wasn’t good enough. Who remembered third?

Maxine pursed her lips. "You're not winning Nationals. Not this year, not any other year. Retire. Do a pretty Waltz at Nationals to celebrate your career and move on with your life."

"We will retire," Oleg said.

"We will not retire." I shook my head, which caused my rhinestone earrings to wag back and forth. One snagged on my upswept hair. I narrowed my eyes at Oleg as I loosened the shiny teardrop.

Maxine sighed. "It's your decision."

She gave us a hug and then left us to find Papa, her husband. "Stan needs help packing up," she said.

Oleg stood and offered his hand. "Let's go."

"I'm not quitting."

"I am," Oleg said. "I am thirty-two, and I am not getting any younger. Let's quit while we are ahead."

I glared at him. "How can you give up? We're so close."

"Last year, we were close. This year, we are far away, and we aren't getting closer."

"I want to win."

Oleg turned to leave. "I am heading up. Knock when you have faced facts."

"I'm going to win," I said as he walked away. "I will win."

Chapter 2

CARLY: STEPPING IN

DOING the wrong thing was not supposed to make me this happy.

There was what I should be doing: working at the ice cream parlor in the small Ohio town I'd grown up in; helping my parents out with Archer, my fourteen-year-old autistic brother; and taking a class or two to chip away at the requirements for my bachelor's degree in special education.

Here's what I was doing—teaching ballroom dancing in New York City.

I blamed it on the ad. One April morning, spitting rain and downright cold, I'd cut through the dance department on my way to a psychology class. I did this often although it didn't save any time. I did it because I loved catching glimpses of the classes. Lines of ballerinas, hair scraped into buns, arranging their legs and arms into acute and obtuse angles. Modern dancers with shaggy ponytails and baggy t-shirts rolling on and sliding across the floor. The odd African class with its infectious drumming and stomping.

I yearned to join them. I'd danced at the local studio until I was fourteen but stopped when my parents needed my help with Archer, whose low-functioning autism required almost constant support. I'd tried to be a good sport about it, but I still danced in my dreams.

That day, I stopped near a bulletin board thumbtacked with audition notices and performance fliers. An ad featuring a man in a tuxedo and a woman in a glittery dress caught my eye.

Sleep in and dance all night in New York, New York.
The Vernon and Irene Castle School of Ballroom Dancing seeks summer instructors to teach wedding couples their first dance.

At the bottom, a name and number to call plus the motto of the studio: *Step in to step out.*

I stepped in with both feet, right then and there, expecting nothing.

What I got was everything.

I spoke to Ralph, the studio owner. He explained the gig, three months of teaching couples how to do the basics for their weddings.

"We put you up for a week in a hotel and train you. You've gotta dance background, so you'll pick up quick. At the end, if it's not working out, we part ways, no hard feelings. If you're good and I'm good, you can hit the floor and start teaching. We've gotta deal with one of the universities, and you can live in a dorm room on the cheap," he told me.

Without thinking, I said yes.

And now, it was another ordinary day in my new extraordinary life.

I slept in, an enormous treat. For as long as I could remember, I'd woken up early. My dad, who stayed up when Archer couldn't sleep, which was most nights, catnapped while my mom changed Archer's diaper and got him dressed. I made a breakfast of gooey oatmeal, the only way Archer would eat it, and a banana smoothie, the only way Archer would touch fruit.

In New York, I had a leisurely breakfast of bagels and coffee before taking the subway, which still exhilarated me with its opportunities for people watching, to the studio in Midtown where I taught students box steps and rock steps and fancy walking steps for their weddings.

The work was engaging but not difficult, and the students, except for a few snippy bridezillas, were pleasant. Time flew, and before I knew it, I'd be on the subway back to my tiny but surprisingly nice dorm room in the East Village.

I loved working at the Castle, the nickname by which the studio was known. Its namesakes, Vernon and Irene Castle, were a famous duo in the early 20th century who'd refined the Foxtrot and classed up the Tango.

The Castle was different from any dance studio I'd ever been in. Without fail, most dance studios were depressing places with stained walls, splintery barres, and fluorescent lighting that made everyone look sepulchral.

The Castle, though, was beautiful. A sheet of caramel-colored wood fanned across the floor, and from the ceiling, a quartet of chandeliers, beaded like a flapper's dress, made everything gleam. The walls were papered in a soothing cream shadow stripe, and benches, upholstered in the same shade, lined the perimeter. It resembled a hotel lobby: elegant, rich, inoffensive.

It was hard to imagine people getting into the sweaty, grueling, and often embarrassing work of dancing, but that's what we did here.

Although I was busy with my wedding couples, I found plenty of time to park myself on a bench and watch the advanced dancers. If he were free, Sam, the other teacher Ralph had hired, would hang out with me.

Sam was from Texas, and he spoke with a slight twang that I found adorable. He was tall and gangly, but he moved with natural, silken grace.

"How do you get that good?" I asked as a couple swept by us to a breezy Frank Sinatra song. Their feet skated across the floor in a straight line while their torsos swayed toward the wall and then leveled out. It was the Feather Step, a signature pattern of Standard Foxtrot.

"Practice," Sam said. He ran his hand through his hair, dark red and bushy, like a pile of fall leaves. "Lots of it."

I longed for an opportunity to get that good. Teaching wedding couples was fun, but it didn't require me to know much more than the basics. And since all I taught were wedding couples, I had no need to learn more than I already did.

I sighed, but it was a small, inconsequential one. I was happy in New York.

My parents were livid when I told them of my summer plans. "Ballroom dancing in New York City?" they'd asked. "What about your studies? What about Archer? We need you here."

I didn't have a good rebuttal, so I'd stayed mute and accepted the darts of guilt they hurled at me.

They were right. I was needed there. It took all three of us to manage Archer, whose extensive needs dictated our days, plus keep up with the demands of everyday life: dinner, laundry, tidying up.

Neither of my parents made much money, and my hometown in Ohio offered little support for autistic kids. I was the support they relied on.

"It's just for the summer," I said lamely. "Like camp, but I'll be getting paid." I'd never been to a sleep-away camp, but it was the best analogy I could find.

It'd been weeks, and they were still upset with me. I'd taken to emailing rather than calling them, so I didn't have to hear the disappointment sharpening their voices.

Day by day, week by week, my old life in Ohio felt further and further away, less and less appealing. I admitted to myself what I'd known since my first day in New York. I wanted to stay.

But how?

When summer ended, so did the job.

Chapter 3

NINA: THE ULTIMATUM

MAXINE HAD TRIED. Oleg had tried. But I refused to see reason. Then I did something stupid. The day after we returned from Baltimore, I challenged Oleg.

"If you won't dance with me, then I'll find someone who will."

Oleg sighed and shook his head.

"What would you have us do?" I asked.

"Open franchise of the Castle."

"Where?" The Castle was a chain of dance studios in the northeast, and most of the big cities were taken.

He thrust his chest out proudly. "Charlotte, North Carolina."

I gaped at him. "Your big plan is for us to move to Charlotte, North Carolina and open a franchise of the Castle?"

"I have done research. It is fastest growing city in United States. We make out big time."

"Can you see us in Charlotte, North Carolina? Two Big-Apple *Russkis* in the South?"

He smiled, a big, shiny one. "You were born in US. And I have been here twenty years," he said. "I am citizen."

A citizen who still drops his articles, I thought.

"It will be nice. Big home with yard. Lots of space." Oleg reached out and rubbed my belly. "For baby." His eyes were glistening. "American dream come true."

"Winning Nationals is my American dream," I said. "My mother scrimped and pinched and saved, so I could become a champion."

"It is your life, not your mother's."

"Do you know how many times I've heard her say, 'One day, my daughter will be winner. From cleaning lady to champion in one generation.'" I said in a passable imitation of my mother's accent. "That's why she came to America. Her life is my life." I glared at Oleg.

I'd worked hard for years to make it come true, and Oleg was acting like a starting a family in a split-level ranch house in a city I couldn't find on a map was some fabulous consolation prize. I shuddered at telling my mother we'd retired before winning Nationals.

"She might forget when she has grandchild."

"My mother doesn't forget. Besides, we can start a family down the road." I paused. "After we've won Nationals." I swept into the bedroom "See you at practice tomorrow," I said over my shoulder.

"I am not coming to practice tomorrow." Oleg flipped open his laptop. "Or day after. Or day after that day."

I pivoted on my heel to face Oleg. "Then don't bother coming home."

He looked at me over the top of his computer. "Do not be silly."

I placed my hands on my hips. "I'm not being silly. If you're not dancing with me, then you're not sleeping with me," I said. "So don't bother coming home if you don't go to practice." I paused and then added for effect. "Ever."

Oleg's eyebrows shot up. "Are you serious?"

I tossed my hair. "I wouldn't say it if I wasn't serious."

I rose early as I always did and made coffee. I drank a cup while waiting for Oleg to get up. When it was time for us to leave for practice, he was still asleep. I called his bluff. I left for the studio.

I wasn't worried. It wasn't unusual for me to go in a little earlier than Oleg. He enjoyed sleeping in and then getting ready in a frenzy of slurping coffee while buttoning his dress shirt as he locked the door behind him.

Two hours later, he hadn't shown up for practice.

Uh oh. I pushed away the worry knocking at my heart and went through the motions of teaching.

He'll be waiting at home, I told myself as I adjusted a student's dance position.

He can't believe I was serious, I reassured myself as I stepped out for a salad.

He knows I'm just upset about Nationals, I consoled myself as I led a group class through the basics of Quickstep.

We worked at different locations of the Castle (Midtown for me and the Upper East Side for him), so I typically didn't see him until late evening.

He didn't come home. I waited up as the clock measured my shock and regret in minutes that ticked into hours.

Tomorrow. This is just to make a point.

He didn't show up for practice or come home the next day or the next day after that.

He'll come around.

Days became weeks, and soon, a month had gone by.

At some point, when I'd been at work, he'd stopped by the apartment and picked up some of his clothes and his laptop. I slept on his side of the bed that night, clad in one of his dress shirts. I cocooned myself in his scent and comforted myself that this would soon pass.

I was too proud to call. I'd issued the ultimatum after all. I did, however, keep my phone by me at all times. Just in case Oleg called.

Our Sheepshead Bay apartment felt vast and abandoned without Oleg. I clattered through it, trying to fill up its blank corners. I pulled *Mastering the Art of French Cooking*, a wedding present from Oleg's mother, from atop the bookshelf. Its spine cracked reluctantly and then invitingly when I opened it for the first time.

As I concocted elaborate meals for one, I tuned the television to reality shows that gave me the illusion of company. I picked at heavily creamed or profusely buttered dinners while perched in front of the flickering screen as nubile young things frolicked in hot tubs and squabbled over boyfriends. I threw away more food than I ate, but I was cooking for a hungry heart, not an empty stomach.

I'd been partnered in life and on the dance floor since I was eighteen, and I was unprepared to handle single life at twenty-eight. I took to spending hours at the Castle, grateful for the hustle of Ralph selling lessons and the bustle of students taking lessons. I chitchatted with the other teachers about innocuous topics: weather, work, the finale of a trashy reality show about waiters/models.

Anytime someone brought up Oleg, I changed the subject.

When there was nobody to talk to and nobody to watch, I looked out the window. The Castle was located on the fourth floor of a fifteen-story building, which meant I was high enough to observe the striders and the dawdlers dance in and out of each other's way but low enough to see faces, some gleeful, some glum, yet all pointed toward a destination.

On more than one occasion, the reflection of Ralph's face would appear in whatever window I was staring out of. He'd pull at the collar of his shirt and then avert his eyes. He was probably aware of my newly un-partnered state, both on and off the floor, and bless his greedy heart, was worried and wanted to do something.

I was right as it would turn out.

Chapter 4

CARLY: QUARTER TURNS

SAM and I had begun eating lunch together while exchanging stories about our teaching successes and snafus. Since we were both green, there were more snafus than successes.

"I got confused again when I taught the Quarter Turns in Foxtrot." He groaned. "I had them start facing Diagonal Center rather than Diagonal Wall. I didn't realize it until they tried it with music. And there they went, cutting across the Line of Dance smack into Nina's students."

Nina was one of the advanced teachers at the Castle. I was in awe of her. She'd been a Nationals Rising Star Standard champion and a bronze medalist in the Open division. She wore her black hair in a blunt pageboy that could have looked severe, but it suited her snapping green eyes and pointy chin. She smiled like a cat, quick and knowing.

"She was nice about it, but still," Sam said. "I was embarrassed." He slurped some Dr. Pepper.

I smiled sympathetically. "I did that yesterday."

And I had, although the studio had been empty at the time, so nobody saw my students crossing the invisible directional circle that dancers followed as if horses around a track. Cutting across Line of Dance was a ballroom dance sin on par with looking at one's feet.

"I won't do it again," Sam said. "Twice is enough for that mistake."

I opened up my takeout container of falafel. One of the delights of New York was the bounty of cheap, tasty ethnic food all located within a few blocks of the Castle.

"How'd you end up teaching here?" I asked.

"After graduating from college, I was planning on working at my dad's business."

I cocked my head.

"Recycling," he said in response to my silent question. "It's huge in Houston, and my dad got in on the ground floor. Now, he has the life. He works in the morning, goes to lunch and then the golf course before swinging by the office to tie up a few things. He's home by five with a whiskey in his hand."

I spread my napkin in my lap. "What happened?"

Sam cracked his knuckles. "We had a fight. I asked him not to bring my new stepmother to my graduation."

"Why?"

"My mom and dad were married for twenty-five years, and she did everything for him. She was devastated when he told her it was over."

I leaned toward him, chewing on some falafel.

"He did this spin on the affair-with-a-secretary cliché. My stepmother is young and attractive, and she works for my dad. But she has an MBA, and my dad hired her to acquire new businesses." Sam didn't say anything for a moment. "She's pretty good at it. Profits are up twenty percent since she started."

"Oh," I said. I wanted to say something more comforting, but nothing came to mind.

"I didn't want to put my mom through that," he said. "My dad was furious. He said my stepmother was family now, and I needed to stop playing favorites with my mom."

I nodded and took another bite of my falafel.

"He said that if I wanted special treatment outside the office, then I'd probably want it inside the office. So he rescinded my job offer."

I swallowed. "That's a tough break. How'd you end up here?"

"I'd taken a ballroom dance class in college, and when I saw the ad, I figured, 'why the hell not?'" he said. "I needed a job, pronto, and New York sounded fun."

He grinned at me, which caused my heart to flutter like a flag in a stiff breeze.

"Have you made up with your dad?" I asked.

"Not yet."

"You will." I patted his shoulder. Our eyes met, but neither of us said anything. Sam looked down, studied his shoes for a moment, and then lifted his eyes to me. He opened his mouth to say something as my cheeks heated up.

The door to the teacher's room swung wide before slamming shut.

The moment was lost.

I took a sip of soda to cover my confusion.

Sam cleared his throat. "So what's it like growing up with an autistic brother?" The tips of his ears were pink.

"Like being on a roller coaster that never stops," I said. "Archer is low-functioning and non-verbal."

I wiped my hands with my napkin. "Intellectually, I know he doesn't understand his behavior. But when he bites me, it hurts physically. And when he rips up my homework that I spent all night doing, it hurts emotionally."

I ripped the napkin between my fingers. "But I couldn't get upset, ever, because he didn't know what he was doing."

I balled up the papery ribbons. "It hurts so much, though, to watch your baby brother hit his head against a wall over and over. It hurts so much to watch him run out the door and into the street as you chase after him, praying no cars are coming."

I tossed the napkin into the trash. "There are good moments, too. He loves cartoons, the old ones like *Bugs Bunny* and *Wile E. Coyote and The Road Runner*. He curls up with me, and we watch them together."

I threw the takeout container on top of the napkin. "I had to grow up quickly. There are only a certain number of hours in the day, and Archer's needs were so immediate that my parents didn't have much left over for me," I said. "I became the third parent."

I squared my shoulders and smiled at Sam, who was looking distinctly uncomfortable. Talking about Archer was always hard. Nobody knew what to say or if they should say anything.

"I learned a lot about patience," I said, ballooning each word with cheer. "Which I'm about to use now as I teach Forward Change Steps in Waltz to students who may or may not remember their right foot from their left."

I stood up and flashed Sam another smile, this one with as many teeth as I could manage. "See you on the floor."

He was gazing at me, his mouth agape.

"Yup," he said finally.

Chapter 5

NINA: RALPH'S BIG PLAN

"NINA, Nina, I gotta lotta problems, and one of them you can solve."

I settled into the leather club chair that rested across from Ralph's desk and lifted my eyebrows. Ralph, to my eye, didn't have a "lotta problems." He ran a successful dance studio that allowed him, a bookie's son from Queens, to live like a king.

Ralph was composed of squares: size EEE feet he shoved into specially made dance shoes, a block of a torso, a brick for a head, and square white teeth that lined up like sheets of toilet paper.

Yet he was rarely without some longhaired, large-breasted beauty on his arm. He had a motto of "try 'em all," and if one girl turned down his advances, he moved onto the next one. He leered at women on the streets, and I'd overheard him discuss how plastic surgery could enhance a female's looks.

For all his gross misogyny outside the studio, Ralph was a surprisingly good boss. He paid his male and female teachers the same, even though male teachers were harder to come by. He'd never tried anything with me or any of the other female instructors, and if a male student acted creepy, he showed the student the door, no questions asked.

Ralph's behavior, though, had less to do with respect for women and more to do with respect for his bottom line. Treating his female teachers well was good for business.

"What's the problem?" I asked.

"You're a terrific teacher, Nina. One of the best I got. But you're about to be one of the only ones I got."

I frowned. The Castle was a hopping dance studio that required a dozen or so instructors to keep pace with demand. Teacher turnover was high, collateral damage for a studio located in New York City where young people juggled multiple dreams and weren't hesitant to abandon one when another looked more promising.

"Who's leaving?"

Ralph sighed. "Everybody," he said. "I got the opposite problem of every other studio owner. Students and nobody to teach 'em." He ticked the leaving teachers off his fingers. "Show, grad school, moving to L.A., getting married, another show." He stopped. "Clown college," he said in disbelief.

I nodded, wondering where this was going.

"I got the advanced students covered. Four Russians are starting on Monday."

Great, I thought. More *Russkis* to remind me of my failed ambitions. I coughed to keep from crying.

"The social students are the problem. I got plenty of folks, but nobody to teach 'em."

Ralph did have a problem. Unlike advanced students who were interested in the process, social students showed up with a goal, usually a wedding. They required patience and enthusiasm and a teacher who could teach the same thing over and over without succumbing to boredom or animosity. It was like waiting tables except waiting tables held the promise of a big tip.

"I got Carly and Sam, but they're leaving at the end of the summer." Ralph leaned forward. "I want to keep 'em. They're attractive, quick, well-spoken. It could take a year before I found two teachers as good."

"How do plan on doing that?"

Ralph rubbed his thick hands together. "I gotta plan." He smiled at me. "That's where you come in."

I blinked. "Me?"

Ralph nodded. "My social teachers don't stay because they're killing time until something better comes along.

I wrinkled my nose. "True, but so what?"

"I want them to compete in the Castle's competition next month."

The competition was ostensibly an event of contested professional and amateur divisions for the studios across the northeast. In reality, it was more a cross between a frat party and a business meeting with all the drinking and talking shop.

"What's that going to do?" I asked.

"I want them to get the dance bug. They won't mind teaching all those wedding couples if they're competing." Ralph reclined back in his chair with a satisfied smile. "I also gotta suspicion they like each other. Listening to some romantic music while holding onto each other might give 'em the push they need. After the event, I'll offer them a year contract and hook 'em up with some coaching." He smirked as if he wanted to high-five himself.

I frowned. Ralph's plan had a lot in common with Swiss cheese. It was full of holes.

"What does this have to do with me?"

"You're going to help 'em. Throw together some routines, polish their technique, encourage 'em to practice after hours."

The whole thing sounded dumb for everybody involved.

"Wouldn't it be easier to keep looking for other teachers?" I asked.

"I've been trying. But these young kids have zero interest in ballroom dancing." He sulked. "I talked to one girl who would've been terrific. She was personable, studied modern and jazz in college." Ralph shook his head. "When I told her we only teach men to lead and women to follow, she told me we're reinforcing outmoded gender norms and that ballroom dancing is a tool of the patriarchy."

He wrinkled his forehead. "What's the patriarchy?"

"It's . . ." I trailed off. A primer in women's studies wasn't going to change Ralph.

"Another guy I talked to wanted to know if he could teach all his lessons via video conferencing."

I swallowed my laugh. "Kids today."

"And even if I get one that doesn't care about that stuff, I gotta train 'em, hope they stick around for a while." Ralph sighed. "Sam and Carly are the best I've seen in a long time."

I yawned, my mind on the *poulet au porto* I would make this evening.

"Will you train them, Nina?"

I shook my head. "I've got plenty on my plate right now between teaching my students and running the Wednesday class and social," I said. *Plus making amends with Oleg,* I thought.

Ralph shifted in his leather chair. "It's none of my business, but I noticed you've been hanging out here more than usual. As someone who's experienced his fair share of . . . " he stopped and squinted, "bumps in the road, the best thing to do is keep your mind on other things."

"I feel great," I said. "Never better," I added with a big smile that was belied by my wet eyes.

"It'll take your mind off things. And sometimes bumps require extra change in your pocket. So, in addition to your teaching rate, I'll give you a bonus—a big one—if they stay."

"I can't get them ready in Standard in time."

"I want you to train 'em in Smooth."

"Smooth?" I asked. "What do I know about Smooth?"

"I'm gonna bet plenty." Ralph's phone buzzed. "So it's settled," he said as he reached for the receiver.

It was not settled, but I left Ralph's office anyway.

That night, I ate the chicken in port that I'd prepared for myself. Then, by myself, I watched a reality show about attractive young people who worked in a beauty salon. As the receptionist argued with the master stylist, I zoomed back on my life and saw what the world saw, a depressed woman alone in her apartment, the same as yesterday and the same as tomorrow.

A tear dribbled down my cheek. *Stupid Nina.*

I picked up the phone to call Oleg but put it back down. My fingers itched to push the buttons, but my pride, an enormous, unmovable mountain forged from ego and ambition, had blocked my heart.

I blew my nose. I was going to take Ralph up on his offer. Oleg might catch wind of my new project. He'd know I wasn't sitting around crying for him. Maybe that could kick start our reconciliation.

If I was going to train Sam and Carly, then we needed to start immediately. The next day, I approached Carly. She was lounging on a bench with her long legs stretched out in front of her. I paused to inspect her; I couldn't decide whether she was pretty or plain.

Today a shaft of pinkish twilight made her ivory skin look dewy and highlighted her high cheekbones.

Pretty.

"Hello," Carly said. She scooted over, so I could plop down beside her. She gave me a generous smile, which I returned. Carly's most striking quality was her unrelenting cheerfulness. Ralph had good reason to want to keep her.

"How are you enjoying the Castle?" I asked.

"I love it," she said without any irony. "Teaching dance is so rewarding."

I tried to remember where she was from. Ohio? Indiana? A place where people spoke sincerely without the cynicism that italicized New Yorkers' conversations.

"What are your plans for the fall?"

Her face fell. "Go back to college. Help out my family." She cocked her head at me. Brown eyes too close together and thin lips.

Plain.

"What are you studying?"

She plucked at the hem of her skirt. "Special education. My brother has low-functioning autism, so I have lots of experience with special-needs children."

"What's your favorite dance?"

Her face lit up.

Very pretty.

"Waltz. Or Foxtrot," she said. "Maybe Tango if I knew more about it."

"None of the Latin dances?"

"I feel like a giraffe with a hip replacement."

I laughed. "Would you enjoy learning more about Waltz, Tango, and Foxtrot?"

Her forehead creased. "How . . ."

"The Castle has a competition coming up in a couple of weeks, and there's a division for newbies called Rising Star."

"Competing?" Carly asked with big eyes. "In what? Who with?"

"Smooth. It's four dances: Waltz, Tango, Foxtrot, and Viennese Waltz," I said. "Imagine if Standard and Latin emigrated to America and had a baby."

"I'm not picturing it."

"Think Fred Astaire and Ginger Rogers."

"It sounds wonderful, but I don't have money for lessons or a dress." Her eyes burned with longing.

"I'll train you for free and lend you a dress.

"Who would be my partner?"

"Sam. You two would be a good fit."

Carly twisted her hands. "I don't know."

"Don't overthink it. Tomorrow. Ten a.m."

She looked up, two splotches of crimson staining her cheeks. "Did Sam agree?"

"He will," I said, confident for no reason other than Ralph seemed confident in his ability to sniff out young love.

Sam was even easier than Carly. I forwent the pleasantries and got straight to the point.

"Competing with Carly? Sounds fun," he said, his accent elongating all the vowels as if they were chewing gum.

Maybe Ralph was on to something.

Chapter 6

CARLY: THE BEST THERE EVER WAS

MAYBE IT WAS ALL the time we spent in each other's arms, or maybe it was the romantic music we danced to, or maybe it was just the excitement of being young and on an adventure in New York, but my heart pinged loud and clear every time Sam came near.

When Nina approached me about competing in August, I'd been intrigued but hesitant. But she'd talked me into it although I wasn't sure what she was getting out of training us.

I asked Sam for his opinion. "Nobody does anything around here for free," he'd said.

This was true. Ballroom dancing was overtly mercenary, and it started at the top. Ralph salivated over new students and their untapped bank accounts. Fresh blood, he called them.

"Maybe it has to do with that husband of hers," Sam said.

Nina never said anything, but the scuttlebutt around the studio maintained that Oleg had moved out of their apartment a couple of months ago. Nina's red eyes and the chalky band of flesh on her ring finger led me to believe that the scuttlebutt was on point.

Sam and I progressed in the beginning, mostly because up was the only place to go. We'd gotten down the syllabus of school figures, and while we weren't exactly sailing through the steps, we could dance a song from start to finish without mortally injuring each other.

"I'm struggling," Sam said during a lesson. He pushed a hand through his auburn hair, which made it stand up. I yearned to smooth it down.

"How can I help?" Nina asked.

He sighed. "I understand what you're saying, but I can't visualize it. What is good Smooth dancing?"

"Come." She walked to the edge of the floor where a computer rested. She keyed in a few words and brought up a video.

I gasped, which I turned into a cough. A man, impossibly good-looking with light blond hair and the classical features of a Greek statue, was dancing Foxtrot with a slender brunette. He led her under his arm, and then side-by-side, they floated through a crisscrossing sequence with their feet.

"Trey Devereux. The best there ever was," Nina said. "Probably the best there ever will be."

Trey Devereux. His name hovered in my head like skywriting as he stroked across the floor. My mouth gaped in an *o*.

Nina winked at me. "Trey has that effect on people."

I slammed my mouth shut and refocused my attention on the video. Even with my rudimentary understanding, I appreciated his attention to details. When he led with his heel, he didn't stick it up like a skyscraper or keep it too low like a ballet dancer attempting a modern dance move.

For as nuanced as his approach was, he produced a huge amount of negative space. His body dominated the air-filled canvas of the dance floor by succumbing to it.

"What do you think?" Nina asked.

"He's exceptional," I said. Seeing him slip and skate across the floor made me want to practice more, more, more.

"Keep going," Nina said.

I fought to locate the right words. "His dancing is a big painting composed of tiny brushstrokes. No detail is beneath his notice, but he uses them in service of the whole."

Nina smiled at me. "Well put." She looked at Sam. "And you?"

Sam scratched his chin. "He looks like a movie star. That has to help. But it's also his partner. She lets him lead everything."

My cheeks warmed. I wasn't letting Sam lead much. I was so concerned about executing the choreography perfectly that I'd forgotten the purpose of ballroom dancing—the leader invites and then the follower interprets, sometimes with imperfect results.

"Who's his partner?" I asked.

"Tamsin Grubbs," Nina said. "He met her at a shag club. She was trailer trash. Trey cleaned her up."

"What's shag?" Sam asked as I studied Tamsin. She didn't look like trailer trash with her regal posture and delicate features.

"It's the Carolina version of Swing."

On the video, the Master of Ceremonies was announcing the six couples who'd made the final.

"From Charleston, South Carolina: Louis Pierre Devereux, III and Tamsin Grubbs."

"I thought his name was Trey," I said.

"Trey is a nickname for boys named after their fathers and grandfathers. It means three," Sam said. "It's so an entire family isn't answering to Louis." He overemphasized the second syllable of Louis, Lou-WHEE, an exaggeration of the name of the former kings of France.

"Where are they now?" I asked.

"They retired five years ago," Nina said. "They won three Nationals titles in Smooth, the only couple to do so."

"Is that a big deal?" Sam asked.

"Most couples retire after two years. They win the title and then defend it for a year to show their win wasn't a fluke."

"What happens after couples retire?" I asked.

"After Nationals, the champions go on a tour where they make a big paycheck. After that, most become coaches or judges. Some open studios or start competitions. No matter what, winning is lucrative," Nina said. "Plus they'll always be Nationals champions."

"Is that important?" Sam asked.

"Winning Nationals is enough to pay your bills for the rest of your life even if you go into another line of work," she said. "People love winners. You start out ahead before you've made a move."

Sam's eyes glinted with something I couldn't read.

"Where are they now?" I asked.

Nina shrugged. "I haven't seen them since their last Nationals. Trey comes from old money in Charleston. As far as I know, he went back there. As for Tamsin, I don't know."

On the screen, Trey and Tamsin were whirling through the opening bars of Viennese Waltz. If I ever had the opportunity, then I would measure myself against this god. His beauty, his talent, and his devotion to hard work were inspiring.

I played with the collar of my blouse. "What's he like?"

Nina scrunched up her face. "Odd," she said. "Exquisite manners, charming, but private. He showed up at the start of his event, and in between rounds, Tamsin and he would go practice. I've never shared more than pleasantries with him."

She tweaked her lips slyly. "I never knew if he preferred men or women, and that's saying something for the world of ballroom dancing where everyone is sleeping with everyone else."

"Who're the current champions?" Sam took a swig of Dr. Pepper.

Nina pulled up a new video. "Park and Ashley Lee."

I didn't know much, but they weren't great compared to Trey and Tamsin: too vertical, cheesy facial expressions. I winced. Ashley had extended her leg in an arabesque, the free foot sickled—the opposite of correct ballet technique.

"They look like they want to be Trey and Tamsin but haven't practiced enough," Sam said with his usual bluntness.

Nina laughed. "They're good in closed position, which is why they won."

"Why didn't Smooth evolve?" I asked.

"No one had a new idea," Nina said.

Chapter 7

NINA: DO AS I SAY

FOR THE FIRST time in a long time, I had no idea what I was doing.

As a Standard dancer, I'd spent my career in the embrace of a leader who, through his body, shaped my body in time and through space. He asked, politely and with finesse; I responded, willingly and with élan. Together, we were the perfect pair—question and answer.

Smooth was a different world from Standard. The man still led and the woman still followed, but the woman had a range of interpretation not available to her in Standard.

When the man spun her out, something he couldn't do in Standard, he lost his corporeal jurisdiction over her. Until she returned to his arms, she could be, and sometimes was, a loose cannon.

That's what I was right now, a loose cannon whizzing through life with no leader waiting, his arms spread, to catch me.

On the dance floor, Oleg had led. Off the dance floor, I had. It'd worked until I butted into his domain. I missed dancing with him, his ramrod posture and slender arms providing the ideal vase from which I could bloom.

I swore in Russian as I headed home alone to my empty apartment. What I missed was Oleg.

That night, with shaking hands, I picked up the phone and punched in his number, digital choreography I'd performed thousands of times. My pride hung its head.

"Nina," he said, his tone like an overcast day.

My heart leaped into my mouth where it stayed. I'd assumed he would be glad to hear from me, pleased I'd made the first move toward reconciliation, and I hadn't made any plan beyond the actual call.

"Nina." Still no sun.

I couldn't think of anything to say, so I hung up.

He didn't call back.

To keep my mind off of what my heart already knew, I threw myself into coaching Sam and Carly. I wanted them to win.

The ethos of Smooth—so American with its liveliness, uniqueness, and riskiness—stood in opposition to how I'd been trained to dance, which was safely and pristinely.

My stomach bounced. I couldn't do myself what I was about to ask Carly and Sam to do. So I employed the edict of parents and dance teachers from the beginning of time. Do as I say, not as I do.

To buy myself time, I spent their first lessons refining the syllabus figures that would make up a quarter of their routines.

They were terrible at first. Carly was overly committed to doing the steps in the order I'd taught them, and she refused to let Sam lead.

"But it's not what you showed us," she said, tugging on her ponytail, light brown and wavy like *café au lait* being swirled with a spoon. "Don't we have to do it right?"

"That doesn't matter. What I've given Sam are suggestions." I threw Sam a pointed look. "Excellent ones, but suggestions nonetheless. Let him decide if he's going to take them or not."

Sam got frustrated easily and required lots of petting to keep working. Carly coddled him and coaxed him and cheered him on, and she never let his mood dampen hers.

Good basics were hard to fake, so I pushed them, breaking down the same techniques again and again.

Foot placement: the position of one foot in relation to the other

Footwork: the part of the foot in contact with the floor

Dance position: five points of connection—shoulder, arm, wrist, hand, and, the most important, the band of skin that ran from rib to thigh

"Again," I said with a pert smile. This marked the seventh time I'd said *again*.

Sam and Carly took dance position.

"Basics are boring," Sam said.

Carly's eyes were sparkling. She adored the details. Perfectionists loved ballroom dancing. There was always something to improve on, excellence just one heel lead or sway to the right away.

"The judges will appreciate a well-danced Natural Spin Turn in Waltz more than a high kick with some waving arms," I said.

The Natural Spin Turn—half a box rotating rightward into a sweeping pivot with a late, quick rise that made a couple hover like a roller coaster at the top of a hill—told a judge everything he or she needed to know. How did the dancers' feet stroke the floor and how did their spines sculpt the air?

After my lessons with Sam and Carly, I watched old Smooth videos from Nationals, lingering over the ones of Trey and Tamsin. I skipped my fancy French meals and reality television shows in favor of a sandwich and my laptop. I studied the evolution of the style and picked apart the dances I enjoyed, searching for phrases I could knit together to create coherent routines.

As bad as Sam and Carly were, I was worse as a teacher, reaching for words, so many words, when a demonstration would affect the desired results more quickly. I walked through all the open work and encouraged them to develop their personality through trial and error. When they landed on something captivating, I added it to their choreography.

I was making it up as I went along, and I couldn't believe Sam and Carly hadn't caught on. I chalked it up to their naivety.

Ralph was right about one thing. It did take my mind off Oleg. I'd coast along for a while, making notes of things I wanted to tell Sam and Carly. Then a Waltz, heartbreaking because it was beautiful, would waft through the studio. Tears would prick in my eyes because Oleg and I had danced to it a few years ago at Nationals, the first year we made the Open final. Then I would remember that I was an almost twenty-nine-year-old woman who hadn't seen her husband since May.

A month after Ralph set this harebrained scheme in motion, he stopped by to check on Sam and Carly's progress.

"How's it going?" he asked.

"See for yourself."

Carly and Sam were dancing their Waltz, a routine that had just begun to gel. Sam rolled Carly out, and then she smacked him in the face.

Sam yelped as Carly apologized profusely.

Ralph grimaced. "How about the other front?"

I shrugged. There'd been no progress. Sam and Carly appeared to like each other, but neither would make the first move.

"It won't take much," he said, gesturing with his chin in Sam's direction. Sam was sitting on a bench, his eyes following Carly with undisguised gusto as she danced the spins with a new position of her arms.

The next day, we worked on Tango.

I put on my best no-nonsense face. "Contrast is key, both in the dances and between the dances," I said. "Right now, your Tango is too muted."

Sam scratched his head. "It feels different than Waltz with all the quick changes of direction and sudden stops. Plus there's no rise and fall as in Waltz."

"I'm not talking about the technique." I paused for impact. "I'm talking about the feeling of each dance. Tango should strike a different chord in the heart than Waltz does."

"Doesn't the choreography do that?" Carly asked. "Waltz swirls and Tango stalks. Foxtrot is jaunty while Viennese Waltz is a whirlwind with all those rotations."

"All those rotations," Sam echoed. "I'm a clock that can't keep up with the time."

I giggled. Viennese Waltz, the fastest dance, was hard in the beginning. Once they got the technique down, it would be one of the easier dances thanks to Newtonian physics and all that an-object-in-motion-stays-in-motion stuff.

I looked at Carly. "Some of the feeling comes from the choreography. But it also needs to spring from in here." I tapped my heart.

Carly blushed as Sam shuffled his feet.

She cleared her throat. "How do we do that?"

"Eye contact," I said triumphantly.

This was, actually, my big plan. If I made them look each other in the eye with a specific feeling, then, perhaps, the emotion would create some motion, like a date or a kiss.

As a Standard dancer who had to keep my head left unless otherwise directed by my partner, eye contact seemed downright racy.

"Instead of performing for the judges and the audience, you're going to perform for each other. Draw eyes to you by having eyes for each other," I said.

Carly's cheeks deepened to magenta as Sam stuck his hands in his pockets.

I blinked innocently. "Let's begin."

I told them how they should look at each other: with passion, with wrath, with undeniable lust. I kept my demeanor cool and professional, but inside, I was tittering like a schoolgirl.

By the end of our lesson, Carly and Sam sported dazed, flushed expressions.

"Be sure to practice. Tonight if possible." I waved at them and then went home to my solitary dinner and winking television.

My stomach burned as I remembered the lesson. It wasn't because I was jealous of young love. Because I wasn't. Not one iota. The whipping cream I'd used in my *potage velouté aux champignons,* more commonly known as cream of mushroom soup, must have gone bad.

Chapter 8

CARLY: FOLLOW!

"I FEEL like you're staring into my soul," Sam said.

I laughed to cover my discomfort. My eye contact during Foxtrot had been a touch emphatic. My crush on Sam had grown to the point where it was impossible to keep contained beneath my skin, which prickled when he took me into dance position.

"Scared of what I'm going to find?" I smoothed my dress, a capsule of navy blue that swung into a wide skirt, over my hips. I didn't dare look at Sam, panicky he'd see my feelings scribbled over me like bright crayon defacing a blank wall.

"Should we try the pivots again?" Sam asked.

I tried for nonchalance. "You betcha."

Smooth pivots: One hand on each other's shoulder, the other streaming behind as if a kite in a breeze. Right thighs pressed together. Left legs reaching backward. Eyes connected. Unblinkingly.

We traced curlicues across the floor, a twin-engine turbine where physicality embodied physics. Sam halted our momentum, and I swept my leg in an airy semi-circle. Instead of releasing me like he was supposed to, he pulled me close.

Nina's admonishment flashed in my head. *Follow!*

So I did. Our eye contact unbroken, we ambled in a tight circle. Then Sam lowered his head and kissed me. I melted into him, yielding to his lead.

It was an awkward kiss at first, but as we cottoned on to each other's pacing and pressure, it grew into a dramatic, impassioned one. Swaggering Foxtrot songs played and played as we kissed and kissed.

The last song on the playlist faded to a close, and reluctantly, we pulled apart.

"That was our best dancing yet." I didn't look at Sam.

Sam shoved his hands in his pockets. "Do you want to get out of here?" The tips of his ears were flaming.

"Let's," I said, my voice thrumming with raw, urgent need.

He grabbed my hand, and we sprinted out of the studio. We abandoned our Viennese Waltz at the edge of the floor, forlorn without bodies to animate its dizzying revolutions carried along by a buoyant triple meter.

That night, we performed a different dance where heart compelled flesh.

Sam and I didn't tell anyone we were together. We didn't acknowledge it ourselves. It was August, and everything in New York stuck together. Sunshine to glass. Heat to concrete. Sam's body to mine.

We lived in a bubble where September didn't exist, only the Castle's competition and the days until it. The light-filled hours were filled with teaching and practicing and the dark ones charged with two bodies that couldn't get enough of each other.

I hadn't been unhappy before in Ohio; it was the life I knew. But now I was happy, and it threw into relief how unhappy I'd been moving between the tightrope of home and school.

My parents had stressed that the only life worth living was one in service of others. "Personal happiness is nothing when compared to the suffering of others. When you've made someone else happy, then you can be happy."

They volunteered at soup kitchens, canvassed for politicians they believed in, and rattled buckets to raise money for impoverished arts organizations. Whenever they could, they took me with them—showing me how a life in service of others should be lived.

Archer's diagnosis of autism had turned their do-gooding instincts inward, but it didn't alter their philosophy. They spent hours researching autism and trying every therapy they could. Although they didn't make much money, when some extra cash found their way into their bank account, they spent it on treatments for Archer. They believed, with all their hearts, if Archer could improve—a few words, toilet training—then every effort would be worthwhile.

I'd acted in accordance with this edict throughout my first twenty years, but the serpent of personal pleasure had seduced me. To return to a life where duty trumped desire seemed impossible.

I swallowed. That's exactly what I would have to do in a few weeks.

Please let me stay, I prayed, ignoring the heaviness in my stomach.

"Have you made up with your dad?" I asked Sam.

He sighed. "Not yet."

I stroked his hand.

"When do you leave for Ohio?" Sam asked.

"I haven't bought my ticket yet," I mumbled.

Sam kissed me, and we slammed the door of here and now on future's clamorous knock.

Our progress impressed Nina.

"You're ready." She winked. "Your connection has improved dramatically."

I opened my mouth and closed it soundlessly while Sam shifted his eyes toward the floor.

Her pale green eyes sparkled. "Don't tell me. You practiced."

"So hard," I said and then clapped a hand over my mouth as, too late, I grasped the double entendre behind my words.

Nina swallowed her laughter. "Dance well."

The Castle's event was similar, as Nina explained, to a typical competition, which had two levels: Rising Star, for newbies like Sam and me, and Open, for seasoned dancers. The Castle's event was different from most competitions. Here, only employees of the Castle could compete.

"What does that mean?" Sam asked.

"It means the level of competition is a lot lower here than out there."

"That's good for us," I said.

"Most of your competitors will be pretty green."

"We're green," Sam said. "Like two unripe bananas."

"Yes, but you trained as if as you were hitting the circuit. Most of these couples will throw together a few routines and have their boss look at them once or twice."

"Thank you, Nina," Sam and I chorused.

~

The competition was held at a fancy hotel on the Upper East Side. Nina met us at the entrance to help us get the lay of the land. She led us through the hotel lobby to an opulent ballroom.

"Wow," said Sam.

That didn't sum it up. Tables for ten draped with snowy clothes were scattered along three sides of the parquet dance floor. A platform holding a podium bookended by two rectangular tables was located against the furthest wall. Rows of crystal chandeliers dripped from the ceiling.

On the dance floor, six couples attired in lurid hues of hot pink, electric blue, and highlighter yellow were finishing up a Mambo to boisterous applause.

Nina gestured to the dance floor. A handful of men and women wearing evening clothes were positioned around the edge. "The judges," she said. "They mark the couples in order of one to six if it's a final round. If it's not a final, they mark the couples they want to recall to the next round. Finals are six couples, semifinals are twelve, and quarterfinals are twenty-four. First rounds vary. If it's a big event, the rounds will be divided into multiple heats of dancers, so the judges can see everyone."

"What's happening now?" I asked. The couples were exiting the floor as a woman strolled around the perimeter, collecting sheets of paper from the judges.

"The scores are going to be tallied."

"How do they do that?"

Nina nodded to the platform. "Do you see the bald man wearing a tuxedo?"

We nodded as the woman in the red dress handed him a sheaf of papers

"That's Papa. He's the Chairman of the Judges."

"Papa?" I asked. The man was punching numbers into a calculator. His fingers flew over the rubber squares.

"His real name is Constantine Papadopoulos, but everyone calls him Papa except for Maxine." Nina saw our questioning looks. "Maxine is his wife. She's also a coach, one of the best." She stretched her lips in a bright, tight smile. "She used to be my coach."

"What does Papa do?" I asked.

"He tallies the marks and announces the winners," Nina said.

Papa was shredding the score sheets.

"That's a lot of power for one person to have," Sam said.

"Not really."

Sam nodded toward Papa. "Could he cook the marks, so a couple he likes wins?"

"It would be hard." She pointed to the dance floor. "Who should win?"

Six couples were taking their place for a Standard Waltz. I swept my eyes over each before returning to the one I liked. Their poise pointed to them as winners.

I dipped my chin in their direction. "Them."

"In the orange gown?" Nina asked.

"That's the one."

"I agree, and the judges will as well."

Papa lifted his head and caught sight of Nina. He waved vigorously at her, which she returned, much less vigorously.

"What happens if it's not so clear-cut?" Sam asked.

"If it's a tie, Papa follows the rules of the skating system," Nina said. "There's not much he can do to throw the competition. Judges talk, so it'd have to be extremely close, just a couple of marks that he could conceivably mis-enter without raising suspicion."

"It seems sketchy," Sam said. "Especially since he shreds the score sheets. There's no way to confirm what he enters is what a judge wrote down."

"Maybe, but what would he get for throwing the competition?" Nina shrugged. "He's been Chairman for ages, and no one's questioned his honesty."

She glanced at her watch. "You two need to get ready." She handed me a garment bag. "One of my old Standard dresses. You're taller than I am, but it should fit otherwise." She passed Sam a suit hanger. "Oleg's tail suit. It's too stuffy for Smooth, but no one here is going to care." She was smiling, but her eyes were damp with hurt.

I wanted to give Nina a hug in sympathy and gratitude, but she gave me a push. "Go change."

I slipped into her old Standard dress. It was green with a hint of blue, like an exotic sea. The long-sleeved lace top clung to my figure while the satin skirt opened in a wide circle. Rhinestones littered the fabric—enchanted dust from a fairy godmother. It was the most beautiful dress I'd ever worn.

I found Nina. "Lovely," she said. She coiled my hair into a topknot and applied makeup with a heavy hand.

Sam appeared, pulling at the collar of the tail suit. "Who needs to breathe?"

Nina tweaked his bow tie. "When he can have good posture instead."

My heart swung into a canter. Sam looked adorable dressed up, dapper and a little sheepish.

Nina handed me a piece of stiff white paper with the number twenty stamped on the back. "Make sure there are no wrinkles," she said as she passed me safety pins.

I pinned the number on Sam's back, feeling as if I was living someone else's life.

Nina hugged us. "I'll be cheering you on."

Sam and I clasped sweaty palms and entered the ballroom. We made our way to the on-deck area, which was crowded with dancers waiting for their upcoming events.

The Rising Star Smooth was tiny, only six couples. I couldn't decide if I was grateful or not for the small size. Fewer couples meant the floor would be easier to navigate. It also meant we'd be more noticeable.

My nerves whirred when the Master of Ceremonies announced our event. Sam guided me to a spot at the end of a long wall, and we took our opening pose for Waltz.

Then we were off. Waltz went surprisingly well, and my nerves slowed from a gallop to a canter. Sam exhaled as the opening bars of Tango thrummed through the ballroom. We struck our opening pose, and then we slammed head on to the meaning of the word *competition*.

Silly me thought competition referred to the placements awarded by judges, first through sixth, a ruler sliding incrementally from best to worst. Every duo danced to their ability, and the judges, through an analysis of style and skill, compared couple against couple to evaluate where each should land.

That was not competition. Those were results. Competition was what was happening right now, right here. It was Darwinian, survival of the fittest, the fleetest, the fastest thinker.

The resource we were fighting over? The dance floor.

Even with six couples, the floor churned with activity: sky-high kicks, endless twirls, ellipses of lavish figures. To dance our routines well, we needed space, lots of it.

Nina had warned us, but still. We had zero experience navigating around other people, and our efforts to avoid collisions were haphazard and hesitant.

Sam veered out of the way of a couple who'd stopped to slice their arms like Spanish conquistadors only to smack into another couple who'd scissored their legs into a deep lunge.

"Sorry," Sam said as he brushed by the couple whose bodies were stretched in an X. Then he groaned. There was another couple in front of us. Fortunately, they took off, and we chased after them.

I crashed into another dancer during some solo spins.

"Sorry," I whispered over my shoulder.

By the end of Tango, we were sweating, profusely, and disoriented, profoundly.

Foxtrot started out auspiciously. Lady Luck smiled down upon us, and the floor beckoned, a blank sheet unattended by other couples. Buoyed by the freedom of dancing unhindered, we executed our choreography well. We may have even smiled.

Then we turned the corner, and Sam got lost. He entered into a sequence that lay twenty-odd bars in the future. Gritting my teeth, I followed. He cursed under his breath, but there wasn't much we could do except keep going. When we got to the end, forty-five seconds earlier than planned, Sam whispered, "Let's pick up from the beginning. So we did half our Foxtrot twice.

It was time for Viennese Waltz, the last dance. Sam and I trudged through our starting poses. I'd never been so tired in my life. Sam appeared to feel the same way. His dance position sagged, and his breath—short, damp puffs of air—pounded in my ear.

I envied his ability to breathe. I couldn't inhale more than a wisp of oxygen, and my body shifted into an unwieldy bag of sand that reluctantly followed Sam's lead.

Finally, it was over. After a quick bow, we plodded off the dance floor.

Sam pointed to a patch of carpet away from the dancers thronging the on-deck area. "Over there."

We slumped to the floor like a couple of drunks undone by Saturday-night shenanigans.

"If there was another round and we were recalled, I wouldn't go," he said.

"Me neither." I collapsed into the wall, unable to muster the energy to sit upright. "Do you think they'd notice if we went to sleep right here?"

"Don't care if they do."

Nina smirked at our shell-shocked expressions.

"What did you think?" she asked.

"It was war," Sam said.

"Except more polite," I added.

"How do you think you did?"

"Dead last," I said.

"Definitely," Sam added.

Nina shook her head. "I don't think so." She paused and then smiled, the arch of her lips like a cat being petted. "I think you won."

She was right.

Ralph took us to the hotel bar for a drink to celebrate. "You kids looked terrific," he said.

I took a sip of wine as my shoulders drooped, my medal scraping my thighs. The post-high I'd felt when Papa announced us as winners was dribbling away. Later this week, I'd get on a plane and return to my old, ordinary life in Ohio.

Ralph rubbed his stubby fingers together. "So I gotta proposition for you."

He laid out his scheme. If Sam and I would sign one-year contracts to work at the Castle, then he'd set us up with a couple of coaching lessons to get us started competing.

"You could be fierce on the circuit." He gestured to the waiter for another round of drinks. "And having a Nationals title has gotta lotta prestige, no matter what you do with your life."

Sam squeezed my hand under the table; I squeezed back as my throat tightened guiltily.

"Yes," we said.

I should have said no. I was needed at home. My parents needed me; Archer needed me. But their needs were no match against my wants, which were dancing and Sam. I was going against everything I'd been taught to do—devote myself to the greater good.

The greater good was my family. It certainly wasn't ballroom dancing in New York. I shivered as I pictured my dad restraining Archer from punching another hole in the wall as my mother typed up a letter to the insurance company begging for reimbursement. Dinner would burn on the stove because I wasn't there to tend to it.

"We have to do it in a year," I said to Sam. "I can't stay away from my family for more than that."

"Let's do it." His face had a vacant look as if he was already living the future after next year's Nationals.

Chapter 9

NINA: YOU CARRY MY DREAMS

SAM AND CARLY DANCED WELL. I'd felt like a proud mama watching them. There'd been some hair-raising issues for sure. Sam's floor craft lacked delicacy as he tossed Carly this way and that as he tried and often failed to avoid oncoming traffic. They'd forgotten half of their Foxtrot, and Carly almost had a heart attack during Viennese Waltz.

But they'd won. Competition was based on comparison, and good wasn't always criteria for winning. Better was, and that's what they'd been with good footwork and great chemistry. Today, it was enough.

Ralph slipped me a check. "Nice job," he said. He grinned, which came awfully close to a leer. I didn't know if Ralph's joy was from the impending expansion of his bank account or his half-baked scheme panning out, but I didn't care. The check had a lot of zeroes.

I beamed back at him. "Thanks."

I was going to miss teaching Sam and Carly. It'd kept me preoccupied throughout the summer, my failures pushed to the side by the more immediate goal of preparing them for the competition. It was a minor endeavor, nothing compared to what I'd lost, but it had been something.

Ballroom dancing depended on contact—a clasp of the hands, the press of two torsos together—to forge connection. And with connection, all things were possible. One person's limits were halved and his or her prospects doubled when paired with another. Four legs rooted into the earth, allowing two hearts and two heads to reach heavenward.

The rest of my life stretched before me, and it looked to be a lonely path I'd tread down, unconnected and on my own two feet.

Oleg had been at the competition. I'd spied him on the other side of the ballroom as the Open Standard was beginning, an event we'd won last year.

My mouth gaped a little, and I touched a finger to my parted lips. He was wearing a dark gray suit with a blue shirt open at the collar. He looked exactly the way he had every day since the first day I'd seen him, studious and poetic.

My mother had not been pleased when I told her of my plans to marry Oleg.

"I did not move to United States for you to marry son of rug salesman (Oleg's father owned a carpet store in Staten Island) because he's not half-bad dancer. You carry my dreams, *zolotse* (my gold). Why waste them on beanpole with receding hairline? In five years, you will hate his guts."

She went on like this for some time, but I stayed firm.

My parents left Russia in the '80s. They were Jewish although neither believed in much of a god. They were happy to proclaim their faith, though, when Russia, seeking compromise with the West, began allowing some Jews to reunify with family in Israel. My parents invented a couple of relatives in Tel Aviv and decamped to Vienna where they applied to come to the United States as political refugees.

They'd been trying for years to have a child with no success. Maybe it was all the schnitzel and beer in Vienna or maybe it was the excitement of their American future, but luck struck. When they stepped off the plane in Queens, I was a gob of cells wrapped in a cocoon of hope and big dreams.

Seven months after they arrived in the steaming, cacophonous zoo of New York, I was born: black-haired, colicky, and prideful from the start.

In America, my parents and I lived as many Russians do, in deep Brooklyn off the B/Q train. Our apartment building had a lobby with peeling turquoise paint and a junky elevator that heaved with a put-upon sigh every time I pushed six. Our small unit overlooked a concrete courtyard where odors from cooking and screeches from arguments wafted in and then stayed, like squatters tucked in for the long winter.

My father drove for a car service, and my mother did a little cleaning. I went to school with all the other Eastern-European children where we navigated the jarring transition of being Russian at home but American in public.

For special occasions, my family headed to one of the Russian restaurants that were located by the water. We chewed through platters of smoked fish, over-dressed salad, and curlicues of beef tongue while attractive young people lip-synced to Russian pop songs.

Sheepshead Bay was the old country in the new, but with heat that worked, grocery stores with groaning shelves, and police uninterested in old men arguing politics.

My father bored of it quickly. He'd moved to America to be American. He wanted to live in a big house, to barbecue burgers, to go about life in a landscape of something other than scruffy brick buildings and elevated subway tracks. One day, when I was six, he dropped off a client at his New Jersey mansion and kept driving. And kept driving. And kept driving. He called from California.

"I have found paradise," he told my mother. "And I am not coming back."

That wasn't quite the last we heard from him, but it was close. Every once in a while a check would show up. He became a bigamist, remarrying under an assumed name and starting a second family.

My mother looked over her options and found them not promising. Cleaning was hard work and didn't pay well. Her arthritic knees, a genetic booby prize she'd passed onto me, were only going to get creakier, her hands more chapped, and for what? So she could sponge the smears off a rich lady's toilet for a handful of dollars? She'd come to America for a better life than she'd left behind.

Then there was me. I was a precocious child, well spoken and attractive. My mother decided she'd pass the burden of success onto me.

She had a good long think about it and concluded that she had two goals. One, work as little as possible for as much money as possible. Two, get me the best of everything.

My mother got in touch with her long lost beauty through the magical powers of powder and paint, dye and diet to emerge an appealing middle-aged woman. She redid our living room to accommodate the tastes of large, tired Russian bottoms with capacious leather sofas, an enormous television, vodka and tea an arm's reach away.

She advertised herself as a gentleman's companion, offering compassion and comfort to men in need of an understanding friend. I actually believed this until I was eleven when I received a rude awakening to the full extent of her work.

One day, as I ate lunch at school, an older boy of thirteen pointed at me. He made a crude but unmistakable gesture with his hands. "My father is doing that to your mother right now."

While there was sex involved, many of the men did come to my mother for the conversation, the ego stroking, and the pretend pleasure she took in their company. They poured out their woes to her, these burly, crimson-cheeked men with hearts that had been battered and bruised by a world unimpressed with them. She kept her rates low to ensure a steady stream of business, and if a man didn't have money to pay, she'd barter.

That's how I ended up dancing.

Arkady Makarov ran a ballroom dancing school, similar to the ones in the old country where children started young. Arkady's wife, a frigid shrew deeply resentful of all the time Arkady spent instructing lithe young women with shiny eyes and dreams of winning big, controlled the money.

Arkady wasn't attractive exactly with his reddish nose and thinning hair, but he was palatable enough to impressionable women with his square shoulders and strong dance position. Yet he couldn't do any of the wooing necessary to embark on an affair with the nubile women who frequented his school.

He heard about my mother and showed up one day, apologetic for his lack of cash but pitifully invested in regaining his manhood.

In desperation, he offered dance classes to me in exchange for my mother's time, three days a week during the hours right after school let out. A time in which his wife would be engaged with picking up their two children, managing homework, and peeling wrappers from snacks.

My mother was intrigued. My presence after school was cutting into her potential profits. Afternoons offered the opportunity to entertain men on their way home from work. She could slowly wean some of her tedious morning clients and replace them with more lucrative ones.

So, at fourteen, I was shuttled off to dance class three times a week. I took to it immediately. The details, the nuance, the subtle but rewarding work of remodeling the human body until it could swoop through space, in time, using minimal effort for maximal effect.

Standard was where I shone. I wasn't tall, which was problematic as Standard girls usually are, but I was slim with a flexible spine and loose hips. In the beginning, I floated between partners, improving my technique and developing my skills, but not settling into a partnership that would allow me to cultivate my potential.

Then I walked into the studio when Oleg was dancing the Foxtrot. Tall with dark hair slicked back from a high forehead, he stroked across the floor in a Feather Step. His long legs ate up space until he'd made it halfway across the floor in four forward paces.

"Who's that?" I whispered to the girl next to me.

"Oleg Fortunov. He moved here from Staten Island. He's looking for a partner."

Oleg Fortunov, I thought. That sounded promising.

My mother's dreams rested on my shoulders, growing heavier each year. I needed a plan for achieving them as it was clear that my scholastic abilities were not up to the task. I was quick but lazy, and I found science and math boring, which meant medicine and finance, the best ways to impress folks from the old country, were out. The liberal arts were also a bust. Reading was tedious and as for writing, I preferred to talk, finding my tongue quicker than my pen.

It would have to be the dancing, which, while not as lucrative as other fields, promised medals to drape around the mantle. Fortunately, my mother didn't mind as long as I was bent on achieving something notable.

So I memorized Oleg's schedule, making sure to position myself around the studio when he was around. Then I ignored him, never looking in his direction nor acknowledging his presence. There's nothing more a man hates than to be ignored, especially one like Oleg, who was enjoying the attention from the girls at the studio.

"Hello," he said in Russian one day as I brushed the suede bottoms of my shoes, so they wouldn't slip on the floor.

"Hello." I answered in English.

He stuck out a hand for me to shake. "I've seen you around. I'm Oleg," he said in English, which was accented, not heavily but noticeably.

I ignored his hand and stepped into my shoes. "I haven't seen you around," I said in Russian. "I'm Nina."

His mouth gaped. He was probably used to women falling over themselves for him. I peeked up through my eyelashes at him. He was gazing at me with eyes wide with interest. My heart zipped into the lively cadence of a Quickstep.

"Do you do everything your way?" he asked.

I smiled. "Ask me to Waltz, and you can find out for yourself."

He did, and it was good. I was a little short for Oleg, but I matched his stride and ballooned my back to fill his dance position impressively.

"Nice," Arkady said as he watched from the sidelines.

We did Tango, Viennese Waltz, Foxtrot, and Quickstep. Those were good too.

I slipped out of my dance shoes. "That was fun.” I tossed him a casual wave. “See you around."

He gawked at me as I sauntered out of the studio.

The next day, he was waiting for me.

"Will you practice with me today?" he asked. His blue eyes were hard with purpose, like two shooter marbles.

I shrugged. "Maybe at the end."

I’d dressed with extra care in my favorite leaf-green skirt and turtleneck top that matched my eyes. I'd added a scent, nothing bold or spicy, just a light floral a man would catch in dance position.

I practiced with a variety of partners as Oleg watched me from the sidelines, his jaw slack with interest. When there were fifteen minutes left, he sought me out.

"Dance with me."

I gazed around the ballroom, pretending to scope out other potential partners.

"Okay," I said in a resigned tone.

It went on this way for some time, Oleg pursuing me, me pretending indifference until he got desperate.

After we'd danced a particularly good round, Oleg followed me home, hiding behind babushkas dragging shopping carts and mothers pushing baby carriages. He wasn't a good spy although that wasn't the point.

When I got to my building, I made a big show of looking for my keys, pulling them out, and then sticking the correct one into the lock. It gave Oleg plenty of time to dash down the block and throw himself on one knee.

He reached for my hand. "Dance with me.” He thrust a tiny diamond in a band of gold in my face. “Marry me.”

"I thought you’d never ask." Inside, my heart bounced happily. Oleg was a good catch, and married couples often did better in competition. Judges assumed the off-the-floor relationship manifested itself in on-the-floor chemistry.

I graduated from high school a few months later, and instead of a graduation party, I had a wedding. Two hundred people at a Russian restaurant paid for by the various men my mother entertained. No detail was overlooked. There were chocolate fountains and engraved invitations, red-rose centerpieces and a dress covered with seed pearls. The expense was only exceeded by the tackiness.

Oleg and I found jobs at the Castle and started competing in Standard. Competing in ballroom dancing was a marathon, staying motivated and working hard even when winning was far away.

Nowhere was this more evident than Standard where progress was glacial. Some of it had to do with technical development, which was enormous in the beginning before drifting to incremental changes that were almost unnoticeable. Couples could sit in second or third position for years, waiting for the first-place couple to retire. Oleg and I knew it was going to be a long road, but we were young and enthusiastic and mistakenly optimistic about the future.

It didn't take long for the luster to wear off with Oleg. Everything he did annoyed me. His arms swung emphatically when he walked as if he were a happy-go-lucky gorilla. I took to walking in front of him, so I wouldn't notice. The forehead that had once appeared so regal now seemed dome-like as his hairline made an alarming beeline for the crown of his head. He snored, he grumbled in the mornings, and he scattered his clothes around our apartment, no matter how many times I showed him the location of the laundry basket.

But beyond these annoyances, he was boring. His heart beat with the rhythm of an accountant. Penny-pinching filled him with a childlike glee that adults usually reserved for more impressive happenings like sun-soaked vacations or lavish meals.

"Look," he'd say. "I found case of bottled water for dollar less. Let's buy five."

I yawned.

He'd flip through dozens of open tabs on his laptop, blissfully comparison-shopping at big box stores and travel websites.

"If we take 5:33 a.m. flight to Cleveland and 9:20 a.m. back to New York, then we save eighteen dollars." Oleg bounced in his seat, a baby on favored grandparent's knee. "Per ticket."

"Bravo," I said, rolling my eyes. Oleg didn't notice; he'd turned back to the computer to see if he could find a lower rate on our hotel room.

Saving money was a good thing, but it was the only thing that Oleg got excited about: not dancing, not sex, and not me.

We taught and we practiced and we competed, and as the years rolled on, he annoyed me less and less. Oleg was a decent, hardworking man who took pride in providing a good living for us. He wasn't jealous or controlling, and he didn't care if I went to dinner with the girls from the Castle or took my mother to get her nails done. He didn't drink to excess, womanize, or lie.

As I listened to the girls at the Castle fret about dates who still lived with mothers and boyfriends who slept with best friends, my husband looked better and better. As long as it didn't cost too much money, he was happy to follow my lead off the dance floor.

He loved me, mostly because he didn't understand me.

My reminiscences retreated as the last dance of the competition, a Quickstep, faded and the finalists walked off the floor. As they wiped sweat from their brows and chugged water, I looked at Oleg across the floor, my heart in my eyes. He felt my gaze and turned his head. Our eyes met, and then he looked away.

Chapter 10

CARLY: DOLLARS TO DUMPLINGS

IT WAS OFFICIAL. Sam and I were together, on and off the dance floor. We found a cheapish sublet decorated exclusively in shades of sherbet in Sunnyside, Queens and threw ourselves into our new lives. College, Archer, and my parents receded into background noise when confronted with the raucous immediacy of life at the Castle.

Ralph was as good as his word and set us up with two lessons a week with Maxine. "She's trained everybody, and if she hasn't trained them, then someone she's trained is training them. All bucks stop with Maxine," he said.

Maxine was a birdlike woman in her fifties with a wedge of tangerine hair and a matching slash of lipstick. She always wore the same outfit of a black turtleneck, slim black pants, and Cuban-heeled, T-strapped dance shoes. A cup of tea was never located more than a few feet from her. Maxine's style was high on physical demonstration and low on words.

"Dancers are special creatures. You need to see it. You need to feel it. You do not need to hear it," she said. "That's what the music is for."

When she used words, she slanted toward the concise and the explicit.

"What are your goals?"

"To win Rising Star Smooth at Nationals," I said, hoping it wasn't so lofty of a goal that she'd pooh-pooh us out of the studio.

"When?"

"Next year," Sam said.

"Why so quick? Most couples take a few years to do that. They develop their style, work on their technique, keep the burnout to a minimum."

"For the challenge," Sam said. He used a confident tone, but he directed his eyes at his feet.

I nibbled my lower lip. Sam was my boyfriend and we spent hours together, but something was motivating his dancing beyond just the dancing.

I couldn't figure it out.

He lived like an open book. He spoke freely to his mother in front of me, and he left his laptop open with his email up. When his college roommate came to town, we went out for drinks, and he introduced me as "my girlfriend, Carly." He didn't even have a security code on his phone.

"How about you, Carly? Why do you want to do it in a year?"

"I have to go back to Ohio—that's where I'm from—to deal with some family things."

When I'd told my parents that I was staying in New York for the year, they'd been furious. They didn't yell although that would've been far preferable to the tactics they did use. In small, hurt voices, they listed all the ways how I was failing as a daughter.

"It's frivolous," my mother said. "Ballroom dancing means nothing in the scheme of things. It's a pastime for people with too much time and too much money on their hands."

"Are you using your gifts to their fullest potential to better the world?" my father asked. "When you go to bed, can you tell yourself that you spent your day in service of others?"

"We need you," they said. "Archer needs you."

"It's just for a year. One year for me to do something exciting and fun before I get back on track." I gasped a little, my lungs fogged with desperation and self-reproach. "It's called a gap year in Europe."

I hugged myself. I didn't have a good argument. Everything they said was true.

The next time I called, they'd reached a consensus. They'd be supportive as long as it was for a year. Then I'd return home, resume my studies in special education, and help out with Archer. "Focus on the skills you can acquire to help you educate your future classrooms of children," my mother said.

Relieved, I sent an email every week to Archer, detailing my life in New York and telling him funny stories about teaching and dancing. As I wrote the email, I pictured Archer in one of his green t-shirts, tag carefully removed to prevent irritating him, sitting across from me while rocking himself.

My heart squirmed guiltily. I didn't know if Archer would understand the email or even where I was and what I was doing, but my parents could read it out loud to him. Maybe it might feel, at least for a moment, that we were all together.

I spun my attention back to Maxine. She was nodding briskly. "You've got urgency. Tap into it. Remember that every action you make should lead you one step closer to the reaction you want."

She eyeballed us. "Samuel Chapman and Caroline Martindale, National Rising Star Smooth champions. It should be the mantra you say every hour, on the hour. Let it drive you when you practice, when you work out, when you're catching the plane to yet another competition in a Midwestern city you've never wanted to visit. Remember, if you don't win, you don't get a second chance."

Maxine was good. I yearned for a boulder to move. That's how pumped up I was.

She was also a quick worker. On our first lesson, we danced through the routines that Nina had devised, so that Maxine could evaluate our choreography and technical prowess.

"Nina did well by you," she said. "She played up your strengths and hid your weaknesses, of which there are many. I had no idea she understood Smooth at this level."

She picked apart the routines: cutting, pasting, copying, deleting. At the end of two hours, we had four competition-worthy pieces of choreography.

After she left, Sam groaned. "I hope I can remember it all."

I'd found a piece of paper and was scribbling Maxine's new routines on it. "We'll remember together," I said distractedly. "Did the Reverse Wave come before or after the jazzy side-by-side section in Foxtrot?"

"After," he said. "I think."

"How'd it go?" Nina asked during our dinner break.

"Maxine said you did a wonderful job with us."

I slurped a noodle, relishing the salty ribbon. There was a ramen shop down the block, which was good, cheap, and filling, the holy grail of food for a competitive ballroom dancer. I couldn't seem to eat enough. Calories in didn't replenish the calories out, which were expended in a blaze of teaching and practicing.

As bad as it was for me, it was worse for Sam. He scouted out dollar pizza parlors and dumpling joints. He scrounged for change, so that he could get an extra slice or a couple more dumplings.

“Look what I found.” Sam waved a twenty-dollar bill that had fallen, forgotten, into the sliver between the wall and a bookshelf in the teacher’s room. "Do you know how many dumplings this will buy?" he asked, licking his lips.

Nina snickered as I gave Sam a kiss.

I settled back into my chair. "How do you become a champion?" I asked Nina.

She scrunched up her face. "Grit, stamina, desire, talent." She shrugged. "The usual."

"Not the abstract, motivational-poster stuff. I want the practical stuff."

Nina bobbed her head from side to side as she thought. "Money," she said. "Lots of it. It's not a popular answer, but it is the answer. It buys you more opportunities, and opportunities are what you need."

Sam crossed his arms and tilted his head toward Nina. "What kind of opportunities?"

"Opportunities to pay for more lessons and to attend more competitions, especially the out-of-state ones where you can get in front of a different judging panel. It buys prettier costumes, a better hair-and-makeup team, new shoes. You don’t have to teach as much, so your body holds up better. Once you win the Rising Star at Nationals, the money gets easier."

"How come?" I asked.

"Companies will sponsor you in return for your endorsement. They loan you dresses, do your hair and makeup for free, and give you shoes. Studios will bring you in for a show, which can net a good check. The studio will bump up your pay because they can charge students more for lessons with a champion."

"Did that happen to you when you won the Rising Star in Standard?" I asked.

She nodded. "And if you win the Open at Nationals, it's even better. Plus, you're a champion, better than anybody else in the country."

Nina had given us the answer, but it presented another set of questions.

The Castle's set up was straightforward—teach a lesson and then get paid. However, this made a dependable paycheck difficult as the number of students taking lessons changed week by week. Some weeks were fantastic, others not so much.

There were ways to create stability. I could put students on a regular schedule or teach group classes, but students got sick or went out of town and group classes could be exhausting and annoying.

If we weren't competing, it wouldn't be a problem. But we also needed to practice for a couple of hours a day, which we did during the mornings when the studio wasn't busy. But practicing took time plus it left us too tired to teach more than four or five lessons a day, enough to live on but not enough to fund competitive ballroom dancing.

It was a cruel equation. Teaching more would net us more cash, but then we'd be too tired to compete, the whole purpose of teaching more.

"How did you get the money to win Rising Star?"

"We got lucky. Oleg had a student, Wanda Steinberg, who wanted to compete."

"Oleg competed with you and his student?"

"There's a whole pro-am circuit that's very popular. Most students are too old or not good enough to compete professionally, so they compete with their teachers. There are medals and championships, and the students take it seriously."

"How did Wanda Steinberg competing help you and Oleg?"

"She paid for herself and Oleg to get to all the competitions, everything from flights to meals. That meant we only had to pay my way."

"It must have been a huge amount of money for her," I said.

"She didn't care. She was old and her husband had died and she had a fortune with nothing to spend it on. She thought blowing it on winning the pro-am title in the senior-citizen Standard division was better than buying another fur or expensive meal."

"Did Oleg mind? Competing with her and then competing with you?" I asked.

Nina shifted her eyes downward. "He didn't mind," she whispered and then swiped at a shiny bead that looked like a tear. She lifted her head, her smile fixed and fluorescent.

"Wanda could be difficult—when you're paying that much money to one person, you think you own him—but she wasn't as bad as some of the others," Nina said. "Some students insist their teachers spend the entire competition with them."

"What happened to her?"

"She passed away a couple of years ago. They buried her wearing her Nationals medal."

As we rode the subway home, I thought over the conversation with Nina. A student would do the trick. But how to find a student? A nice one?

It would have to be me who found the student. No one was going to want to compete with Sam. He was, at best, a mediocre teacher who was indifferent to the needs of his students. He used the same scripts for the same steps, never varying his words or tone. I'd started teaching at the opposite end of the studio, so I didn't have to listen to him.

"Down like an elevator on one, now up like an escalator on two, three," he'd say as he plodded through the rise and fall in a Waltz box.

Down like an elevator on one, now up like as escalator on two, three, I'd recite along mentally. I dropped my vocal register to a *basso profundo* when I said *down* and then raised it several octaves on *up*, as Sam did.

With the exception of our practice sessions, where he executed everything full out, Sam was a sluggish dancer. He walked through all his demonstrations, and he never used hip action during the Latin dances. He made all his female students learn East Coast Swing even if they wanted something else because he didn't have to hold a formal dance position with lifted forearms.

"Have you heard of Swing?" he asked every new student. "You're going to love it."

Anybody who studied with Sam became an adroit Swing dancer and not much else.

Ralph had Sam's number and booked him with wedding couples or new female students who didn't know any better. Every once in a while, though, he'd have to teach someone more advanced who insisted on Waltz or Cha Cha, dances that required a modicum of effort. His face darkened into thunderclouds as he led Miss Chang into a Natural Spin Turn or Mrs. McDonald through the Three Cha Cha Chas Forward and Back.

"I hate teaching," he said when we got home. He'd had a taxing day of instructing dances other than Swing. He flung himself onto the sofa and tossed his arms behind his head, while I sprinkled cereal and streamed milk into bowls. We'd landed on cereal as our go-to dinner since we were too tired to cook at night.

I handed him his bowl. "I thought you enjoyed dancing."

I backed away carefully from the sofa. Sam had dumped his open laptop on the coffee table, its edge dangling in space, just asking to be hit. I nudged the laptop until it was resting safely on the coffee table. The screen blinked to life and up popped an article on gold prices.

Boring.

Especially in the face of our life, which, while grueling physically, was interesting and exciting.

"Correction. I enjoy dancing Smooth with you. But teaching sucks." He said sucks as if he were blowing a raspberry. "It's arduous being on my feet all day, holding dance position. The women are heavy, like bricks in a skin suit. And then, it's not enough to dance with them. They want to talk. All the time. About their husbands, their kids, their jobs, their mothers."

I patted him on the knee.

He groaned. "I'm a day laborer in a dress shirt listening to hens cluck," he said. "This is not the life, not the life at all."

I disagreed. I loved teaching.

Students came in with the same stated goals—dance at their daughter's wedding, have fun on a cruise, meet new people, but most were looking for something else. Sometimes it was tied to their ego, the need to be extraordinary at everything. Other times, it was to try something new and reengage with life. Often, they were driven by loneliness.

Ballroom dancing was inherently social, but steps replaced words and beats ironed out pauses. The shy, the awkward, and the weird found a home where good rhythm or a barn of a memory vanquished their shyness, awkwardness, and weirdness. Some got good while others stayed middling. Everyone, though, had fun.

As a teacher, I gave what I could where I could with a hug, a ready ear, a sympathetic nod. I loved seeing their eyes brighten, a smile spread across their face, a thankful chuckle. I found humor to be the most useful tool, a laugh being the shortest distance between two people.

My parents had drilled into me that the best life was one lived in service of others. But this wasn't what they meant. Ballroom dancing was a rich man's sport, and my students were bankers, lawyers, doctors, or executives.

They might possess aching hearts or bruised spirits, but they had full bellies, intact faculties, and bulging bank accounts. I was taking wealthy people's money in exchange for teaching them how to Foxtrot. And if I went the extra mile and offered them comfort while doing so, that was nice and all. But still. There were people with real problems and real needs whom I could be helping.

The back of my throat vulcanized into hard rubber. In my head, my parents' voices escalated.

Have you made the world a better place?

When you go to bed, can you feel good about yourself?

We need you. Archer needs you.

I silenced my parents' disapproving commentary and turned to solving the money problem.

I didn't have a student who seemed interested in competing. They were happy to show up once or twice a week, take their lesson, and then go about their lives. I broached it with one or two only to have it shot down.

I needed to find one soon. The season loomed, just a few months away. We couldn't get out onto the floor without costumes, and those were a huge chunk of change. Plus we needed to get to competitions to wear those costumes and that meant even more money for airfare, hotels, and meals.

"What if we can't get it together to compete the way we need to? Do we go another year?" I asked. My parents would flip out if I stayed for another year, but Ohio felt far away from New York. So far away that nothing seemed better than staying in New York for another year to work at the Castle and be with Sam.

"It has to be a year." Sam hardened his jaw as his eyes glinted with determination.

Chapter 11

NINA: PIOTR, JÜRGEN, AND FRED

NATIONALS–THE Nationals Oleg and I were supposed to win—dawned on a steamy day in early September when people fought summer's languid, lingering heat by turning their attention to holidays and bonuses and pumpkin spice lattes.

I didn't know what would be worse, staying at home to pretend it wasn't happening or attending to watch the funeral of my dreams

I went. It was the same as it was every year. A hotel near Penn Station hosted the event. It was always a laugh to see commuters do a double take at men in tail suits or women in risqué Latin costumes having a smoke outside or running to the bodega for a soda.

Nationals stretched over several days to accommodate the number of events it would host: professional, amateur, and pro-am. The last evening presented the Professional Open events, which would crown one couple in each division the best in the United States.

In a country where what someone did was more relevant than who someone was, winning Nationals meant something. It could be monetized, and its impact followed the champion for life. People loved winners.

I pushed through the heavy doors and walked into the ballroom, alternately hoping to see someone I knew and praying I could watch from a quiet corner.

I immediately bumped into Papa. His bald head gleamed through the few remaining strands he'd combed over it, and his belly strained against his cummerbund. Rumor had it that he used to be handsome when he was young, but that was hard to believe. In the eleven years

I'd known him, he'd looked the same, only with more hair and less belly.

Papa gave me an appreciative look. I'd dressed carefully in a long gown of clinging black jersey. The dress showed nothing with its long sleeves and high neck yet revealed everything.

"Nina, my dear." He extended his hand, which I took. He grasped it tightly while gazing into my eyes. "Don't you look lovely tonight?"

"It's nice to see you." I removed my hand and discreetly wiped it on my dress. "How's life treating you?"

"Better now that I've seen you."

Internally, I rolled my eyes. I'd known Papa for years, and he'd always been flirtatious with me. Nothing untoward, but a lingering glance here, the press of his hand there had convinced me of his interest.

Flattering to me, but useless for him. The last ten years I'd been married to Oleg, and now, even without him by my side, Papa held no interest. He was old, he was unattractive, and he was married to Maxine, my former coach.

Papa might be Chairman of the Judges, but in reality, he was little more than an empty suit. His position, seemingly full of power and prestige, might excite some newbie, but his job consisted of little more than glorified data entry.

As a coach, a good one, Maxine had all the power. Papa may tally the scores and announce the results, but everyone was loyal to Maxine. She made them better, more competitive; Papa just reported the fruits of her labor.

I smiled, feeling sympathy for him.

He leaned toward me. "Are you and Oleg doing a retirement dance tonight?"

I shook my head, blinking back my tears.

He rammed his eyebrows together. It looked like two fuzzy worms were kissing.

"You should. You deserve the fanfare. Rising Star Standard champions and Open bronze medalists."

The tears were threatening to spill.

"Let the winners enjoy the fanfare." I tried for a devil-may-care tone, but the tension in my jaw transformed the words into the mewling of a bereaved baby.

Papa placed a hand on my shoulder, which made the situation worse.

"Excuse me," I said. "I see someone I want to say hello to."

"If you need anything, let Papa know." He gave me a meaningful look, which I brushed off like a piece of lint.

I walked a little further into the ballroom. None of the events had started, but the space hummed with animation and expectation. I painted on a smiley face—toothy grin and big, welcoming eyes.

I made my way through the tables strewn around the perimeter of the dance floor. They teemed with well-dressed people, relaxed because their events were done, excited because they were about to witness the best ballroom dancing in the United States.

None of the championships had started, so competitors cluttered the on-deck area. Women in short fringed dresses swiveled their hips in sensuous figure eights. Men in tail suits stroked across the floor, subtly bending their knees and then rising onto their toes to create the stone-skimming-across-a-pond action of Foxtrot. Smooth couples held hands and marked through their Tango choreography, lifting and placing their feet as if jaguars tracking dinner.

My stomach clenched. This was the first year I wasn't with them. Oleg and I had a pre-competition routine. I did my hair and makeup before we got dressed. Then, we went to the practice room and ran through our routines. Next, we headed to the ballroom and checked in with the on-deck captain, affectionately known as door bitch.

On-deck captain was a thankless job, wrangling easily distracted, often late, sometimes grumpy competitors into line by the number pinned on the gentleman's back. The on-deck captain had to wheedle and beg and scream to get a heat of competitors on the floor before starting the process over again. Herding cats would be easier.

After we checked in with the on-deck captain, Oleg would find a quiet corner to mark through our routines. I preferred to burn off steam by chitchatting with the other dancers. Keeping my mouth going provided a much-needed outlet for my jangling nerves.

From years of talking to anyone and everyone, I knew tons of people. People who now gazed at me kindly, people who now ignored me, people who now gestured at me to sit with them.

Why had I come? I wished for rescue. I didn't want to be seen by anybody who'd known me before, when I was someone.

"We're so glad to see you."

I pivoted to my left. Carly and Sam, looking impossibly young in their dress-up clothes, were beaming at me.

I smiled, thankful for their presence. I missed teaching them, but if they were going to hit the circuit, then they needed a real coach like Maxine. "Enjoying the event?"

Carly clapped her hands together. "It's wonderful. Everyone is talented and so friendly."

I giggled at Carly's enthusiasm, unvarnished with cynicism or cheek. They really did grow them differently in the Midwest.

Sam shoved his hands in his pockets. "We're going to try to win the Rising Star Smooth in a year."

I lifted my eyebrows. "A year? Trey and Tamsin are the only couple to have done that."

"It's ambitious," Carly said. "But we're willing to work hard."

Sam put his arm around her and pulled her close. He kissed the top of her head as Carly glowed, a light bulb illuminated by happiness and a new adventure.

I clenched my teeth. Carly didn't remind me at all of my younger self, excited and optimistic, at my first Nationals. Not even a little bit.

And I definitely wasn't jealous of the future that lay in front of her. I only wished her and Sam the best.

"Good luck," I said and turned my attention to the dance floor. Open Standard was beginning.

For years, Standard had been one of the least popular divisions in the United States. To even step out onto a competition floor, regardless of any desire to place well, took years of practicing. When Oleg and I had competed our first year at Nationals, there weren't even two-dozen couples, just enough for a quarterfinal.

Now, the ranks had swelled. I looked at the line stretching across the on-deck area. I didn't know most of the couples. Virtually everyone from my time had retired.

Round after round unfolded. Waltz, Tango, Viennese Waltz, Foxtrot, and Quickstep. Mellifluous, dramatic, venerable, insouciant, and spirited. The dancers ranged from good to awe-inspiringly great.

I spotted the winners in the first round. Their dance position, magnificent like an ocean liner, provided a ballast against the woman's head, which traced the arc of a rainbow. Their technique was strong, but that wasn't enough to win. This couple had brilliant musicality.

Timing is straightforward and uncompromising in ballroom dancing. Step meets sound using quarter notes. Fourths get halved into eighths, doubled into halves, or, plenty of the time, stay as they are: quarter, quarter, quarter. But a beat, a fraction of a second in real time, can be attacked in myriad ways in dance time—early, late, smack in the middle.

This couple toyed with the music, two frisky mice that teased the old tomcat. Holding here, hastening there, they arrived everywhere almost, but not quite, late. They used their bodies the way award-winning actors use speech—meaning forged through pacing.

As couple after couple swept by me, I stopped feeling sad and started feeling inspired. My feet itched to move; my arms yearned to take dance position. I wanted to dash to the Castle, just a dozen blocks away, and try what I'd seen. Since I'd hung up my dance shoes, my right knee had stopped aching. My body felt fresh and up to the challenges of competitive ballroom dancing.

Papa announced the placement of the finalists (all *Russkis*) and then the winners, whom I'd correctly predicted. As the couple bowed, their excitement flashing off of them like a Fourth of July sparkler, I made a decision. I was going to look for a new partner.

The next day, I called Maxine to help me put the word out.

"I wouldn't recommend it," she said. "Even if you find a partner, do you want to start over? Because that's what's going to happen. The judges will ignore your past successes and treat you as if you're any other new couple."

"I miss dancing," I whined.

"Find a student who wants to compete. You can dance and get paid for the pleasure of doing so.

"I want a professional partner."

Maxine sighed. "I'll ask around, but I wouldn't hold my breath."

While she looked for partners, I got myself back in shape, which was harder than it sounded. Without a partner to practice with, I was forced to dance by myself. Vadim, the nicest of the *Russkis* Ralph had hired, took pity on me.

Vadim was the first man I'd met who was both handsome and redheaded although he did nothing for me romantically. He lapped me around the floor a few times in between lessons. I would have been embarrassed if I weren't grateful. Vadim competed in Latin, but he'd trained for years in Standard. He boasted crisp, clean technique, and his kindness helped me regain my skill.

Maxine was as good as her word, and before I knew it, I had three tryouts lined up.

Piotr was first. He was shorter and plumper than most Standard competitors with their sleek, lanky bodies. His English was nonexistent, so we chatted in Russian as we put on our shoes. He'd recently moved here from St. Petersburg, and he was struggling to adjust to American life.

"Why does everyone smile all the time?" he asked.

I was smiling as he said this, which I quickly flattened into a frown. "Americans believe in projecting confidence and happiness. A smile does that." In my head, I quoted the Russian proverb: *Smeh bez prichiny—priznak durachiny* (The laugh without reason—is the sign of stupidity).

"It is disingenuous." Glowering, he stood up and offered his hand. "Shall we?"

I accepted his grip.

"Maxine said you're former Rising Star champion and took bronze medal in Open last year."

"All true." I smiled before knitting my eyebrows together to affect a sterner expression.

Within two bars (a Natural Spin Turn) of Waltz, the tryout was over. Piotr was a good sport and danced some Tango and Foxtrot with me before admitting what I already knew. I wasn't good enough for him.

"This isn't right for me." He attempted a smile, which appeared as a straight line, to lessen the sting.

"Me either." I didn't smile.

The next one will be better, I thought.

Jürgen was an Austrian who'd moved to the United States to pursue a master's degree in civil engineering. He found his classes boring, and a chance stroll by a dance studio was enough to reignite his adolescent passion. He was young (twenty-three), attractive (long-limbed with a swoop of dark blond hair), and a strong dancer (a youth champion before he'd turned his attention to his studies).

He was also an utter asshole.

We were well matched physically, and when we took dance position, I felt a shiver of excitement. We danced no more than a handful of bars, before he stopped.

"You're not letting me lead." He stuck out his lower lip.

I gaped at him. All I was doing was letting him lead. We didn't have routines, so I was depending on the changes in his body to inform me of my movement.

And I'd thought things were going well.

"Let's try again," I said with a grim smile.

This time we'd gotten through no more than a couple of bars before he stopped.

"You're not letting me lead." He glared at me, and the features I'd found attractive just a few minutes earlier mutated into slits with two burning coals for eyes.

"Let's try Tango," I said.

Tango went better. We made it through most of a song before Jürgen stopped. By this point, I'd guessed why he was stopping. He was rusty and didn't know what to do next. It was easier to stop and blame me rather than admit his failings.

He opened his mouth, but I held up my hand.

"Let's not try anymore."

His face, blazing with anger, frosted over. Muttering under his breath, he grabbed his shoe bag.

Bang.

He'd slammed the door behind him.

I slumped onto a bench, exhausted even though we'd danced for no more than a few minutes.

The next one will be better, I thought although I doubted the value of my positive thinking.

I'd known Fred for years. He discovered ballroom dancing as a student at MIT, and although he worked full-time as a mathematics professor, he used his free time to compete professionally. Most people like him would register as an amateur, but he said that being out on the floor with the pros made him better. Fred was close to forty, but he showed no signs of wanting to retire.

"The only way I'm leaving the floor is on a stretcher," he'd said on more than one occasion.

He was delighted by the opportunity to try out with me. I swallowed my pride. I was a Nationals bronze medalist while Fred had barely scraped into the quarterfinal.

Within two bars (a Natural Spin Turn) of Waltz, the tryout was over. I was a good sport and danced some Tango and Foxtrot with Fred before admitting what I already knew. He wasn't good enough for me.

"This isn't right for me." I attempted a smile to lessen the sting.

"It was a long shot," he said. "It sure was fun to dance with you, Nina."

I smiled for real, impressed by his honesty.

Maxine called.

"How'd the tryouts go?"

"No one was right," I said.

"I'm sorry, Nina. The world changed. All we can do is adapt."

"Thank you," I whispered.

"If I get wind of something, I'll let you know."

When I got home that night to my sad apartment with my sad

dinners and my sad reality shows, I collapsed on the sofa and had the type of cry that comes in waves.

The storm would slow to a drizzle, and then an image (winning Rising Star at Nationals, the first time I took dance position with Oleg, a random competition in Seattle where the stars aligned and we danced so perfectly that I thought I was dreaming) would flash like a zigzag of lightning imprinting itself on my heart. The tears would intensify, and I found myself right back to where I started—a twenty-nine-year-old woman sobbing alone in her apartment.

I reached for a picture of Oleg and me, taken at last year's Nationals. We looked happy, our bronze medals swinging around our necks, the promise of our dreams coming true in a year or so. It seemed impossible this was how it had turned out.

I studied my husband's face, studious and poetic. I missed Oleg. My entire adult life save these last six months had unfolded with him by my side.

I wanted him to rejoin me in our dance, but I didn't know how to ask.

Chapter 12

CARLY: THE LOOKALIKE

I WAS LATE.

The line at the dumpling shop was longer than usual. By the time I ordered, paid, and ate, it was five minutes past when I should have started my lesson. Students hated late teachers. Dance lessons weren't cheap, and even missing a few minutes cost students a chunk of change.

I tore into the building, breathless and sweating, as I recited my apology in my head.

The doors of the elevator were closing.

Oh no.

With no time to wait for the next one, I thrust an arm into them before they shut.

Nothing happened.

I jostled my arm and then pitched my entire weight against the doors, trying to force them to part. Without warning, they thundered open, and I plunged into the rectangular abyss.

There was only one person in the elevator, a man with silver hair in a three-piece suit. I smashed into him, and we staggered into the back wall. For a long moment, we stayed there, trying to find our equilibrium. Then I slapped a hand to the wooden paneling to steady myself and leaped off of him.

"I'm so sorry," I cried. "Are you okay?"

"Oof." He lurched himself to standing.

He looked at me, and then his face paled.

"Are you sure you're okay?" I asked. The expression in his eyes—pinched and haunted—was frightening me. "Should I call for someone?"

He shook himself. "I'm fine. Startled but unharmed. You certainly know how to make an entrance."

I smiled ruefully. "Like a deer jumping in front of a car."

He laughed, and then the elevator pinged for the twelfth floor.

I groaned and pushed four.

"Do you work at the dance studio?" he asked, his eyes still tormented.

"The Castle: Step in to step out." I recited the tagline automatically as the doors closed.

I didn't think any more of the incident until Ralph called me into his office a few hours later.

"Carly, Carly. I gotta lotta news for you." Ralph had stretched his meaty cheeks back and was baring his teeth. He resembled an avaricious teddy bear. Only one thing made Ralph this happy. Money.

"You do?"

"A guy came in today and bought a hundred lessons."

My jaw dropped. "A hundred lessons?" Most new students did packages of five or ten to see if they enjoyed it. A hundred was unheard of for a new student. Especially a student who'd never taken a lesson.

"He said you ran into him in the elevator, and you talked him into dance lessons."

"I did?"

"He was wearing a three-piece suit. Has silver hair," Ralph said. "Name's Jason Justus. He's a financier and was in the building to visit his lawyer."

"I did run into him. Literally."

"So I gotta tell you, he seems nice, but he recently lost his wife."

I inhaled. "Did he say what happened?"

"Car accident. A drunk driver hit her."

"How traumatic." I didn't know Jason Justus, but my heart went out to him.

"That's not the only thing."

I cocked my head.

"He showed me a picture of the wife. You're a dead ringer for her."

My shoulders slumped. "Ralph, do you think this is a good idea? Maybe Nina should teach him?"

"He bought the lessons on the condition they be with you."

I nibbled my top lip. "I'm not comfortable with this."

"I told him the rules. We gotta strict no-fraternization policy between teachers and students. He said he understood."

"Okay," I said uncertainly.

"Look at it like this. You're gonna give a grieving man some solace."

The whole thing creeped me out, but there was no way Ralph was refunding the money unless Jason Justus gave him a reason.

Jason showed up for his first lesson in a gray three-piece suit, shiny with nerves.

I smiled, hoping to calm his apprehension. In the abstract, dance lessons sounded great, but when confronted with the actuality of moving one's body in time to music, many students froze.

"If you thought the entrance was impressive, wait until you see the exit," I said. My words glimmered with briskness and brightness—my best teacher voice.

"Such grace, such poise as you tackled me to the ground."

"The Castle is a special place. We only accept the strongest, the toughest recruits."

"Jason Justus, reporting for duty."

"Your first mission, Private Justus, is the Foxtrot. Don't let the silly name fool you. This is a sly, elusive dance that fells even the bravest who attempt to tame it."

And off we went.

Jason wasn't the worst student I'd ever taught, but he was far from the best. He had an ear for music, which helped, but he had no memory for steps. I would do a warm-up dance at the beginning of each lesson to see what stuck from the previous one. Often, he drew a blank.

"He's going to be good for another hundred lessons." Ralph practically licked his lips after watching me teach Jason the Quarter Turns in Foxtrot for the third time. After a month of lessons, Jason had only made incremental progress.

Jason was affable and respectful, but I never forgot he was taking lessons because I reminded him of his late wife.

It seemed he couldn't forget either. Every once in a while, I'd catch him staring at me, his grin drooping and his eyes hooded.

The whole thing felt sad and macabre, but I pushed forward. Maybe Ralph was right, and I was providing solace to a grieving man.

Sam thrust his jaw in the direction of Jason, who was heading to the elevator after a lesson. "He's our solution."

I shook my head. There had to be a better way than preying on a widower's grief.

Chapter 13

NINA: A FULL STOP

WITHOUT DANCING, mine or other people's, to preoccupy me, melancholia took root. Winter came earlier than usual, which didn't help. It was a brutal one, with an excess of snow and sleet. Watery beads and frosty pinwheels streamed to the earth. The city amassed nature's gewgaws into filthy puddles and mounds of gray snow that rested, mountain-like, between the grimy cars parked on the streets. Temperatures plummeted to the single digits and then stayed there like a cold the world couldn't shake.

I bought a new coat, a luxurious camel-colored one with a slouchy neck and sash at the waist. I huddled into it, my barrier against the weather that made me feel as if I was walking through a torrent of tears. I took to sleeping with the light on to counter the nights that stretched out like a quilt patched black with my regret and loneliness.

To combat the gloom, I became excessively social. I caught up with people I hadn't seen in years because I'd been busy dancing. I accepted every invitation tossed my way, even if meant doing something I hated like chugging beer at a grubby dive bar.

The one person I avoided was my mother. I employed a litany of excuses. *I'm sick, I'm working, I'm out of town.* When I did see her, I kept it short and sweet. A pedicure where we read fashion magazines or a swing by her apartment to drop off a quiche I'd made.

"How is everything?" she'd asked.

"Great!"

She tilted her head at me, her eyes sharp, her eyebrows raised, but I kept my smile fixed and my tone bright.

"Never better." I'd add for good measure.

For New Year's Day, I invited the teachers from the Castle to my apartment.

Some traditions from the old country stuck, and New Year's was one of them. For years in Russia, no one could celebrate Christmas or Hanukkah, so New Year's became the important holiday of the winter solstice. Families and friends exchanged gifts, toasted to health and wealth, and ate from platters brimming with savory and sweet treats.

For the last ten years, I'd spent New Year's with Oleg's family in Staten Island. We'd always had a grand time. His mother was surrounded by men: her husband, Oleg's younger brother Nikolai, Oleg's grandfather. Even the two dogs were boys.

She took to me immediately. We cooked in the kitchen, gossiping and giggling about our menfolk. His family had always gone full out for New Year's with expensive bottles of champagne, top-of-the-line caviar, and platters of smoked fish. We drank and laughed and ate ourselves silly.

This year I was on my own.

Every once in a while, staying in the game of life required a full stop and the gift of that full stop—a fresh start. New Year's was going to be my full stop, so I could write a new story, one that didn't involve me crying yet again in my apartment alone.

Planning for my party kept me busy as I decluttered and rearranged and updated. I found some fancy throw pillows (vibrant red-and-pink paisley) and a few vases (two red, one pink), all deeply discounted to add some zing to the neutral hues of my apartment that I'd begun to find depressing.

My heartbeat slowed into a sad march. I wouldn't be able to impress Oleg with my bargain hunting.

Ralph rented a limo for the staff and himself. They arrived en masse, leaving a jumble of wet boots and overcoats in the hall, a place that smelled of meals cooked twenty years ago.

I put out a spread that was half Russian and half American. Caviar, crème fraîche, and blinis mingled with wedges of cheddar cheese and bowls of corn chips. I'd bought a cake from the fancy bakery on Avenue X and looped chocolate-chip cookies around the base. Vodka was a drink that transcended borders, so I ordered a case.

"It's a different world down here," Sam said, chomping on a chip.

My lips twitched as I imagined what a Texan like Sam thought of Sheepshead Bay. Old people in thick-soled shoes poked through the stores as glossy-haired young adults, conspicuously clad in designer clothing, thronged the restaurants and bars. The signage was in Russian as was the conversation. The side streets held enormous brick apartment buildings, plain and faintly hostile, like something Stalin would approve of. No one smiled although deep emotion teemed behind those scowls: wrath, ardor, bone-deep sorrow.

"Does anyone speak English?" he asked.

"The younger generation does." I shrugged. "As for the older generation, they don't need it."

Sam shook his head in wonder.

Ralph pulled me aside. "I gotta tell you, you did a nice job here." He tugged at his shirt collar. "The holidays, they, uh, can be tough."

I widened my burning eyes. If I kept them open, then I wouldn't need to blink away the tears that crowded them. Ralph's sympathy had been a prizewinner's punch to my gut.

"Thank you for coming," I said in a stately voice and walked away.

Carly, wearing a red sweater frilled with lace at the hem, laughed at the appropriate moments and tossed back a shot of vodka with everyone, but her shoulders were stooped and her eyes looked vacant.

When Sam got up to chat with Vadim, I slid into his chair. "How'd it go?" I asked. She'd gone home to visit her family for Christmas.

"Not good," she said in a thin, colorless voice. "My parents are struggling with Archer. He just started to go through puberty, and he doesn't understand what's happening. He's having daily tantrums, and he isn't sleeping. At all."

I patted her on the arm. "That's tough on everybody."

She pushed up the sleeve of her sweater. Three vicious scratches, crimson and dotted with scabs, trailed from her elbow to wrist. "War wounds."

I gasped.

"My parents are in worse shape. They didn't want me to come back." She sighed. "Obviously, I did." She plucked at the lace on her sweater.

I didn't know what to say. The situation seemed traumatic for everyone involved. Grasping for something to say, I said, "That's a pretty sweater. Did you get it for Christmas?"

The corners of her lips lifted. "From Sam." She shot a fond look over at him, who was clinking glasses with Vadim. Sam's cheeks matched Vadim's scarlet hair.

"*Na Zdorovie*," Vadim said and then tossed back his shot.

"Nasty . . . whatever." Sam swilled his shot and slammed his glass down. "Woo-hoo," he shouted.

I winced. "Is he trying to keep up with Vadim?"

Carly giggled. "Tomorrow's going to be rough for him. Good thing it's Sunday."

Using the two measuring sticks of a successful party, intoxication and elation, I could safely call my New Year's gathering a triumph. Everyone, including me, was tipsy and happy from the booze and laughter.

"This is the way to start the year we win Rising Star," Sam yelled as he staggered out the door leaning on Carly's arm.

Carly steadied Sam. "Thank you," she called over her shoulder.

She looked better than she had at the beginning of the party. Maybe it was all the alcohol, but her eyes were lively and her indefatigable smile was anchored back in place.

When everyone left, I washed glasses and threw food-encrusted napkins in the garbage. I should have been tired, but a post-party high had buoyed my spirits. I grabbed a notepad and a pen.

New Year's Resolutions

1. Get Oleg back.

Chapter 14

CARLY: THE GRIND

BY THE TIME January rolled around, Sam and I had established a groove with the 7 train acting as the artery we moved along. We woke early, before the promise of sunrise, and took the subway into Manhattan. We huddled among the bike messengers, the short-order cooks, the delivery men, and the cleaning ladies. These were the people whose invisible industry provided the infrastructure for the more visible, lucrative industries of Midtown Manhattan like banking, fashion, and theater.

New York had become a frozen jungle, so Sam and I twined our bodies together for warmth as we stood on the crowded train. He clasped the rail, and then I clasped him as the brindled brick buildings of Queens with their red-painted fire escapes streamed by.

Although we spent all our hours together, we still took pleasure in each other's company. It was the first adult relationship for both of us, and even with the first flush of love gone, we were enjoying ourselves immensely.

Maybe it was because of our goal to win Nationals, but we turned everything into a competition.

"I bet I can clean the bathroom faster than you can do the kitchen," he'd say.

I ran for the mop. "Overconfident much?"

We raced to see who could climb the stairs fastest at the 46th Street Station, and who could fold the laundry the quickest. We had dumpling-eating contests, which Sam won. At night, we collapsed into bed where there was no competition, just two young, hungry bodies whose hearts pounded in time with one another.

Sam was open and honest like one of those big Texas skies he'd grown up under. He liked what he liked and didn't care about the rest. He followed all the Houston teams avidly, so on Sundays, we headed to a bar with longhorns on the wall and a gigantic Texas flag stretched above the bar. We watched whatever game was on while drinking beer. It was a sociable place, and once people found out we were ballroom dancers, they'd buy us beers if we'd do a few steps.

"Something fancy," a beefy guy in a Texans jersey would yell, so we'd dance a few bars from our Tango or Waltz.

"Woohoo, beers for the hoofers." The bartender would slam two glasses in front of us with foam oozing down the sides in pathways that reminded me of the Feather Steps and Three Steps of Foxtrot.

They had dollar wings, and the server, a blowsy bottle-blonde who had to be pushing fifty, threw some fries in.

"Y'all remind me of my kids," she'd say as she pushed a basket heaped with hot, salty, crinkle-cut fries toward us. We devoured everything and then squeezed our greasy hands together under the bar.

It was fun for very few dollars although I felt guilty living in New York and never seeing anything save our apartment, the studio, and the bar. I tossed it off. We were busy, and we were happy.

The one thing I couldn't toss off was the money. The season was starting in a few weeks, and we were in intense training mode, which Sam referred to as the grind.

"Rinse, repeat. Rinse, repeat," he said, scowling, as yet another morning dawned, and we headed in early to work yet again on our dancing.

I pushed him against the wall of the subway station and kissed him, a passionate, tongue-down-the-throat kiss. "That's not part of rinse, repeat," I said.

"Nope." He grabbed my hand, and we sprinted to our apartment. Our dancing didn't improve that day, but Sam's mood did. Every couple of weeks, when his complaining reached a fever pitch, I'd remind him that our bodies could practice in other ways.

Ralph was so pleased with the addition of Jason Justus to the student roster that he sprung for an extra lesson with Maxine. To ensure that we moved forward rather than pay to have Maxine tell us the same thing twice, we took her earliest lesson slot. Then we practiced until the students started rolling in.

"We'll work in themes: footwork one lesson, dance position the next. We need to get the basics up to par before you hit the floor," Maxine said. "You should plan to make your debut in early February."

On the days we didn't have lessons with Maxine, we practiced what she taught us, which meant reviewing the same thing over and over. To keep from arguing, we developed short cuts.

"Whoa, Nelly," Sam said when I rushed into a step without letting him lead it.

"Sam cannot play it again," he said when his exasperation peaked.

Sometimes, we'd remember that we were young and in love. "Cheek to cheek," Sam or I would say, and we would drop whatever we were doing and slow dance as if we were grandparents at a wedding.

Sam gifted me with a notebook after he saw me struggling to keep track of all the scraps of paper I'd scribbled Maxine's notes on.

"Gold," he said as he dropped it in my lap. "The color of that medal we're going to win."

On the cover, he'd scribbled, *Sam & Carly: Rising Star Smooth Champions*. He'd drawn a heart around it like a besotted middle-schooler. I gave him a big kiss; he'd given up a lot of dumplings for this.

We improved, quickly.

"You're doing well," Maxine said with a brief smile. "We need to talk about your look."

"Our look?" I asked.

"You want to present a visual calling card, so the judges can recognize you."

"Have you thought about a dress yet?"

I scraped the floor with my toe. "Sort of."

"Sticker shock?" Maxine asked.

I nodded.

"Start with something simple. You can add rhinestones as you go." Maxine took a step back and studied me. "Long-sleeved but backless. Red or orange. Your coloring is a touch muted, so you're going to need a bright color to stand out."

Even simple dresses were a fortune. A fortune we did not have.

Maxine brushed a hand against my hair. "You can get away with doing your own hair and makeup. Look online for videos and then practice. That'll save you some money."

Saving money was good, but we needed cash in hand, as in now, to hit the floor in February. That night, Sam and I counted the small stash of bills we'd squirreled away in a coffee mug.

I pressed out the creases of the few bills we had. "We're not even close."

"You have to ask Jason."

"It feels immoral, preying on his grief for our benefit." I stopped. "It is immoral. Can't we think of another way?"

"What other way? There are only so many hours in the day. Ask him. If he says no, then he says no."

I bit my lip. "He's not going to say no."

"Nope. Maybe competing will get some of those steps to sink in."

After my next lesson with Jason, I asked him to go to the office with me.

"Am I in trouble, Miss Martindale?"

"You did throw a number of rocks around today." I'd taught Jason a pattern in Rumba called Progressive Rocks with weight shifts that advanced incrementally. He'd done well with it although I doubted it would survive until our next lesson.

Sam had planted a seed, and I grew my argument around it.

"It's been a pleasure teaching you, and as your teacher, it's my goal to help you become the best dancer you can," I said.

"You're not giving up on me?"

"Quite the opposite."

Jason grinned, which made him look no older than thirty. I still hadn't figured out his age. He had silver hair, but the smooth skin and twinkly eyes of a young man.

"I've been brainstorming ideas about how we can improve your kinesthetic memory," I said carefully.

He laughed. "You mean help me remember what I've learned from one lesson to the next? Let's call a spade a spade."

I smiled, grateful for his good humor. "Pretty much."

"You've been patient and creative, but I might be a lost cause." He caught sight of my head, which was shaking no. "If I take enough lessons, something is bound to stick."

"You need a goal. There's nothing better than urgency."

He leaned toward me. "What kind of goal?"

"Competition." Under the table, I tugged at the hem of my skirt.

"Isn't that for professionals?"

"Before the professional divisions, competitions host events for students to compete in with their teachers." I let the information sink in. "It's fun, and you can win medals . . . and stuff," I finished up lamely.

Jason gazed at me intently. "How does it work?"

I explained how competitions were structured. We'd fly to whichever city was hosting one; Jason would dance in the morning against other men of his age and level. In the early evenings, Sam and I would compete in the Rising Star division.

"So it'd be the three of us traveling together?" he asked.

I nodded.

Jason didn't say anything for a minute, his eyes unreadable. Then he nodded. "I'm in."

After Ralph went in to handle the finances with Jason, I found Sam.

I attempted a happy face. "He's in."

Sam plunked a kiss on my head. "We're in it to win it now." I relaxed against him and pushed my guilt into a back corner of my heart.

I found a red dress with a low back and long sleeves in the spirit of Maxine's suggestion. The dressmaker suggested I pair it with an ornate necklace since I couldn't afford to have the dress covered in rhinestones.

"Bring it back every couple of weeks," the dressmaker said. "We'll start with the cuffs and the neckline and then add from there. By Nationals, we might be able to do something with the skirt."

I gulped as I wrote my check. It could buy us enough dumplings for a month.

With my dress in hand, we were officially in it to win it. Having solved the money problem meant we could concentrate on the part that mattered—our dancing.

But we'd plateaued. We'd made all the big advances; now we had to focus on the minutiae. I adored practicing the same thing over and over, perfecting the hundreds of particulars in each action.

I didn't think I'd ever get tired of ballroom dancing where the details had details. I loved how an inch this way or a twist that way could create ease and beauty.

To keep Sam, who grew bored easily, on track, we spent no more than fifteen minutes on each dance. At the end of the hour, we'd cycle back around and pick up where we left off in each dance. It was imperfect, and many issues lingered, unfixed, until Maxine got hold of them.

On the plus side, our dances developed evenly. We didn't get sucked into spending most of our time on Waltz, some of our time on Tango and Foxtrot, and none of our time on Viennese Waltz.

Sam's short attention span would be what got us noticed. We began to pick up placements in Viennese Waltz. Foxtrot and Tango soon followed. Waltz took a while.

When we started competing, time sped up, and as a result, life flattened into a collage of indistinguishable airports, hotels, and coffee shops.

"I thought traveling was supposed to be fun," Sam said as we waited with our luggage for a cab yet again in the heartland. "But it's just the refrain on a song that never ends."

Jason grinned. "Why do you think travel magazines only show pictures of the destination and never the journey?"

I'd been nervous about competing with Sam and Jason, but Jason's presence ended up a blessing. Sam and I stayed on our best behavior. We never let the stress and tedium eat at us, and we didn't devolve into bickering or tantrums as other couples did.

Jason was a kind companion, treating me with deference and Sam as a kid brother.

"Think fast," he'd say as he tossed Sam a Dr. Pepper in between rounds.

"Shall we dance, my lady?" he'd ask when we lined up for our heat.

"You looked great out there," he'd say after we finished the Rising Star event. "They should have canceled the competition and crowned you as winners."

This was after we'd finished dead last.

After watching other students in action, the ones who treated their teachers like slaves or the ones who lusted after their teachers, I became even more grateful for Jason. The only thing he wanted was laughter, from me at his jokes and for him at my jokes. I did both willingly. Jason and I shared a similar sense of humor.

Once Jason discovered Sam had majored in business, they spent flights chatting about industry topics I couldn't follow. I pretended to be interested in the beginning, but later I took to dozing, delighted by the empty time and space to relax.

As Sam predicted, Jason improved. Faced with the possibility of performative failure, some of the steps began to stick. I set goals for us: the Corte, a flashy beginner dip in Tango, for a competition in Cleveland; the Simple Twinkle in Foxtrot where the duo moved from facing each other to profile for one in Phoenix.

Jason performed better than I expected. He competed in the Newcomer division, which made for a wildly mixed bag of other novice men in his age range. I hadn't been sure which age group to put him in, so I handed him the form to fill out.

"A lady never asks a man his age."

He checked a box and handed it back to me. "I'm younger than I look."

I blinked. Jason was barely thirty.

"I thought you were younger than this," I said, to cover my surprise. "I had no idea I was teaching a man of your age and stature."

Jason winked. "Is it the suit?"

"Of course. Only the youngest and hippest men wear three-piece suits."

He preened, as a joke, and then explained. "I started wearing them in college. I was getting together a team of investors, but everybody thought I was too young to manage their money. So I found the most conservative, old-man suit possible," he said. "It worked, so I made it my uniform." He pointed at his hair. "Although I don't need it now."

Jason's repertory was limited, but he maintained consistent timing, the most important element in ballroom dancing. He placed in the middle of the pack, occasionally inching up to a bronze medal.

"I like him," Sam said after we'd traveled with Jason a few times.

"Me too."

I'd grown fond of Jason. The three of us had fun together, and it was nice to have someone to root for us.

"He's going to make some lucky girl a good husband once he's worked through his grief," I said.

Sam wrapped his arms around me. "Not this girl."

I laid my head against his chest. "Not this girl."

Chapter 15

NINA: OLEG'S BIG DEAL

THE RUMORS STARTED before I had a chance to hatch a plan. At first, I didn't pay them any mind. They were wisps of gossip, thin and unsubstantiated, blowing around the teacher's room like tumbleweeds.

But then the wisps coalesced into one piece of news that vibrated like a heart about to shatter. Oleg had moved on.

I bit my lip as I studied my New Year's Resolution. It was going to be a lot harder if the rumors were true.

I paced around my apartment as I rejected one idea after another. A lot of time had passed. Too much time.

I cursed my pride. I should have reached out months ago. Instead, I'd let the argument fester until it'd grown snarled with disease. All because I was too chicken to admit I'd acted hastily.

Honesty was my best option. I would apologize and ask if we could start again. Maybe I would even move to Charlotte to open a franchise of the Castle although I hoped that could be renegotiated. Maybe we could find something in New Jersey or Long Island.

My pride, always robust, had shrunk in the face of my loneliness and failure. It made a pitiful stand when I reached for the phone on Valentine's Day, but I batted it away like a noticeable but not particularly exasperating mosquito.

Oleg had been good about Valentine's Day even though it was a made-up holiday with jacked-up prices. I'd always received a dozen red roses delivered to the Castle plus a box of fancy chocolates would be waiting for me at home.

This year would mark the first time that I'd receive nothing. Oleg might not have been original, but he'd been consistent.

Plenty of girls over the years left work with wet eyes when their boyfriend or husband sent them nothing. Oleg had made sure I knew that I was loved.

"Nina," he answered. "I was about to call."

This was promising. "You were?"

"I come this weekend and get rest of my stuff, okay?"

I gulped. "Your stuff?" Many a weepy evening, I'd taken comfort in the fact that most of Oleg's stuff was still at our apartment. *It's just a break,* I'd told myself. *Every couple needs one now and again.*

"My stuff. Remember how you threw me out because you would not face facts?"

"Oh, that. I didn't mean permanently," I said foolishly.

"I have moved on with life. Next week, I go to Charlotte."

My eyes bulged. "What?"

"Next week, I go to Charlotte," Oleg said again. "You have moved on, no? With dancing? With life?"

My pride rallied. "Of course."

Although, of course, I hadn't, and Oleg knew this. The ballroom dance world was small enough that he'd heard through the grapevine that I was alone, on and off the dance floor.

"Good. I will bring someone to help with things."

"Nikolai?" Nikolai was Oleg's brother who still lived in Staten Island with their parents. Although older, Nikolai was the beta version of Oleg. He was not as tall, not as attractive, and not as talented.

"Ksenia. She will go with me to Charlotte."

I dropped the phone.

"Nina?"

Tears were gathering, and my nose was running.

I picked up the phone. "Does Saturday work?" I asked through my sniffles.

"Are you crying?" Oleg asked, his timbre high with incredulity.

"Allergies." I swallowed a sob that threatened to escape. "February is terrible for them."

He snorted. "You are liar."

"I do look forward to meeting Ksenia," I said in a grand voice before hanging up.

I sank to the floor, weeping. Oleg had moved on? In not even a year? While I'd been pining for him and his bargain shopping?

I beat my fists against the floor as if I were a small child, astounded by the unfairness of it all. I'd lost Nationals and my husband in not even twelve months.

It was not supposed to turn out this way. I was not supposed to be almost thirty, divorced with no Nationals title. I'd put the time in; I'd put the money in. I'd worked hard, and I'd paid my dues.

I was woefully unprepared for my labor not to bear fruit. I'd gotten everything I wanted in life, convinced that if I wanted it enough and worked hard enough it would be mine. Wasn't that the formula for being a winner?

But when the dream failed to manifest, I'd acted out against the person I loved most. And now I was going to pay, big time.

I buried my head into my hands. The future looked grim, and I wasn't sure how to fix it.

On Saturday, Oleg came over with Ksenia.

I checked her out. Feathery blonde hair crowning pointy features. Slender with small bones still covered in baby fat.

A gosling.

"How old is she?" I hissed in English.

Oleg crossed his arms. "Eighteen. The same age you were when we got married."

"But you were twenty-two."

Ksenia gazed at us blankly.

"Does she speak English?"

"She will learn."

"How did you meet her?"

"It does not matter."

"At a party? A restaurant? Your family?" My tone was escalating to a shriek.

"It does not matter."

An image of Oleg excitedly deal hunting on his laptop popped into my head. "Online?"

He nodded and made a big show of heaving a handful of dress shirts in dry cleaning bags out of the closet.

I glanced at Ksenia again.

She was wearing a cropped white t-shirt that showed her belly. A pleather white jacket. Tight light blue jeans with a white belt. Patent leather white boots. She played with the strap of her knockoff Chanel purse. One of the Cs had come loose and was drooping like a frown. She flipped it. A smile.

No Russian-American girl would be caught wearing this cheap, out-of-season, dated outfit. It was the clothing of someone trying to emulate an American.

My eyes widened as an unwelcome thought took root. "Is she a mail-order bride?"

Oleg flushed. "We have love connection. Ksenia is very understanding."

I clenched my teeth. While I'd been crying into one of Oleg's shirts, he'd been hunting for a replacement.

"You went shopping for a wife?" I shouted. "What about me?"

"You told me not to come home."

I stared at my feet as I cursed my stupid, useless pride.

"I will need help in Charlotte to open studio. I must find space, train teachers, advertise." Oleg's eyes brightened to the azure of a summer day. I pictured him joyfully evaluating this location against that one, a thousand open tabs promising the perfect deal

"Is she a dancer?" Out of the corner of my eye, I evaluated Ksenia's athletic potential. She was twirling the C around in circles as her tongue pushed out of her lips. She didn't look much like a dancer.

Oleg shook his head. "She wants to be wife and mother." He smiled. "I will focus on business, and she will focus on home. A partnership."

I looked around for something to throw at Oleg, but nothing epic enough was within arm's reach.

"That is the last of it." Oleg pointed to the pile of dress shirts on what used to be our bed. "My lawyer will contact you this week with papers. I need to move quick, so Ksenia can stay."

I willed myself not to cry. "Enjoy Charlotte."

"Nina, it is wonderful city. People are friendly, and everything is cheap."

My bottom lip was trembling. I willed it into submission. "Good luck," I said, showcasing all my teeth.

Oleg gestured to Ksenia, who leaped to her feet. She grabbed a handful of hangers and slung them over her shoulder. Then she grasped a duffel bag with the other and walked to the door.

In spite of my grief, I raised my eyebrows, impressed. The gosling was strong.

"Wait," Oleg said to Ksenia in a strident voice he'd never used with me. He turned to face me.

The tears were pushing at my eyeballs. I wouldn't be able to hold them back much longer. The words I wanted to say—I made a mistake, I want you back—couldn't breach the big, swollen balloon of my ego.

So I stuck out my hand instead. "We had a good round."

He shook it and kissed my cheek as if I were a loser in the competition line up and he the winner, shining his munificence upon me.

Oleg left, and I stood, weeping and alone, officially un-partnered for the first time in more than a decade.

Chapter 16

CARLY: HOUSTON

NATIONALS WAS GETTING CLOSER and closer, and Sam and I were getting better and better, placing second or third in most competitions. But second or third was not first, and we were gunning for first.

"It's the reason I keep going." Sam kneaded his shoulders. "The voice in my head that says 'From New York, New York, couple twenty, Samuel Chapman and Caroline Martindale, National Rising Star Smooth Champions.'"

Only one other couple had won the Rising Star in a year, Trey Devereux and Tamsin Grubbs. Whenever I had a few minutes, I watched their old videos, to study their technique, their style, their poise. In truth, I studied Trey and ignored Tamsin. Something about him had bewitched me.

Sam groaned as I pulled up yet another video of Trey and Tamsin. "Not that guy again."

"I learn something every time I watch him," I said as, on the video, Trey stalked with Tamsin across the floor in Tango in an Open Reverse Turn, a box with no close of the feet.

They were in Shadow Position. Both faced the same direction, but the woman was side and slightly in front of the man. It created a contrapuntal effect as the woman could use her free arm to swish through the air slower than the staccato action of the feet.

The video zoomed in for a close-up of Trey, his face magnified to godlike proportions.

"What it's like to be that good-looking?" Sam asked.

Tiny, restless balls of electricity rattled through my stomach as I studied Trey. "Probably amazing. Plus he won Nationals three times, and he's rich."

"I bet he lives like a rock star, thigh deep in women, fast cars, and gold medals." Sam slumped on a bench as he tipped a can of Dr. Pepper down his throat. "Must be nice."

I turned off the computer and danced over to Sam. "You know what would be nice? A kiss before we run Waltz again."

We kept at the grind, but we'd run into a wall, a hard, unyielding one—DeShawn Porter and Nicolette Jackson. DeShawn and Nicolette were an African-American couple, one of the few on the circuit. They'd been competing in Rising Star for close to a decade, had been in the final for a couple of years, and were finally on track to win it.

Their story was mythic, repeated by competitors at every event DeShawn and Nicolette showed up to. Both had come from broken families and impoverished neighborhoods in Washington, D.C. They'd emerged unscathed thanks to a few strokes of luck that included admission to a charter school and a government-funded after-school dance program that stayed afloat through their teenaged years.

A ballroom dance studio owner had attended an open house where DeShawn and Nicolette performed a jazz duet to a medley of disco tunes. He'd offered them jobs as soon as they walked off stage.

While DeShawn and Nicolette may have escaped the cycle of violence and poverty, their friends and family hadn't. They were constantly dipping into their paychecks to help this sister out with rent or buy that cousin diapers. The government-funded after-school dance program that had done so much for them had been unceremoniously slashed when a new political party took office, so DeShawn and Nicolette taught classes for free in troubled schools.

Beyond that, they were nice people. They'd befriended Sam and me during our early days on the circuit. After our first competition, when we placed last and they won, they'd invited us out for a drink. We'd gotten in the habit of going out with them and a few other dancers after our event to talk shop and unwind.

DeShawn and Nicolette were short on cash and time, and it'd taken them years of competing at regional competitions and one or two large ones before they amassed enough momentum to win. This was supposed to be their year, and what a year it was supposed to be —a triumph for hard work and willpower, a victory for humanity when the first African-American couple won a Nationals title.

Everyone wanted them to win, me included, which was a problem.

Because there could only be one winner.

"Maybe we back off? DeShawn and Nicolette can win this year, and we'll work toward next year," I said to Sam.

I loved this plan. My desire to return to Ohio, not robust before, had dwindled to nothing, a thought that made me convulse with guilt. I wanted to stay in New York with Sam, teaching and dancing.

My parents, though, would flip out. Archer's transition from boy to man was taking its toll on them as he became more violent, mostly toward himself but to them and his surroundings as well. Christmas had been a chilling experience, and I begged my parents to find an aide for a few hours a week.

"You know what happened last time," they said. "We'd never forgive ourselves if it happened again."

When Archer was eight and I fourteen, my father had walked into find the aide, a sweaty guy in sweatpants, touching himself inappropriately in front of Archer.

My parents hit the roof. They refused to leave him home alone with anyone other than family, which meant them and me. Although my life hadn't been normal before, this put a serious wrench in it. I quit dancing. After school, I returned home to help out where I could by cooking dinner or watching Archer while my mother fought yet again with the insurance company over his therapy.

I had an idea, though, that might make it okay. If Sam and I got engaged, then they couldn't say much. Ballroom dancing in New York was selfish. I did it for myself. Falling in love was out of my control. It happened to me.

Getting engaged wasn't that far-fetched of an idea. Sam and I made a good couple. Even with the stress of competing, our relationship remained strong and happy. We didn't argue; we made each other laugh. We lived together and danced together in easy harmony. Taking our relationship to the next level was a logical step.

Sam shook his head at my idea, eyes glinting with resolve. "It has to be a year."

"Why?"

"Because we said so." Sam looked at his feet, and the thought that he was hiding something bobbed through my head.

But what?

~

We presented our dilemma to Maxine.

"I've known DeShawn and Nicolette for years. They're a lovely couple, very inspirational."

"But we want to win," Sam said.

"If you want to win, then you can't let the personal stories of the other competitors sway you." Maxine cocked her head at us. "It's a ballroom dance competition not a who-has-the-most-heartwarming-life-story competition. That said, the judges will be on the lookout for any reason not to mark you first. You have to win it outright."

"What can we do better?" Sam tapped his foot, impatient for the answer.

Maxine snapped her brows together. "Run rounds. As many of them as you can. It has to be automatic, so when you get to Nationals, you dance well, no matter where you are mentally or emotionally.

So we did. At night, when the studio cleared out, we ran as many rounds as we could stand. It was good for our physical stamina, but it was even better for our mental endurance. We became pros at pushing through everything: fatigue, grumpiness, self-criticism, memory lapses.

Sam groaned as I started the music for yet another round. "I'll remember these routines for the rest of my life," he said.

One of the biggest and most important competitions before Nationals was fast approaching in Houston.

"Are you inviting your mom?" I asked Sam.

"Nope."

"But she hasn't seen you dance."

Sam called his mother every Sunday night, a point I considered adorable, and kept her briefed of every up and down we'd experienced that week.

"I'm inviting my dad."

I blinked. "Your dad?"

"And my stepmother. They want to meet you."

"They do?" I smiled, pleased my hint had taken root.

I'd taken to leaving magazines out with the pages flipped to pictures of engagement rings I liked. It was cheesy and faintly desperate, but Sam had seen them and not said anything, which I took as a promising sign.

I'd written a plan about what our long-term relationship could hold. If we won Rising Star at Nationals, we could move up to the Open level. We would get engaged and then married a year or so later.

Maybe in a couple of years, we would win Nationals and Sam

could stop teaching. There were lots of other options for him. He could open a studio, become a judge, or run a competition. He'd majored in business, and there was plenty of money to be made in the industry. As for me, I wanted to be a coach.

My cheeks lifted in an excited grin. This would be a wonderful life. Maybe we could even settle in Ohio down the road and help out my parents with Archer.

Sam shifted his feet and looked sheepish.

"Did you make up with your dad?" I asked.

"This is the olive branch."

"I can't wait to meet them."

On the plane ride to Houston, while Jason and Sam chatted about business topics I couldn't follow, I daydreamed about engagement rings and Nationals titles and a cute little house filled with cute little kids with Sam's hair and my eyes.

Due to its size, the schedule at this competition unfolded differently than most competitions. Ordinarily, Jason and I danced in the day, and then Sam and I competed that night. Here, Sam and I would dance one night, and then the next day, Jason and I would compete. He'd come in early to cheer us on.

"I have a feeling you're going to win this one," he'd said when I explained the schedule.

Buoyed by our future, I danced with extra energy, reaching a little more, smiling a lot more.

"What's gotten into you?" he asked as we waited to be recalled for the final.

"I'm enjoying dancing with you today."

"Don't overdo it."

I patted him on the shoulder.

We breezed through the final, and then we won. It was our first win, which thrilled us. We took all the dances but Waltz. DeShawn and Nicolette hadn't competed, so we were unable to gauge how our dancing stacked up against theirs.

Afterward, I met Sam's dad, who provided me with a guide as to what Sam would look like in thirty years—appealing in a gangling, honest way with a small paunch and a bald spot the size of a quarter on the top of his head.

Sam's stepmother couldn't be more than five or six years older than Sam. She had fluffy blonde hair and a ready smile; she was also visibly pregnant.

I squeezed Sam's hand when I met his stepmother. Sam's desire to protect his mother at his graduation made me love him more. He'd showed me a picture of his mom, and she, bespectacled and mousy-haired with a kind, tired smile, couldn't hold a candle to his glamorous stepmother.

"How do you remember all those routines?" Sam's stepmother laughed. "I'm still working on keeping my left foot and right foot straight."

Sam's dad kissed me on the cheek. "I'm happy to meet you, Carly."

He embraced Sam. "I'm proud of you, son."

All had been forgiven.

Sam and his dad went out for steaks while his stepmother went home to rest. I headed to our room and ordered a burger from the hotel's restaurant, a treat I justified in favor of our win. I fell asleep quickly, full and happy from food and the future.

The next morning should have been a joyous one, but Jason was in low spirits. We met for breakfast as we always did before he competed. A scowl, though, replaced his jovial smile, and he couldn't muster more than a lame laugh at my jokes.

"Spill the beans, Mister. The cat's got your tongue," I said. "I want to know where he is, so I can pull his tail and get it back."

He looked at me, his face white against his silver hair. "It's the anniversary of my wife's death."

I clapped my hand over my mouth. "I didn't know."

"I know you didn't. I came because I hoped it might make me feel better." He sighed. "I was wrong."

"I'm so sorry." I'd grown fond of Jason, and I wanted to offer comfort but I couldn't find the right words.

He stared into his coffee cup.

"What happened?" I asked. I'd read it was important for people to talk about their loss. I didn't know whether this was the right thing to do, but it was the only thing I could think to do.

"A drunk driver," Jason said. "But it's my fault."

I wrung my hands.

"We were having dinner at a Chinese restaurant we'd been to a hundred times before, and I was ignoring Kim. I was checking email, taking calls, answering texts. She was a spitfire, and this didn't sit well with her. She'd asked me to dinner because she had something to tell me. When I showed more interest in my phone than her, she left."

I nodded, picking at my nails under the table.

"She grabbed a cab home. Not even two blocks later, a drunk

driver t-boned the car. He survived. Kim and the cabbie didn't." He traced the rim of his coffee cup. "At the hospital, they told me Kim's news. She was pregnant."

He looked up at me, his neck corded, his eyes spooked. "I killed my wife and future child because I wasn't paying attention."

My eyes pooled at the injustice of life. I stood and opened my arms. "You didn't, Jason. You really, really didn't," I said over the knot in my throat.

He accepted my embrace, and we stood there for a minute, maybe more, hugging. When we pulled away, I extended my hand. "Mr. Justus, will you do me the honor of accompanying me in the Foxtrot. Don't let the silly name fool you. This is a sly, elusive dance that fells even the bravest who attempt to tame it."

He laughed. "I'm familiar with this beast. You introduced me to it on our first lesson, and I have yet to slay the Foxtrot. Maybe today will be the day."

We danced, and Jason did well, better than he'd done before.

"Thank you," he said as he gazed at the array of bronze and silver awards he'd spread in front of him. A gold medal for Foxtrot winked from the center of the pile.

I touched Jason's shoulder. He was a nice man who'd make some lucky girl a good husband once he processed his grief.

~

On our next lesson, Maxine sauntered toward us with a big smile.

"Good job, kiddos." She gave us each a hug. Then she pulled away and gazed at us with sober eyes.

Sam and I shifted uncomfortably.

"You're so close that you can taste it," she said. "This is where couples get distracted. They start thinking about the future after they win Nationals."

It was as if she read my mind. I bit my lip, embarrassed I'd been so obvious.

"Don't," she said.

"What needs work?" Sam asked.

"Waltz. It's the best dance for most couples because they spend so much time on it. But we've worked differently, and now you've got a problem. You're not coming out of the gate strong enough."

"I want to win all four dances," Sam said. "If we're going to beat DeShawn and Nicolette, we need to do it from the first step.

I peeked at him out of the corner of my eye. His forehead was creased, and he was shuffling his weight back and forth like a basketball player before the big game. He'd been acting shifty lately, slamming down the lid of his laptop whenever I came close.

Something was going on, and fingers crossed, it had to do with us.

Chapter 17

NINA: THE IMMIGRANT'S SONG

"YOU CARRY MY DREAMS, *ZOLOTSE*."

This was the refrain from my childhood that had followed me into adulthood. My father leaving complicated everything. With nobody else to cheer on, my mother had turned her spotlight on me. She made sacrifices, endured hardship, and literally prostituted herself all because she believed my success would make it worthwhile.

I was not given a choice. I was given an ultimatum.

This was not a new story.

It was not even an interesting story.

Take any cab in New York, visit any dry cleaner, order takeout at any ethnic restaurant and listen to the driver, the clerk, the short order cook. He'll tell you about the sacrifices he and his wife made.

They left the old country, the familiar and friendly country, to come to America for their children. Many of those people steering cabs around the grid of Manhattan, pressing shirts to starchy excellence, or frying yet another batch of wontons had prestigious jobs before they emigrated like scientist, professor, government official.

Why leave?

Because tomorrow held more promise than today.

America, in particular, held the promise of extraordinary, wish-upon-a-star success where one's religion, one's family, and/or one's political beliefs didn't matter.

These immigrants believed in the narrative of success. Hard work. Personal sacrifice. Delayed gratification. These attributes would manifest themselves in something greater than what they left behind, perhaps a big house, a trip to Disney World, a bonanza of shopping options for something as simple as a pair of sneakers. Plus, they could keep what they enjoyed from the old country: the god, the holidays, the family name, the food.

Ask the cab driver, the dry cleaner, the short order cook about their kids. The pride will gleam like a beacon from their eyes, and the slouching lines of their face will arch into a smile.

Straight *A*s, magnet high school, perfect SATs, Ivy League University, prestigious graduate program, and then computer programmer, banker, lawyer, and the end all, be all of immigrant dreams—doctor.

Out will come the pictures of grandchildren, who know nothing of the hardship and insecurity experienced by the grandparents. The expectations, though, they will remain the same. You will pay back our sacrifice with your success.

Like a well-tended investment, children, also known as dreams, performed moderately to significantly well and would continue to pay dividends—read, bragging rights—into the foreseeable future. The parents patted themselves on their back, pleased and a touch relieved that the risk had netted the imagined rewards.

I'd gone about it differently, skipping the practical fields of math and science for the more fanciful one of dancing, but the goal was the same. I was to pay the interest on my mother's dreams until I could remit the balance in full.

Now I had to tell her that her dreams had gone bust on my watch. And in the most ironic way possible. Because my parents emigrated too soon.

I kept the truth from her for over a year. It sounds hard, but it'd been easy.

I told her that Oleg and I were taking a year off from competing.

"Maxine wants us to get new routines and polish our technique. We want the judges to forget about us for a little while, so we can take them by storm next year."

My mother, who knew nothing about dancing except that I was good at it, hadn't blinked. "So you'll be champion year after next."

Through gritted teeth, I'd said, "Of course."

As for Oleg, that had been even easier. My mother didn't care for him, finding him boring and ridiculous with his incessant chattering about deals. Oleg reciprocated the feeling, finding my mother overly opinionated and under-educated.

They both were right about the other, so I kept their interactions to a minimum, mostly my birthday and her birthday.

Last year, for my twenty-ninth birthday, I'd told her that Oleg had a cold. It was August, so we'd gone for a leisurely dinner on one of the boats that lapped Manhattan.

For her birthday, I used some of the bonus money from Ralph to take her to an expensive spa. As for New Year's, she assumed Oleg and I would be spending it in Staten Island as we always did.

Now my mother wanted to throw me a thirtieth birthday party at one of the fancy Russian restaurants by the water.

I declined. She insisted.

The day before she was going to make the deposit on a party for fifty, I called her. I didn't have the guts to tell her in person.

I didn't say hello, just threw the pie in her face.

"Oleg and I broke up. Both on and off the floor." I steeled myself for the barrage of guilt bombs she was sure to throw. My mother had been in the presence of a rabbi maybe three times in her life, but she was well versed in the rituals of being a Jewish mother.

She gasped and then paused, the silence before the song.

"When?" she asked.

"Last year." I opted not to varnish the truth. "The divorce was finalized a few months ago."

"And you did not tell me?"

"No."

"Why not?"

"I didn't want to disappoint you, Mommy," I said through a choked sob. "I'm sorry." I hung up the phone and slumped on the floor. I was crying again. I'd really become quite boring.

Thirty minutes later, my buzzer squawked.

"Who is it?"

"Let me up."

I swore in Russian. It was my mother. Naturally. I'd cut off her opportunity to guilt me over the phone. She took her Jewish mother duties seriously. There was no choice of ignoring her. Even if I denied her entry, she'd wait downstairs until someone else opened the door. Then she would bang on my door until I opened up.

Might as well get it over with, I thought.

I opened the door.

My mother swept past me. She was pushing a cart, the kind babushkas used. "You have been looking thin."

She walked into the kitchen and unloaded her wares. "Beef

stroganoff, roast chicken." She set the dishes on the counter. "Green salad, bean salad, rolls, butter, cheese, crackers."

My mother placed a lemon torte from the fancy bakery on Avenue X on a shelf.

"That's a lot of food," I said.

"You need it. You have been carrying big burden for long time."

I reluctantly reached for plates and silverware.

She reached into another bag. "Red wine, white wine." She slammed the last bottle down. "Vodka."

"Thank you," I said, unsure of what was happening. When were the guilt bombs going to be thrown?

She faced me. "You had tragedy, and you did not tell your mother?"

I stood before her, shaking a little as I anticipated the criticism.

"That is only thing that I'm upset about."

"I didn't win Nationals. I'm never going to win Nationals," I pushed back the sobs that threatened to engulf me. "And I'm almost thirty and divorced."

The sobs won. For the first time since it happened, I dropped my guard and cried in front of another person. Through the stream of tears, I told her everything.

My mother wrapped her arms around me as I wept. "It is okay, *zolotse*. That bean-counter beanpole was not much. As for Nationals, it was ballroom dance competition."

She stepped away and looked at me. "This is America. Dreams are cheap. Find new one."

Chapter 18

CARLY: TOO NICE

A YEAR HAD FELT like an impossibly long time, and then, suddenly, it was over. Nationals had arrived, and Sam and I were as ready as we could be.

"Dance well," Maxine said. "It's been a pleasure."

Although Nationals were held in New York, Sam had suggested we book a room at the hotel where the competition was held.

"My treat," he said, not meeting my eyes.

Neither of us mentioned life after Nationals, which I took as a favorable sign. I didn't want to leave. Returning to Ohio seemed impossible after my time in New York.

Sam appeared to feel the same way. He hadn't said anything about going back to Texas. A couple of times, he'd slammed his laptop closed when I'd wandered near him.

Engagement rings, I'd thought, crossing my fingers.

"Here we are," said Sam when we opened the door to a room that approximated every room we'd stayed in throughout the year.

I made a dramatic leap over the entrance. "Step in to step out."

Sam laughed and followed me in. We had a couple of hours to kill before the competition started. Mine would be filled with hair and makeup while Sam watched television or read business articles online. We'd only do a short warm up. We had multiple rounds to dance, and our energy needed to peak in the final.

Nationals was so big that Jason had danced a few days earlier. He won bronze in the Newcomer division. His ability to dance in time had held him in good stead although his memory had only improved incrementally.

"Bronze." Jason fingered the disc that swung from his neck. "Who'd have thunk it?"

"I thunk it. Multiple times." I gave him a hug. "Congratulations."

"Thank you, Carly." All the affability drained from his face. "You did a lot for me this year."

"My pleasure," I said lightly as I pushed back the thought that all I'd done is resemble his late wife.

I went to the bathroom to do my hair and makeup. I'd gotten faster at doing it over the year, but it still took time. Since it was Nationals, I wanted it to be perfect. Sam flipped on the television, and the sounds of a baseball game drifted into the bathroom.

Sam knocked on the door. "I'm going to grab a sandwich. Do you want anything?"

"No thanks."

I applied my lipstick, a Cupid's bow of scarlet, and exited the bathroom. I headed to turn off the television. Sam had placed his laptop next to it, top thrown open, front half dangling precariously off the console table. A can of half-drunk Dr. Pepper rested next to it.

"Not a good place for your laptop, Sammy boy," I said. I grabbed the laptop, intending to move it to the nightstand when the screen blinked to life.

The tab was opened to a travel website.

Thank you for your purchase, Mr. Chapman.
Details for your one-way trip to Houston are listed below.

I gasped. *One-way trip to Houston*?

I scrolled down. It was wrong, but I didn't care.

Sam was leaving tomorrow. By himself.

The door opened, and Sam walked in. "You'll never guess who I saw in the lobby. That guy from the videos, Trey Devereux."

His eyes drifted to the laptop in my hands, and then he caught sight of my face. Under his breath, he swore. "You know," he said flatly, like an out-of-tune piano.

"I went to move the computer to a safer place. You left the tab up."

"I'm an idiot," Sam said to himself.

Tears were gathering in my eyes. "Everything was going well." My voice wobbled like a bum knee.

"This has been a good year. An arduous year, but a good year."

"What went wrong?" I struggled to get the words over the bump in the back of my throat.

"Nothing went wrong. But I'm ready to go home." Sam sighed. "Boy am I ready to go home," he said. "My dad offered me a job in Houston after the competition. He was impressed that I managed so well on my own. He told me, 'Chapman Recycling needs a winner like you.'" He smiled to himself. "No more teaching and way more money."

"What about us?"

"This was never a long-term thing for me. I thought it was the same for you. We'd have a year and then move onto the lives we were supposed to be living." He scratched his head. "Don't you want to go back to Ohio? To school and to Archer?"

The right answer was yes, but it wasn't what I wanted at all. I wanted to stay in New York and dance with Sam and be with Sam.

"Why was it never going to be a long-term thing?" Tears drove wet paths through my powder and blush. "I thought we were in love."

Sam plucked at his tie. "Because I don't want to marry you, Carly. Not now, not later. You're too much like my mom. You're sweet, generous, always trying to make somebody else happy."

I gaped at Sam. "Aren't those positive qualities?"

"In the beginning, they are. My mom sacrificed everything for my dad, and it made their relationship uneven. My mom always giving, my dad always taking," Sam said. "And he began to resent her. He wanted someone who would stand up to him."

"He dumped your mom because she was too nice?"

"That's my take. He met my stepmother, and she was his equal. Smart, funny, vibrant."

"You don't think I'm smart, funny, or vibrant?" I let Sam's laptop slide out of my hands onto the bed. I didn't bother to turn it over once it landed on its side.

"You are now. But not in twenty or thirty years, after you've sacrificed yourself for me. Working a dead-end job, so I can get an advanced degree. Taking care of the kids, so I can work late hours. Hosting parties, so I can impress business associates. You'll wear yourself out. You won't have developed yourself or created anything for yourself."

"How do you even know that's what's going to happen?"

"It happened to my mom and dad. My mom dropped out of college and worked as a secretary, so my dad could pursue his degree and then start his business. She played golf, so she could make nice with my dad's friends' wives. She joined the boards of charities because my dad asked her to," Sam said. "Then my dad didn't need her anymore. He'd made it. And he wanted someone who was his equal, not his assistant."

I sank onto the bed, my heart cracking into a thousand fragments that wedged themselves deep into my gut.

Sam lifted his chin. "I'm going to marry the second wife first, so I don't hurt someone the way my dad hurt my mom."

"What makes you think I'm like your mother?"

"Look at how we practiced. Everything was designed for my success and happiness, not yours. We worked on dances in fifteen-minute increments because my attention span couldn't handle anymore. We moved on from a step when I wanted to, even if you didn't. You found Jason and asked him to compete even though you didn't want to. During the entire year we've been together, you've always gone along with what I wanted."

I wiped my hands on my cheeks, sticky from tears and eyelash glue. "When were you going tell me?"

Sam looked sheepish. "After we won Rising Star. I figured the title would take the sting out of it." He checked the clock. "Speaking of which, we need to warm up. Go fix your face."

We were supposed to dance? After Sam just broke my heart? Because I was too nice?

I shook my head.

"We can't have come all this way and not dance," Sam said.

"I don't know if I can," I whispered.

He shifted from foot to foot. "I'm sorry it happened like this. But we have to dance. If we don't, it'd be as if we dropped the football at the one-yard line."

I couldn't paste a smile on my face and dance four rounds with the man who'd dumped me for being too nice. The walls of the hotel room inched closer and closer to me. Suffocating with shock and despair, I dashed out of the room, not sure where I was going, but it definitely wasn't to the ballroom to dance with Sam.

"Carly," he yelled.

I slammed the door behind me.

Chapter 19

NINA: LIPSTICK TO THE RESCUE

I TUGGED my dress over my hips. Unlike last year's dress, widow's weeds for a ballroom dancer, this one saluted my single status. Pink chiffon connected at one shoulder that then crested to my mid-thighs. I paired it with dangly silver earrings and silver heels. I left my bangs down but twirled the rest of my hair into a bun.

I couldn't compete with the young girls anymore, but for the first time in a long time, I didn't feel sad about it.

My mother's words chimed. *Find a new dream*. I doubted I'd find it at Nationals, but I wanted to support Sam and Carly. Last year plus a few weeks, they'd been slumped against a wall at the Castle's competition, bushed after a one-round event. Now they had a better than good chance of winning Rising Star.

I was running late thanks to the stupid Q train, but I had to pee. I jogged to the bathroom, tossed open the door, and reached to open the nearest stall.

I stopped.

Someone was crying, the heartbreaking, my-life-is-over kind.

I knew it well, having cried like that for the past year.

It was probably some newbie who'd had a bad experience. The competition floor could disenchant after the comfort and camaraderie of the studio.

I tossed my head from side to side. The Rising Star Smooth was about to begin, and I wanted to watch Carly and Sam dance through all the rounds. Yet my compassion chimed.

"Are you okay?" I asked.

"Nina?"

"Carly?"

The stall door opened. Carly stumbled out, wearing her red dress that finally sparkled the way a proper ball gown should. Makeup streaked her cheeks, and tendrils were pulling loose from her bouffant hairdo.

"What's wrong?" I asked. "The competition is about to start."

"Sam just dumped me."

"He dumped you? Before the competition?"

Carly nodded, her brown eyes dripping like mud. "He's leaving for Texas tomorrow. Without me."

"Mu'dak."

Carly widened her eyes at me.

"It means asshole in Russian." I gave her a hug. "What happened?"

She poured out the story as I got angrier and angrier on her behalf.

"He broke my heart. How can I pretend that everything is okay for four rounds?"

"That's exactly what you're going to do."

I hugged her again and then took her hand. I led her to the ballroom, and then I pressed my ear to the door.

"Will the first heat for the Rising Star Smooth please take their places?" said the Master of Ceremonies.

"What heat are you in?"

"The second."

"So we have a minute and a half."

I reached into my purse and pulled out a tissue. I dabbed at the streaks on Carly's cheeks. "Listen to me. You put your time and money, your heart and soul, your body and brain into winning this. Not dancing doesn't just punish Sam. It punishes you."

I pulled out my lipstick. I smeared a little over the pads over my fingers and then stroked it onto her cheeks. "Dance for yourself. You deserve to win."

I dragged the lipstick over her frown, lifting it upside down.

Inside the ballroom, the Master of Ceremonies said, "Thank you, competitors. Let's welcome heat two to the floor."

"I'll meet you after the first round to do a proper fix of your face. The judges will mark you and Sam through regardless."

I opened the door and pushed her through. "Dance well."

Chapter 20

CARLY: THE CURTSY

I SPRINTED from the door to the on-deck area. Sam was pacing in circles, his face woven in tight lines.

He exhaled when he saw me. "I'm sorry. I am."

I had a lot of things I wanted to say to Sam, but what I said was, "Let's go win Nationals."

Maxine's advice to run rounds held us in good stead. We did not dance our best. There was no way we could dance our best with all the emotion stewing beneath the surface of our skin. We did, however, execute everything the way we'd been taught to with no blips of memory or bobbles of technique.

Although I hadn't known Sam the person as well as I thought I had, I did know Sam the body backward and forward. As he did me. He led me the way I enjoyed being led, assertively but not aggressively. I followed him the way he enjoyed being followed, landing dead in the middle of the beat, not too early nor too late.

In between rounds, we stood mutely away from each other, at odds with every prior competition where we'd clasped our bodies together and joked with the other dancers.

As we walked on for the final, my sorrow and horror at being dumped right before Nationals reared up. Last year, we'd been so excited, brimming with plans and new love.

Now here we were, hard work about to pay off, but I didn't care. Once this round ended, I was going back to Ohio to live out my life of duty. Not that Sam cared.

He caught sight of my face, which was heavy with the promise of rain.

"It's the last round," Sam whispered as he led me to a place on the floor to start. It was the first thing he'd said to me since he apologized. "Let's not blow it now."

The opening bars of Waltz sounded. The DJ had selected a mournful one with a delicate violin melody. As I glided my arms through our opening sequence, tears pounded at the back and then the front of my eyes.

"Just four more dances," Sam murmured as he picked me up in pivots. "We can do it."

When he released me into some solo spins, I remembered that Trey Devereux was in attendance.

So I danced for him. Trey Devereux couldn't know nor would he care, but I dedicated each action to him and performed every motion for him. He'd inspired my dancing, and I used the final to tell him how much he had meant to me.

Sam whistled. "That was good," he said under his breath as we spun to a close in our Viennese Waltz. "Some of our best."

I ignored him and directed my attention outward to Trey Devereux.

For you.

I sank into the final bow.

Chapter 21

NINA: NOTHING TO LOSE

I STOOD at the back of the ballroom for a better view. The Rising Star Smooth final was in full swing. Carly's mouth had a weird twist at the corners, but otherwise, Sam and she looked powerful, elegant, and technically solid.

It was no contest.

"Nina, still as beautiful as ever."

I shifted my eyes from the dance floor to my right. A devastatingly good-looking man, tall and slender with light blond hair, was lounging against the wall. He smiled at me, a dazzling curve in a face of geometrical planes and angles.

"Trey Devereux," I exclaimed.

He reached out and grasped my hand. He brushed a dry kiss atop it as a tiny flame flickered in my abdomen. Trey had to be at least thirty-five, but his impact remained undiminished.

"It's been years," I said.

"It feels like yesterday," Trey said absently. He'd fixed his eyes on the competition. I followed his gaze. Carly and Sam were skimming through their side-by-side section in Foxtrot: a cross of a foot, an extension of the other, a tricky turn that started backward to end forward.

It was the choreography I'd given them. I mentally patted myself on the back.

I turned back to Trey. He was still watching Carly with an intense, almost feral look in his eyes.

I pointed at Sam and Carly. "They're breaking up."

They'd taken closed position to perform a Reverse Wave. Sam stroked backward in a subtle semi-circle as Carly stepped forward, her head cocked rightward.

"Both on and off the floor?" Trey asked in a careless tone.

"Sam is moving to Houston to work at his dad's recycling business."

He picked at some lint on his tuxedo. Then, his lips parted, he leaned toward me. "What's she like?"

"Bright. A hard worker. Nice." I paused, remembering all the ways Carly had indulged Sam to keep their partnership throttling forward and how Sam had chosen to repay her. "Too nice."

The Foxtrot ended, and the Master of Ceremonies announced the finalists.

"From New York, New York, Samuel Chapman and Caroline Martindale."

Sam turned Carly out, and she curtsied, placing her right hand over her heart in a show of gratitude. The crowd roared their number —*twenty*.

I peeked at Trey. "Caroline Martindale," he was saying to himself.

"She goes by Carly."

He nodded.

"Are you coming back?"

He gave me another luminous smile that didn't reach his eyes. "The world is a mysterious place."

That would be exciting, I thought. *Trey Devereux back on the floor.*

I turned to say good-bye, but he was immersed in Carly's Viennese Waltz.

I went to find Maxine and congratulate her on Sam and Carly's win, let her know that Sam was quitting. It took some time to make my way through the crush, but I got to her as Papa announced the winners.

"Taking first in all four dances, from New York, New York, couple twenty, Samuel Chapman and Caroline Martindale."

"Nina," Maxine said. "The kids did it."

"I'm happy for them."

She smiled. "They won Waltz. Finally."

Sam and Carly bowed to hearty applause.

Maxine poked me as Trey strode by us. "Is that Trey Devereux?"

"In the flesh."

"It's been at least five years since I've seen him. What's he doing here?"

"He's coming back."

She waved her arm. "Trey," she called. "Trey."

Trey's eyes were fixed on Carly, who stood at the edge of the dance floor, her gold medal dangling forlornly from her hand.

He reached her, his lips arching into a smile, as his eyes hardened with determination.

My scalp prickled. *Watch out, Carly.*

"Don't you look beautiful tonight, Nina."

I turned to see Papa, who, between the tuxedo and the belly, resembled an Emperor penguin.

He leaned in. "Do you have a minute?"

I peeked at Maxine. She was talking to the couple who'd won Rising Star Latin.

They were *Russkis.*

Naturally.

I forced a smile. "Anything for you."

"Come with me." Papa led me to a quiet corner of the ballroom. He plunked down in a chair and spread his legs to allow his belly space to settle. I sank into a chair beside him, daintily pulling down my dress, so it wouldn't ride up.

"What do you know about Jorge Gonzalez?"

"He's a Latin dancer." I'd seen Jorge at competitions for years, but I'd never gotten to know him beyond perfunctory hellos and cheek kissing.

"He used to be a Latin dancer. He and Amber called it quits last year. They went from being second to not making the final in a matter of months."

"*Russkis*?" I asked. Oleg and I hadn't been the only couple affected by the Russian invasion.

Papa nodded. "He was pretty torn up over it. All those years plugging away wasted."

I cocked my head sympathetically. I knew the feeling.

"He's moving back to New York from San Francisco in search of a fresh start."

I studied my nails, painted peony pink to match my dress. I had a chip on the right pinky. "What kind of fresh start?" I yawned. What did Jorge Gonzalez have to do with me?

"He wants to compete in Smooth."

I raised my eyebrows. "That's a bold move for a Latin dancer."

"He thinks he can bring something new to the field."

I shrugged. "Maybe he can."

"He needs a good partner. Someone who can help him with the Standard elements." Papa stared at me, his brown eyes unblinking. "Someone like you."

My mouth dropped. "Me?"

Papa smiled. "You did a terrific job with Sam and Carly."

Smooth with Jorge Gonzalez? What might that be like? Awful? Hilarious?

Papa leaned toward me. "Maxine sees him as a son. She would take a big interest in the partnership."

Maxine and Papa didn't have any children. Maxine, in particular, treated her couples as her kids by clucking over them when they suffered hardship and celebrating every small accomplishment.

Papa threw me a meaningful look, another unblinking one. "As would I."

I lowered my head to hide my instinctive eye roll. What could Papa do for us? Read our results with extra gravitas?

I looked up at him through my lashes. He was staring at me, slack-jawed and starry-eyed. Did Papa think I was flirting with him? I rearranged my features into benign disinterest, but it altered nothing.

He placed a hand on my arm. "Think about it. You have nothing to lose and everything to win."

Chapter 22

CARLY: LOOKING AT THE SUN

WE WALKED off the dance floor, goal complete. When we hit the carpet, Sam turned to me. His face, dear and familiar for so many months, was now foreign and vaguely repellent. His lips were uplifted with self-satisfaction. He'd gotten the job done and was ready to collect his reward. Which was not a Nationals title nor me. It was a corner office in Houston and a McMansion where he could return home every night to his future wife who wouldn't put her happiness before his. This year could be bookmarked as a story to pull out from time to time when he wanted to impress a girl or charm clients.

Winning Nationals was nothing more than a pit stop on the way to his real life.

He kissed my cheek. "Good luck."

"You too," I whispered.

He strode to the door, auburn hair gleaming under the mellow fire of a dozen chandeliers. People tried to waylay him, to congratulate him, to snap a photo of him, but he didn't stop. His business here was complete.

My shoulders slumped. We won, but I'd lost. There was nothing left to do but go to my hotel room, wash my face, and fall asleep. I could go to the bar and revel in the congratulatory envy of the other dancers, but I wasn't up for that.

Tomorrow I'd buy my ticket to Ohio and return home to keep my side of the bargain with my parents. I should be grateful for having had the year, but now, the only thing I wanted to do was cry and cry because I'd only had the year.

"I don't believe I've had the pleasure," a voice like burnt honey said to my left.

I swiveled and then blinked a few times to make sure my eyes weren't deceiving me. There, in the flesh, was Trey Devereux. I'd watched his videos a thousand times, but they left me unprepared to see him face-to-face.

I took his proffered hand while my heart slammed against my chest. He lifted my hand to his lips and swept a dry kiss over it. I squeaked, a tiny, imperceptible one. His presence was overwhelming, like looking at the sun.

Trey lifted my arm in an elementary spin to the left, and instinctively, I followed. He drew me into dance position, a lighter and broader frame than Sam's, aluminum instead of iron. My body snuggled into his as our peaks and valleys fit into each other. He shifted weight, and I, helpless, moved with him. His body was a live wire to which I sparked.

He inhaled sharply and then leaned toward me. "Would you like to dance?"

Chapter 23

NINA: THE RUNAROUND

SO I THOUGHT ABOUT IT, weighing possible rewards against potential embarrassments.

Papa was right. I had nothing to lose by trying out with Jorge Gonzalez. And if the partnership did work out, Maxine wouldn't let us get on the floor until we were ready. I bit my lip at my pigheaded refusal to take her advice about retiring last year.

Where had that gotten me? A now ex-husband who'd moved to North Carolina with an eighteen-year-old mail-order bride. I would follow her instructions this time.

I cobbled together a thumbnail sketch of Jorge. I knew the most important thing, which was the same thing everyone knew. His persistence was legendary. The story of his start in ballroom dancing had been recounted so many times that it'd taken on the fuzzy contours of myth.

Jorge was a poor kid from the Bronx, the son of a cleaning lady and a low-level drug dealer who was serving a long sentence for being in the wrong place at the wrong time. He'd been introduced to ballroom dancing through a program that brought classes to middle schools in disadvantaged neighborhoods.

When he'd gotten to ninth grade, he'd been furious to discover the program didn't run in high schools. So he took the B train to Bryant Park and walked up Sixth Avenue until he got to the Castle, which was owned by Papa and Maxine.

"How do I take lessons?" he'd asked Maxine. Maxine gave him an up-and-down look. He was a scrawny fourteen-year-old kid in low-rise jeans, a baggy t-shirt, and work boots.

"You don't," she'd told him, not unkindly.

He was undeterred. He showed up the next day after school, clutching a roll of paper towels and a bottle of window cleaner he'd bought at the dollar store.

"Let me clean the mirrors for a class."

Maxine opened the door for him. "We have a person for that."

He showed up the next day with a broom and a dustpan.

"Let me sweep the floor for a class."

Maxine sighed. "We have a person for that."

He showed up the next day with a rag and furniture polish.

"Let me polish the furniture for a class."

"We've got a—"

Jorge grinned. "No you don't." He swiped his fingers over a small table in the lobby that held copies of the group class schedule and then flicked his hand in the air. Gray fuzz clung to his fingertips.

Maxine was Jewish on her mother's side, and when someone showed up three times asking for an introduction to the faith, you weren't supposed to turn him away. Jorge had shown up four times. She relented.

"What time do you get out of school?"

"Two."

"Come in at three and do some light cleaning. Touch up the mirrors, sweep the floor, and restock the cups by the water cooler. At four, one of the teachers will give you a lesson. Then scram before the evening sessions start."

Jorge had pumped his fist.

He'd kept up his end of his bargain and Maxine hers, but he didn't scram at five. Instead, he made himself indispensable. He helped the old ladies buckle their dance shoes, he poured water for group class attendees, and he danced with the single ladies at the socials.

"We're never losing him, are we?" Maxine asked Papa. Jorge was gamely leading a woman six inches taller and seventy pounds heavier than him in a Rumba.

Papa shook his head. "He needs some dance shoes. I don't know how he's so light on his feet in those work boots."

Maxine offered him a pair the next day.

Jorge turned them down. "Let me earn them, fair and square."

So she invented work for Jorge. He alphabetized student folders, watered plants that she picked up on her way into the studio, and organized the lost and found where she planted a couple of dress shirts in Jorge's size, tags removed and the fabric balled up to suggest previous ownership.

At sixteen, he'd gotten his GED and come on full time as a teacher at the Castle. At twenty-one, he'd moved to San Francisco to compete in Latin with Amber Morimoto, a promising but temperamental dancer. Maxine and Papa had given him their blessing.

Right around this time, Maxine and Papa had sold the Castle to Ralph. I'd started soon after, but I had never gotten to know Jorge.

I roused myself from Jorge's origin story. Amber and he had won the Latin Rising Star the same year Oleg and I had won the Rising Star Standard. That put him at thirty-three or so.

Did we even have the stamina to win Nationals at our age? The desire? The commitment?

I was going to find out.

I called Papa. "I'm in."

"I'll set it up. And if Papa can do anything to help, let him know."

Internally, I sighed. Papa's infatuation, mild for so many years had taken on alarming strength since I'd been single.

"That's sweet of you," I said in a chirpy voice.

"I mean it." Papa stopped for a moment. "I've watched you through the years, and you are a lovely, determined woman. If there's a place for him to help, Papa will." A husky edge tinged his words, a womanizer crooning sweet nothings to his next conquest.

I rolled my eyes. "It's good of you to offer. I've got to run, but I'll see you on Tuesday for the tryout."

Maxine and Papa were coming with Jorge to the Castle on Tuesday to facilitate our tryout as if we were teenaged newbies rather than seasoned competitors in our thirties.

Tuesday dawned, a blindingly sunny day, where the glare reflected off the steel-and-concrete buildings in hot white quadrangles. I arrived at the Castle early, mostly to give myself time to cool off. Jorge was there, warming up, his face set in resolute lines. He was wearing a black dress shirt and black pants. His muscles, the result of daily weightlifting, bulged.

My eyes lingered on his biceps, which swelled like two stressed syllables.

Jorge wasn't handsome, exactly, but there was a lot to like about his spiky black hair and skin the color of a perfectly toasted piece of bread. He wore a small gold hoop in his left ear.

"Hey," he said, walking over to me with his hand outstretched. "All those years of seeing you at competitions, and here we are."

I grasped his hand, snug and warm like a mitten. "Life. You think you have its number, and then it does a number on you." I smiled.

He returned it, a casual, easy one.

I relaxed a little. Jorge was nice. This was not to be underestimated in the ballroom dance world where, simply because they were appointed leaders, some men became assholes.

They couldn't help it. To follow well, a woman turned her body and soul over to her partner. Leading revealed the moral fortitude of a man. If he was a jerk, then dancing with him, no matter his skill, would be a pain. Everything would be the follower's fault, interpretation the value that mattered in the partnership. If he was nice, then dancing with him, no matter his skill, would be a pleasure. Everything could be debated, consensus the value that mattered in the partnership.

Maxine clapped her hands to get our attention. "You two bring the raw ingredients of Smooth. Today we see how they blend."

It should have been awful. It could have been hilarious. Maxine tossed together some simple phrases more appropriate for students than for veteran dancers seeking to win the Open Professional Smooth at Nationals.

We started with one wall's length of choreography in Viennese Waltz: an opening pose, a long ribbon of basics that rotated right and then left, a rollout where I twirled away from Jorge, some elegant side-by-side steps to a dip. Last, a runaround where we gripped each other's shoulder with our right hands and cantered in a stationary circle like a merry-go-round.

We were dreadful and wonderful in our own ways. Jorge struggled in closed. His dance position—rounded, too hulking—lacked the sleek stretch and streamlined edges of a Standard frame. As for his footwork, he entered steps with toes and exited with heels, a stutter to a thud, the opposite of correct technique, which created a fluid, gentle action.

I did my best to fill in for his deficiencies in closed. I bent my knees a little more than normal to keep his footwork from throwing us off, and I glued my body to his to maintain contact.

Jorge, though, shone in the open portions. He easily coordinated his arms with his legs, and he instinctively used his body to frame and enhance me. Problem was, there wasn't much to frame or enhance. My arms hung limply by my side, and I was counting—*counting*—as I attempted, and then failed, to execute the elegant side-by-side sequence.

When Jorge turned me out for a series of solo turns, I veered out of control into a bench resting against the wall. Hoping to salvage the moment and, most importantly, my pride, I plopped on the bench and posed as if I were a showgirl.

Maxine should have nipped it in the bud then and there, but she had us try the phrase with music. Somehow, some way, we made it all the way until the dip. As I arched over Jorge's arm with him gazing at me from above, I almost swooned. Forgetting about technique, we segued into the runaround, our eyes locked, our right sides pressed together as our free arms streamed above us.

Our bodies had connected like a cliché.

Forever or four bars of music, it was hard to say how long, but at some point, our runaround skidded to a stop. Jorge brought his lips close to my ear. "Let me dance with you."

I nodded, too overcome to respond.

Maxine stopped the music. She pursed her lips and narrowed her eyes at us. I peeked at Papa. His mouth was agape, and he wasn't blinking.

My stomach dropped. The jig was up.

"I have a good idea," Maxine said.

Chapter 24

CARLY: FIT FOR A PRINCESS

WE HAD our official tryout the next morning under the watchful eye of Trey's coach. Cyrus had a plummy British accent and round gold-framed glasses, which he peered over as Trey led me through the Standard syllabus and then some easy Smooth choreography.

Trey's presence continued to dumbfound me, but this turned out to be advantageous. I didn't think; I just did, and Trey deployed my body without effort, an arrow to his perfectly hewn bow.

"You've got potential, dear girl," Cyrus said. "Trey wants to win his fourth Nationals. How hard are you willing to work to make that happen?"

"Very," I said in a breathless, girlish timbre. I tried again. "Very." Closer to my normal voice but still too high and nervous.

Cyrus nodded at Trey. "I'll let you two work out the details." He smiled at me. "I look forward to seeing your progress."

Trey outlined his expectations. I would relocate to Charleston, which he pronounced CHAH-l-ston, and live with him and his mother.

"Mama's incapacitated." He waved a hand. "You won't be seeing her much."

I forced myself to meet his eyes, impenetrable silver discs like dimes.

My only job would be to train. Everything would be provided for me including meals, clothes, entertainment, and living quarters.

"I have a big house," Trey said. "Even a ballroom. You'll find you don't need to leave much."

I said little beyond *yes* and *okay* although my stomach sloshed with the hot, sticky soup of exultation. It sounded like a fairy tale. A handsome prince had swept into my life, unbidden, and was whisking me away to his beautiful palace where we would while away our days dancing.

"Bring nothing," he said.

So I did just that. I vacated my sublet. As for my belongings, I'd acquired very few in New York beyond clothes and the odd book or tchotchke. I stuffed everything in a box and asked Nina if she would hold on to them. The last thing I tossed in was my Nationals Rising Star medal.

It made no sound when it hit the soft mass of clothes.

Nina raised her eyebrows as I passed the box to her. "He said not to bring anything?"

I nodded.

"What are you taking?"

I pointed to my purse, which held my phone, a few toiletries, some personal items, and my wallet with my driver's license and cash for cab fare to and from the airport.

"That's it?"

"Trey said he would have everything I needed."

She wrinkled her nose. "That's odd, no?"

I tugged at my hair. It was odd, but I was determined to do what he asked. What was I leaving behind anyway? Some cheap clothing and a few replaceable trinkets. They were nothing compared to the opportunity to dance with Trey Devereux. "You said he was odd."

"I did say that." Nina smiled although her eyes looked worried. "Keep in touch. I can't wait to hear how it's going."

Jason was bewildered when I told him.

"You're moving to South Carolina to compete with and live with some guy who you spent an hour dancing with?"

I explained who Trey was and why it was so special, but it was lost on him.

"Nina will teach out the rest of your lessons," I said as brightly as I could.

Jason's backbone wilted. I scraped my feet against the floor. He was still grieving, and Ralph had been right that my looks had given Jason solace.

"I don't care about the lessons," he said, more to himself than me. Then he squared his shoulders. "Best of luck, Carly. I'll miss you."

I was a coward and didn't call my parents. Instead, I sent them an email rhapsodizing about the extraordinary opportunity. I included few details beyond the fact that I'd be relocating to Charleston, a city even further away from Ohio than New York.

Trey even has his own ballroom! I wrote. My parents would find this inane, but at least they'd know I wouldn't want for anything.

A plane ride of a couple of hours separated Charleston from the cookie-cutter sameness of the Ohio suburb I'd grown up in. An even shorter trip separated Charleston from the neon dreams and concrete reality of New York. Yet this was a world distinct from any other.

I hung my head out of the window as the cab driver languidly made his way to Trey's home near The Battery. The homes, painted the colors of little girls' Easter dresses, sagged with voluptuous, profligate beauty.

The air—top note sweet, bottom one fetid—rustled with paper: old money, invitations to balls, the social registry. And then there were the accents that lingered over some letters and ignored others, a queen choosing favored courtiers.

The cab driver pulled up in front of an enormous antebellum mansion painted a strident coral. Black-shuttered windows peeked like curious eyes from behind the three gabled porches that wrapped around the house.

"Here you are, miss," the cab driver said, his quartet of words a tune of old-timey music.

I shoved my tongue back in my mouth and paid. With nervous fingers, I pushed open the gate, ornate whirls of wrought iron, and then walked up the flight of stairs to the door. I grasped the brass knocker in the shape of a pineapple and slapped it against the door a few times.

I was unsure of how hard or how long I should knock. I waited for a few agonizing minutes before lifting my hand again. The door opened just before my fingers closed over knocker.

I dropped my arm to my side as my eyes landed on an elderly man in a white jacket and black pants.

"You must be Miss Martindale," he said. "Won't you come in? I'm William, the butler."

A butler?

"Um, hi." I issued a firm command to my rickety legs to behave, and then I stepped into a palatial entryway. A chandelier the size and shape of a small planet dangled over my head.

William gestured to his right. "Why don't you take a seat in here? I'll let Mr. Trey know you've arrived."

"Here" was a large room bedecked with heavy velvet drapes in jade green. Chairs and love seats with dainty walnut frames were strewn about. I perched on one near the door.

I placed my purse in my lap but that didn't feel right, so I put it on the floor. That didn't feel right either, so I moved it to the table next to me. That really didn't feel right, so back into my lap the purse went.

"Carly."

I swiveled my head.

Trey Devereux, unbearably good-looking, was striding into the room. He extended his arm, and I placed my trembling hand into his cool one. He gifted it with a dry kiss.

"How was your flight?"

"Fine," I stuttered.

He pointed to my purse, which was slumped in my lap as if it were a dead cat. "Is that all you brought?"

"Yes?" Had I misunderstood what bring nothing meant?

He smiled, but it didn't reach his eyes. "Good."

"Let me introduce you to my mother. Then I'll show you to your room, so you can rest. Tomorrow we jump in with both feet."

Trey led me down the hall to a room decorated with lavender-sprigged wallpaper. Knickknacks—cut-glass perfume bottles, silver picture frames, lacquered boxes, and china dolls—littered the surfaces. The main attraction, though, was Trey's mother who sat on a velvet sofa next to a table crammed with bottles of pills.

Trey's mother was fantastically obese. Corpulent, a word I'd learned for the SATs, sprang to mind. Swags of fat dangled from her arms in fleshy leg-of-mutton sleeves. Her bosom scraped the top of her thighs, and her neck consisted of three rolls, like a snowman.

Although it was only four in the afternoon, she wore a fancy caftan of magenta satin. Her face was heavily made up with squiggles of eyeliner and splotches of rouge. Her hair had been tinted blonde and was arranged in a nest of curls.

"You're my son's new dance partner?"

I nodded as I tried to minimize my gawking.

Her eyes flitted over me. Her cheeks wobbled as she puckered her lips thoughtfully. I guessed what she was thinking. Next to the exotic plumage of her son, I was a little brown wren.

"Be sure to do what Trey asks you to do. He knows best."

"I know. I will."

Trey offered me his arm. "Come." He led me up a curving staircase. He pushed open a door, and I followed him inside. "This is you."

This bedroom had none of the suffocating glamour of Trey's mother's room. The floor was a warm walnut, and the walls were painted peach. The room was broken up into two parts with a bed near the windows and a small sitting area of a love seat, a coffee table, and a television by the door. A crystal vase of white calla lilies had been placed on the nightstand, and a jumble of throw pillows in shades of tangerine and cantaloupe rested on the bed.

My bedroom in Ohio had bright pink walls and a matching coverlet; it hadn't been updated since I was six. As I'd gotten older, my love of bright pink had turned to intense hatred, and I avoided spending time in my bedroom except to sleep. It'd felt like being trapped in a throat lozenge. I'd asked once or twice for it to be updated, but it fell too low on the list of our family's priorities to ever get done.

"Do you like it?" Trey asked.

I pinched myself to make sure I wasn't dreaming. "It's a room fit for a princess."

"I'm glad."

Trey grazed my shoulder with his pointer finger, and I faced him.

"I'm looking forward to dancing with you," he said.

"Me too."

"It's going to be grueling, Carly. There's a reason why I'm a three-time champion. Try as hard as you can, and we'll do just fine."

I nodded emphatically.

"William will wake you at seven for breakfast."

"Thank you, Trey."

"Enjoy your evening." He closed the door behind him as my eyes bobbed after him.

I'd thought Sam and I had worked hard on our journey to win Rising Star, but that had been child's play compared to the routine Trey had devised for us.

William knocked at seven with an egg-white omelet, cut fruit, whole-grain toast, and black coffee. In the morning, we alternated between yoga and boot camp for an hour, and then Trey drilled me on the syllabus. I did the same figures, again and again, reciting aloud the footwork or the foot placement.

During lunch, a chicken Caesar salad or a turkey club, I reviewed what he'd taught me. In the afternoon, we danced. No routines yet, just lead and follow. Trey taught me how to interpret the subtle cues of his body, how to relax, how to listen, how to wait, and how to trust.

At night, I took a shower and curled up on the love seat, too spent to eat much of the grilled fish and vegetables William delivered to me. I flipped on the television for company before I fell asleep. I'd stopped dreaming; my mind was too tired to arrange my thoughts into a cogent narrative.

Everything I needed filled the closet and shelves. Workout gear, practice outfits, some dressy clothes, dance shoes, cosmetics, hair ties, every toiletry under the sun. A selection of current novels rested on a shelf near my bed, and at least three-dozen DVDs of movies and popular television shows were arranged on a console table.

I'm living a fairy tale, I thought every time I retired to my room after dancing with Trey.

The next day and then the day after next, we did it all again.

Trey was an exacting but patient teacher with rich, detailed knowledge. He never yelled at me or mocked me or even appeared frustrated with me.

"Again," he said all the time.

Sometimes, "Better."

Once, "Good."

I tried to figure him out. His room was above mine, and I listened for any small sound to clue me into this cipher of a man. In the morning, he rose early, showered, and then dressed in the same outfit of blousy gray pants and a white dress shirt with a discreet monogram —LPD, Louis Pierre Devereux—on the cuff.

He spent his daylight hours dancing with me before eating dinner with his mother. Then he returned to his room to take another drawn-out shower. Long after every house on the street had gone dark, he was up, pacing around his room in ellipses, arcs, a figure eight. He listened to the radio, shows where lovelorn souls called in to confess their feelings and request a song that represented their yearning and despair.

Who was he yearning for?

What was he despairing from?

Was it Tamsin? They'd danced together for five years.

Did he miss her?

Was he wondering what mistake he'd made by asking me to dance?

Trey appeared utterly devoted to the dancing. He didn't go anywhere, and no one came to see him. The only people who showed up at the mansion were staff: gardeners, a woman to clean, a companion who made up his mother and watched television with her.

The common denominator among the help? They were old, with grizzled hair and wrinkled brows and bowed spines.

I'd tried to strike up a conversation about the weather or exchange pleasantries with them, but they ignored me. Bewildered, I gave up after a few efforts. I didn't know what the decorum of the South dictated, so I shrugged it off as a faux pas on my part.

"You don't need to do that, Carly," Trey said when he'd chanced upon me chatting up a delivery man.

Trey didn't seem to have any hobbies. Every once in a while, I'd see him in the garden on his laptop, his brow creased. If I squinted hard, I could make out a spreadsheet that he kept plugging numbers into. My heart jumped out of the window and into the garden where it kept him company.

Not that he noticed or cared.

Chapter 25

NINA: BOY MEETS GIRL

WE FOUND out what Maxine's idea was after Jorge had relocated to New York.

"Every couple who's won has been emulating Trey." She paused. "With good reason. Trey—and I say Trey because it was always him; Tamsin was nothing more than a blank canvas he used to color in with himself—worked with each dance in an abstract way. He distilled the emotion into motion. It was beautiful. It was powerful. It lacked, however, passion and a narrative.

"What does that mean for us?" I asked, acutely aware of Jorge standing beside me. Since our tryout, I couldn't forget the image of our runaround, his brown eyes meeting my green, something important taking root deep inside me.

I gave myself a small shake. I was absolutely, completely, most definitely not at all interested in Jorge. We were too different. Not to mention that my last dance partner had been my husband and look at well that had turned out.

"You two are going to tell a story. Each dance will be a chapter."

Jorge wrinkled his brow. "What kind of story?"

"The oldest story known to man. Boy meets girl."

"That doesn't sound like much of a story," I said.

Maxine shot me an amused look. She seemed to think that the possibility of romance lay between Jorge and me. I wanted to laugh at her matchmaking spirit. The only thing we had in common was a desire to win Nationals.

"That's Waltz. Boy and girl argue, Tango. Boy and girl make up,

Foxtrot. Happily ever after, Viennese Waltz. Each routine will start in the position of the last routine to create a through-line. We'll embed a few iconic images in each dance to tip everyone off.

Maxine got down to business, crafting not just sequences but stories.

Waltz. A meet-cute entrance where we backed into a runaround. I spun out; Jorge followed. A small pause as our hands clasped—*hello, you*. Then Jorge swept me under his arm. A closed-position sequence. A *développé* where I unfolded a leg as Jorge lunged, my head pressed against his chest as he hugged me close. Pivots with intense eye contact.

We ended in a dip, Jorge tracing the outline of my jaw with his fingers.

Maxine clapped her hands. The lesson was over. I sank into a bench, my aching body second to my head, which throbbed from trying to remember everything. It'd been a while since I'd learned a new routine. Especially one this challenging.

"Let me get you some water," Jorge said.

He appeared a moment later with two cups of water. I clinked mine against his.

"Na Zdorovie." It came out like a whimper.

He grinned tiredly and pushed his hand into his left hip. *"Salud."* His was more robust than my toast but not by much.

We sat slumped side by side as we downed the water. I rubbed my right knee, a niggling pain, not enough to be worrisome but enough to be noticeable.

Maxine perched beside us. "You did well today. Practice, practice." She stopped for a moment. "But that's not going to be enough. For this to work, you have to address your weaknesses. Jorge, drill the syllabus, every day, no exceptions. Nina, get yourself to a ballet class. Those arms look like broomsticks."

Over the next week, Maxine choreographed Tango, Foxtrot, and Viennese Waltz. Viennese Waltz ended with Jorge on his knee, my left hand in his—a marriage proposal.

Jorge and I might not know much about Smooth, but we could tell that Maxine had a good idea. In truth, a great idea. No one had brought anything new to Smooth since Trey and Tamsin.

Maxine had been my coach for years, and she'd always been a terrific one: specific, concise, frank. Oleg and I had developed steadily and stylishly under her guidance.

In a dozen years, though, I'd never seen her this fired up. Her omnipresent cup of tea remained untouched during our lessons. She requested that we take her first slot, which was late for office workers but early for ballroom dancers.

"I want to work with you when I'm fresh, not when I'm tired from eight lessons."

Jorge and I had looked at each other and shrugged. I'd miss the sleep, but I knew what becoming a champion required.

Maxine wanted us to win. If we won, then she did too. She'd been a successful dancer and was a well-respected coach. But this was an opportunity that didn't come around too often—to radically alter the discipline.

Legacies were tricky things in dance where the impact lived in one body passing an idea on to another. Maxine had the opportunity, if we won, to write her idea far into the future.

The three of us were in it to win it together.

Maxine had us work inside out, emotion and then motion. For each step of the foot, for every lift of the arm, there was a corresponding feeling. For each feeling, there was a motivation that came from the story.

"Nina, you're still upset at Jorge. He broke your heart in Tango," Maxine said. "Jorge, though, wants your forgiveness."

We were working on Foxtrot.

Maxine paced for a moment. "Anger is a pointy emotion. It prickles." She looked at me. "Think of a time when you were so angry you wanted to throw something."

Easy, I thought, remembering when Oleg brought his eighteen-year-old mail-order bride to our apartment.

"Forgiveness, though, is a curve: the bow of a head, the bend of an arm reaching out." She spun her gaze to Jorge. "Find a memory when you had to go to someone, hat in hand, and beg for forgiveness.

His eyes lit up before they dulled with sadness.

"We ended Tango with you two back-to-back," Maxine said. "We'll start Foxtrot there. Nina begins on her own." She gestured toward Jorge. "You watch her go and realize your mistake."

She danced through some choreography: a step across with one foot and a low kick of the other, a punchy solo spin, a knotty sequence of footwork and jabbing arms that connected to the cadence of Foxtrot.

I danced it for her.

She narrowed her eyes. "More points."

Maxine added jounces of the hip and extra flex in my elbow. Then she had Jorge stroke across the floor with rounded arms. He scooped me up in a Natural Weave, a bouncy pattern that rotated one way before backing out the other way, as I looked away from him.

"We have to feed the narrative into the ethos and technique of Smooth," she said. "The judges won't bite otherwise."

At the end of the session, she gave us a meaningful look. "For this to work, you must practice the feeling every time, even if you're just marking."

So we did, and what we practiced on the dance floor affected my life off it as Jorge's presence began fracturing my dreams. Runarounds slanted from vertical to horizontal, and our dance position compressed from wide to close.

I shrugged it off. We were spending a lot of time together. It was natural that he'd appear from time to time. Or every night.

I told my mother I was competing again when she dropped by my apartment with a box of Russian chocolates she'd picked up. Although months had passed since the divorce, she still thought I was too thin. As I chewed through a square of chocolate and praline, I filled her in on the details. She was worried.

"Second chances come with high price tag, *zolotse*," she said. "You put in same effort as first time, but you are older and wiser. Those qualities are not good when chasing dream."

"Why not?" I asked. Being older and wiser seemed like useful capital to bring to a second chance.

"When you are older, you are more tired. When you are wiser, you are more cautious. Winning needs energy and chutzpah." She patted my hand. "Those are things of youth."

I wanted to disagree, but the ache in my knee stopped me. Since Jorge and I had started dancing together, my knee had begun whining. I iced it every night. Just to be on the safe side.

"I feel great," I said.

My mother eyed me doubtfully. "Then why are you rubbing knee every time I see you?"

I yanked my hand away from my knee, which I'd been massaging. "Just a little soreness. It's no big deal."

"Why not find different dream?" she asked.

"Because this is the dream I've had since I was a teenager." The frayed lace of frustration edged my words.

Most of me was grateful that my mother hadn't held it against me when I told her of my failures. Part of me, though, wished she would push just a little more.

I was older and wiser, and yes, more tired and more cautious than

I was a few years ago. Hearing her on refrain in my head—*You carry my dreams*—would be a useful impetus if the going got tough.

Who was I kidding?

The going was going to get tough. The question was when.

I touched my knee, which hummed with pain—minor but noticeable. Very noticeable. Hopefully, the tough going could wait until the end.

"Just wait and see," I said. "Jorge and I are going to win Nationals this year."

I didn't believe it when I said it, but I did mean it.

Chapter 26

CARLY: SUNDAY

ON SUNDAY, I awoke in a frantic fit. It was after nine. William hadn't knocked on my door the way he normally did. I threw on some clothes and balled my hair into a bun. I pricked my ears to see if I could ascertain any sounds of life as I zipped to the ballroom, but the lights were dark and the sound system was off.

I bit my lip. Had Trey given up on me after a week?

I made my way downstairs, my knees weak and woozy from a hard awakening. I peeked into the sitting room that I'd waited in my first day, but no luck. My last option was the garden. I found him there, sitting at a table, the laptop in front of him. Spreadsheets spilled across the screen.

I ran to him. "I'm so sorry." I pushed the last bobby pin into my hair. "I woke up late. I should have set the alarm, but William has been so good about knocking at seven." The words careened out of me, one barely enunciated before the next overtook it.

I'd been too frantic to put on shoes, so I stood before him in bare feet, one hand clasped to my breastbone, the other clutching my dance shoes. Although it was October, the sun was blaring down, and sweat beaded at my temples.

Trey looked up and noted my feverish eyes, hastily assembled bun, the shoes dangling from my hand. "I told him to let you sleep. It's Sunday."

"And?" I asked uncertainly.

"It's your day off."

I exhaled. "Oh."

Trey's lips tweaked at the corners, and for one bright moment, it reached his eyes, the sun sliding out from a cloud only to be obscured by another. "I forgot to tell you." The honey in his voice was sweet with apology.

I curled my toes, the stone cool and soothing beneath my heated distress. "It's okay."

He rose and pulled out a chair for me. "Sit."

I sank into it, feeling ridiculous and juvenile. It was Sunday, the one day most people didn't work in the ballroom dance world. I did know that.

"I'll ask William to bring you some breakfast."

"Thank you."

So I had a whole day to do nothing. I glanced at Trey. Was I really supposed to do nothing, or should I try to curry favor with him by reviewing steps or practicing?

He seemed to read my thoughts. Meeting my eyes, he said, "It's a free day. You've earned it, Carly."

I nodded.

He picked up his laptop. "Enjoy."

"Thank you," I said. Trey strode off, his hair gleaming almost white in the sun.

After I'd eaten breakfast, I tried to figure out how to spend my free day. Maybe I could take a walk? The pastel parade of homes framed by palmetto trees I'd seen from the cab looked enticing.

I wasn't a prisoner here, but I couldn't imagine walking out the front door without telling someone—Trey—where I was going, a thought that made me fidgety with discomfort. I lacked the courage to knock on his bedroom door and interrupt whatever he was doing to tell him I was going for a walk.

So I lolled on a bench amidst the profusion of bright flowers. A stone path bisected the garden into quarters, and a fountain of a little boy spurting water out of his mouth rested in the intersection.

The sun warmed my body, and the rigors of steps and techniques that clogged my every waking thought melted to the sidelines. Like a lazy cat, I fell asleep.

"Carly."

I blinked awake. Trey stood above me. "Hello?" I asked, unfolding my spine from a curve to a line.

"You've been here a week, and you haven't asked for anything. Do you need something, anything?" he asked. "I want you to be happy."

"Do you have a computer I could use? I want to let my parents know I'm okay, and I don't have a signal on my phone."

"Where are you from?"

"A small town in Ohio. You won't have heard of it."

"Follow me."

Trey led me to a study with heavy, dusty mahogany furniture and glass-fronted bookshelves laden with leather-covered tomes.

"There you go." He pointed to an antique desk with a blocky, old-fashioned computer. "It's a slow connection."

I sneezed as dust flew up my nose. "Thank you."

"Let me know if you need anything else."

I pulled up my email. There was a short one from Nina checking to see how I was settling in. I dashed off a reply long on assurance and short on particulars. There was also an awkwardly phrased one from Sam wanting to know if I'd seen his Texans jersey.

Sorry, can't help. I moved to Charleston to dance with Trey Devereux. Hope Houston is treating you well.

I didn't sign it.

Sam probably wouldn't care, busy as he was in his new life, but at least he'd know I wasn't crying into that Texans jersey for him. We'd only been broken up a few weeks, but it felt like years with all the changes in my life.

My parents had sent an email from Archer. He wanted to know when I would be coming back to Ohio. *Mom and Dad need the help,* the email said before he signed off *Love, Archer.*

Sighing, I typed in a reply.

Dear Archer,

Good job with your stickers this week. I am so proud of you!

Did Mom and Dad tell you I'm in Charleston, South Carolina? I'm dancing with a new partner named Trey Devereux. He's a three-time Smooth champion. That's a big deal! It's like earning all your stickers for three weeks in a row.

He's teaching me a lot. You should see your big sister now. She has a mean Fallaway, Slip Pivot, Double Reverse Turn. I hope you can see me dance one day! Tell Mom and Dad hello, and let them know that I'm doing well.

Love,

Carly

I hit send and my email shot through cyberspace to disappoint my parents once again. The daughter they'd taught to be of service to the world had abandoned their principles to pursue ballroom dancing, a useless, silly endeavor that pitted human against human in a competition that did nothing to move society forward.

I wrung my hands. I hadn't been home since last Christmas, which both relieved me and worried me. I wanted to see Archer's face, his eyes brown like mine, hang out with him on the saggy sofa in the living room and watch some *Sylvester the Cat*. But I wouldn't leave if I visited, and I couldn't imagine not returning to Charleston.

To Trey.

The niggling feeling I'd felt when watching him on video had developed into a full-blown crush. Crush, though, didn't capture the intensity and complexity of my feelings.

I was in love with Trey, a thought that filled me with deep dismay. Trey could never love me back. I was completely unsuited to him, too plain, too boring, too childish.

Too nice, I thought bitterly, remembering Sam's criticism.

I wasn't even sure if he was straight. It took a couple of weeks before I got an answer to that question.

Ricky, our boot camp instructor, was—for real—a former Marine drill sergeant. He had a shaved head and wore camouflage cargo pants. He cut the sides out of his t-shirts, so his muscles, bowling balls barely restrained by flesh, protruded.

Ricky was also flamboyantly gay, which made for some jarring transitions.

"Easy-peasy push-ups coming right up," he said in a singsong voice while bouncing on his toes. Then, in a mean, booming tone that reverberated around the bedroom Trey had repurposed into a fitness studio, "Drop and give me twenty. Now."

Ricky couldn't seem to figure Trey out either. I caught him staring at Trey while we were doing squats, Ricky's attractive all-American features creased with confusion. One day, Ricky chanced validating his intuition. During a two-minute plank, Ricky corrected Trey's positioning. He left his hand lingering on Trey's lower spine. Trey paled and pushed it off.

Not gay.

Ricky never tried it again. But every once in a while, I'd catch him staring at Trey with yearning eyes.

It wasn't just Ricky. Fran, our yoga teacher, had it bad for Trey although she was too professional to try anything like Ricky had. She was, also, at least forty with a little girl's body and a little boy's haircut.

Fran would lose her patter when Trey struck Warrior One and then transitioned into Warrior Two. To help her out, I inhaled and exhaled a little louder than necessary, which roused her from her stupor.

It would have been funny if I weren't so besotted myself. Trey had become the sun around which I orbited. It wasn't just his astonishing looks, which I'd assumed would lose their potency when I was confronted with them every day.

They didn't.

It was Trey as a whole. His outward appearance served as the final resolution for the other extraordinary aspects of him. Trey was the most exceptional person I'd ever met.

At the end of practice, I'd rub my sore calves, imagining myself in the soft cocoon of my bed. Trey, though, would pace around the ballroom, ready to dance another couple of hours. Although I placed him in his mid-thirties, he had none of the issues that plagued older dancers like bad knees or an aching back.

He escorted me to my room after every practice. "You did well today, Carly," he'd say, his hand cool and dry against my sticky back as he guided me through the door. "Have a good night."

"You too," I'd say brightly as he closed the door behind him. I wished I could think of something more engaging to say, anything that would make him linger for just a minute more.

Although I'd been here for over a month, Trey had never presented another version of himself beyond the one that was charming, patient, and hard working. I measured myself against him and strove to be cheerful, diligent, self-reliant, and the best dancer I could be.

Maybe then, he'd treat me as more than an imperfect piece of clay that required his diligent manipulation.

Trey was also meticulously private. I lived below him, and I still knew next to nothing about him. I didn't know where he'd gone to school, who his friends were, if he'd been in love. He offered no invitation to ask, so I stayed quiet and offered no information about myself.

Everything was strictly professional.

Which was not at all the way I wanted it to be.

Chapter 27

NINA: OF THE EARTH

RALPH HAD BEEN DELIGHTED to welcome Jorge at the Castle.

"I always got space for a teacher like you." Ralph's eyes blinked like a winning slot machine.

Jorge picked up a full teaching schedule, and we spent our days dancing, either together or near each other. Even when we weren't dancing, I knew where he was in the studio: standing a dozen feet to my left, fiddling with the volume of the sound system; sitting three seats down from me in the teacher's room, discussing soccer with Vadim; calling his mother as we rode the elevator after practice, him chatting in the rat-a-tat of Spanish.

It was annoying, but it didn't matter because I was absolutely, completely, most definitely not at all interested in Jorge. I liked men like Oleg. Russian men.

Jorge possessed none of Oleg's grave charm and mathematical approach to life. If Oleg was a triumph of rationality and well-considered actions, Jorge was the opposite. He was constructed of the earth and sewn together with the bright thread of zeal.

The only thing he took seriously was his dancing. As for the rest, he treated it with casual enthusiasm. When I got frustrated, which was more often than I was comfortable with, he'd make goofy faces and ask me to teach him Russian curse words.

"We got to make it fun, Nina," he said. "It's too hard otherwise."

So I taught him curse words and giggled at his pronunciation, which was more liable to offend a Russian than the actual content of the word. He taught me some salty phrases in Spanish, and I had fun making him laugh when I employed them.

Jorge spent money freely. Every morning, he showed up with bagels.

"You need it," he'd say as he shoved a cushiony ring glistening with melted butter in my direction. I never did find out how he knew that I preferred butter and not cream cheese on my bagels, but I ate it gratefully. He plied the staff with pizza and wine on Fridays because he'd gotten paid and it was the end of the week and, hey, we should celebrate.

We opened a checking account together (not unusual for a competitive couple who shared a number of business expenses but not living ones).

"Let me take care of it," he said. "I got a head for numbers."

I thought about arguing, but I was too tired from teaching and practicing, so I deposited my share every week and didn't think about it. When I checked the account some weeks later, my eyes widened. It had ballooned impressively.

When I asked him about it, he grinned. "There are two ways to go about making money. I can scrimp by working for my money or I can invest by having my money work for me. I don't like saving pennies to make dollars, so I figured out how to add pennies to make dollars.

"How'd you learn?" I asked with genuine interest. Since Oleg left, I'd been stuck managing my money. I wasn't a profligate spender, but I had very little left over at the end of the month. More money would be helpful, especially with all the costs of competitive ballroom dance.

"Real estate in San Francisco is crazy," Jorge said. "When I moved there to dance with Amber, the only place I could afford was an hour away from the studio. On my way in, I listened to shows on money. I made some mistakes in the beginning, but I figured it out." He laughed. "I do okay for myself although I'll never be like that Jason guy you teach. He's a genius."

I was teaching Jason. He was pleasant but distracted, and he canceled more classes than he took. Even when he did take a lesson, he'd often leave early, something he'd never done with Carly.

"I've got to run," he'd say, his eyes fixed upon the clock.

"See you next week," I'd say to his departing back.

"Sure thing," he'd call over his shoulder.

No sure thing, I thought.

Ralph had been disappointed when I told him that Jason wouldn't be buying any more lessons, but there wasn't much either of us could do. I didn't resemble Jason's late wife.

I bent my head to Jorge. "Will you teach me what you know?"

He did, and I followed his advice. And, at the end of the month, I found myself with a little more money than the month before.

Jorge cared little for the faux politesse that characterized ballroom dance, a sport and an art that was British at its heart. He swore when he made a mistake. He clutched me in a bear hug when something went well. He turned the music up, and he danced full out, every time. He perspired profusely and without embarrassment.

"You don't mind, do you?" He'd shown up in a tight t-shirt that clung to his muscles rather than the dress shirt favored by Standard and Smooth competitors. "Cuts down on the dry cleaning."

"Not at all." I busied myself buckling the strap of my shoe, but I couldn't seem to get the silly spoke through the hole. After the third try, Jorge knelt down beside me.

"Let me," he said. "This hole?"

I nodded, my cheeks warm.

I'd expected his earthiness to annoy me or even disgust me, but it was enlivening after all the dry, diplomatic, dress-shirted men I'd danced with. So I shrugged it off and didn't flinch when I pressed my head against Jorge's wet t-shirt as he cursed because, yet again, he'd landed heel first. He had very sweet-smelling sweat.

Jorge also lived up to his reputation. His persistence was, in fact, legendary. No matter the day, he woke at six and headed to the gym where he lifted weights for an hour. Then he came to the Castle where he drilled the syllabus with a dour-faced German woman who worked as an examiner for a teaching organization. If we didn't have lessons with Maxine, we practiced. He taught a full schedule, with a grin on his face. He needed one thing to keep going.

"Tea?" I asked the first time he put a pot to boil.

"Maxine got me into it," he said sheepishly as he measured out some Orange Pekoe. "Less jittery than coffee, but enough caffeine to keep me going."

"I'll take a cup," I said. Just to be sociable.

We practiced and we joked and we spent our days touching or close to touching, but when night came, we turned, back to back, toward our respective boroughs—the Bronx and Brooklyn.

"See you tomorrow," he'd say over his shoulder.

"Bright and early," I'd say as we both got on the B train, him heading north, me heading south, Midtown our only common meeting ground.

Jorge pulled me aside after we'd been dancing together for around six weeks. "Now that the honeymoon's over, we got to figure out how we're going to manage," he said.

"Manage what?" I asked before swallowing some tea. Jorge had taken to making me a cup at the beginning of practice. I returned the favor by making him one at the end.

"Getting along when we dance." He stopped and took a sip of his tea. "Me and Amber had some big blowouts."

"Why?" I asked. Oleg and I had rarely argued. We worked on what Maxine gave us, and if there was a point of contention, Oleg would defer to me until we saw Maxine.

"Amber and I came from different backgrounds. She's from money while I'm a broke kid from the Bronx."

I nodded. I didn't know much about Jorge and Amber's partnership beyond it had followed a similar trajectory as the one Oleg and I had followed. Lots of hard work to win the Rising Star and then stalling in the Open division before being ignominiously ejected after the Russian invasion.

"Amber's dad is a CEO of a big tech company in Silicon Valley, and her mother is a trial lawyer. Amber grew up getting everything she wanted, and if she didn't get it, she'd been taught to argue for it." Jorge wrinkled his brow. "Sometimes I think she liked to argue more than dance. It got worse and worse as we went along."

"I'm sorry," I said, and I was. I'd seen plenty of couples over the years fall into this trap.

"I'm not educated like Amber is, but I know things."

I shrugged. "I don't have a college degree myself."

"I look at it like this. You got skills I don't have, and I got skills you don't have. Let me help you, and I'll let you help me," Jorge said. "Let's not make it into a competition between us." He gestured an arm to the window. "We got plenty of competition out there."

"Works for me." Arguing sounded like something that took a lot of energy. Getting along would be far preferable. I smiled at him. "We'll be on each other's team."

"I knew you'd understand." He looked down and then back up at me. "Another thing."

I tipped my head to the side. "Okay."

"I don't think we should get involved because—"

"Of course not," I said, cutting him off, my lips squished into a tight line.

It took a couple of practices, but we arrived at a system that worked for us. First, I worked with Jorge on the Standard technique and figures before he helped me with the open portions. Then we spent a chunk of time applying everything we learned from Maxine. The last twenty minutes, we ran two rounds. During our free moments between lessons, we'd run a dance to keep the information fresh.

We practiced the emotion every single time. It'd gotten to the point that, when we danced, we were in love, forever style. We always had a moment at the end of Viennese Waltz—gazing into each other's eyes, Jorge proposing—where we would have to shake ourselves loose from the story. To alleviate the tension, Jorge would crack a joke or I'd make a suggestion about something we should ask Maxine.

Our chemistry didn't go unnoticed.

"Looks good," Vadim said. "Like real love." He paused. "Is it real love?" He winked at me.

"Don't be silly," I said in an airy trill. "We're just dance partners. Nothing less and definitely nothing more."

Our schedule was exhausting. Only a year and some change had passed since I was a competitor on the circuit, yet it seemed a lifetime ago. Maybe it was all the new information or maybe it was dancing with a new partner or maybe it was the fact that I'd turned thirty, but I couldn't remember feeling this type of bone-deep fatigue.

I rubbed my knee. I hadn't been to see a doctor, too terrified of what he would tell me. My mother had passed on her arthritis to me, and it'd burrowed deep into my right knee. I hadn't mentioned anything to Jorge or Maxine. Because there was no need to worry them about something that needed no worrying. I wasn't going to let it be a problem. Not even a little one.

I counted the months to Nationals. There were nine. That wasn't so many. When I wasn't dancing, I would rest. My social life could wait until next year. *Mastering the Art of French Cooking* went back on the shelf. I made soup on Sundays, which lasted me through the week. Sleep trumped everything, so I gave up on cleaning. I let dirty dishes pile in the sink, and colonies of dust bunnies took up residence on the floor.

My mother was horrified when she stopped by.

"If I'd known you were coming, I would have tidied up," I said, a touch defensively.

"Are you tired, *zolotse*?" Her eyes glinted knowingly.

"I feel wonderful," I said with as much gusto as I could muster. I was not going to admit to my mother that she was right. I was feeling distinctly low on energy and short on chutzpah these days.

My mother pursed her lips and hired a cleaning lady for me. She also took to leaving nourishing meals.

"If you want to become champion, you must eat," she said as she dropped off a casserole. "You need noodles, protein." She pointed at the split pea soup I'd made. "That is food for sick person."

Like a snowball, the days rolled forward, picking up speed as the season loomed. What kept me going? One thing. Jorge and I were getting better. Each practice was stronger than the last, and winning, doing what I'd set out to do all those years ago, seemed like a real possibility.

Our efforts pleased Maxine. "You're going to be ready when the season starts."

"To win?" Jorge asked.

"The judges decide that. Park and Ashley Lee retired, but rumor has it that Trey Devereux is returning." She widened her eyes at me. "With Carly."

"I know," I said.

"He's already won. Three times." Jorge scratched his head. "Why would he come back?"

Maxine shook her head, her orange hair rustling like the skirt of a flamenco dancer. "No one knows." She tweaked the corners of her lips. "It's going to be an exciting season for Smooth."

Chapter 28

CARLY: DANCE POSITION

AFTER SIX WEEKS, Trey's coach Cyrus visited.

"You've done marvelous work, Trey. The partnership is poised and powerful." He turned to me. "Well done."

I smiled, pleased but way more relieved. I didn't know what I'd do if Cyrus found me wanting.

"What will you do for routines?" Cyrus asked Trey.

"Freshen up the previous ones to suit Carly."

"So you're keeping the old look."

Trey drew his eyebrows together. "Should I change?"

"That's your decision. My job is to help you be the best version of whatever you choose to be."

"Mastery and purity are my hallmarks. I want to give the judges what they expect."

Cyrus turned to me. "What do you think?"

"Trey's the expert."

Cyrus studied me. I returned his gaze timidly.

"How old are you?"

"Twenty-two."

"Do you like Charleston?"

"It's nice, I think. I haven't seen that much of it."

"What do you do for fun?"

I traced a circle on the floor with the tip of my shoe and then retraced it. "I practice."

Cyrus chuckled. "Outside of practice."

"I sit in the garden."

Cyrus peered over his gold-framed glasses at me. "At twenty-two, your idea of fun is sitting in the garden?" he asked. "I'm sixty-four, and that's not my idea of fun."

"Yes." I was disappointing Cyrus, and I didn't know why. Wasn't I supposed to devote myself, body and soul, to dancing?

"Could you be a good girl and ask William to put on some tea?"

Once I exited the ballroom, I yielded to temptation and tacked my ear to the door.

"Are you pleased?" Cyrus asked.

"Very. Carly's a hard worker and cheerful, always cheerful," Trey said. "It's been more pleasant than I expected."

That was . . . good? What had he been expecting?

"She needs a longer leash," Cyrus said. "She can't just be an extension of you. She needs to bring her own flavor to the partnership." His voice had a sharp, unyielding edge like a ruler smacking an obstinate student's wrist.

I strained my ears, but Trey remained quiet.

"Take her out. To eat, to see a show, to walk by the water," Cyrus said in a softer tone. "It would be good for you both. You work too hard, dear boy."

I held my breath to hear what Trey said, but a siren wailed and it was lost.

"She's lovely, and her devotion to you is touching," Cyrus said. "Nurture her, so the rose can bloom. If you make it all about the flower, the roots will wither. And we know how well that turned out last time." The edge, sharper than before, had returned.

I fled down the stairs, nervous they'd open the door and realize I'd been eavesdropping, as questions popcorned in my mind.

What happened last time?

Was Cyrus alluding to Tamsin?

Where was Tamsin?

Trey never brought up his former partner. I'd expected him to have photos up or, at the least, mention her from time to time, but he acted as if she didn't exist.

Had he been in love with her?

Was he still in love with her?

I hoped not.

On Saturday, at the end of practice, Trey sat on the bench, unlacing his shoes. I was walking through the notes he'd given me on the alignment of the Open Reverse Turn, Lady Outside in Tango—a box with passing feet that revolved counterclockwise.

Alignment acted as the road map to ballroom dance steps. Using Line of Dance as its north star, alignment dictated the position of the feet in relation to the room.

I muttered, "Right foot back in Contrary Body Movement Position to Diagonal Center, Left Foot to the side and slightly forward pointing down Line of Dance . . . "

I lost my focus as a flutter of movement caught my eye. Trey was waving at me.

He patted the spot beside him. "Sit."

I jogged over, parked myself beside him, and lifted my face expectantly.

"You've been here for over six weeks."

I nodded, unsure of where this was going.

"I'm pleased with how well everything is going, how beautifully you're dancing."

"Thank you," I said more as a question.

"I want to celebrate our partnership. May I take you to dinner tonight?"

I looked down and then up at Trey. "Yes." I didn't trust myself to say anything more.

He smiled, and it almost reached his eyes.

"I'll knock at seven." He reached out a hand and traced the outline of my bun with his pointer finger. "Wear your hair down."

One of the delights of my partnership with Trey was a wardrobe crowded with pretty clothes. For years, my sartorial purchases revolved around functionality and price, with the latter always, always being the prime factor. I felt like a princess when I threw open the closet door every morning.

Most of the clothes were for practice, a rainbow of jersey dresses, skirts, and tops that moved easily, but a small collection of cocktail dresses hung in the back. While everything was meticulously laundered and pressed, giveaways pointed to previous ownership. A snag here, some dropped stitches here, an almost unnoticeable rip in the hem.

Tamsin's, I thought. It made sense. We were of similar height and coloring.

After weighing several options (burgundy velvet, too matronly with its long sleeves; lavender silk, too girlish with its sweetheart neckline), I landed on a stretchy tank dress constructed of black lace. It showed off my legs, something I had a lot of, and its severely cut bodice minimized the need for breasts, something I did not have a lot of.

At seven on the dot, Trey knocked—slow, quick, quick, slow. He was wearing a navy blue suit, a pink dress shirt, and a blue tie dotted with pink. He was, as usual, extraordinarily good-looking and so clean.

"Wavy," he said as he brushed his index finger against the beige waterfall I'd draped over one shoulder. "I wouldn't have guessed."

"Pink," I said, tapping his shirt cuff. "I wouldn't have guessed."

He frowned at me.

I winked. "You always wear white."

He half-smiled and offered the crook of his elbow. "Shall we?"

I twined my arm through his. We walked the half-dozen blocks to the restaurant, a sleek outfit with high-backed chairs, white tablecloths, and large canvases of horses that hung on velvet-covered walls. Ivory candles in small brass lamps winked from each table.

I settled into the chair and smoothed my dress. My stomach bobbled up and down, excitement with a chaser of apprehension. I hadn't eaten at that many nice restaurants.

"May I order?" Trey asked.

I closed the menu. "Please."

Used to counting pennies, I would have ordered the cheapest thing on the menu without paying attention. When the server came over to take our order, she gulped as she made eye contact with Trey.

My heart pounded in understanding. I'd spent the last six weeks with him, and he still dazzled me. My empathy ebbed when she turned to me and sniffed.

I was found wanting.

She refocused her attention on Trey. "The duck breast is good as are the pan-roasted sea scallops."

Trey listened politely and then placed our order. He didn't share the wine list with me, but I gathered he'd ordered an expensive bottle.

"Very good, sir," the server said, her face brightening as she calculated the tip. She brought the bottle over quickly. Red wax dribbled from the seal down the sides, and the looping script of the label was in French.

Trey tasted the wine and nodded his approval. The waiter splashed some in my goblet, an enormous bowl perched on a slender stem.

He extended his glass to me. "To our partnership."

I clinked my glass against his. I took a sip, eager to try expensive wine for the first time.

Hmmm.

It tasted like every other glass of wine I'd had.

Maybe I did it wrong.

I took another mouthful, this time letting it linger on my tongue before swallowing.

Still regular old wine.

Trey gestured toward my glass. "What do you think?"

"It's nice." I was hedging.

He cocked his head at me.

"The distinction between swill and fine wine is lost on me." I leaned forward conspiratorially. "Don't tell anyone here."

Trey laughed, the creaky *ha ha* of rusty gears grinding to life. He pushed his glass aside. "I'm not much of a drinker myself," he said. "Daddy died of cirrhosis of the liver when I was nine, so I stay away from the stuff."

He lounged in his chair as I picked at my napkin. Now that we were out together, I had no idea what to say. The only thing we ever talked about was dancing. Actually, Trey talked; I listened. The canyon of silence between us felt infinite, unconquerable.

"How did you start dancing?" I asked in an anxious rush.

"Cotillion."

"What's that?"

"It's a Southern tradition for children from well-to-do families. It's a cross between dance classes and charm school. I started in sixth grade."

I tried and then failed to imagine Trey as a sixth grader. He seemed as if he'd been born mature.

"I can't picture you as a sixth grader." I forced myself to meet Trey's eyes.

"Once upon a time I was, and I was a sixth grader who loved to dance. I'd stay after class and pester the instructor with questions. She didn't know much, only enough to teach the basics, but she did her best to answer my questions."

The waiter placed our first course in front of us, lobster-and-corn chowder. I took a spoonful. Now this I could appreciate, liquid satin adorned with chunks of rosy lobster.

"How did you go from cotillion to three-time Nationals champion?" I asked after swallowing.

"Instead of going to a normal high school, I had a tutor. I was a quick learner, so there were hours during the day when I had nothing to do. Mama remembered that I'd enjoyed dancing and found me a teacher."

Trey closed his eyes. "Margaret Foxworth. She had to be at least sixty years old, but she knew the Standard syllabus backward and forward. She was a tiny, shriveled nut of a lady, but she spoke with this big bellow. During our lessons, she sat with her handbag in her lap and drilled me on the basics." He smiled, a real one. "I still hear her in my head."

I smiled back at him, delighted by the scrap of personal information.

"When we'd dance together, she had me rewind the music if I made a mistake." He swallowed some soup. "It could take me an hour to dance a two-minute Waltz."

"So you're a high schooler being bossed around by a grandma who'd smack you with her purse if you stepped with a heel instead of a toe. What happened next?"

"I went to college in Virginia. I majored in art history, a useless but interesting degree."

I opened my eyes meaningfully.

"Colonial portraiture," he replied to my silent question. "I can regale you with tales about all the traveling artists who would arrive at plantations with the entire picture painted save the face."

"18th-century Mad Libs, painterly style?"

He laughed again, a little less creaky this time.

"Something like that. On the weekends, I went to Washington, D.C. There was a British couple who owned a studio. I took lessons from the wife. She's the one who convinced me to try Smooth. Up until that point, I'd only done Standard and a little Latin," he said. "Which was not my forte," he added.

"It wasn't mine either. So many hips, and so many directions those hips are supposed to move in." I smiled at him.

He returned my smile. "That's how I felt."

"Latin was a bust, but you discovered Smooth," I said. "When did you decide to compete?"

"I was having a marvelous time in Virginia, so I stayed for a while. I got a master's degree and was contemplating a doctorate in antebellum art, a useless endeavor, but Mama had become incapacitated. So I came home."

The waiter placed our entrees, the recommended scallops, in front of us. I carefully cut a small piece of one and placed it in my mouth. I chewed, but I was not at all interested in the creamy texture or the crackling sear. I wanted Trey to tell me more about himself.

"I'd met Cyrus at the studio, and when I told him I was leaving, he suggested I give competing a go. I came back to Charleston with the intention of becoming a Nationals champion. It took some time to find the right partner and train her. But I did it." He said the last words with a sense of finality, the chord at the end of a long hymn.

Tamsin Grubbs. Was Trey still in contact with her? I wanted to ask, but Trey's tone held me back.

"What did you do while you were retired?"

"A whole lot of nothing," he said. "I took up running and entered every race I could. I read. Took a class or two."

I placed another small bite of a scallop in my mouth. I was way too excited for food, but I felt I should make a stab at eating the delicious meal.

"How about you, Carly? How did you start dancing?" The heat from his gaze felt claustrophobic, like wearing wool on a summer day.

"Pretty much like every little girl. I saw *Swan Lake* and wanted to be a ballerina. I took ballet and jazz and even a few tap classes at the local studio. I loved it. I was never happier than when I was dancing, but I had to stop when I started high school."

"Why?"

"My brother Archer has low-functioning autism. As he got older, it was an all-hands-on-deck situation," I said, avoiding specifics. "There wasn't the time or the money for dance classes."

I twirled the stem of my wine glass. "In college, I used to cut through the dance building, so I could watch the classes. I missed it so much, but I didn't have room in my schedule," I said. "A year and a half ago, I saw an ad for summer teachers at the Castle. I called, and Ralph, the studio owner, hired me on the spot. I never looked back."

"What do your parents think about you living in Charleston and dancing with me?"

"That it's frivolous," I mumbled, not meeting Trey's gaze.

His silvery eyes bored into me. "Are you in contact with them?"

"They send me an email every week from Archer. He's nonverbal, but they pretend he writes it. It says things like I did well with my stickers this week, and mom and dad wish you would come home, Carly."

I swallowed. I should go home, keep my end of the bargain, but my heart, beating for Trey, had overpowered my sense of duty.

"What do your parents do?"

"My mom is a freelance grant writer, and my dad is a counselor at a juvenile detention center," I said. "They wanted me to become a special education teacher." In a small voice, I said, "Obviously, I didn't do that."

"Did you want to be a special education teacher?"

I wrung my hands together. "Not really. But my parents believe the only life worth living is a life lived in service of others."

Trey stopped with his fork halfway to his mouth.

"My first memory of Christmas is when I was five. After opening presents, we went to a soup kitchen to serve dinner to the homeless. My job was to stand by the rolls and wish everybody a happy holiday."

I didn't add how terrifying the experience had been. Men—some clean, some not, all with dead, sad eyes—listened to my well wishes as their bent spines spoke to the inanity of my words.

I sat up straight. "It was a good lesson. There's always somebody less fortunate than you." I arranged my features to read as happy, which was not at all how I felt about that memory.

Trey put his fork down. "What did you want to be?"

"I never got a chance to find out." I looked down. "Archer needed so much support that our household revolved around him." I took a deep breath. "Our town didn't offer many resources for autistic kids, so my parents depended on me. They suggested I become a teacher since it has regular hours and summer breaks. It would allow me to help out at home." I tugged at the corner of the napkin, snowy white and so soft, in my lap. "Special education was the natural fit."

Then, without warning, the cork popped off the resentment I'd bottled up for years and years, and out spewed a jet of caustic vinegar. For the first time ever, I told someone how I really felt about how growing up alongside Archer.

"I tried to be perfect. I didn't complain about giving up dancing or never having a birthday party or a sleepover with my friends. By the time I got to high school, though, I was tired, so tired, of being perfect. It didn't get me anything beyond five minutes of my parents' undivided attention or the occasional compliment." I said, staring at my lap. "So I began lying because I was desperate for any type of social life. I baked cupcakes that I sold for autism research. I dyed the frosting green since Archer liked that color. I put up a stand at football games and school dances. I only baked two dozen because I could sell that many in fifteen minutes and spend the rest of the time with my friends or a boy I liked."

I came up for air but dove right back in. "I lied and told my parents it took the entire time to sell twenty-four cupcakes. In college, I lied about the start and end times of my class and invented group projects, so I could meet friends for coffee or go on a date."

My volume had risen to a quiet shriek although my eyes stayed focused on the napkin spread across my legs. "Then I started leaving. First it was for the summer and then for the year until I won Rising Star. Now I'm here with you, and I don't know if I'm ever going back."

I dropped my pitch to its normal volume. "I love my brother, I do. But I couldn't give up dancing. Not for the second time."

I pushed my uneaten scallops around my plate as I replayed my words in my head. The word I'd used the most was *I*. I twisted in my chair. "I'm so selfish," I muttered. I raised my eyes and looked around the restaurant, so beautiful, and then for the first time in minutes, at Trey, also so beautiful.

His face was arranged in a smooth curtain of bland politesse. "Dessert?"

I shook my head miserably. It'd been going well, and I ruined it.

We didn't say anything as we walked home through the streets of Charleston, the bright, elegant houses at odds with my black mood. Trey held the door open to the mansion and then escorted me up the stairs.

"May I come in?" he asked as we approached my door.

"Okay," I said, my hand clumsy as I turned the knob.

Trey followed me in and then closed the door behind him.

"Sit?" I swung an arm toward the love seat, feeling moronic. It was his house; he could sit where he wanted.

"I'd rather stand." Trey took off his jacket and placed it over the back of the love seat. Then he loosened his tie, lifted it over his head and positioned it on top of his jacket.

I stood by him, unsure of what was happening.

Trey placed his pointer finger under my chin and steered my face until I was looking at him. "Your happiness is important too, Carly. Don't let anyone tell you otherwise."

I dipped my head up and down. After my outburst, I didn't trust my words.

His finger traced the outline of my jaw as I shivered. "Are you happy here? Are you happy with me?" he asked.

I stared at Trey with burning, yearning eyes. "I'm so happy."

"I'm glad."

Like a conductor setting the downbeat, he reached down and

pulled my dress over my head. I stared at him for a moment before bending my head forward, so my hair cascaded down my chest. The lack of carbs and intense exercise had whittled away what little curves I'd had.

"Lovely," he said in a faint, faraway voice.

He unbuttoned his shirt and removed his pants. I gulped. His body was a flawlessly cut gemstone, all hard planes and defined edges.

Trey offered his hand, and I placed my damp one in his dry grip. "Follow me?" he asked.

He strode to the bed and lay down before pulling me on top of him. He placed his right hand on my shoulder blade, and I ringed my left around his deltoid. We were in dance position.

Trey tipped his body to the left, and I rolled until the right side of my body was on the bed. I extended my leg backward as I arched my back, a comma dripping with desire. Then he rotated me across his body until we both were looking up at the ceiling, me in front and to his right—Shadow Position. He guided me to lift our clasped left hands to the side and then up in the air.

Using intense eye contact, we went on like this for sometime in our languid naked dance, none of the muss, fuss, or mess of actual sex, yet intense, sensual, and honest in the way sex was. At some point, we returned to dance position. I placed my head on Trey's heart, overcome by the beauty and oddness of him.

"We can't get distracted, Carly. We have to maintain our focus and keep our energy up," he said.

I nodded against his chest, my body sagging with disappointment.

"You understand?"

"I do." I did although I didn't want to. Trey was telling me that our only physical relationship would be dancing.

He brushed a dry kiss against my forehead. "I'm glad."

Trey continued to take me out. For dinner, for walks along the Battery, to the opera for my birthday where he lent me ruby earrings and then danced with me in the garden until the wee hours of morning. We chatted, he held my hand, and I made him laugh as often and as easily as I could.

It felt as if we were dating except we weren't. That hallmark of dating—verbal assertion of feeling validated by specific physical declaration—was missing.

My love, huge to begin with, flourished. I'd always thought love a finite thing, a place with defined walls, a ceiling and a floor, what I'd felt with Sam. My love for Trey, though, expanded infinitely, the universe rushing to meet borders that didn't exist.

It was impossible to keep hidden beneath my skin, which was porous to begin with. Trey knew; he had to know. Everything I did, everything I said, and everything I wanted was designed to please him. He would never love me back in the same way, but I didn't care. My love, a massive wave of reeling emotion, only required a beach upon which to land.

If Trey accepted my love, then that would be enough.

Chapter 29

NINA: IT SOUNDS LIKE A JOKE

"THE SEASON IS RIGHT around the corner," Maxine said.

"Are we ready?" Jorge asked.

"As ready as you're going to be. You need to get out on the floor and show the judges what you're doing. If it's not working, we need to rethink immediately. And if it's working, we need to make it better, as quickly as possible."

My left knee shook in terror while my right knee wobbled in pain. The last competition I'd danced in was the one in Baltimore where Maxine had told Oleg and me to retire. I wiped my palms, clammy with ambition and nerves, on my skirt. The enormity of what Jorge and I, a Latin boy and a Standard girl, two kids born of immigrants, from the outer boroughs, were trying to do hit me hard.

"Costumes?" Jorge asked as he massaged his left hip. He'd done this before, but he was doing it with more frequency and intensity. I wanted to ask him about it, but it might draw attention to all the rubbing I was doing to my knee. So I kept my mouth shut.

"They need to bold and sexy." She swiveled her gaze to me. "I know you're used to being covered up when you dance, but now isn't the time to be demure."

A dressmaker volunteered to sponsor us due to our previous accomplishments. Maxine went with us to the first appointment. She selected primary colors: stoplight red, swimming-pool blue, sunflower yellow. The silhouettes featured cutouts, low backs, plunging necklines, and slits in the skirt.

It was nothing compared to a Latin costume, but my cheeks

burned self-consciously the first time I tried on the ball gown Maxine had chosen. If these slivers of fabric tacked together could even be called that. The dress consisted of two tiny diamonds of blue satin for the top attached to a large triangle of skirt, slashed with a thigh-high slit.

"I feel like a showgirl," I said when I walked out of the fitting room. "I'm ready to join a kick line."

"Sell it, darling," she said. "None of this will work if you don't believe in it."

Jorge had his own problems. He pulled at the sleeves of his blue suit coat. "How can anybody dance in this much clothing?"

He took dance position with me, our torsos pressing into each other. "I can't feel your body," he said with a grumble. "How am supposed to lead if I'm separated by all this fabric?"

My cheeks heated up although he meant it benignly.

"Practice, practice," Maxine said.

Practice, practice was all we did. We had so much information to apply—from Maxine and from each other—that we pushed running rounds to the evening. Long after everyone left, we would stay in the studio, running round after round.

It could have been awful. It was late and we were tired, but when one of us would droop, the other would swoop in with a joke or a cup of tea.

Our deficiencies were so pronounced that, out of desperation, we committed to everything together. He supported me; I supported him.

"I got you," he'd say as I arced over his arm into a death-defying dip.

"Wait," I'd say when he'd try to rush into yet another heel-toe exit.

"Use me," he'd say when I dropped into a dramatic lunge, my lone support his strong, warm grip.

"Elbows," I'd say when his dance position sagged.

Our first competition should have been terrible. Plenty of it, in fact, was terrible.

We made our debut at a tiny event in Rhode Island. It was February, and the sparkle and sociability of a ballroom competition added much-needed vitality to the landscape of gray frigidity.

There weren't enough dancers to fill a six-couple final, just two other couples who'd been around forever but never progressed beyond the quarterfinal at Nationals. They looked at competing as something fun to do a few times a year, so they stuck to small competitions where their friends could root them on.

"You're competing?" one of the women asked through a mouthful of pink lipstick and chewing gum. "Together? In Smooth?"

We smiled. "It sounds like a joke," I said. This had become my go-to when we were confronted by the surprise of others.

She spat her gum into a napkin and tossed it in the trash. "Trey Devereux is coming back."

"It's going to be an exciting season for Smooth." I'd co-opted Maxine's line to cover my dismay at the challenge we were up against. Trey was unbeatable. And while Carly might still be green, she'd work insistently to get to his level by Nationals.

A picture of Carly watching videos of Trey slipped into my head. She'd looked like a tween in raptures over a rock star. I couldn't wait to find out if dancing with and living with Trey had tamed her ardor or fed it.

Jorge and I were pulsing with nerves when the opening notes of Waltz sounded. We performed stiffly, uncomfortably until we got to the moment where we clasped hands for the first time—*hello, you*. As we gazed into each other's eyes, the violin swelling, we remembered our promise. *Let's help each other*.

So we did. When I whirled out of control in Tango, veering precariously across the line of dance into the path of another couple, Jorge spun after me. He picked me up in dance position and entered into the closed portion of our routine.

We were back on track.

He forgot an entire wall of our Foxtrot, but I followed. When we got to the ending, music was still playing. He cursed under his breath.

"The runaround," I whispered. So we did the runaround again and managed to hit our ending pose.

We were back on track.

Viennese Waltz was the roughest. Jorge forgot everything he knew about footwork, which created a series of bumps rather than the silken ride it should be. My arms, stiff and aching, flopped rather than floated. We gritted our teeth and kept going.

We were back on track.

For all the mistakes we made, and they were big, embarrassing mistakes, something else was happening. We were happening. All the chemistry we'd practiced bubbled up, out, and into the ballroom.

The audience noticed. By Tango, they were chanting our number, fifty-two. By Viennese Waltz, all eyes were on us. With only three couples to compare, the judges had plenty of time to watch, and watch us they did. Over clipboards, their curious eyes followed us everywhere.

After we bowed and walked off the floor, exhausted but exhilarated, Jorge grabbed me into a bear hug, which I returned. I relaxed against him, thankful for his strong arms. I was so tired I could have gone to sleep right there.

Maxine found us. Her eyes were glittering. "Rough but exciting," she pronounced. She cocked a head toward the judges who were parked at a table, waiting for the Open Latin event to start. The judges, who habitually wore polite but jaded expressions, were gossiping energetically. "You got their attention."

We won although it wasn't a big deal. Even though we weren't very good, the other couples were worse, and better was the only currency that mattered in a ballroom dance competition.

The season had begun.

It wasn't enough to get out there and dance, hitting any and every competition. A couple had to strategize to maximize their time and money, which were limited even for the best dancers.

Where should they compete? In their backyard or across the country?

When should they compete? Every weekend? Every other weekend?

What competition should they compete at? The small ones or the big ones?

The circuit was chockablock with options. A smaller competition in West Palm Beach with a distinguished judging panel or a large one in Kansas City attended by all the dancers in the Midwest? An underwhelming competition in New Jersey that would cost little in the way of time and money or a prestigious one in Las Vegas that would involve considerable resources?

Every competition was a pace forward toward Nationals, the only competition that actually mattered.

Maxine wanted us to hold off on the bigger events for a few months.

"Hit the regional competitions. Let the judges get to know you in an intimate environment. It'll buy us some time to clean up the technique."

She tilted her head to Jorge. "Footwork, my son. Get your heels and toes straight." Maxine swung her gaze to me. "Arms, Nina. They're flapping like chicken wings."

We followed Maxine's advice. We took planes, trains, and buses to the far reaches of the U.S to attend tiny competitions. Jorge and I spent so much time together that our relationship naturally progressed to the next level—friends.

Before our trip to San Diego, Jorge asked me if I liked movies.

"Sure," I said and then laughed, a little embarrassed. "Although I see maybe three movies a year."

Jorge grinned at me. "Same here. We work late, and then spend our weekends on the road competing."

I wrinkled my brow. "The last movie I saw was in August."

I blinked. That was six months ago. I'd gone with Carly, Sam, Vadim to see a midnight showing of that summer's blockbuster in which a traffic cop discovers he has super powers.

It was as dumb as it sounded, but we had fun passing around mini bottles of vodka that Vadim had secreted in Carly's purse, much to her surprise. Carly and Sam had been in intense training mode for Rising Star, and the jokiness had lightened their mood.

"That's about the same for me," Jorge said.

"Why movies?"

He smoothed his spiky hair. "Because pretty much the only thing I've done as an adult is dance. It's time to catch up on life."

"What did you have in mind?"

"We have all this dead time getting to and from competitions," he said. "Let's watch movies together."

I was intrigued by Jorge's idea. Oleg had always spent our trips on his laptop planning our next trip, joyfully shifting among dozens of open tabs. I'd flipped through fashion magazines and napped.

I exhaled, nostalgic but not sad.

"Should we start at the beginning and work our way through?" I asked.

"Let's watch the best movie from each year. By the time we get to Nationals, we should be up to the 21st century."

So we watched movies: silent ones, film noirs, sweeping epics. Besides filling up the gigantic time suck that took place between New York and competitions, the movies proved to be useful to our dancing.

"I'm learning things," I said after we'd watched *Gone with the Wind* on the way to yet another competition in the Midwest.

Although we were on a plane with flight attendants bounding up and down the aisles, the romance had swept me up. When the camera panned in for an impassioned kiss between Clark Gable and Vivien Leigh, I peeked at Jorge who'd been staring at me. Both of us hastily turned our eyes back to the screen as my stomach bounced.

"About acting," I said brightly.

"Same here," Jorge said.

"The best actors convey so much emotion through their faces without actually making faces."

He nodded. "I wish I'd done this years ago." He laughed. "I made a lot of stupid faces when I was dancing Latin."

I winked at him. "I had the opposite problem. I didn't make any faces."

He gave me a half hug, and I shivered, which was silly. I was absolutely, completely, most definitely not at all interested in Jorge.

At the hotel, we'd gotten into the habit of leaving the door unlocked between our rooms.

He'd poke his head in my room. "Can you pin my number on?"

I'd stick my head in his room. "Do you want some tea?"

He'd open the door a few inches. "I'm going to get a snack. Want to come?"

I'd pull the door all the way open. "Let me put my coat on."

He'd walk through the door into my room, and then shut it behind him. "I'll wait here."

It was easy and it was comfortable, and I looked forward to the travel time that bookended competitions. Not that it meant anything beyond the fact that we were two people who spent a lot of time together in pursuit of the same goal.

Maxine kept her ears pricked for feedback.

"Nothing we don't know already," she said. "Full steam ahead."

News of our partnership flew far and wide. The only person who I doubted knew of its existence was Carly. We'd exchanged emails in the beginning, but Carly's answers left a lot to be desired.

I'm learning so much, she'd written. *Trey's a wonderful teacher.*

Then she'd sign off.

As I'd gotten busier, I'd dropped off on my correspondence.

A competition, our first big one, was approaching in Washington, D.C. I'd gotten wind that Trey and Carly would be there, so I emailed Carly to let her know I'd see her. I missed her. Even though we were competitors now, I wanted us to be friends first.

Rumors whirred that Trey kept her under his thumb. At competitions, no one had exchanged more than a hello with her since she'd departed for Charleston. Vadim had seen her a few weeks ago at an event and confirmed this.

"Who is this Trey Devereux? He looks like prince but has

personality of toad." he said. "I'd like to talk to him. See what he did with our Carly."

Carly was a great favorite of Vadim's. He'd struggled his first weeks teaching at the Castle. Americans weren't used to the Russian style of teaching, which was blunt and demanding, and Vadim couldn't understand why his students left crying.

One day, Carly had caught wind that it was his birthday. To cheer him up, she'd brought in a small cake and a cheap bottle of champagne. After lessons were done for the evening, she'd gathered the staff to sing "Happy Birthday." It was when every cent counted for Sam and Carly, so the gesture far exceeded its dollar amount.

Thereafter, Carly had taken to teaching near Vadim. Without saying a word or issuing a criticism, she showed him how to teach to an American clientele—sunnily and with an abundance of positive feedback. Vadim had cottoned on and softened his approach. Now he was a popular teacher with more students than he could manage.

"What happened?" I asked.

"I see her at on-deck area. I go over, say hi, ask her to get drink after competition, but this Trey Devereux grabs her hand and takes her to practice room. I think, big mistake. He thinks I'm hitting on Carly, doesn't know we're old friends. So I try again and ask both of them. He doesn't give her chance to answer. Just says, 'Maybe another time' and pulls her away, like she's dog on leash."

Vadim's nostrils flared. "Asshole." His accent pumped up the word to the proportions of a steroid-addled wrestler.

I laughed internally. Vadim's anger exceeded the slight. His feelings for Carly were probably more than platonic. Carly might never be the most beautiful woman in the room, but her thoughtfulness and cheerfulness would always keep her supplied with a steady stream of suitors.

"When I see her this weekend, I'll tell her you said hello," I said.

Chapter 30

CARLY: AN EXCITING SEASON FOR SMOOTH

WE'D GOTTEN BETTER.

Correction.

I'd gotten better. The relentless work had paid off, and I was dancing like Trey did, with power, elegance, and clarity. Although I still lived in my head, reciting everything Trey had taught me, my body had grown to trust his, and I responded instinctively to even his most minor of invitations.

"Getting there," he said after a particularly good practice.

"Less like driving a clunker and more like a two-door hatchback?" I asked.

He laughed, only a little creaky. "At least a midrange sedan." His eyes widened as if he'd done something unexpected before he recomposed his features into their mask of indifference. "I'd like for us to make our debut soon."

"Okay." I twisted my hands. I wasn't feeling ready, but Trey was the boss.

"I wouldn't suggest it if I didn't think we were ready. You've done well, Carly."

"Thank you," I said in a small voice that belied my racing nerves.

We made our debut at a smallish competition in Raleigh in the middle of February, on a day so warm that it felt like the middle of summer. People were falling over themselves when they saw Trey. We couldn't walk more than a few feet without being waylaid by a competitor wanting to chat with Trey.

No one phrased it so bluntly, but beneath everyone's bonhomie and it's-good-to-see-yous, the big question throbbed. Why come back? Why risk the legacy?

Trey deflected them with various answers. "I missed dancing" and "I haven't danced to my full potential" were the ones he employed the most. To Papa, he said, "I couldn't resist this girl and her beautiful dancing."

I doubted any of these answers were true. For all the rigorous practicing, Trey didn't take pleasure in dancing. He approached it dutifully, resolutely, meticulously, but not with joy or curiosity.

He's maxed out his potential, I thought.

He was so clean, so polished, so consistent, the routines a recording rather than a live rendition, that there wasn't much for him to work on. Cyrus reminded him every now and again of some trivial point or offered a suggestion to accommodate me, but for the most part, he was content to let Trey be. Adding anything more would gild a lily that was already too perfect.

We won that competition. We won the next and the next and all the next after that, smaller events that barely stretched to a one-round final. Cyrus met us at the competitions, and afterward, he and Trey holed up together to go through the copious notes they had for me.

I worked as hard as I could to apply their corrections. I carried around a small notebook to jot down their comments, which I reviewed at night. For as battered as my body was due to the endless practicing, my head had it far worse.

Each tap that stick made to drum required me to display multiple strata of knowledge from the cock of my head to the part of my foot in contact with the floor. Then there were the hundred other subtle sways and small shapes between my crown to toe because Trey's dancing abounded with texture—tiny, elegant motions that coalesced into one big, flawless action.

To keep my mental space clean and clear, I'd given up on external stimuli. That meant no television, no books, just the occasional email to Archer on Sundays. Instead, I reviewed and practiced, practiced and reviewed. And when I was too broken for that, I collapsed in bed and visualized our routines. If the world came to an end, I wouldn't know or care. My single concern was to manifest flesh to sound, so I could be Trey's equal.

Because then, maybe, hopefully, he would love me a little, a small gesture in return for the humongous treasure chest I wished to drop at his feet.

One Sunday, I went to write my weekly email to Archer, hoping my parents wouldn't twist the knife of guilt too much, and found an email from Nina.

Big surprise! Will see you soon.
Nina xxoo

The fatigue crashed around me like a curtain at the end of a show, so I replied with a question mark.

She responded. *You'll see.*

I found out the next weekend when we decamped to Washington, D.C. for our first largish event, a semifinal.

The cherry blossoms had reached their peak bloom, and I stuck my head out of the cab, drinking in the rosy profuseness that lined the streets. I wished I could take a walk among them, but my time was already accounted for with hair, make-up, practicing, and competing.

Trey saw my face. "They're pretty aren't they?"

"So pretty," I said.

He smiled at me, and it reached his eyes as it did these days when we were together. "Maybe some time, we can do something other than compete in these cities we visit." He took my hand and squeezed it, which I returned. He didn't release his grip, just let our hands rest on the seat between us as my heart jiggled happily.

Trey was pleased about the opportunity for us to dance more than one round. "It'll be good for you to dance two rounds. You can relax into the routines and enjoy the challenge of doing the steps the same way but in a new way."

He was probably right, but I was more excited about the ball gowns. When Trey announced his return to the dance floor, his old sponsors rushed to him like a bevy of debutantes seeking the most eligible bachelor. They plied him with an endless stream of free costumes, dance shoes, and hair-and-makeup sessions in exchange for his endorsement.

He kept it simple for himself, black suits with a tie and flower in his lapel that matched the hue of my dress. He'd chosen pastels for me. "You're too delicate for vivid, garish colors," he told me. "I want you in the soft colors of a rainbow after a storm."

So I wore hues of lemon and mint and sky. Because the fervor surrounding Trey's return trumpeted like a bugle, I had a new dress for every round. It was a big change from the one red dress I'd carted all around the country when competing with Sam.

At this competition, I'd wear a dusty rose dress with sheer sleeves and a plunging back for the semifinal. For the final, I had a high-necked lavender one with an ornate rhinestone belt.

Trey directed the hair-and-makeup team before each competition. "Carly should look like an ingénue: young, fresh, innocent. No dark colors, no thick glosses or powders."

He requested that my hair be simple and elegant. No bouffants, no complicated braids or curls. I wore elegant French twists and classic chignons ornamented with a flower that matched Trey's.

I was never going to be beautiful, but made up, with my hair upswept and attired in a gorgeous dress, I felt, at least, like I passed muster next to Trey, who stopped traffic as if he were a matinee model.

In Washington, D.C., as we took the elevator to the ballroom, an audacious little girl of seven or eight patted Trey on the arm.

"Will you marry me when I grow up?" she asked as her pigtails bounced.

"Sure thing. What's your name?"

"Makayla."

"Nice to meet you, Makayla," he said. "Now don't you break my heart by marrying someone else."

Trey appeared unperturbed by the attention. I couldn't tell whether he'd stopped noticing it or if he'd chosen not to notice it.

Nina answered her cryptic email by the on-deck area.

"Carly," she said and gave me a careful hug as to not muss my makeup.

Trey kissed Nina's hand.

"Are you coming back?" I asked, taking in her cobalt blue dress with its bikini top and full skirt with a slit. This was sexy for Standard.

She nodded. "In Smooth." She flashed her cat-like smile at me. "We're competitors now."

"Who are you dancing with?" Trey asked. Impassivity glazed his features, but his eyes sparked.

In the months we'd danced together, I'd gotten better at reading Trey. He rarely moved his facial features, but I'd learned how to gauge his emotions. The mask had holes for eyes and a mouth, and I paid keen attention to them. I was determined to uncover the real Trey.

"Jorge Gonzalez."

Trey blinked.

Nina laughed. "Sounds like a joke, a Standard girl and a Latin boy take on Smooth."

"I look forward to dancing alongside you," Trey said. "Good luck."

"You too."

Nina and Jorge were in a different heat than ours for the semifinal. Trey watched them with interest, his jaw hardening as the dances were ticked off.

They were uneven but teeming with extravagant emotion, daredevil tricks, and a flamboyant narrative. No one was dancing like this. Everyone was doing us, just not as well as we did us.

They had issues, big, noticeable ones. Jorge was dreadful in dance position, his frame squat and crooked. His footwork offended. He used heels when he should have used toes and toes when he should have used heels. Nina struggled in the side-by-side sections, lost without a leader manipulating her every movement. Her arms, used to being anchored in dance position, lacked the expansive flourishes that characterized Smooth.

Jorge and Nina had another thing going for them—intense chemistry. I didn't know what the status of their relationship was off the floor. On the floor, though, they looked as if they had the hots for each other, and it had nothing to do with the story they were telling. Jorge took exquisite care to frame Nina, and she pasted her body to his in closed position, making sure that they never lost body contact. Even when one made a mistake, the other didn't sulk. Instead, they worked as a team to move forward, eyes and hearts turned toward each other.

After the semifinal ended, Trey turned to me. "Run and change your dress as quickly as you can. Meet me in five minutes in the practice room."

We didn't stay to hear if we'd made the final because of course we'd made the final. So had Jorge and Nina.

Trey had seen something in Nina and Jorge's dancing that was causing him dismay. We ran through our routines and he issued corrections, but his mind was somewhere else.

We won that competition and the ones after it, but Jorge and Nina were exciting the judges with their novelty and passion. They moved up the ranks quickly, and soon, they were placing second or third.

When Cyrus came to town, Trey asked for his opinion on Jorge and Nina.

"No finesse but utterly compelling to watch. This idea of theirs, to make each dance a story, is original. They're different from everybody else."

"Maybe we should change it up a little?" Trey asked, his eyes bright with ideas.

"It's too late for that, dear boy. Dance your best and let the chips fall where they may."

Trey pressed his lips together.

He's worried, I thought and then shivered.

If we lost, it would be my fault.

Chapter 31

NINA: AMANDA BELLOWS' BLUE DRESS

I HAD A FOUR-LETTER PROBLEM–PAPA. True to his word, Papa did take an interest in the partnership between Jorge and me, emphasis on me. I'd unleashed a monster that day at Nationals when he pulled me aside to discuss trying out with Jorge, an indefatigable, lovesick one that followed me around like a puppy.

Papa began stopping by the studio in the mornings when we practiced. He'd recline on the bench and sip coffee as we danced. Nothing was going to happen; nothing could happen. Jorge was present as was Ralph. Still, it was unsettling to have Papa there.

Ralph's mouth flopped open the first time Papa showed up. "You here to take a lesson or something?" he asked.

"I'm keeping an eye on the kids for Maxine." Papa smiled, an easy, noncommittal one. "You don't mind, do you?" Although he phrased it as a question, he issued it as a statement.

"Suit yourself."

Papa had been Ralph's boss back in the day, and although Ralph had owned the studio for a dozen years, he couldn't seem to shake old habits.

Great, I thought as Ralph turned the corner to his office.

In reality, Papa kept an eye on one kid—me. His eyes, shiny with desire, followed me anywhere and everywhere. Occasionally, he'd throw out a comment or a correction to us, proof that Maxine had, in fact, requested his presence, and he wasn't here just to ogle me.

Jorge caught on that something was off about Papa's visits, but couldn't sniff out the real reason.

"Has he ever done this before?" Jorge asked.

"Not with me."

"Me either."

I didn't mention Papa's interest in me. It wasn't as if he'd propositioned me or touched me inappropriately. He'd been flirty, but nothing had crossed the boundary from innocent infatuation to wily seduction. No law said he couldn't look. He just couldn't touch.

There was no way he was touching.

I brought it up to Maxine during one of our coaching sessions.

She smiled fondly. "Stan enjoys stopping by from time to time. He misses the studio." She patted my arm. "It's nice for him to hang out with you kids. Being Chairman of the Judges is a slog."

So much for that.

I ignored Papa, hoping he would recognize my disinterest and let it go. I greeted him briefly when he showed up and then turned my attention back to Jorge. My indifference to Papa, though, had the opposite effect; it stoked the flames of his ardor.

Then he began his push.

One day, as Jorge and I neared the end of our practice session, Papa knocked on Ralph's door.

"Okay if I take the kids out to lunch?"

"They could use the fun," Ralph said.

Papa waylaid us as Jorge and I were making notes about issues we wanted to discuss with Maxine.

"Ralph gave me permission. I'm taking you two to lunch."

"I have to teach in half an hour," Jorge said.

I didn't have a lesson until mid-afternoon.

Great, I thought.

"That leaves Nina." Papa offered his arm to me.

The studio was filling up with teachers and students. I searched for a reason to turn down his invitation but couldn't find one. Declining would be uncomfortable with all the people around. Plus, Papa was Maxine's husband, and he was Chairman of the Judges. I couldn't say no without having an excellent reason.

I had no reason much less an excellent one.

Internally, I sighed and then gritted my teeth. "It must be my lucky day," I said as I took his arm.

He guided me to a fancy Midtown restaurant that specialized in seafood. Men and a few women in business attire wheeled and dealed as they spooned clam chowder into their mouths. They washed down underhanded arrangements with sips of expensive

Sancerre and then prepped themselves to return to the office with espresso.

A few men were dining with women like me, dressed up but not in suits. I was wearing a forest-green A-line skirt and a matching scoop-necked top, an outfit unremarkable for the ballroom dance studio, but one that registered as dressy and vaguely inappropriate for a weekday lunch.

As Papa settled into the seat across from me, the waiter flashed me a knowing grin. I didn't return it.

Great.

He thought I was a mistress.

"Drink?" Papa asked.

I shook my head.

"Live a little."

"I have to teach in a few hours." I turned to the waiter. "Iced tea, please," I said firmly.

I ordered one of the cheapest things on the menu, salmon with whipped potatoes. Papa pressed his lips together when he heard my choice, but I was not going to take advantage of the situation. I wished Jorge were here. His presence would lighten the mood considerably. He would banter with Papa, and I could ignore the smarminess emanating from Papa.

I pinched myself. I depended on Jorge on the dance floor, not off. I pinched myself again and then for good measure, added another one. I really needed to stop thinking about Jorge when we weren't dancing.

Papa leaned forward. "It does me good to spend time with young people," he said.

At thirty, I wasn't exactly young as my creaky right knee could attest to, but I rolled with it. Papa had to be over sixty. Age, like beauty, rested in the eye of the beholder.

"My pleasure," I said.

The waiter plopped down our entrees. Papa had ordered squid-ink linguine, which looked like a tangle of slimy black worms.

"I've known you a long time, Nina. At least a dozen years. Am I right?"

"I started right after Ralph bought the studio."

"It's been a pleasure watching you grow up."

I cut a piece of salmon and shoved it into my mouth. My plan was to eat and leave. I was not comfortable with the direction this conversation was heading.

Papa sucked down a noodle. "Jorge too."

I swallowed some potatoes.

"It seems like yesterday that Maxine and I opened the Castle. Now it's been there for thirty years."

"A lot of great dancers have passed through its doors," I said.

Papa reached for his phone and then handed it to me. "We just got these digitized."

I flipped through his pictures. Papa as a young man with a big mustache and even bigger grin, the unmistakable swirly print of the Castle's logo behind him. The hearsay was true. Papa had been handsome in a swarthy, wolfish way. A picture of Papa and Maxine, who looked about sixteen, competing in Latin at Nationals. I snickered at Papa's catsuit. A headshot of Papa wearing his gold medal. He and Maxine had won Nationals twice before Papa retired. Maxine had continued to compete, placing in the Standard final and winning Smooth as one of the original innovators of the style.

I handed the phone back to Papa. "Thank you for sharing."

I relaxed a little. Maxine was right. Papa was lonely. Being Chairman of the Judges was a slog with little reward beyond the paycheck and the empty prestige.

I cut another piece of salmon, more slowly this time. Seeing the old pictures had touched me. For all the world's technology, dance remained an oral form, passing down its secrets from teacher to student.

I was lucky to have Maxine as a coach. She'd been on the ground floor of every ballroom dance development in the United States. The least I could do was entertain her husband for an hour or so.

"A lot has changed," Papa said.

"But one thing has stayed the same," I said.

"What's that?"

"Everyone still wants to win Nationals."

Papa stared at me with brown eyes, hard and penetrating like cold chocolate that could chip a tooth. "Is that what you want Nina? To win Nationals?"

"Isn't that what everybody wants?"

My mother's words clanged through my head. *This is America. Dreams are cheap. Get new one.*

But even with that advice, I couldn't shake my desire to win Nationals. The dream had been with me for so long that I didn't know who I was without it. Maybe if Maxine hadn't thrown me together with Jorge, a new dream could have taken root. But the old one, battered and bruised but still standing, pounded in my heart with the same insistence. I'd told myself so many times that I would be a Nationals champion that it felt as true to me as my name.

Papa shook his head. "Not true. I've been Chairman of the Judges for a dozen years, and I've learned a lot, watching from that dais. Plenty of people think they want to win Nationals. Some people think they deserve to win Nationals. But most of them, in their heart of hearts, don't care."

I scrunched up my face at him. "Really?"

"Even the ones who win Nationals don't care. They see it as winning at the craps table in Vegas. Show up, look pretty, and hope Lady Luck takes a shine to you."

"Are you saying some champions don't deserve to win?" I asked, a forkful of potatoes paused halfway to my mouth.

"I'm saying most champions win because they get lucky. They dance a little better than the rest. Maybe God blessed them with good looks or exceptional musicality. But on a different day, with a different judging panel, with a different costume, most might not win."

This was a bold statement. One that went against the common narrative of hard work, dedication, and stamina. Plus money.

"Even if it's due to luck, they're still Nationals champions," I said.

"What is a Nationals title worth?" Papa asked.

"Money-wise, a pretty penny. Plus a lifetime of prestige. Everybody knows that you're a winner."

He smirked. "Who won Nationals before Trey and Tamsin?"

I tipped my head from side to side, thinking. I threw my hands up. I couldn't remember.

"The Bellows."

I scanned through my memory. "Ted and . . ."

"Amanda," Papa said.

"That's right."

"What do you remember about them?"

"Ted was English, and Amanda had red hair." I searched for something more.

"Anything else?" Papa slurped some more noodles. "How about their dancing? How about the way you felt when you watched them dance?"

I'd been a newbie when the Bellows won, engrossed in my quest to win Rising Star. Even still, I must have watched them dance dozens of times, waiting for my event to be called or sticking around for awards to be announced. Yet I couldn't land on a single image of them dancing. Even when I trained Sam and Carly, I'd spent most of my prep time watching videos of Trey and Tamsin.

"Amanda had a blue dress I liked," I said. "It had peacock feathers around the hem."

"It was green," Papa said.

I widened my eyes. The dress had definitely been blue. I decided against saying anything. Papa was getting up there, and his memory might not be what it was. So I nodded.

"Don't you think that's strange?" Papa wiped his lips. "They won Nationals twice in Smooth, the division you're competing in, and the one memory you have of them is a dress Amanda wore."

Now that Papa brought it up, it was strange. "I guess they never made much of an impact on me," I said.

Papa lifted up his lips triumphantly. "That's why it's not enough to win Nationals. Do you know where Ted and Amanda are now?'

"No clue."

"They own a dance studio in Boise, Idaho."

"That's not so bad," I said.

"It's fine. But think of the time, money, and energy they put into winning Nationals. And now a top competitor . . . " Papa nodded at me, "can't recall their dancing and barely remembers who they are." He gestured for the waiter to bring two coffees.

In spite of my desire to make it a quick lunch, I was intrigued. I had no idea Papa had turned his job as Chairman of the Judges into one as a philosopher where he rhapsodized about the meaning of winning Nationals.

"Dance disappears the moment the music stops," Papa said as the waiter dropped off our coffees.

I stirred a spoonful of sugar into my cup. "Like life."

"That's why winning Nationals means nothing most of the time. That's why, when push comes to shove, the winners leave it up to luck."

"That's awfully pessimistic of you." I took a sip of coffee.

"I said most of the time." Papa poured some milk into his mug. "Not all the time."

I put my cup down. "When does it mean something?"

"When the dancing lives on after the music has died."

I frowned.

"Who's the best Smooth dancer of all time?" Papa asked.

"Trey Devereux." I sighed. "Obviously."

"Why?"

"Because he created a new way of seeing the dances. And then he did it well."

Papa smiled, showing off pointed canine teeth tinged gray from his linguine. "He was a trailblazer. Nobody's had a good idea since then." He gazed at me. "Until you and Jorge."

"We're working hard," I said, not sure I was following where Papa was going with the conversation.

"Winning Nationals can be an end or a beginning. You can collect your medal and ride off into the sunset to open a studio in Boise, Idaho, or you can do what Trey did by radically altering the discipline and influencing competitors for years to come." Papa stopped and blew on his coffee. "Nationals was just the launching point for his dancing. He knocked himself far into the future."

His eyes met mine for a long moment, the brown warming like chocolate heating in a pan. "You and Jorge have the same potential. You could inspire generations of dancers in the future." He sipped his coffee. "But you'd have to win. Nobody cares about second place." His eyes didn't leave my face as his words sank in.

Papa was persuasive. When put like that, winning a Nationals title was a stroke of luck that ultimately meant nothing. The legacy of winning was what mattered.

"Trey's back," he said.

"We saw him a few weeks ago."

"He looks terrific. And Carly's a good fit for him. She's a much more intelligent dancer than Tamsin ever was."

"Do you know why he came back?" I asked.

"He told me he saw Carly and couldn't resist dancing with her." Papa gulped the last of his coffee. "Could be true. But he showed up at Nationals looking for a partner. He must have a compelling reason to come back. And I doubt it's because he missed dancing."

Papa leaned back in his chair. "He's going to be almost impossible to beat even with the fresh approach Jorge and you have taken. I've seen the marks, every single one of them, for twelve years," he said. "Your risk-taking may get you rewarded in smaller events, but at Nationals, the judges will swing to what they know and love. And what they know and love is Trey Devereux."

I knitted my brows together. This was depressing stuff. But there was always next year.

I rubbed my knee, which was pinging. Not alarmingly but noticeably.

Papa waved his hand for the bill.

I reached for my purse to throw some cash on the table, but Papa put his hand up. "It's on me."

"Thank you," I said.

"I've liked you for a long time, Nina. I've liked Jorge for a long time. I want to you to know what you're up against."

He escorted me outside the restaurant and then turned to face me. "It was nice having lunch with you." He kissed my cheek, a light one that barely made contact with my skin. Even still, I recoiled.

Papa walked away, waddling a little. I slowly turned to head back to the Castle. He'd given me a lot to think about.

Chapter 32

CARLY: THE TWINKLE THAT LOST ITS LUSTER

THE WEEKS TUMBLED BY, one somersaulting after the other in an indistinguishable stream of practice and then compete, compete and then practice.

I worked as hard as I could, improved as fast as I could. One question spurred me on. Why had Trey returned? He could quit, immediately, and keep his legacy of undefeated Smooth champion untarnished.

There was an urgent reason, and it had to do with the spreadsheets Trey worked on when we weren't dancing.

As with the whirl of a kaleidoscope, the antebellum glamour that had wowed me so much in the beginning had transformed into distinctly threadbare, down-at-its-heels shabbiness with patchy carpets, moth-eaten drapes, chipped furniture, and water-damaged parquet.

All of the rooms save for the ground floor, the ballroom, and the rooms used by Trey, his mother, and me had been shuttered. I couldn't imagine what it cost to keep this place going. More money than I'd ever make in my lifetime.

Ballroom dancing wasn't cheap either. Many of our expenses were covered due to Trey's reputation. Still, plenty of cash was needed for one competition from flights and cab fare to hotel rooms and room service because we never, ever ate anywhere but our hotel rooms. Even with the prize money, which could be substantial, Trey was, at best, making a tiny profit not worth the time and energy it required.

He did not ask me for money, nor did he give me any money from our winnings. Trey paid for everything. The last time I'd handled cash was when I'd taken a cab from the Charleston airport to the mansion. I'd been worried in the beginning, wondering what he expected from me in the way of financial contribution. Gradually, I stopped noticing, and it'd become second nature to leave a list with my modest needs (shampoo, bobby pins, hand lotion) for William to take care of.

My suspicions were confirmed one Sunday evening when I went to send Archer my weekly email. Trey had fanned an array of bills by the computer. I didn't mean to look, but the blocky print, the ominous red color, and the imperative language made it impossible not to look. OVERDUE, PAST DUE, PAY NOW OR ELSE.

I clapped my hand to my mouth. I didn't open any of the envelopes although I could have. The letter opener, its tip topped with a pineapple, had already done its work, slicing through the envelopes, so Trey could confront their dire news.

I ran a finger over the opener, its steel blade cold and unbloodied by anything other than the truth. Trey was broke.

After our afternoon practice on Monday, instead of walking through the corrections Trey had given me, I sat down beside by him as he unlaced his shoes. I cleared my throat.

He looked up at me. "It seems like you have something you'd like to say," he said.

I nodded. Trey waited, his features sphinx-like.

I shuffled my feet. I was finding it hard to form the words to say what I wanted to say. "I, um, I wanted to thank you. You've shown me so much kindness."

"It's been my pleasure."

I wiped my sweaty palms on my skirt. "I haven't been contributing financially to our partnership, and I want that to change."

Trey's eyebrows shot up. "What makes you think you need to do that?"

"Because it's not fair for you to carry the weight of both of us. I'm a good teacher, a trained teacher, and I could teach lessons a few evenings a week," I said. "It wouldn't be much money, but it could defray some of the expenses."

Trey was already shaking his head. "I don't want you teaching, Carly, while we're competing. It's hard on the body. You're a thoroughbred horse right now. Even advanced students will knock bad habits into you," he said. "Plus, it's tiring, being cheerful for the parade of students who will lay their woes on you." He stroked my hand with his index finger as my skin rippled. "It's nice of you to offer, but no."

I smiled mischievously. "Even cotillion?" I asked. "I've heard enthusiastic sixth graders aren't so bad; they just ask a lot of questions."

"Even cotillion," he said firmly, and then, it registered. He laughed, and it sounded almost well oiled.

I took advantage of the lightness and stepped in with both feet. "Why did you come back?"

"Because I missed dancing. Because I didn't feel I'd reached my full potential." Trey recited the answers with practiced finesse.

"I don't believe you," I said in a rush.

His mouth gaped slightly. "Why not?"

"Because you've gotten as good as you'll ever be, which is the best the world has ever seen. Cyrus doesn't even give you corrections anymore. As for missing the dancing, I can't prove it, but I don't think so. There's no joy, no curiosity in it. You're a record, the same all the time, every time."

"Are you criticizing me?" His face remained impassive, but his gray eyes sparked, dead wood against hot flint.

"Absolutely not. You're perfect all the time, in every way. It's daunting showing up every day and trying, then failing, to match you." I hesitated. "But we spend so much time together. I get a different read on you than anyone else."

"Does it matter why I came back? Winning is what matters."

"It matters to me," I said.

"Why don't you tell me why you think I came back?" His features stayed inscrutable, but his mouth was pressed into a flat line.

I took a long, courageous breath. "Because you need the money." I snaked my hands together and then wrung them.

Trey inhaled sharply. "How did you guess?"

"You left some bills by the computer in the study," I said. "I wasn't snooping, I promise, but I couldn't pretend not to see what was there in black and white."

And red.

"I forgot you use that computer sometimes," he said to himself.

"I email Archer every Sunday."

He swiveled to me. "Your first instinct was to help me by working yourself to the bone?"

I ducked my head. "Yes," I said slowly.

I couldn't read Trey's reaction. Had I breached some invisible doctrine of the South with my Midwestern approach—frank acknowledgment of hardship with an offer of humble assistance?

"That's generous of you," he said.

"If we win, will it fix things?"

"Some but not all."

I sagged against the wall. "Oh."

"Seeing as you already guessed, I might as well tell you," he said. "Mama doesn't have much of a head for figures. She made some bad investments, and then the market collapsed. If she'd told me earlier, I could have salvaged things, but she didn't understand why the money stopped flowing until just a little while ago."

Trey pressed his pointer fingers against his temples. "I acted as quickly as I could by selling, consolidating, paying off, but it wasn't enough. I needed to do something big, something extraordinary."

He laughed mirthlessly. "But I have the skill set of a 19th-century gentleman, which is to say I'm useless in the 21st century. The only thing I know how to do well enough to monetize is dance. Between the sponsorships and the prize money, competing doesn't cost anything, and sometimes even nets a few dollars. If we win Nationals, there's a big check at the end plus the tour and commercial opportunities. And, after that well dries up, I can do something with my win, which I didn't do last time. This time, I'll get my adjudicator's license and use the momentum from the win to start judging. It won't be enough, but it would provide an income stream until I can sell the mansion."

"Sell the mansion? But it's been in your family for generations."

"That's the problem. My family hung onto something that made less and less sense as the years ticked on. Who needs fourteen bedrooms?"

"When are you going to sell?"

"As soon as Mama passes."

"Is she sick?" I asked. "From what?"

"There's a whole mess of technical terms, but in short, she's eating herself to death."

I spluttered.

"She's been at it for a while, and she's getting close to succeeding. My goal is to keep her comfortable here until she dies and make sure that William gets the retirement he deserves. Then I'll sell, pay off the debts, and downsize."

"Can you do that? Kill yourself with food?"

Trey averted his eyes. "She's been trying since I was thirteen."

I sat awkwardly beside him, not sure what I should say or do. He rose and turned to me. "Enjoy your evening."

"You too," I murmured.

Knowing the weight of Trey's burden intensified my role in the partnership. If I wasn't good enough, then a whole lot of people lost. And they were going to lose a lot more than a shiny medal.

I picked at my dinner as I brainstormed ways to improve my dancing. That, though, lacked a commercializing factor. There weren't many ways to improve efficiently and effectively beyond what I was already doing. Getting better took hours and hours, and even with all the time I was putting in, there wasn't much more I could do. It took time for a body to absorb, to apply, to manifest, to exist. Speeding up the process would turn to vinegar what could be fine wine.

I sighed and turned off the light. At least sleep was something positive I could do.

A knock awakened me. Slow, quick, quick, slow and then again as the bang on the door increased in volume.

"Come in," I said, tossing on my robe. I'd taken to sleeping naked since I danced so much in my sleep.

Trey pushed the door open. "May I stay with you a while?" he asked. "I could use the company."

In the moonlight, his face shone, smooth and cool, a porcelain mask. His voice, though, was tight and small, all the honey stopped up in the back of his throat.

I sat up and pulled my hair over a shoulder. "On one condition."

He stopped mid-stride. "What's that?"

"If an opportunity comes up for me to help, one that doesn't affect our routine or our goals, then you let me take it." I raked a hand through the beige rope of hair that dangled down my torso. "Nothing is going to happen, but on the off chance it does, I want to pay you back for all the kindness and trust you've shown me."

Trey covered the distance to the bed in seconds. "You're one in a million," he said.

I stuck out my hand. "Do we have a deal?"

"You drive a tough bargain, Miss Martindale." Then he grasped my hand and placed one of those dry kisses on top of it.

I plumped up the pillow I'd been using and then scooted over. He slid into bed as I slipped out of my robe. He offered his left hand, which I accepted with my right. He placed his other hand on my back, and I positioned mine on his shoulder. Dance position. Our position. I rubbed my cheek against his chest as he stroked my hair. I let the beat of his heart lull me to sleep.

I'm happy, so happy, I thought as I fell backward into the soft black cushion of slumber.

It felt like a minute, but it must have been hours, because sunlight was streaming through the windows and William was knocking.

"I slept?" Trey asked as he blinked awake. Then he tensed.

William knocked again. "Miss Carly? I have your breakfast here."

I giggled. "You've been caught red-handed."

The whole thing struck me as hilarious. We'd slept together in the most benign way possible, and Trey, a grown man in his own home, was worried about offending the propriety of his butler.

Trey shoved his hair out of his eyes. His mouth moved, but no words came out.

I pushed him out of bed. "The closet."

He struggled to his feet and darted into the closet.

"Please come in," I said, each word stiff and pressed as if it were a freshly starched collar.

William entered and dropped off my tray on the coffee table. "Have a good day, Miss Carly."

I waited until William's footsteps disappeared down the hall. "You can come out."

Trey exited the closet and grabbed his robe, looking at me the whole while.

I beamed at him, my eyes two headlights of bliss.

He got to the door and then stopped. "Thank you, Carly."

"My pleasure."

He fiddled with the doorknob.

"You'd better go. You don't want to run into William on the stairs in your robe. He might tip over from the shock."

Trey smiled, a huge one that lit up his face from the inside out. "See you at yoga."

He didn't come every night. He didn't come most nights. But once in a while, when he needed release from the worry and stress that pinstriped his days like bars of a jail cell, he came to me. We didn't talk, just draped ourselves in a soft, casual dance position. I laid my head on his chest and let the metronome of our combined heartbeats hush us into sleep.

I didn't expect anything to come of my promise to help. It was a soul's bright penny of hope tossed into the wishing well of an indifferent universe. Somewhere, somehow, someone plucked my copper out of the many clogging its waters and saw fit to answer my request.

One day, as Trey and I were finishing our morning practice, William knocked. I had my notebook and was clarifying a few details on our Viennese Waltz.

"There's a call for Miss Carly."

"A call?" I dropped my notebook. "Archer. Which way do I go?"

"The study." William stood out of the way to let me pass.

I dashed down the stairs, my heart tap dancing against my chest. Something terrible had happened to my little brother, and here I was worried to distraction about the state of my Viennese Waltz.

"Hello," I gasped into the receiver.

"It's good to hear your voice. How's the South treating you?"

"Jason," I said.

"You're worked up. Don't tell me. You're overcome by the sound of my voice. You've been wondering about the state of my Foxtrot. Let me tell you, it's poor. So poor that I need a tune up."

"Jason," I said again, sinking weakly against the mahogany desk as my heart rate returned to normal. "How are you?"

"Not so good as I've been trying to tell you. My Foxtrot is in a state of disrepair. My Twinkle has lost its luster."

I laughed, delighted to hear from him. "How can I help? Do you want me to talk you through it over the phone?"

"What would be the chance of me getting a face-to-face tune up? I've got business in Charleston."

"I don't know. Could I get your number and call you back?"

He recited his number and then a second time to make sure I'd written it down correctly.

I walked back upstairs to the ballroom. Trey was sitting on the bench, staring into the distance. He jumped up when he saw me. "Is everything okay?"

"All good," I said. "I have a former student who has some business in Charleston, and he wants to take a lesson."

Trey pressed his lips together.

"You promised."

"I did."

I handed Trey the piece of paper with Jason's number scribbled in my bubbly print. "Call him. Set it up."

Trey did, and Jason showed up a few days later in a three-piece suit with a big smile. I told William not to bother, and I met Jason at the door. We embraced quickly.

"Is this a set to *Gone With the Wind*?" he asked.

I nudged him and pointed to the green drapes. "Scarlett's dress in its original form."

We did a double lesson. Jason was the same as he always was, sweet, earnest, a musical but forgetful dancer.

The time flew, and before I knew it, Trey was watching from the sidelines as I taught Jason, for at least the fifth time, the Sweetheart in Swing. Trey leaned against the wall with his arms crossed, a small smile playing at the corners of his lips, as Jason mixed up which arm he should initiate with.

At the end of our lesson, Jason spun me out and bowed deeply.

"My lady," he said in a throaty baritone at odds with his typically joyous tenor.

I curtsied. "My lord," I said in a high-pitched, pretentious accent.

"To whom do I direct my payment. Carly Martindale? Caroline Martindale? Lady Martindale of Foxtrot Corner?"

"Trey will take care of you."

Jason directed his gaze at me, his eyes hard and demanding. "I want to pay you, Carly."

"Trey will take care of you." I forced a breezy tone. I couldn't do anything with Jason's check. I'd had a bank account in New York, but it didn't have any branches in Charleston. Then there'd also been a merger with another bank, and I wasn't completely sure where the few dollars I did have saved were stored.

"Next week?" he asked me. He ignored Trey. Jason was the first person I'd seen unaffected by Trey.

I tilted my head to Trey who nodded. "I'd love to," I said.

After Jason left, Trey knocked on my bedroom door and stuck his head in. "Does he really have business in Charleston every week?"

"I doubt it."

"Why does he come?"

"I look like his late wife."

Trey blinked. "Has he tried anything?"

"Jason knows the rules."

Trey closed the door and then opened it again. "You're a good teacher, Carly. Kind and patient."

Jason came most weeks, and I looked forward to his visits. My life had telescoped to such an excruciatingly small bead that I'd forgotten how much I enjoyed teaching.

During one of our lessons, Jason stopped in the middle of a dance.

I'd rolled the volume knob too far, and a militaristic Tango—marching rhythms, rousing melody—was drubbing at the walls.

"Too loud and revolutionary?" I yelled.

Jason pulled me into a deep dip as I looked backward toward the toe of my extended leg—the Corte. When we returned to vertical, he let go and put his hands on my shoulders. He leaned in close and stared at me. "Are you okay, Carly? Is he treating you okay?"

I gaped at him. “Trey treats me like a princess.”

"Do you need anything? I mean anything from a box of chocolates to a plane ticket home."

"I'm happy here, so happy. And it's even better now that I can teach you." I smiled at him. "I've got a special step for you today . . . " I trailed off.

Jason held my gaze. "If you need something, would you let me know?"

"Of course," I said, puzzled by Jason’s concern.

"Anything," Jason said. "I mean it, Carly." He looked around the ballroom with its peeling wallpaper and scratched floors. "It's not normal you being here, all alone with this guy, his obese mother, and a butler, for heaven’s sake. No one else in the ballroom world is like this. They're all teaching, practicing, and taking coaching at studios, places with decent lighting.”

As if on cue, one of the lights blinked in the ballroom.

“It’s like the beginning of a horror movie,” Jason said, more to himself than to me.

"Trey is exceptional. There's a reason why he's a three-time Nationals champion," I said.

Jason sighed. "If you're happy. But don't forget my offer.”

Chapter 33

NINA: KNEES AND HIPS

PAPA'S WORDS ricocheted throughout my head. Winning Nationals was the thing I'd been gunning for since I was a teenager. With the disappointments of last year fresh in my memory, I'd been ecstatic to receive a second chance.

But, as I was realizing, second chances were double-edged swords. The blade was finely honed from past experience. Turned outward, it could swipe at the competition, but turned in, it could slice a wound that still festered. Failing a second time would be worse than failing the first time. And this time, I understood what winning was really about. It wasn't about the moment when they slipped the gold medal around my neck. It was about the moment I'd had with Sam and Carly when I showed them a video of Trey.

I'd said, "Trey Devereux. The best there ever was. Probably the best there ever will be."

Trey would die at some point, but his ghost would live forever on the dance floor.

This time, I was dancing for my future self. I navigated seas of wooden parquet with sails made of satin and chiffon, buoyed by the promise of landing in a place where I would be immortalized in generations of dancers to come.

This was the immigrant's dream writ large.

"Why do you want to win?" I asked Jorge one day when we took a break for tea.

"No one's asked me that question." He laughed. "We bust our asses every day, but for what?"

"Right," I said.

He turned to me. "How about you? Why does Nina Fortunova want to win?"

I cleared my throat. "I had an interesting conversation with Papa. He said that winning is either the end or the beginning."

Jorge crinkled his forehead.

I gave him the gist of what Papa had told me. Jorge sipped his Earl Grey tea thoughtfully as he listened.

"Papa said Trey Devereux is going to be almost impossible to beat."

He nodded. "Trey knows how to win." He interlaced his fingers and squeezed his hands together, which made his muscles flex impressively.

My thigh seared with pain. "Ouch," I exclaimed. I'd tipped my cup and splashed tea on my leg.

"Let me." Jorge stood and retrieved a paper towel. I blotted at the stain. Keeping my head down to hide my warm cheeks, I said, "We need a reason to win. Something that will sustain us from now to the final."

He pushed his hand into his left hip. Using the pads of fingers, he pressed and released, a pianist playing a familiar melody. "I stopped dancing for myself a long time ago. It made quitting too easy."

I raised my eyebrows at him.

"Dancing is hard. If I want to feed my ego, there are easier ways to do it," he said.

"You've got a point," I said. I'd danced for years to satisfy my mother's admonishment: *You carry my dreams.*

"Who are you dancing for?" I asked.

"A whole bunch of kids I don't know."

I cocked my head toward him.

"I'm a poor kid from the Bronx. Most of us are more liable to find ourselves in jail than . . . " He arced a hand around the elegant ballroom. "My mother did her best to keep me on the straight and narrow, but it gets hard in high school." He took another sip of tea. "Who knows what would have happened if I hadn't talked Papa and Maxine into letting me take lessons."

I balled up the paper towel in my hand.

He pointed north. "I live in the Bronx because I got to keep it real. The difference between the people up there and the people down here is that up there, they're browner. So they don't get as many opportunities. I'm not any more special than the next Puerto

Rican kid. The only difference is that I made an opportunity for myself."

He took another mouthful of tea. "If I win Nationals, I can show what one opportunity can do for a brown kid."

"So we're dancing for the future?" I asked.

"It's what gets me up every day."

He slipped his arm around my shoulder and pulled me until I was clinched against his chest. "Let's show them what two scrappy kids from the outer boroughs can do."

I didn't say anything, just relaxed in his embrace. I was absolutely, completely, most definitely not at all interested in Jorge, but it was nice to be held. Especially by someone who had strong arms and a tender touch.

The future beckoned promisingly to Jorge and me, but the present reared to point out the undeniable. Jorge and I were breaking down. Not our dancing, which grew by bounding leaps every day.

"You're going to make a Standard dancer out of me yet," Jorge said as he danced through the closed section of Foxtrot by himself: Feather Step, Reverse Turn, Three Step. Travel Diagonally to Center, rotate three-quarters, travel Diagonally to Wall, an elegant four bars of skimming across the floor akin to an ice skating sequence.

"I couldn't agree more," I said, lying through my teeth. Jorge was never going to be a Standard dancer, but his technique had progressed from offensive to inoffensive. It had not, however, progressed to transcendent, nor would it. Jorge just wasn't built for Standard.

"Next up, Nina Fortunova will perform the dual role of Odette/Odile at the Metropolitan Opera House," I said as we finished our Waltz. My arms had improved tremendously. I was never going to be as graceful as some of the female competitors, but Jorge suggested my arms stay in constant motion out of closed position, which helped.

Our progress delighted Maxine.

"It's going to get close," she said. "I predict that within the next month or so, you two will start taking a dance away from Trey and Carly." She stopped and looked at us. "Tango, probably. It's their weakest dance and your strongest."

Jorge and I smiled at each other, and not for the first time, I thought what nice eyes he had, dark brown, almost black, like espresso, but kind too. I pinched myself. Lots of people had nice brown eyes, and I wasn't gushing about them.

"Don't slack off." She gave us a pointed look. "At all."

I wanted to cry. My knee hurt. All the time. Even when I slept. I swallowed aspirin by the handful, but it alleviated little to no pain. Jorge didn't seem to be in any better shape. His hip was bothering him more and more, and I'd caught him a couple of times wincing in pain.

Nationals were still a few months away, and the idea of maintaining our relentless pace felt impossible. Dancing in one's thirties was no picnic. Particularly, when one's income came from teaching dance, an on-your-feet, high-energy job.

"How are you feeling?" Jorge asked me at the beginning of every practice session.

"I feel great," I'd say. I'd taken to practicing in pants a few days a week to hide the knee brace I wore. "How are you feeling?"

"Never better," he'd say.

It was a gigantic game of chicken. Neither of us would admit to the other that our bodies were crumbling, two sand castles confronted by the inevitable tide of aging.

One of us was going to have to force the issue, but it wasn't going to be me. If I said the words out loud, then they would be true. So I wrapped the wool around my eyes like a balaclava and invested in a bottle of aspirin the size and shape of a cookie jar.

I was tired, all the time, from teaching, from practicing, from competing, from being in constant, grinding pain. I used my intellectual discipline to keep from caving into the mewling of a body that was begging me to say uncle. I projected myself into the future to meet the me who'd won Nationals. She was happy and excited and said lots of encouraging things to keep my morale up.

I still hadn't seen a doctor. I already knew the diagnosis, arthritis exacerbated by intense physical activity. I also knew the remedy. Stop dancing or face a knee replacement later down the road.

After Nationals, I told myself. Then I'll take it easy. I visualized white beaches and turquoise oceans and a chair in which I could park myself, not moving beyond lifting a cocktail dewy with condensation to my lips.

The idea of coming back for the next season was unthinkable. I took a calendar and counted the days until Nationals. There were over a hundred. At the end of each day, I scratched an X through the square. No matter the result of Nationals, I was going to retire. Knee replacements weren't the simple matter that hip replacements were. I did have ambitions of walking when I was in my forties.

Finally, the issue forced itself.

Maxine pulled us aside after a lesson. She didn't mince words. "You're both fighting injuries. How bad?"

"I feel great," I said, the words big but hollow, a Fabergé egg that, when flipped open, would reveal the bitter pill of truth.

"Never better," said Jorge.

Maxine shook her head at us. "Don't lie to your mother. Spill the beans."

Neither of us said anything.

Maxine tossed her orange hair and pointed at me. "Right knee." She turned to Jorge. "Left hip."

"Arthritis," I whispered.

"Labral tear." Jorge's shoulders slumped. "The doc says I need surgery."

Maxine pursed her lips grimly. "It's not easy dancing in your thirties," she said. "It's even harder when you switch styles and partners, and then set yourself the goal of winning Nationals."

We nodded.

"If you don't win this year, can you maintain this pace for another?"

Jorge and I looked at each, and our eyes, brown to green, earth meeting flora, told the truth to the other.

"No," we said together.

Maxine inhaled and then held it for a moment before releasing it. "Okay then." She set her jaw.

With the cat out of the bag, Jorge and I relaxed our vigilance around each other. We added short breaks to our practices. At the end, he made me a baggy of ice while I set up a heating pad for him. My mother continued to drop off casseroles and cluck over me. I wrapped up part of her casseroles and brought them in for Jorge.

"Noodles, protein," I said, quoting my mother. "We have to keep our energy up."

A few days later, he passed me a plastic container. "*Sancocho*. Puerto Rican beef stew." He winked. "To keep our energy up."

We grinned at each other. "Mothers," we said together through our laughter.

I showed him the calendar, and at the end of the day, I scribbled one diagonal and then he the other. The Xs strung across the weeks, evoking Throwaway Oversways, a splashy Standard pose in which couples stretched their upper bodies and one leg away from each other. A Throwaway Oversway was the best type of step, beautiful but laden with symbolism, revealing the tension between personal freedom and romantic love.

Papa continued to drop by our practices. Afterward, he'd throw us a couple of suggestions. He wasn't a coach, but he knew his stuff. And as Chairman of the Judges, he tallied each and every mark from each and every judge. He knew what was working for us and what wasn't.

I didn't know if this was ethical, but as Chairman of the Judges, Papa knew the rulebook inside and out. We weren't exchanging money for his services and he wasn't on the dance floor judging us, so it could be chalked up to friendly interest on his part.

In reality, I knew why he was there. His eyes followed me everywhere. Once or twice, Jorge had looked at Papa suspiciously, but Papa had just smiled back blandly.

"Looking good, kids," Papa had said.

Papa took me out to lunch every couple of weeks. He always asked Ralph first and he always included Jorge in the invitation, but most of the time, it ended up being the two of us.

While his interest in me remained intense, he hadn't pressed for anything more than the opportunity to sit across from me and break bread. In spite of my doubt and discomfort, I'd warmed to him.

He was lonely and under-appreciated. As a beloved coach and maker of champions, Maxine received all the petting while he gazed down upon things like an impotent god.

"I miss being in the thick of things," he'd said to me more than once. "If I could do it again, I wouldn't have accepted the position of Chairman of the Judges."

Papa regaled me with stories of the early days of competitive dancing in the United States. He showed me pictures of some of the original legends and told me their stories.

"Grover Ferris. The first US Latin champion." Papa passed me a photo of a lithe man with a pouf of yellow hair in a purple catsuit. The camera had caught him in the middle of a stag leap, his legs hooked and split, one arm over his head, the other curved in front of him.

I handed the picture back to Papa. "Was his Paso Doble as good as they say it was?" I asked.

He nodded. "Grover's Paso Doble is the best I've seen. And that's saying something, because I've been watching the Paso Doble for close to forty years."

"Where is he now?"

"Died of AIDS in the '80s." Papa scowled and pushed a forkful of roast chicken around his plate. "We lost a lot of good people to it."

I murmured something comforting. Papa looked upset, as if Grover had died recently rather than decades ago.

"It's one of the things about aging," he said. "Things that

happened years ago feel fresh, and things that happened last week have already receded into the past." He ate a bite of his chicken. "When you get older, there just aren't that many new experiences to be had."

I sipped my iced tea. Sometimes I was reminded of my mother listening to a big, overly sensitive man spill his heart. But then again, I wasn't doing the other thing my mother did for money, nor would I.

"You should watch Grover's videos. His dancing puts into perspective what being a Nationals champion means," Papa said. "That's why we're talking about him today."

I twirled my straw around in my glass.

"You and Jorge are looking good. It's getting closer and closer every competition. If you win, you'll inspire a whole new generation of dancers."

Discreetly, I rubbed my knee. Nationals was exactly a hundred days away. Jorge and I had drawn the *x* together today after practice.

"We can do it," Jorge had said, emphasizing the word *we*.

"We can," I'd said, stressing the word *can*.

Papa leaned across the table toward me. "Are you and Jorge going to stick it out for another season if you don't win?"

I shook my head.

"Why not?"

"We're both struggling with chronic injuries. This is our one shot."

For a moment, Papa's eyes narrowed and glittered before rounding into the contours of concern.

"Is there anything you can do?"

"I can stop competing," I said. "Which I'm doing after Nationals, win or lose."

He reclined back in his chair, smiling. "So you have to win."

"We have to win."

"If I can do anything to help, I will," Papa tilted his head and met my eyes squarely. "Papa knows how thankful you'd be."

My stomach coddled at Papa's veiled concern. If it was close between them and us, Papa would make sure we won. But it was going to going to cost me something. I remembered my mother's words: *Second chances come with high price tag, zolotse.*

I touched my knee, which was particularly crunchy today.

Please don't let it come to that.

Chapter 34

CARLY: THE THUMBPRINT IN THE MOON

"I'M SURPRISED to see you here."

I turned my head. Nina was walking to the sink beside me.

"Hello," I said.

I turned on the faucet and mechanically placed my hands in the trickle. I was flopping with fatigue. It'd been an excruciating three rounds, and the results were disappointing. We'd won, but Jorge and Nina had taken Tango from us. I wanted nothing more than to go upstairs, take a short, scalding shower, and then tumble into a blissfully blank sleep where none of this mattered. Trey, though, had the key to my room, and he'd been waylaid by Papa.

"Congratulations," she said.

"Thank you."

"I didn't think you two would be here."

"Why not? Nationals is less than three months away." I squirted soap, a lurid pink, from the dispenser into the palm of my hand.

Nina furrowed her brow. "Didn't Trey tell you?"

I placed my hands under the faucet and mechanically rubbed them together. "Tell me what?"

"Tamsin Grubbs died this week. They found her outside one of those rent-by-the-hour motels in Tampa."

"Oh." I rinsed my hands under the water and tried to process Nina's news.

"From an overdose. Heroin. Trey had to go identify the body."

Trey had left town for a couple of days, which startled me. He'd said that he had urgent business, but he'd be back in time for us to fly to Boston. He hadn't offered any details beyond saying it didn't concern our dancing. He wanted me to rest and practice, so I did. His mouth had looked tense when he returned, but he acted as if nothing was out of the ordinary.

I turned off the faucet and reached for a paper towel. "That's awful."

"She didn't have any identification on her, just a picture of Trey and her at the first Nationals they won. The police officer went to a ballroom studio in Tampa, and they told him who she was."

I twisted the paper towel in my hands. "That's a long way to fall. Three-time Nationals champion to dying in a fleabag motel. What went wrong?"

Nina shrugged. "I don't know." She patted her hair and then turned to face me. "Are you enjoying dancing with Trey?"

I tossed the paper towel into the trash. "I love it."

She eyed me doubtfully. "Really?"

"Really," I said hotly.

She touched my shoulder. "Does he treat you okay?"

I made strong eye contact. "Trey treats me like a princess."

"You deserve nothing but the best." She smiled at me. Her red lipstick streaked her right front tooth. "There's a pro party tonight. Are you coming? I'd love to catch up."

"I'm too tired."

"For an hour. Let's have some girl time."

"I can't."

"How about a quick drink in the bar? On me."

I shook my head. "Thanks, but no."

Since I'd started dancing with Trey, I'd never done anything after a competition save return to my room, take a shower, and go to bed. Trey had never told me I couldn't go out after a competition, but I couldn't imagine him approving if I did. He wanted my focus on dancing, and I wanted to do whatever he wanted. So I stayed in.

Anyway, we always took the earliest flight available to Charleston. I tried to get as much sleep as possible before another wearying day of travel that preceded another wearying week of practicing and then yet another competition.

I would have enjoyed catching up and finding out if her intense chemistry with Jorge had led to an off-the-floor romance. Now, though, that I knew the cause of Trey's trip, I wanted to get back to him as soon as I could.

Her eyes flashed as if I'd answered some question she'd been harboring. "Take care of yourself, Carly." She swept out of the bathroom.

"You too," I said to the door closing behind her.

Trey was waiting for me by the elevator. We went upstairs, and he unlocked the door to my room.

"Come in?" I asked. "Just for a minute?"

"Anything for you." Trey's tone was mild, but his lips were stitched together in a sad, tired line.

I closed the door. "I heard about Tamsin. I'm so sorry." I peeped into his eyes; the gray was fogged. I shrank back. "That's all." I bit my lip. I wanted to offer comfort, to be present for Trey, but this was obviously the wrong way to go about it.

"Who told you?"

"Nina. I bumped into her in the bathroom."

He inhaled sharply. "What did she tell you?"

"Where they found her. How they figured out who she was. That you were the one to identify the body."

Trey pressed his index fingers to his temples. "I'd hoped to spare you." He sat down on the bed facing the window. He patted the white duvet beside him. "Sit."

I perched myself next to him as Trey looked out the window. The moon dangled in the black sky, a milky curlicue that looked as if a thumbprint had blotted out the rest.

"What do you know about Tamsin?"

"Not much. You met her at a shag club. She wasn't much better than trailer trash. You cleaned her up, and then you two dominated the field until you retired."

Trey exhaled. "It's more complicated than that. I was on the search for a partner, but I wasn't having any luck. Nobody was right. They were too tall, too short, wrong coloring, too heavy in my arms, too light, not willing to relocate to Charleston," he said. "I decided to see if I could find somebody raw, train her from the start, so we could create this vision I had of Smooth."

I nodded.

"I'd heard about this shag club, so one night I stopped by. My expectations weren't high, but I had nothing to lose. Tamsin caught my eye as soon as I walked in. Right height, right look, musical, good instincts all around. I watched her for a couple of songs, and then I asked her to dance."

I shivered as I remembered the first time Trey asked me to dance. It was one of the most important moments in my life.

"We danced, and it was good. She was a supple piece of clay for me to work with." Trey gazed at the moon before continuing. "Then she opened her mouth."

He sighed. "She'd dropped out of high school at sixteen, but she stopped learning a long time before that. She called the Viennese Waltz, the Vietnamese Waltz. She worked as a bartender at a dive bar. She'd never been outside of Charleston. The only thing she'd ever worked at was her tan. Her biggest success in life was not getting pregnant." In a low voice, he said, "I should have known better, but I was desperate to start dancing. So I asked."

I shifted my weight toward Trey, hoping he would look at me but his eyes were fixed on the moon.

"She was thrilled. A scion of an old Charlestonian family wanted to compete in ballroom dancing with her. It was a dream come true that she didn't know she could have," he said. "It was fine in the beginning. The novelty and the glamour sustained her through her first Open Nationals, but she wanted to quit after we won. She'd gone further than she or anybody thought she could ever go. She wanted to parlay her win into something substantive. A husband, a house in the suburbs, a fun story to tell at barbecues."

Trey paused. "I insisted, though, on a second Nationals. We had to show it wasn't a fluke. It was rough. I got more and more intense as we went along. She resented me the whole time. But she kept going, and we won again. This time, she was done."

He stared at the moon for a long while without saying anything. "I was blinded by my ego. I wanted to win a third time. No one had done it, you see. So I bribed her. With money."

Trey dropped his head into his hands. "She'd come from nothing, and the amount of money I was promising her was huge. But even with that carrot, she couldn't. She was tapped out. She started sneaking out and skipping practices and hanging out with a rough crowd."

He lifted his head. "I'll never know for sure, but I think she started using around this time. I should have let her quit, but I wanted that third title so badly."

I ignored the moon and kept my eyes on Trey. He needed to know he wasn't alone.

"We won, but she was lost," he said. "I gave her the money, set her up in an apartment, checked on her every couple of weeks, but it was too late. For a while, she'd call, mostly to ask for money, but it'd been at least year since I'd heard from her." He pressed his hands together.

"Until this week." Trey looked out the window. A smoky wisp of a cloud passed in front of the moon. "Now she's dead. Papa asked for some pictures of us to run them with the obituary in the Nationals program."

I didn't know what to say. I felt sorry for Trey and for Tamsin.

"I was too hard on her. Too exacting, too demanding." Trey turned his head to me, his beautiful features stretched with sorrow and regret. "She wasn't strong and smart like you, Carly. I didn't have the connection with her off the dance floor the way I do with you."

He took my hand and kissed it. "You would tell me if I was being too intense?"

"I would."

Trey squeezed my hand, and I squeezed back. He released our grip and draped his arm around my waist. He pulled me close, and with his free hand, he guided my head onto his shoulder. Then he placed his head on top of mine.

We stayed like that for a while, staring at that moon, light chewed up by darkness, silent but alert in our wake for Tamsin.

Chapter 35

NINA: POOR LITTLE RICH GIRL

MY PLATE WAS full with one big main of Nationals plus a side each of Papa and my knee. Pain and anxiety fringed my days, and the grating misery eroded my self-confidence. The bright spot in all of this was Jorge.

Although the pressure hung heavy over us, thick and heavy smoke from the fire of our ambitions, we kept our time together light but focused. We'd made a tacit commitment never to argue and never to devolve into grumpiness or pettiness. We showed up as the best version of ourselves, which enabled us to climb a steady slope of improvement.

Maxine nodded approvingly. "I wish all my couples could get along as well as you two do. What's your secret?"

"We're on each other's team," Jorge said. "Sometimes I'm the coach and Nina's the player. Sometimes it's the other way around."

"We help each other to help ourselves," I said.

"But with no score-keeping." Jorge rubbed my shoulder with one of his warm hands. My skin melted to his touch, butter on a hot pan.

Maxine's eyes twinkled mischievously. "It's working well."

I'd been swimming along in seas rougher than I would have preferred but manageable until a tsunami blew in on a westerly wind —Amber Morimoto, Jorge's former partner.

Jorge met me by the entrance to the Castle one day.

I wrinkled my brow at him. "Hello?"

We had a routine, one that provided stability and comfort to us both. He drilled the syllabus for an hour before we practiced. I came in thirty minutes early, ate the bagel Jorge left for me, and practiced the *port de bras* I'd learned in ballet class. If the teacher needed to see him with a partner, I would abandon my bagel and/or *port de bras* to dance with him.

We'd never deviated from this.

"Hey," he said, and then ran a hand through his hair, which made it stand up, black velvet piled the wrong way. "Do you mind if a friend watches us practice?"

"What friend?"

"Amber."

I raised my eyebrows. "She's in town?"

He nodded. "We, uh, have been on and off for a while, and we just got back on. She wanted to come see what we're up to."

My heart sunk. He was dating Amber? I reached into my chest and pulled my heart back to its original position. Why should I care who Jorge dated?

"She's looking forward to meeting you," he said as he walked into the ballroom.

Meeting me? I'd competed alongside Jorge and Amber for a decade. Surely she knew who I was.

Amber was half Japanese and half white, and she was a good dancer. Her most salient quality, though, was her wealth. She stunk of money.

She was pretty in the way rich girls are pretty: ultra slim thanks to a chef-prepared diet of fruits and vegetables made yummy; a sheaf of glossy hair that could double as a fur coat; and porcelain skin nurtured through expensive creams and lotions laden with exotic, hard-to-pronounce ingredients.

She wore an outfit that read as rich girl don't care: snug designer jeans, a white tank top favored by rednecks, and no bra. An orange bag, slouchy and stamped with the conspicuous label of a high-end fashion house, rested beside her like a pampered dog.

Jorge and I walked over to Amber as I prepared my smile and readied my polite chitchat.

"Amber, you remember Nina Fortunova?"

She looked up from her phone. "You look familiar."

"As do you," I said jokingly. She was joking, right? "I remember when you and Jorge won the Rising Star Latin. That was the year I won Rising Star Standard."

"Oh, I never paid much attention to Standard." She yawned. "Too stiff and boring."

Jorge shifted uncomfortably from foot to foot beside me as I gaped at Amber. Clearly, money did not buy manners.

"How long are you in New York?" I asked as I crossed my fingers that she'd be leaving soon, say, this afternoon.

"Dunno," she said. "As long as I want."

I turned to Jorge. "Shall we get to it?"

"Let's," he said.

We tried to have a regular practice, but Amber's presence was like the threat of rain. She didn't say anything in the beginning, just fixed her eyes on us as a smirk played around her lips. With resolute cheer, we went through Maxine's notes from our last coaching session. Then it came time for me to work with Jorge on his Standard technique. That's when Amber started to get restless.

She took a phone call (a phone call!) and gabbed with someone on the other end about a vegan bakery that made, like, the best cupcakes ever.

"Babe, can you take that outside?" Jorge asked.

She ignored him.

Gritting my teeth, I kept going.

We switched. Jorge worked with me on arms in Foxtrot, my weakest dance. Something about the swinging Americana of it never sat right on my body. Specifically, the open sections where we needed to evoke a fancy-free Fred-and-Ginger couple. I did worse than usual with Amber watching.

"Tomorrow," I said with as much enthusiasm as I could muster.

"Tomorrow," Jorge said, his typically easygoing tone tight with stress.

"Shall we run a round?" Usually, we did rounds at night, but we had plenty of time left over in today's practice since neither of us had succeeded at applying corrections.

Jorge went to set up a playlist for us. Although our bodies were old and aching, we ran our rounds back to back to keep our stamina high. At competitions, there'd be a twenty-minute break between rounds while the recalls were tallied, which we'd use for water and rest. In the studio, however, that would take forever, so we ran round after round.

Midway through our first Tango, Amber got up and wandered across the floor to the coffee machine. She fiddled with the buttons before putting a hand on her hip.

"Babe," she said. "How do I work this?" She gave the coffee machine a poke.

"Let me finish this round, babe," Jorge said, still dancing.

"How do I work this?" she asked, each word the shrill peal of a bell.

"Sorry," he said to me. We stopped, and he made Amber a cup of coffee as I walked through our Foxtrot and Viennese Waltz by myself.

We ran another round but were too distracted for it to be effective.

"Tomorrow," I said.

"Tomorrow," he said, his forehead crumpled.

Before the studio closed for the night, Jorge pulled me aside. "I'm sorry about today. It takes Amber some time to warm up to new people."

I didn't say anything.

"It was hard for her when we quit. We were close, and then we were far away."

"I know the feeling."

He smiled ruefully. "I know you do."

"Why doesn't she find a new partner?"

"Nobody wanted to dance with her. She can be kind of difficult."

That's an understatement.

I repeated Maxine's suggestion to me. "Maybe she could find a student to compete with. It would keep her on the floor."

"Amber's never had a job. Her family is loaded like you can't imagine."

"I gathered." I revisited my mother's words. "Time for a new dream. This is America, after all. Plenty of dreams are out there for the taking."

"That's what I told her." Jorge shook his head. "But when you've got that much money dreams are harder to come by."

I frowned as I processed his words. He was right. If you were never hungry, then there was no reason to fight to eat.

He sighed. "She's also not too happy about me dancing with you."

"Why?" I asked. It wasn't that uncommon for couples to split up on the floor but stay together off the floor.

"I've been pretty happy dancing with you, Nina. We get along, and we get better. It sounds simple, but it isn't."

"Agreed."

"I wish we could have found each other years ago before we both were busted." He massaged his hip as I thought of my knee.

"Life. It gives you what you want just as it takes away what you need," I said, waxing philosophical. All the lunches with Papa were rubbing off on me.

"Right," Jorge said. "Anyway, Amber is worried that something more is going on. That's why she wanted to come and watch."

"But nothing is going on."

"That's what I told her. But she needed to come see for her own eyes."

"Is she satisfied?"

He shook his head.

My hands dropped to my sides. "Why?"

"Get a load of this. She thinks we're too nice to each other."

I didn't know what to say, so I laughed.

"She's being stupid," Jorge said. "She's seeing things that aren't there, but she refuses to believe me."

"Is she coming tomorrow?"

"She's got to be on her best behavior. Otherwise, I'm kicking her out."

"See both of you then," I said as brightly as I could and left.

Amber attended our practices every day. She sat on the bench and watched us dance and played with her phone. As the days ticked by, my loathing of her evolved into pity. Amber may be rich, but she was not young. She was older than me and probably older than Jorge by a few years. Silver threaded her mane of sable, and when she smiled, once, at Jorge, crow's feet radiated from the corners of her eyes, which were alternately sad or angry.

Poor little rich girl. She'd never held a job and had no idea how to occupy her days beyond watching her boyfriend practice.

I remembered how gloomy and adrift I'd been last year and how the Castle acted as a harbor of positivity for me. Ralph had smoothed over my "bumps" by having me train Sam and Carly. The staff had helped me through my first New Year's alone by filling my apartment with their presence and raucous laughter. Every day, I'd had a place to go to, people to talk to, and a profession that gave me self-worth. Amber carried an expensive handbag, but I felt much richer than her.

My pity didn't last long.

"Babe," she said during one practice. "Don't you think she should place her arms over her head instead of putting them to the side? She's kind of short. It might help the judges see you better."

Jorge and I skidded to a halt. I was shaking with outrage and surprise. "She" was not doing a damned thing that Amber Morimoto suggested.

"Babe, no," Jorge said. "Maxine gave her those arms. We can't change them."

"It would look better." Amber buried her face in her phone.

"Sorry," Jorge whispered to me and squeezed my hand. I squeezed back. Not because I liked Jorge, because I did not, not at all, but because Amber had lifted her eyes from her phone and was glaring at us. Specifically, she was glaring at me.

We made it through another half a dance before Amber butted in.

"Babe," she said. "You should tell her to lift her leg higher. It looks dumb that low."

We were working on a runaround where I stayed in place, one leg lifted and hooked. I hadn't been the beneficiary of ballet training when I was younger, so my flexibility, while more impressive than the average person's was not on par with a ballerina's.

Amber had been a ballerina when she was younger, her skill honed at the finest schools money could buy. She'd switched to ballroom her first year in college, not talented enough to pursue a career as a professional ballet dancer. All the ballet training had left her with extravagant flexibility, which Jorge and she had used regularly in their routines.

Maxine had suggested I leave my leg a few inches above the floor rather than lifting it to knee-level—what my moderate flexibility allowed for.

"If the leg isn't high, it's better left low. We'll make it about the emotion," she'd said and directed us to gaze into each other's eyes as Jorge clasped my hand to his heart.

Jorge looked at Amber. "Stop, babe. Please."

"It does look dumb," she said. "I'm just trying to be helpful. I want you to win."

My blood, boiling and bubbling, coursed through my body, as my fingers curled into a fist.

Jorge led me to a corner far away from Amber.

"I don't know what's gotten into her," he whispered.

I knew what had gotten into her, and Jorge did too. Jealousy. The serpent had wrapped its scaly coils around her heart and was crushing it, hard and pitilessly.

For one moment, I stepped into Amber's shoes and felt her pain.

Would I act like this? I asked myself.

No, I would not, I answered myself.

I'd done plenty of things I was not proud of, but I'd never, nor would I ever, demean someone like this.

She was old and scared and hurt, but I was old and scared and hurt too. My empathy, not great to begin with, evaporated.

"Three strikes," I hissed to Jorge. "She's got one more, and then one of us is leaving."

The anger, youthful and vitalizing, heated my cheeks. I felt like the Nina from a couple of years ago, the one with a husband who hadn't replaced her with an eighteen-year-old mail-order bride, the one only two places away from a Nationals title in Standard, the one who believed in herself, her talent, her vivacity, and her ability to manipulate life like a piece of clay.

Jorge stared at me, his eyes dazed and intrigued.

I placed a hand on my hip. "I'm not joking."

"You aren't," Jorge said as a statement not a question.

I smiled. "Shall we take it from the top of Waltz?"

We took our opening pose.

"Amber," I said. "Would you be a sweetheart and press play?"

If this were a movie, there'd be a slow pan to Amber, contrite, pressing play. Instead, real life happened.

"Push it yourself," Amber said as she swiped at her phone. "I'm busy."

All the girlish vigor I'd felt dried up. I was back to being the Nina I was now, a thirty-year-old divorcée with a busted knee and a tattered dream. My shoulders collapsed, and I wanted to slink into a corner so I could cry and cry. I was tired of trying this hard and being in this much pain. I just wanted it to be over.

Please let me win. I prayed to a god my ancestors hadn't believed in for decades. *Please let the effort mean something.*

"Let me," Jorge said.

He strode over to Amber. "Come with me, babe." He extended his hand, and with wide eyes, she took it. He escorted her to the lobby. He opened the door and then gave her a gentle push out of it. "Go shopping or something. I'll call you later."

Amber, her mouth slack with shock, exited.

Jorge walked back to me. His face was set in determined lines although his eyes looked tormented. "Shall we?" He offered the crook of his elbow.

I hooked my arm through his. "Let's."

Amber didn't come to any more practices. Jorge, though, showed up the next day with a forehead crosshatched by worry.

"How are you feeling?" I asked.

"Never better," he said.

I grasped his shoulder, warm and sinewy to my touch. "Let me go make some tea."

Chapter 36

CARLY: THE RING

NATIONALS LOOMED LARGE; two flips of the calendar page and it would be here. I didn't know if I wanted it never to come or to come tomorrow.

Several times over the searing month of June, a man in a sleek black suit showed up. Trey let him into some of the upstairs rooms, where they had low, muffled conversations that I strained to hear. Then last week, a moving van showed up. While we were practicing, picking apart and then putting back together our Tango, men tramped up and down the stairs, their arms laden with furniture. At one point, they banged into the door of the ballroom. Trey winced before his features recomposed themselves into their normal inscrutability.

"Again," he'd said to me. Along with *good morning* and *good evening,* it was one of the only words that left his mouth these days.

I continued to teach Jason a few times a month. He brought some much-needed levity into my week. He forgot everything he learned, which made lesson planning easy. The only issue was how much Jason loathed Trey. At the end of every lesson, he would try to write his check to me.

"Trey will take care of you," I'd say brightly. He'd glance at Trey, leaning against a wall with his arms crossed, and then Jason would scowl.

"Do you need anything, Carly?" Jason would ask as he wrote out his check. "Anything at all?"

"I have everything I could ever want," I'd say, shooting a worried look at Trey. He couldn't think I was complaining to Jason about him.

Trey was spending more and more time with me. After dinner, he'd join me in my room. William brought us decaf coffee with a dollop of cream but no sugar, served in porcelain cups stamped with an intricate print of blue roses. We listened to music—pop, light classical, some jazz—while holding hands. He scooted me close to him, so we could sit thigh-to-thigh, chest-to-chest. He'd leave after an hour or so, to shower and to pace the same well-worn pathways around his room.

Before retiring, I cracked the door, and in the darkest hours of night, he would slip into my room and then into my bed. We assumed a loose dance position as ferocious summer storms ripped apart the night sky with pitchforks of lightning and thwacks of thunder.

Trey got what little sleep he could before the sun rose, throwing its unforgiving light into the tiny den of comfort we'd forged in each other's arms. In those dark, hushed hours, our feelings stitched together through the press of our hands, I was happy, so happy.

Two worries kept me up until Trey came to me. Nationals, obviously, and post Nationals. Was Trey going to thank me and then book me on the first flight to Ohio?

Please let me stay here, with Trey. The prayer chimed in my heart on a never-ending loop.

During a coaching session, I caught Cyrus eyeing me thoughtfully. At the end, he pulled me aside.

"Trey, be a good boy and ask William to put on some tea." After Trey left, Cyrus sat on a bench and pointed to the space next to him. I placed myself beside him, smoothing down my skirt.

"You have something on your mind," he said.

"Just winning Nationals."

Cyrus shook his head. "Something else is going on."

I laced my fingers together.

He peered at me, his eyes big with curiosity. "Your secrets are quite safe with me, dear girl."

My secrets were certainly not safe with him, but my anxieties had unraveled my resolve.

"What happens after Nationals? If we win, we go on tour, but then what? And if we don't win . . . " I gulped. Not winning was unthinkable.

"I imagine Trey has some type of plan," Cyrus said.

"Does that plan include me?" I whispered.

"Are you in love with him?"

"It's not normal how I feel," I said, putting into words what had been swimming beneath my skin for months.

"You can't love someone like Trey and expect it to feel normal." Cyrus patted my hand. "How do you feel about him?"

"I would do anything for him."

"Anything?"

I nodded miserably. Then I said what every person thought when they saw us together. "I'm not pretty enough for him."

"Don't sell yourself short. You've got nice bones, and you clean up well. Besides, Trey has all those good looks, and how happy do you think they've made him? Not very, I can tell you that much." During the last sentence, Cyrus' voice had taken on a white-hot edge as if he wanted to hurt someone for hurting Trey.

I twisted my intertwined fingers.

"Why do you want to win Nationals?" Cyrus asked.

"I want to win for Trey. He has to win."

"That's not a good enough reason. You have to want to win for yourself. Becoming a champion is no easy feat. It requires endless reserves of stamina and grit, the ability to sacrifice any and every desire, no matter how big or small, for the goal. Wanting to win for Trey is not enough to sustain you through the next weeks."

I didn't say anything.

"You've held up admirably, but things are about to get harder. Harder than you can imagine. Find a reason."

I clenched my jaw. *My reason is Trey.*

Cyrus seemed to read my mind. He sighed. "Keep digging. It'd be nice if at least one of you wanted to do it for the dancing." He sent me away, so he could have tea with Trey.

To tell Trey my secrets, I thought.

A few nights later, Trey came to my room. Instead of slipping into bed beside me, he pulled back the covers, placed his hands under my hips, and rotated me a quarter turn until my legs dangled over the bed. I hadn't closed the drapes, and moonlight streamed through the window, glazing everything with its pale magic.

He took his pointer finger and ran it, leisurely but purposefully, from the crown of my head all the way down my torso, symbolically splitting me open like a melon, my insides pink, slick, and pulsing with what he already knew. I danced for him, I lived for him, I loved for him.

"You are lovely," he said, the honey in his voice tied up in knots. He knelt, spread my legs, and then buried his head in between them.

I moaned as the fluttering, like the restless motion of a hummingbird's wings, increased in tempo and temperature. The heat and excitement swirled into one desperate, insistent goal, and I shuddered.

He rose abruptly and sprinted out of the room as I lay there, a guttered candle, my flesh dribbling off my bones.

"Please stay," I whispered, but Trey was gone. A cat, he came and went as he pleased even as I held my arms wide open for him.

Thump, thump. His footsteps were pounding up the stairs as my heart galloped after him. Squeak. He'd pushed open his bedroom door. Clink, then tinkles and more tinkles. He'd turned on the shower.

It took at least a hundred minutes for my delirious body to mellow into sleep, but I eventually dozed off to the pitter-patter of Trey in the shower.

The next day was the Fourth of July, for which I was grateful. Trey had suggested we take the day off.

"It'll be the last one we get," he'd said. "We can watch the fireworks from the balcony."

At the time, I hadn't cared. I would spend the Fourth of July thinking about dancing with and loving Trey. This was one step removed from how I spent my days, which was dancing with but still loving Trey.

Now I exhaled, relieved for the respite. I wasn't up for seeing him, for spending so much time close to his body with last night fresh and feverish in my memory. It'd happened, but why had it happened?

A knock—slow, quick, quick, slow—interrupted my reeling thoughts.

"Come in," I said. I threw on my robe although the knock was Trey's.

He walked in, wearing a dark gray suit and lavender tie. His face, unreadable as usual, looked pale, and ash smudged his under eyes.

"Good morning, Carly."

"Good morning," I said, my unease lifting the words up to a coloratura's range.

"Will you have breakfast with me in the garden?" he asked.

I nodded.

"Wear something pretty."

After he left, I jumped up and threw open the closet door. All I had were pretty, girly clothes. Even my workout gear was pretty with sheer panels and lace insets.

I landed on a pink dress, its shade reminiscent of a ballet slipper, sleeveless but with a long, full skirt. Its cold, slippery fabric clung to my heated skin.

I brushed my hair and let it hang loose, always a treat since I wore it up so much. I hadn't had so much as a trim since I'd been in Charleston, and it'd grown long, cascading to the small of my back. I applied some light makeup while wishing for some jewelry to wear. The dress could use some oomph.

Coiling a lock of hair around my finger, I entered the garden. Sunlight gushed over the foliage, a drunk's lavish compliments. The tangles of yellow and purple and red flowers glistened, and the water in the fountain wavered, coaxing and incandescent like a mirage. Everything was illuminated, most impressively Trey, whose blond hair sparkled as if it were a crown.

He stood and offered me his hand, which I took. He issued a dry kiss over my damp skin. I swallowed; last night was dangling like a canopy in the front of my mind.

Trey pulled out a chair for me. I settled myself and took in the table, which was groaning under the weight of a feast fit for at least eight people. Toast with whorls of butter, fluffy scrambled eggs, fruit salad, a platter of smoked salmon and capers.

"Wow," I said.

"William outdid himself."

"He did."

Trey smiled at me, but it didn't reach his eyes, which teetered with nerves. "I asked him to." He reached for a bottle. “Champagne?" He didn't wait for an answer and poured a stream of fuzzy gold into a crystal goblet.

I closed my hand around the delicate stem of the glass.

"To our partnership." He clinked his glass against mine.

I took a sip, appreciating the bubbles that smashed like little rocks against my tongue.

Trey set his glass down and sought out my eyes. "You've become special to me, Carly. I've enjoyed our time together, both on and off the dance floor."

"Thank you," I mumbled. “Me too.”

He handed me a small black leather jewelry box. "If we win Nationals, I want us to continue our partnership."

Dumbly, I stared at the box and then reached for it with shaking hands.

"Open it," Trey said.

I flipped back the lid and gasped. Nestled in white satin was an antique ring. The center stone was an enormous sapphire with tiny, perfect diamonds studding its perimeter.

"It's beautiful," I managed to get out. Was Trey proposing? I wasn't sure I was following the script.

He lifted the ring out of the box. "Allow me." He slipped it on my fourth finger, left hand.

Trey was proposing. My heart stuttered, and my breath disappeared into the fervor of my emotions.

"It's been in my family for generations," he said. "My grandmother was the last person to wear it. She lived with us until she died. I had a nanny, but my grandmother was the one who took care of me. She read me stories and took me to the park. She's been dead a long time now, but I miss her every day."

He pulled back and studied the ring. "I had to guess on the size, but I think I did okay."

My hand, heavy with jewels and expectations, drooped.

"Would you want that, Carly? To continue our partnership if we win Nationals?"

I beamed at him. "So much."

He smiled, and it reached his eyes where it stayed—a ray of sun slamming into a prism. "I'm glad," he said as he removed the ring and put it back in the box.

Both of us picked at the breakfast, gazing at each other over our champagne glasses, and then Trey pushed back his chair. "Enjoy your day, Carly." I stayed sitting in the garden, happy but baffled.

Trey wanted to marry me. It was a strange proposal, no talk of love or commitment, just continuing our partnership. But he must love me. At least a little. He wanted to spend the rest of his life with me. As for me, I loved Trey, so much so that my love would be enough for two people with plenty leftover.

A shadow loomed over me. "The missus would like to see you." Startled, I looked up to see William hovering above me.

I struggled to my feet and followed him to Trey's mother's room, a place I'd not been since the day I arrived.

"Miss Caroline Martindale," William intoned as if he were presenting me to the Queen. Trey's mother looked the same as she had the first day I'd met her: dripping with jewelry, smeared with makeup, and smothered in fat.

She pointed to a delicate armchair upholstered in periwinkle velvet. "Sit."

I perched on the edge of the seat, my back ruler straight.

"My son tells me he aims to marry you if you win Nationals."

I nodded and then smiled, a little obsequiously. I wanted her to like me.

"If I'm going to bless this union between Trey and some nobody from Ohio with do-gooder parents and a retarded brother—"

"Archer isn't retarded. He's autistic." I corrected her automatically.

She pursed her lips "An autistic brother, then I want something."

I widened my eyes. I didn't have anything to give her. She knew that seeing as I was living under her roof and on Trey's dime. "What do you want?" I asked.

"A grandchild. The sooner the better." She gestured toward the clutter of pill bottles. "My health is not robust."

I gaped at her.

A baby?

Images surged through my mind. Little fingers gripping my big finger, tiny socks, a silver rattle, sweet lips blowing raspberries. Chubby legs taking their first hesitant steps. A gummy smile and a voice saying *mama, mama*. My eyes moistened, and I reached to brush away a tear.

A baby. Trey's baby.

I loved this idea.

"I thought you'd like that." She shifted her enormous girth. "There might some difficulties."

"Difficulties?" I echoed.

"My son has always been exceptional, even when he was a boy. When Trey's father died, I started taking Trey out and about with me. To dinner parties, to the theater, to galas. He was such a good-looking boy and always polite. People couldn't believe he was a child. He could hold his own in conversation. Unsurprisingly, people treated him as older than he was."

She reached for a silver picture, a swoop of fat bobbing from her upper arm. She handed it to me. "Trey at eleven. The ballet, I think."

I studied the photo. Trey wore a tuxedo, his lips spread in an impish grin. This little boy looked like Trey, but he seemed nothing like the reticent, sphinx-like man I loved. He stood next to a beautiful, voluptuous woman, clad in a low-cut black velvet gown.

I blinked. The woman was Trey's mother.

"As you can see, Trey has always been charming and good-looking."

"Yes," I said, unsure of where she was going with this.

"When he was thirteen, one of my friends took a shine to him. She would have him over for tea, so she could show him things."

She narrowed her eyes at me and cocked her head. "Are you following me?"

I cleared my throat. "Not really."

"The kinds of things that a woman of experience shows a young man."

"Like how to pull out a chair for a lady?" I asked stupidly.

"Don't be obtuse, Caroline. My son has known how to that since he could walk." She sighed. "Adult things."

My mouth fell open. "When he was thirteen?" I asked in a faint voice.

"Trey has always been mature for his age," she said. "In retrospect, he was a touch young for such things. After a few months, my friend rather abruptly moved on to other preoccupations. Trey, naturally, was quite upset. He'd always been such a lively boy, and it was as if someone turned out the light."

I took a shaky breath.

"I thought a change of scenery would do him good, so I sent him to an all-boys boarding school a few hours away. One of the teachers there took such an interest in Trey. Always had him stay after class, so he could show Trey things. Well, some of the boys stumbled on them one day. They ribbed Trey for a few days, and then they told the headmaster. The headmaster didn't like it one bit. So he fired the teacher and sent Trey home."

I was shivering violently as if I'd been caught naked in a blizzard. "Trey. Victim. Not once but twice," I said through gasps. I couldn't form a coherent sentence.

Trey's mother stiffened. "My son is not a victim. He is exceptional. People are drawn to him."

The showers, the insomnia, the pacing, the self-imposed isolation, the chasteness of our relationship, the rapid departure last night: It made sense now. Trey had been abused. Twice.

"Where is the woman, the teacher?" I croaked. "Are they in jail?" My tongue had become an unwieldy anchor that refused to budge under the wave of my staggering horror.

"My friend had breast cancer a few years back and found religion shortly thereafter. As for the teacher, he got married and moved to Georgia to work at a military academy.

My stomach clenched, and the contents of it, that gorgeous, special breakfast, roiled threateningly. I balled up my fists. I wanted to punch

Trey's mother. Then I was going to find her friend and the teacher, and I was going to hit them, again and again, as hard as I could.

"When Trey came home, he was withdrawn. He wouldn't eat, couldn't sleep. I was beside myself with worry. Finally, I remembered how much he'd liked cotillion. He'd stay after and badger that poor teacher with questions. So I found an instructor, and that perked him up," she said. "I'd hoped as he got older that he would get interested in the things that boys his age were interested in. Skirt chasing, drinking, raising Cain. But he was all about the dancing. After he won his third Nationals, I thought maybe he'd find a nice girl and settle down. But he's so devoted to me. Never wanted to go out or spend time with people his own age."

She gazed at me. "He's always been mature for his age," she said again.

He's always been mature for his age, I repeated to myself. I shoved my fists under my legs for fear I might start pummeling her.

"Then he met you. You've been good for him and good to him. I haven't heard him laugh this much since he was a boy," she said. "I daresay he's fonder of you than practically anybody in the world, save myself naturally."

She fluffed her hair. "You're a smart girl, a nurturing girl. Figure out what he needs, so you can have that baby you want."

She gestured for me to leave. "Be sure to win Nationals." She trilled the words as if she was a musical theater soubrette.

I stood and, with wobbling legs, exited. I paced around the hall, my thoughts a jumble of angry impulses and muddled replays of Trey's mother's revelations.

"Carly," Trey said. He was walking down the stairs, but I'd been too agitated to notice. His eyebrows were knitted in concern. "Are you okay?"

"I came from talking to your mother."

"What did she say?"

"She wants a grandchild."

Trey's face was unreadable. "She told me that too."

"She said there might be some difficulty."

"What else did she say?" Trey's lips were trembling.

"She told me about the woman when you were thirteen and then the teacher at the boarding school."

I looked at him with wet eyes. "I'm so sorry, Trey."

His eyes were glassy, his shoulders hunched. He was an animal caught in a trap.

Brusquely, he grabbed my arm. "Let's go practice."

"It's the Fourth of July."

He pushed me toward the stairs. "Come on."

"I'm really not up for it. Tomorrow, I promise."

"We're going to practice." His jaw was set, and his gray eyes were frozen.

"Okay, okay." I followed him up the stairs into the ballroom.

"Waltz," he ordered.

Mechanically, I struck the opening pose.

"Lower your right arm an inch. Lengthen your spine. That's too much. You're pulling up too far from the floor. Relax your shoulders," he said. "More. More. More." His voice was hard and relentless, a hammer hitting a stubborn nail.

I fought to apply Trey's corrections.

"Point your right foot. Your ribs are sticking out. Relax your shoulders."

His volume grew louder until it was ricocheting off the walls of the ballroom. I was caught in a firestorm of imperatives, and I couldn't find cover. Nothing I did was right.

"Please slow down, Trey. I can't do everything at once."

He ignored me. "Your left foot is too turned out. More curve in the wrist. Relax your shoulders." He screamed the last correction.

During a sequence of solo spins, I lost my spot, thrown off by the barrage of criticism, and veered precariously toward the wall.

"Find the straight line with your feet."

Trey strode over to me. His eyes were flashing, and his mouth was contorted into a cruel sneer. "How many times do I have to tell you? Because every time I tell you the same thing, it means you're not moving on to the next thing."

"I'm doing the best I can," I said. "Can we call it a day and try again tomorrow?"

"Do it again."

I performed the spins again as he roared, over and over, "Find the straight line."

I couldn't focus, and I tripped.

"Again."

"I can't." I wrapped my arms around myself. "I'm telling you, Trey. I can't."

His mouth fell open, and for a moment he stared at me, his eyes bulging. Then he turned on his heel and left.

Trembling and irrational with distress, I returned to my room.

William brought me dinner, which I declined. I lay in bed as day evaporated into night, too dazed by the last twenty-four hours to think or feel anything logical. I burrowed under the covers and clutched a throw pillow to my chest, a velveteen tube of light orange that reminded me of a popsicle. My hot tears oozed down it.

I caressed my ring finger, remembering the weight of the engagement ring, how beautiful it was, how much I wanted what it symbolized—Nationals champion and Trey. In other words, the happily-ever-after ending.

Trey's signature knock roused me. "May I come in?" he asked.

I didn't answer.

"Please."

I stayed silent, scared of what he wanted.

"I know you're in there, Carly."

I buried my head in the throw pillow.

"Let me in," he said. "Please."

I sighed and steeled my shattered nerves for whatever was coming. "Okay," I said.

Trey opened the door and stepped in the room. My heart seized again at how good-looking he was. He jogged to the bed as he unknotted his robe.

I rolled over, and he slid in beside me. He offered his left hand to me. I placed my right hand in it. We took a loose dance position, and I laid my wet cheek on his chest. Outside, a boom sounded. The fireworks had started.

"You've been crying," he said.

His acknowledgment sent my already whirling emotions into a tizzy, and the drizzle escalated into a downpour that splashed onto and then puddled into the cavity of his breastbone.

I finally understood my parents' tireless love and fervent advocacy for Archer. To love someone so singular, so distinct from oneself, so incompatible with the world at large, required stepping off the well-lit, well-trod path of normalcy and onto a shadowy orbit that might never resolve itself in a straight line of here to there. Love would always be an endless cycle of all journey and no destination.

"Are you quitting?" Trey asked.

I shook my head emphatically. "I'm in it to win it."

"All of it?"

"Every bit of it."

His chest collapsed as he exhaled. "I'm glad."

He kissed the top of my head. "You are one in a million."

Then he pulled me up until we were eye to eye. Tenderly, he pressed his lips against each cheek. Then, with his lips wet with my passion and compassion for him, Trey kissed me, our first real one. Outside, fireworks—splatters of red, white, and blue—imprinted themselves against the inky sky.

Chapter 37

NINA: SALSA DANCING

JORGE and I caught a second wind. We got closer and closer until we were very close.

One week before Nationals, we danced in San Francisco, the city Jorge had called home for a dozen years. Former students, prior coworkers, friends, an old boss or two all flocked to the competition. Jorge had been a popular teacher and competitor, and everyone who knew him or had known him came out to show his or her support.

One person was missing—Amber.

"Is she coming?"

"I asked her to."

I stroked his forearm. "I'm sorry."

Amber seemed like a lot of trouble for not much reward. I didn't think this because I wanted Jorge for myself. I thought it because it was true. What was the point of being rich if it couldn't buy you any of the stuff that mattered? Like, say, the ability to cheer on your boyfriend and his dance partner at the competition before Nationals?

Amber never showed up. Jorge looked for her and sent texts. When it became apparent she wasn't coming, he said to himself, "So that's that." His spine bowed, and then he squared his shoulders.

He grinned at me with relieved eyes. "Let's dance," he said and offered his hand. I placed my hand into his warm, safe grip.

"Let's," I said.

We danced well, probably the best we'd ever danced. And with the crowd on our side, we'd taken Tango and Viennese Waltz from Trey and Carly. Rule Eleven, the tie-breaking procedure, decided the event, not in our favor, but we hardly cared. A Nationals victory lay inches from us. We only had to keep our momentum hurtling forward.

After the competition, Jorge popped his head into my room. "Do you want to go out? Blow off some steam."

"I should ice my knee," I said.

He threw me an easy smile. "Later. We could use some fun."

I smiled back. "Let's go dancing," I said. "For fun."

We went to a small but jumping Salsa club around the corner from the hotel. Sticky bodies, blaring music, and riotous laughter filled the postage-stamped space.

"It's not my best dance," I said.

"Who cares," he said.

With the small of his hand on my back, Jorge led me to the bar and ordered two sangrias. It was too loud to talk much, so we smiled at each other as we drank, and then he led me out to the dance floor.

"For fun," he said.

"For fun," I echoed.

Then we danced. The floor pulsed with so much activity that we couldn't do much beyond a few basics. My body trusted Jorge's implicitly from spending the last year near it, next to it, pressed up against it, so I followed effortlessly and happily.

Partner dancing was fundamentally social. Even with no speech, it was a dialogue, words transformed into changes of weight and direction. Emotion and meaning were conveyed through the bend of a knee or the pop of a hip. Even when surrounded by other people, it was private, two hearts turned toward each other, two heads bent to the same task at hand.

On that crowded, clammy, cacophonous dance floor, Jorge and I had a heart-to-heart talk.

I like this; I like you, he told me as he led me into a Cross Body Lead with Underarm Turn, a quick directional switch of 180 degrees that ended with a cyclonic spin.

I like you; I like this, I responded as he slipped under his arm and then lifted it for me to swish under.

I'll help you; you'll help me, he said silently as he did a basic while arcing his left arm over his head and then returning to dance position.

I'll help you; you'll help me, I replied as he guided me into another Cross Body Lead, his body acting as an open door that I walked through, knowing he was behind me and when I turned around, he would be in front of me.

We were a team, two bodies that committed to everything together.

We danced and danced, talking the entire time about how good we were together, how easy it'd been for us, how we weren't going to stop even when we hung up our dance shoes.

The music ebbed and the lights brightened and the club thinned out, but we stayed on the dance floor in each other's arms, moving so we could communicate. Finally, when we were the last couple left, winners in a dance-a-thon we didn't know we'd entered, we stopped.

"For fun," Jorge said, out loud, as he wrapped his arms around me.

"For fun," I said and lifted my face to his.

We kissed. No leading, no following, just instinct.

Jorge and I ambled back to the hotel, luxuriating in anticipation of our new dance we would perform. And then, once we got my room, we took our time until we couldn't anymore. We went off time in a frenzied, unrestrained show of passion.

Sated and joyous, we slept on our sides, backs pressed together.

In dance position, the power came from the back, rather than the arms. The muscles were bigger there, stronger there. A dance position initiated from the back provided support and safety. One commenced and maintained through the arms could sag and wiggle, a loose connection from which anyone can escape. When dancing with another, firmness and freedom weren't mutually exclusive.

Jorge and I had each other's back.

I drifted off, hugely thankful, because I'd grown up, and gratitude seemed a more appropriate reaction than the self-congratulatory validation of my younger self when something wonderful happened. And this was something wonderful.

A tinkle of Salsa music roused me. I opened my eyes, confused. Were we still at the club?

It was Jorge's phone.

"Where?" he asked, his voice thrumming with insistence. "I'll be there as soon as I can."

I sat up, a little embarrassed but mostly happy. "What's wrong?"

"It's Amber. She swallowed a bunch of pills last night."

I opened my mouth, but no sound came out.

"She's okay, but she's asking for me."

"Go," I said, finally finding my words, or, in reality, a word.

"I'll be in touch," he said as he disappeared through the unlocked door between our rooms.

When he left, I pulled my knees to my chest. Tears streamed down my face and into the indentation where Jorge had slept.

I was being silly because I absolutely, completely, most definitely not at all interested in . . .

Who was I kidding? I was in love with Jorge, and I had been for a while.

Chapter 38

CARLY: THE PROBLEM WITH PERFECTION

WHAT HAD BEEN unthinkable just a few months earlier was now a distinct possibility. We could lose Nationals to Jorge and Nina.

There was nothing we could do beyond what we were already doing, which was practicing as much as possible and dancing as well as we could.

We had a problem, though, and it had nothing to do with the quality of our dancing.

"You've arrived, dear girl," Cyrus said after our last coaching session before Nationals. "You two look marvelous together: sparkling, flawless, and beautiful." He smiled. "A diamond in a golden setting."

"Will it be enough?" I asked, slumping on the bench. I was so tired that I could barely hold my eyes open. Trey had added extra time to our practice sessions, and my body was struggling to keep up.

Cyrus threw up his hands. "The judges decide that."

The judges, though, didn't seem interested in us. "Perfectly safe and safely perfect," one snipped to another as Trey and I stood behind them, waiting for the elevator.

They hadn't seen us, and Trey didn't give them a chance to. He'd grabbed my hand and pulled me to the stairs. We stopped taking the elevator after that. We climbed industrial staircase after industrial staircase, leaving a trail glittering with rhinestones and tears in our wake.

They were interested in Jorge and Nina. Everybody was interested in Jorge and Nina. No one said anything to Trey or me, but we overheard plenty practicing between rounds and observing heats. "So exciting, so emotional," people said over and over. And the worst, "I can't stop watching them."

They still had glitches in their technique, but they'd addressed the larger issues. The judges, gauging by the results, seemed willing to overlook their minor errors in exchange for the heat and flash Jorge and Nina brought to the floor.

Perfection, when confronted by passion, was obviously overrated

Trey was in a dark place, and I'd given up trying to elicit a smile or a laugh from him. There'd be plenty of time for that after Nationals.

If we won.

It seemed impossible that my happiness rested on a few flicks of the judges' pens.

Although Trey had folded deep into himself, we remained in constant contact. He held my hand everywhere, between heats, on the airplane, in the morning as we climbed the stairs to the ballroom. On Sundays, when we returned from a competition, we sat in the garden, our heads on each other's shoulders, our arms laced around each other. The thick, stultifying heat of the Charleston summer pressed down upon us.

The tension and worry lapped over us, but even its relentlessness couldn't erode the joy I found in Trey's arms.

I wasn't particularly religious, but I prayed every night, kneeling beside my bed as if I was a dutiful child. *Please let us win,* I begged over and over. *Trey's been hurt enough. Don't hurt him anymore.*

In the larger scheme of humanity, my appeals for mercy were silly. People were starving and dying and suffering, all at an incomprehensible magnitude, and I was praying to win a ballroom dance competition so I could keep a man. I was glad that no one save God and I could hear my pleas.

My parents had dropped the pretense of sending emails from Archer and wrote me long missives that alternately implored and guilt-tripped me into coming back to Ohio.

We need your help. Archer needs your help. Your family is more important than a ballroom dance competition. Please come home immediately.

Everything they wrote was true. The problem was that Ohio was no longer home. Trey's arms were, so I stopped reading and replying to their emails. After Nationals, I'd figure something out. Maybe I could fly home a couple of weekends a month to give them a break.

Archer's face flashed in my mind, the little peach fuzz he'd had the last time I'd seen him now darker and thicker. I twisted my hands. I missed Archer intensely although I couldn't imagine being away from Trey for even a few days.

It was selfish; I was selfish, putting a ballroom dance competition ahead of my family, who desperately needed me. Trey needed me too, I rationalized.

One week before the future would be decided, disaster struck in San Francisco. We danced well. At this point, we always danced well. Trey had tuned my body so completely to his that I moved instinctively to his every command, unrestrained by mental chatter or emotional apprehension. We'd become one person spread over two bodies. If I hadn't been sick with worry, I would have enjoyed dancing. Instead, it was a means to an end.

Dancing well was barely enough; we tied with Jorge and Nina. We took Waltz and Foxtrot, and Rule Eleven decided the event. Luckily, in our favor.

Jorge and Nina didn't appear to care that they'd come in second. They'd taken two dances from the exceptional Trey Devereux, and this elated them. The chance to win Nationals rested so close that they could reach out and feel the weight of the gold medal in their hands. I tried to be gracious when I congratulated Nina. If she hadn't trained Sam and me two years ago, then I wouldn't be here, with Trey, but worry and self-interest stained my words.

"What can I do better?" I asked Trey when we returned to Charleston.

"You can't do anything better."

"There has to be something."

He shook his head. "It's between fire and ice at this point. The judges either like what we're selling, or they don't."

I closed my eyes. I wanted there to be something—anything—I could do, one achievable goal to which I could spin my focus.

"What's the plan if we don't win?" I asked, my pitch barely audible.

"There isn't one," Trey said.

Chapter 39

NINA: PAPA'S QUESTION

JORGE WAS GONE for almost a week, one of the longest of my life. I didn't know what to do, so I did what I always did. I showed up at the studio to practice and to teach and to take comfort in the camaraderie of the other teachers.

Maxine called me.

"It's bad luck right before Nationals," she said, her voice a pill of sympathy and bitterness. Maxine lost, too, if we lost.

"It is," I said.

Maxine sighed. "Amber was always high strung."

"So I've seen."

"Dance your best. Even if you don't win, you and Jorge have accomplished something significant this year. You should be proud." She rallied herself. "I'm proud of you," she said, the perky peaks doing nothing to cover the valley of her disappointment.

I thanked her and hung up. Accomplishing something significant wasn't the same thing as winning. And if we didn't win, we would never be anything more than a blip on the radar.

Jorge returned to New York the day before our event.

"It's been a mess," he said.

"Is she okay?" I asked.

"Physically, yes. Mentally, not so much." He sighed. "Her shrink called it a cry for help."

A conveniently timed cry for help, I thought and then gave myself a stern shake. Amber must have been in a dark place, one blacker and bleaker than I'd ever been in, to do something like that.

"She begged me to stay." He pressed his hand to his forehead. "I couldn't. We've put so much into this."

"Do you need to go back?" I asked, enunciating each word as if I were a programmed robot.

"I don't know," he said. "She's got the best care money can buy. She's got her parents by her side. If I stayed, it would have been good for her but bad for you and me." He paused. "Whose happiness matters more?"

I squeezed his hand. "Nobody wins in this situation."

He squeezed back. "I want us to win."

"Me too. But it's been a great experience whether we win or lose." My tone was peppy, but my meaning was hollow. I wanted to win, more than anything, so Jorge and I could write ourselves into the future.

Trey didn't need to win. He'd won three times, which guaranteed him a place in the imagination of future dancers. If he won, it would be another tick in the column for how things had always been, not what they could be—two scrappy kids pulling themselves up by their bootstraps through persistence and hard work to arrive as champions. If we won, our dancing, our story would inspire another generation. If we lost, well, then we disappeared.

I hoped Carly was holding up. She was tougher and smarter than Tamsin had ever been, but she'd looked distinctly worn-out and hollow-cheeked at the last few competitions. In between heats, Trey held her hand as she stood obediently beside him. I remembered Vadim's words—like dog on leash.

Win or lose, I was going to track her down after Nationals and make sure she was okay. Carly had always been gregarious, and the change in her personality since dancing with Trey was alarming.

Papa came to watch our last practice.

"You kids look terrific. I can't believe how far you've come in a year."

I rubbed my knee, not that it did anything beyond making me feel as if I was doing something, anything, to salve the pain. Even with a week off, it still throbbed like a heartbeat, steadily and incessantly until death. Jorge slumped on the bench next to me, the knife-edge of his hand kneading his hip.

"Lunch, Nina?"

Papa didn't wait for an answer. He guided me to an upscale Chinese restaurant. I picked listlessly at some lo mein as he droned on and on about how this would be his fortieth Nationals. At this point,

I'd heard all of Papa's stories. Most of them, three or four times. I hoped he wouldn't bring up Grover Ferris again. I'd heard about Grover Ferris' Paso Doble at least twenty times.

I gave up on feigning interest in Papa. All I could think about was how tomorrow, I would know if I was a winner or a loser.

"It's going to be close," he said. "Closer than I've ever seen before."

"Probably," I muttered.

"If it's close, I can help." He stared at me unblinking, his face mild but his eyes keen. "Do you want me to help?"

I toyed with the napkin in my lap, running my fingers around the edge of its hem. The stitches had broken loose at a corner. I stuck my finger in the tiny pouch it created.

I was tired and in pain and on the cusp of my last chance to win Nationals. The man I loved was potentially returning to California to be with his rich, crazy girlfriend. I'd worked for so long and so hard, and all I had to show for it was an empty apartment with an empty bed. Winning Nationals was all I had left, and at this point, I didn't care if I won it fair and square. One or two marks in the wrong direction would designate me as a loser for the rest of my life. So I looked to the future and found it bright if I won Nationals."

"Yes." I looked Papa in his eyes. "I want you to help."

He sat up straight and smiled with shiny, spiky incisors. "That's a good decision to think about the future," he said. "You'll be amazed at how little the past can matter once you get to the future."

I swallowed and nodded and thought about how long I'd carried this dream. If Papa fudged a few marks in our favor, then he was only helping Jorge, Maxine, and I write a history that would resonate later. Plus I'd finally repay my mother's sacrifices. Saying yes was made of win.

"I know how thankful you'll be," he said. "And I'll want to accept your gratitude immediately. That way you don't get busy and forget about poor Papa."

I stared at my feet. I knew exactly what type of gratitude he expected. I cleared my mind. I would think about that when and if I had to think about it.

He leaned back in his chair. "I've liked you for a long time, Nina. I'm glad I have an opportunity to show you how much I like you."

Chapter 40

CARLY: THE THUNDERSTORM

I HAD A PREMONITION, and it was a terrible one. I'd never been one to trust intuition over good-old fashioned facts. The treacherous mountains of life were easier to navigate if I looked outside myself, acknowledged the landmarks and potential pitfalls with steely-eyed realism, and then responded accordingly. Head over guts, this was how I lived my life. I'd learned that from growing up alongside Archer.

Maybe it was the immensity of my love for Trey or maybe it was the minuteness of my world or maybe it was the intense pressure of Nationals, but my brain was addled. It refused to acknowledge rational thought, and instead, was in a panic thanks to a red-hot alert issuing from the bottom of my belly.

You're not coming back.

This thought sent me into a tizzy. Because the one thing in the world I wanted was to come back to Charleston with Trey, to be with Trey.

Nothing logical supported this feeling. I'd been with Trey when he bought our tickets, two round-trip tickets from Charleston to New York. Even if we lost Nationals, we were returning to Charleston. Together. What happened after that was hazy, but I was coming back to Charleston, no matter what.

My premonition, though, only increased in potency.

You're not coming back.

The night before Nationals, I lay in Trey's arms, fitting myself into the landscape of his bone and sinew. Neither of us could sleep; neither of us even tried. Instead, we took what comfort we could from each other's body and breath. Trey brushed kiss after kiss on the top of my head as I pressed my cheek into his chest, memorizing these few inches of him: the hard planes of his muscles, the clean smell of his skin, the steady thump of his heartbeat.

Don't forget that I love you, I told his heart. *Because I love you more than I will ever love anyone.*

Trey didn't have a plan if we lost Nationals, but I did. He could get his adjudicator's license, and I would teach as much as I could. We would get married, something small and simple. I didn't care about the wedding, just its purpose—to be Mrs. Louis Pierre Devereux, III, Trey's wife. I would do whatever Trey needed, so I could get pregnant as quickly as possible. That should mollify Trey's mother to the point where she might not mind leaving the mansion. We could sell and move somewhere smaller. It could be a shack on the beach for all I cared as long as Trey called it home.

Together, we'd work it out. Plenty of people went through financial difficulties and emerged from them unscathed. We were hard working and energetic, and most importantly, we had each other.

Trey had to know that. As long as we had each other, nothing else mattered. Money could always be made, but love was only found. And we'd been so lucky to find each other.

Another thunderstorm raged outside. Every few minutes, the bedroom illuminated with spooky white light, and then thunder, terrifying in its vigor, smashed over our heads. I'd been through plenty of thunderstorms, but this one felt particularly savage, as if God was out to get Charleston.

I silenced my thoughts, which were silly and useless, and rotated my head to take in the bedroom. Its contours were fuzzy in the darkness, but I knew them so well that my imagination sketched in the black holes.

"A room fit for a princess," I'd said when Trey led me into it. And it had been a room for a princess with beautiful dresses and sweet dreams and an odd but perfect prince. I'd always thought my capacity for happiness had been sized ordinarily, but with Trey, it proved to be colossal. Even now, anxious about what the next twenty-four hours held, I was happy, so happy, to be with him.

A Y-shaped branch of lightning flashed outside, and the room brightened, as if a ghost had settled in for the night. My intuition blared, loud and clear.

You're not coming back.
I am, I told myself firmly. *I am coming back.*

Chapter 41

NINA: TEA AND ASPIRIN

MAXINE HAD SUGGESTED black for the final of Nationals. "It's the color of champions," she said. "The dancing must be responsible for the result."

I thought of Amanda Bellows' blue dress with peacock feathers and agreed. "Black it is." Plus Jorge looked good in black. It matched his hair and made his skin look like salted caramel ice cream. Not that it mattered.

I adjusted the necklace of the dress Maxine had selected. This one wasn't quite as revealing as some of the dresses I'd worn in the past, but it was still a big change from my Standard days of long sleeves, high necks, and full skirts. This dress was fashioned from shiny, silky black velvet that reflected rainbows like a pool of oil. Swoops of ebony beads hung from my throat to my chest. The fabric was split from my neck to my waist, and a cut opened the skirt from ankle to crotch.

I looked beautiful but vaguely frightening, as if I were an evil queen or a dark angel.

Or a seductress, I thought, my mouth dry as I remembered how all this might play out. I pushed it out of my head. I'd think about that when and if I needed to think about it.

Jorge pushed through the adjoined door to our rooms. "We look like bank robbers," he said when he saw my dress.

"Or Nationals champions," I said.

His eyes twinkled. "I like that better."

I gestured to the nightstand on which I'd placed two cups of tea and a pile of aspirin. "Our last supper."

"Perfect for two old-timers like us."

"Bottoms up." I clinked my cup against his. I swung a half dozen aspirin into my mouth and chased it with a swig of tea—Prince of Wales, smooth and mild. Jorge did the same.

"When this is over, I want to talk to you," he said. "I thought some things over when I was in San Francisco, and I need to tell you something."

For a second, I forgot about everything that was about to happen and gazed into Jorge's eyes. We might be different on the outside, but on the inside, we were constructed of the same stuff: immigrant dreams, personal ambition, the ability to rejigger a goal and then try, try, and try again. Together, we'd learned and practiced the most important rule for any couple—treating us as sacrosanct.

It'd been easy for us because it'd been a pleasure. I enjoyed giving to Jorge, knowing that he would always return the favor. Our partnership had unfolded as a series of good turns, happiness tossed back and forth in a sacred game of catch.

It was a very nice way to be.

I smiled and then frowned. *He's going to tell me he's returning to San Francisco, to Amber.*

Of course he was going back to Amber. She needed him; I only wanted him. I had so many things I wished to tell Jorge, but they would have to wait.

So what I said was, "Let's go win Nationals."

Chapter 42

CARLY: THE WHITE DRESS

NATIONALS, the event that had defined the last two years of my life, arrived. New York was unseasonably cold for early September with a sky that matched the concrete sidewalks. After the oppressively sweet heat of Charleston, I struggled to get warm and to stay warm. I burrowed into the light sweater I'd brought with me. I wished I'd thought to ask Trey about the weather before we left.

Please, please, please, I prayed. I stared unseeingly out the window as the cab driver whizzed through the familiar streets. Trey looked outside his window. Our hands, interlaced as they always were these days, rested on the seat between us.

Trey felt my hand trembling in his. Wordlessly, he took off his suit jacket and handed it to me. I burrowed into it, grateful for its warmth and for the way it smelled like him, so clean. He opened an arm, and I snuggled up next to him.

Although Nationals was a multi-day competition, we flew in the day of our event, Open Professional Smooth, and win or lose, we'd leave the next morning. I'd silenced my intuition with a grim talking-to. I was coming back to Charleston no matter what.

I gazed into the future to gauge our emotional state, but no clear picture presented itself. I hoped for jubilation, exhilaration, probably relief as we headed back to Charleston where our new life of marriage and a baby awaited. Perhaps, next year, Nationals would pass unnoticed as our dance position increased to accommodate a child.

It seemed impossible that a year had gone by since the last Nationals. I smiled, a wise, rueful one, as I remembered how naïve I'd been when my emotions followed a scallop of up, down, up: exuberance at competing with Jason and Sam, horror at being dumped by Sam before the Rising Star, and then extravagant joy when Trey asked me to dance.

We got to the hotel, and the hours melted away in a blur of practicing, hair and makeup, and then the early rounds. Before it even registered, I was changing for the final. Trey had selected a white dress for me, a nice change after the procession of pastels I'd worn all season.

I smoothed the dress over my hips and studied myself in the mirror. The top was fashioned of lace, an intricate pattern of flowers and curlicues while the bottom, diaphanous chiffon, swirled around me. Except for some modest décolletage, the dress left little skin showing beyond my head and my hands.

I found Trey pacing outside the ballroom. I stopped for a moment to acknowledge him, to admire him, to adore him—this person I loved more than anyone in the world.

I will do anything for you.

Enormous cheers erupted from the ballroom. DeShawn Porter and Nicolette Jackson had won the Rising Star Smooth. For a moment, I stepped outside my worries to send them telepathic felicitations. *Congratulations. You deserve it.*

Trey turned. "Carly." He strode over to me. "You look like a bride." He took each of my hands, kissed them, and then held them to his chest. We gazed at each other, hearts in our eyes. I had so many things I wished to tell Trey, but they would have to wait.

So what I said was, "Let's go win Nationals."

Chapter 43

NINA: THE SECOND GENERATION

JORGE TOOK my hand as we exited my room. My heart beat against my chest, the bang, bang of a kettledrum. A year ago I'd come to Nationals to root on Carly and Sam. I'd been newly divorced and on the lookout for a new dream.

It seemed impossible that that girl was now this girl. I'd found a new dream. The only question was whether I could make it come true. Jorge seemed to read my thoughts. He gave my hand a gentle squeeze, which I returned.

We walked toward the elevator with matched paces, two soldiers off to fight a polite but pitched battle. At the push of a button, the doors sprung open. The interior was crowded with people heading to the ballroom to watch the professional events. Jorge and I fought our way inside.

"Nina," said someone to my left.

I turned my head to see Jason standing behind me with a genial smile. He'd finished out his lessons with me months ago, and I hadn't seen him since. He looked exactly the same with his silver hair and three-piece suit.

"Jason," I said. "I didn't know you would be here tonight."

"I couldn't resist the opportunity to watch my teachers duke it out." He said it in a light voice, but his eyes looked worried.

"It's going to be epic." My breezy words were belied by my serious expression. "It's been a while since you've seen Carly. Last year, right?"

Jason looked down. "I saw her last week."

"You did?"

"No hard feelings, Nina. You were a good teacher. But I was attached to Carly. I've been flying to Charleston to take lessons with her a few times a month."

"That's nice," I said, not caring. Everybody knew why Jason was attached to Carly, and it had nothing to do with Carly's teaching aptitude.

He furrowed his brow. "She's in a bad situation. That guy . . ." He scowled. "I don't care how happy she says she is. Trey treats her as if she's his prisoner."

The elevator dinged. The ballroom and my future lay a dozen or so steps to my right. If it weren't the final round of Nationals, the most important night of my life, I might have asked Jason more questions. Instead, I shrugged as Jorge led me out of the elevator. Jason's words, like a footprint on the beach, were washed away by the tide of more immediate concerns.

"Good luck," Jason said to my back.

Maxine was waiting for us by the door to the ballroom. Her eyes were glittering, and she was tugging on a lock of her tangerine hair. She studied us for a moment. She brushed a piece of invisible lint off of Jorge's jacket and resettled the waterfall of jet beads that dripped from my neck.

"Thank you for everything," I said, my words a little broken. Maxine had been a presence in my life for a dozen-plus years. I was deeply indebted to her. After all of this was over, win or lose, I was going to take her out to dinner and tell her how much she meant to me.

Maxine glanced at Jorge. "You've got Tango in the bag," she said, her tone low and urgent. "Do what you need to do in Viennese Waltz."

Jorge jerked his head in understanding. "I will."

I swung my gaze between them, my eyebrows raised. I wasn't following their cryptic exchange. There wasn't much we could do beyond dancing our best and hoping the judges bought what we were selling.

Plus the deal I'd made with Papa. I wiped that from my mind. I would think about it when and if I had to think about it.

She gave us each a quick hug. "Dance well."

Jorge opened the door to the ballroom, and we stepped in. When we stepped out, we'd know whether we were winners or losers.

My mother and Jorge's mother stood up and waved at us. My mother was wringing her hands, and Jorge's mother was gripping the back of her chair. They were nervous for us, probably more nervous than we were. Both of them had emigrated over thirty years ago from countries thousands of miles apart to end up here—watching their most precious asset try to win Nationals.

We were different and we were doing something different and we'd worked hard and we wanted it, so much.

Would it be enough?

Chapter 44

CARLY: TAKING THE LEAD

DANCING functions as a primer in the limitations of the human body. A dancer discovers, quickly and harshly, that effort is useless in the face of genetically programmed bone and muscle. One could try, even improve, but DNA trumped exertion and desire every time.

But what if a dancer was Trey Devereux, whose DNA was silk trimmed in gold, whose labor provided his bone and muscle with a much-needed avenue for expression?

Limits, then, displayed themselves outside the body through other people, canned music, a slippery floor. When confronted with these issues, what did a dancer like Trey Devereux do? He pivoted to a new position to avoid the couple in his path, turned to the music in his head, relied on his technique to manage the expanse of wood that operated as an ice rink.

What, then, could throw Trey Devereux off?

Desperation that manifested itself as self-doubt.

We drew Tango for our dance on, our weakest dance. Nothing we could do. Thirty-four was the second number called for the final. It was the way the chips fell.

It started off fine. We'd done the moves a thousand times, maybe more. We completed the long wall of striking poses and closed work before segueing into the short wall, a trajectory filled with tricks: a drop, a dip, and a drag where I unfolded my left leg across Trey's chest, which he caught and then leaned me into a split as I curled into a deep backbend.

Trey slipped during the drag. A slick square of parquet, a

rhinestone caught under his shoe, a bulb from the chandelier that shined in Trey's eye, I didn't know why except that it happened.

He'd slipped before. Even the sun slips on snow. The recovery is what mattered, and Trey always recovered, his mistake one dissonant note in a melody of sweet ones.

This time, he froze—a full stop.

Trey's eyes widened. His mouth trembled. His features paled and slackened. The mask had dropped. For the first time, Trey showed the world the petrified little boy he was. All thanks to a twist of genetics that had made him too beautiful for this dark world.

My heart ceased mid-thump. He was spooked.

A beat of music passed and then another, another, another.

For the first time ever in our partnership, I took the lead.

With superhuman effort and a prayer of gratitude for all the boot camp and yoga we'd done, I yanked myself from upside down to right side up. I improvised some quick flourishes with my arms and manipulated us into dance position.

"Open Reverse Turn, Lady Outside," I whispered into Trey's ear, but he didn't move. Our saving grace was that the music faded. I rolled myself out and bowed as Trey looked at me dazedly. I hooked my arm through his and guided him off the floor.

When we reached the safety of the carpet, away from the gimlet eyes of the judges, I turned to him and took the loose dance position we slept in.

"It's okay. It's okay," I whispered in his ear. Trey remained frozen against me as the third couple recalled to the final finished their Foxtrot, and the Master of Ceremonies announced the fourth couple.

I inhaled, my breath rattling like cold wind through a shattered window. I stayed in dance position but looked into his eyes. They were glassy and unfocused. He was somewhere far, far away from here, from me.

I took his cheeks in my hands and tugged his face until we were nose to nose. His eyes wouldn't meet mine.

"We're at Nationals. We have to dance soon."

Nothing.

I tried again. "Trey, it's Carly. We're at Nationals. We have to dance soon."

Nothing.

My legs were quivering, and my teeth were chattering. If Trey didn't come back, then we were not dancing the final.

The Master of Ceremonies was recalling the fifth couple to the round. I had to do something.

I wrapped my arms around him and yanked his body, stiff and unyielding, to mine. I brought my mouth close to his ears.

"I will never let anyone hurt you," I said over and over as a Waltz, romantic and melancholic, reverberated around us.

Then there was one last couple to be recalled to the final, Jorge and Nina, also dancing Tango. A lucky draw where Jorge's footwork wasn't quite as offensive and Nina's arms registered as forceful rather than stiff.

I spun Trey around so he could watch and then I slipped in front and to the side of him, shadow position. In his ear, I whispered, "I love you."

Something—the music, Jorge and Nina, my recitation of love—roused him, and he shook himself.

"Carly?" he asked.

"We're about to dance the last round at Nationals."

"We have to win."

"I know."

He reached for my hand and kissed it, and then the Master of Ceremonies asked everyone to the dance floor for the final.

Chapter 45

NINA: THE LAST POSE

I DON'T KNOW if we danced well in the final. I do know that we danced with our hearts hanging out of our chests. I told Jorge everything: how much I loved him, how thankful I was to have danced with him, how sorry I was that we didn't meet years earlier when we were agile and untouched by life.

He told me the same, and we danced the way we'd learned to dance with each other, always helping because we were on each other's team. In Waltz, he saved me when I overshot a lunge. I held him back when he tried to depart a Chasse From Promenade, a rolling hill of a step, with a heel that would likely kerplunk.

"Let me," he said when I wobbled in Tango during a pose where my leg pierced the air. He steadied me, and we were back on track.

"Let me," I said when he rose and fell too much in Foxtrot. I steadied him, and we were back on track.

Then it was almost over. Viennese Waltz. Our best dance after Tango thanks to the happily-ever-after narrative and the lack of dramatic rise and fall, which hid Jorge's footwork problems. Jorge positioned us near Trey and Carly, a strange choice since we usually started far away from them. A silent gentleman's agreement. We did our thing, and they did theirs.

But Jorge had forced the issue. We were going to compete head on, win it fair and square. We started in front of them, the ballroom dancer's version of higher ground. Then I stopped paying attention to them and refocused on us. I told Jorge over and over through every pose and each pace what I'd known since our tryout but had been too scared to say.

I love you.

He understood me because during our last pose, Jorge on his knee, my hand clasped in his, he whispered, "I love you, Nina."

The music was dying.

But I was soaring.

Chapter 46

CARLY: VIENNESE WALTZ

WE DANCED SUBLIMELY: Waltz, Tango, Foxtrot, each movement expanded to its maximum potential, each action scoured clean of technical debris. I lost my humanness and became a celestial being, the moon to Trey's sun.

Then Viennese Waltz. One-hundred seconds, plus or minus, of circles, rotating left before right, right before left, all traveling counterclockwise around the Line of Dance.

Jorge and Nina, by tacit agreement, usually chose a starting position at the opposite end of the floor from us. It was good for them and good for us. Their technical flaws didn't register quite as profoundly when executed away from Trey's brilliance, and our more subdued performance wasn't overshadowed by their profuse emotion.

For this Viennese Waltz, they set up to our left and a little in front us—claiming Line of Dance for themselves. Not ideal, but manageable since we had several opening poses that would buy us time until they moved.

The music started and we started, but we couldn't get going. Jorge and Nina were in our way at every moment. When we wanted to travel, they stayed in place. When Trey pivoted us to a new direction to avoid running into them, they went the same way. At one point, they'd boxed us into a corner so tightly that we were forced to sway side to side, like a couple of high-schoolers at prom.

Finally, we got far enough away from them to open up into our routine, but it was too late.

The music was dying.
And so was I.

Chapter 47

NINA: IN MY MOTHER'S FOOTSTEPS

WE WON!

Jorge and I won Nationals, two ethnic kids from the outer boroughs. When they called the results for second, I knew.

Rule Eleven had decided the event, but who cared.

Jorge grabbed me, and we hugged as Trey and Carly went to collect their silver medals. Tears spilled down both of our cheeks, and I couldn't catch my breath, too overwhelmed by the enormity of the moment. Then Papa announced it, validating the champagne of joy that was jetting through my body.

"Placing second in Waltz, first in Tango, second in Foxtrot, and first in Viennese Waltz, from New York, New York, couple fifty-two: Jorge Gonzales and Nina Fortunova."

Jorge clasped my hand and hiked it high in the air as cheers detonated throughout the ballroom. The next few minutes were a blur of kisses and congratulations and gold medals draped around our necks.

For this one glorious moment, Jorge and I existed in the space and time where we were the best. We'd written ourselves into the future. After pictures were completed, Jorge and I walked off the dance floor and stood for a moment, holding hands as we drank in the moment.

I turned my head to the right. My mother, born in Moscow, and Jorge's mother, born in San Juan, were bawling into tissues. Neither of them spoke much English, but winning was a universal language.

I turned my head to the left. Maxine was bouncing on her toes as she collected congratulations from those around her. It was her win just as much as it was ours.

I turned my head into the ballroom. People were applauding and cheering and raising their glasses to us.

I turned my head toward Jorge. He was muttering a prayer of gratitude through the exultant tears that were still streaming down his cheeks.

I turned my head to the dais. Papa was smiling. Then he met my gaze and nodded.

No, no, no, no, no. Freezing rain fell on the firecrackers of my happiness.

I turned my head toward the door of the ballroom. I wanted to run out of it and back to the time when I told Papa I wanted his help.

Trey was at the door, his hand clasped around Carly's wrist as she fought back tears. He flung open the door and towed her out behind him.

Jason, his suit jacket flapping, was chasing after them, his jaw set.

I turned back to Papa. Maybe I'd misunderstood. I held my breath and cocked my head toward him. He nodded again, this time more emphatically.

I gasped silently.

Jorge slung his arm around me. "We did it."

No, we didn't.

"We did." I strove for the tenor of a champion, overjoyed and munificent, but my words sounded thin and unconvincing.

Jorge stepped back.

"I'm just overwhelmed," I said as an explanation, adding some fullness to the words so they rang true.

He kissed the top of my head. "We're going to have some major celebrating to do."

I burrowed into his side, and for a moment, I forgot everything except how much joy our partnership had brought me.

Then I turned my gaze back to the dais. Papa was getting up, his eyes fixed on me.

I nudged Jorge. "Go tell Maxine thank you. I'll talk to Papa." I walked to the door, mechanically accepting the well wishes that rebounded off me.

Papa found me by the door. "Congratulations."

"Thank you."

"Are you grateful?"

"I am," I said, choking on the fear that had misted up from the bottom of my belly.

"There are a lot of people who want to congratulate you. But I know you're going to let Papa express his admiration first." He smiled at me, showing off his pointed incisors slippery with saliva.

I flinched. I felt caught in a fairy tale. I was the character who'd failed to understand the ramifications of her bargain with an unsavory cad. Unlike a fairy tale, there'd be no prince to save me. I was on my own, and I was no match for the wolf determined to collect his end of the bargain.

"What's your room number?"

I didn't say anything, just looked at him with big, pleading eyes.

"What's your room number?" he asked, his tone a cold caress. "You promised that Papa could be the first to express his admiration." He leaned toward me. "You remember, don't you?" He said the last as a statement rather than a question. Then he gazed at me meaningfully. "You had nothing to lose, and you won everything."

I recited it, almost inaudibly as I remembered how Papa had talked me into trying out with Jorge using similar words.

"Tell everyone you're going to change," he said. "You can meet them at the bar later."

"Okay," I said, as if I was begging for my life.

"I'm looking forward to this." He reached out a hand—the hands that would soon be touching the most intimate places of my body, the last of which were touched by Jorge—and stroked my forearm. Vomit pooled in the back of my throat as I understood what, exactly, I was about to do. I was going to betray Jorge, Maxine, and the entire system of ethics on which ballroom dancing was founded because my desire to win trumped everything.

I hated myself.

It doesn't have to mean anything, I told myself as I made my way to my room. *It won't mean anything. You will do it, and then he will leave. No one will know. He won't tell, and you definitely won't.*

Once in my room, I executed the actions of changing like a computer program.

I took off my medal and placed it on the console table. I took off my dance shoes and tossed them by the bed. I took off the black ball gown and hung it up. I took off my makeup and applied a light moisturizer. I took off the rhinestone comb that had held my topknot in place and ruffled my hair with my fingers.

All the while, my feelings were reeling.

My mother had come to the United States, so I could have a better future. She'd literally prostituted herself, so her daughter could become a champion. And now that champion was going to prostitute herself.

The apple didn't fall far from the tree, I thought grimly as Papa rapped on the door.

I tossed on the black satin cocktail dress I planned to wear to the bar, carefully chosen to evoke the gown I'd worn for the final.

Maybe I could talk him out of it? The thought lit up again and again like a firefly, a bright dot of hope in the darkness of reality.

"Nina," he said when I opened the door. "What a quick-change artist you are."

I let him pass as my mind scrambled for an excuse, any excuse, to put this off or, even better, not to do it. Ever.

He walked to the console table and picked up my medal. "Gold," he said. "The color of champions."

I opened my mouth to say something, anything, but no sound emerged.

"Come here," Papa said.

I somehow made my body take the dozen steps to him.

"You aren't having second thoughts, are you? You wouldn't make poor Papa go downstairs and tell them there's been a mistake, would you?"

I shook my head.

Papa smiled as I recoiled. "I didn't think so." He placed a finger on my lips. "Shh," he whispered. "It's just between you and me."

I nodded.

"Turn around," he said.

I pivoted. He slowly dragged the zipper down. My flesh pricked to the cold air and the hard truth of the situation. The dress fell to the floor, and I waded in its slippery black pool.

Papa lifted my hair and planted a kiss on the back of my neck. Then, as I shivered in shame, he kissed each vertebra. When he got to the small of my back, he stopped. For a brief moment, a firefly flickered, and I thought he'd come to his senses.

He placed something over my head. A cool metal circle slapped against my naked chest. It was my Nationals medal. I ran my fingers around its circumference. I'd worked hard for it, but I hadn't been good enough to win it outright. So I was going to pay the tax of a loser.

My mother's words boomed in my head. *Second chances come with high price tag, zolotse.*

I flinched at the rustle of a coat being removed, the pop of a button, the metallic scrape of a zipper being pulled down.

No, no, no, no, no. I fought back terrified tears.

Papa placed a hand on my shoulder and spun me to face him. I looked down as my hair drifted in front of my eyes, a blackout shade from which I refused to peek.

"I've waited a long time for this," he said. "I remember the first time I saw you. Long Island. A small competition. You were all of eighteen. You wore a pale yellow dress and had a rose in your hair." He brushed his hand against my locks. "You were beautiful and full of life. 'That's a special girl,' I thought to myself."

I didn't look up.

"For years and years, I'd attended competitions, watching couples dance, and I had yet to see anyone like you." He placed both his hands on my cheeks and lifted my face until it was inclined toward his, my hair falling back to my ears. "You still are special. I've enjoyed watching you grow up from a beautiful girl to the beautiful woman you are now."

He kissed me. I didn't respond.

He pulled back. "Let's try that again. Think about how grateful you are to Papa. How happy you are to be a champion."

It's choreography, I told myself. Nothing more, nothing less. Go through the motions. They do not require emotion to be effective.

So I banished my heart and soul to somewhere far from here and became a body. I followed the steps: a hand here, a head there, flexion in the knees, extension of the arms. I attended to the rhythm, a few slows and then all quicks. I varied my alignment: facing Line of Dance, backing Line of Dance, pointing Diagonally to the Wall. I swung and swayed, a professional skilled in the figures of lovemaking.

Finally, thankfully, it was over. Papa collapsed on top of me, breathing heavily into my ear. His noisy sucks of air prevented me from hearing the door open between my room and Jorge's.

My hands rushed to my mouth as I half-screamed, half-wailed. How could I have been so stupid? I hadn't locked the door between my room and Jorge's. It'd been second nature for so long to leave the door unlocked that I'd stopped thinking about it.

He walked in, swinging a bottle of champagne from one hand and two glasses from the other.

"Plenty of people are waiting to buy us drinks, but I thought we could . . . " his voice trailed off and his grin, full of promise, turned into a pucker of confusion as he saw, and then comprehended, what was happening.

"It's not what it looks like," I cried.

Jorge, mouth now agape, backed into his room as the bottle of champagne and two glasses slipped from his fingers. I winced at the thud and then the back-to-back cracks as our celebration shattered against the floor. Then my heart followed, tumbling to the pit of my stomach where it smashed against my regret and self-hatred.

Because it was exactly what it looked like.

Chapter 48

CARLY: CHOOSING

WE LOST.

When they called the results, my muscles froze into shocked, rigid hunks of meat. Trey stiffened and gasped before regaining his composure. He pushed me forward.

We collected the check that would not be enough, dropped the silver medals around our necks where they hung like anchors, kissed the other couples, posed for pictures with the finalists. All the while, we acted as if nothing was wrong with second place, that it wasn't going to impact the rest of our lives.

Finally, it was over, and we walked off the floor, my thoughts careening in concentric circles.

The largest, slowest circle: *How did we lose?*

The middle, faster one: *It was all my fault.*

The small, tight one where my anxiety spun, a roulette wheel in a tizzy: *I'm going to lose Trey.*

My eyes burned from holding back the tears that threatened to stream down my cheeks. Trey needed me to succeed, and I'd failed. Massively. I wanted to throw myself at his feet, beg for his forgiveness, offer my help in any way I could.

Please let me stay with Trey. It was the only thought that mattered.

Trey, his hand a vise-grip on my wrist, dragged me out of the ballroom and then down the hall, his fingers biting into my flesh. I struggled to keep up. My high heel caught in my skirt, and I stumbled. He yanked me up.

"Walk, Carly," he said. We reached the elevators, and I slowed down. No one was around. They were all in the ballroom congratulating Jorge and Nina.

Trey wrenched my arm. "Keep going." I couldn't hold the tears back, and they spurted down my cheeks.

He hauled me down a long hallway until we got to a door to the stairs. He threw it open and then pushed me through. Trey let the door slam behind him, but someone or something caught it before it banged shut.

"Where are you taking her?"

Jason stepped through the door. He appeared pale against the darkness of his suit, but his voice was mellow and steady.

Trey ignored him. "Walk, Carly."

I placed a foot on the bottom stair and groped for the railing.

"I can solve your problems, Trey" Jason said. "In return, I want one thing."

Trey looked over his shoulder at Jason. "What do you know about my problems?"

"Enough."

Trey released me. Without his support or the railing to hold onto, I crumpled to the floor. I folded my knees to my chest and buried my head in them. Then I collapsed against Trey, the one thing I cared about in this stupid quest to win Nationals. My piercing wails boomeranged around the stairwell.

Please don't let me lose Trey, I prayed over and over as Jason said something to Trey. My sobs were too noisy for me to catch it.

Trey said something about cotillion.

Cotillion? I thought wildly. *Why are they talking about cotillion?*

I buried my face in Trey's leg. *I love you. I will do anything to keep you.*

"Carly." Jason loomed above me. So many tears blurred my vision that it looked like he was melting. "You're coming with me."

He gently placed his hands under my armpits and lifted me to standing. My knees buckled, but Jason snaked an arm around me. "We're going to walk, one step and then another. We'll do it in a social Foxtrot rhythm: Slow, Slow, Quick, Quick."

"I'm not going anywhere without Trey," I said.

Jason opened the door and helped me through it. "Where's Trey?" I shrieked. "I want Trey."

"He's behind you, Carly." I looked over my shoulder. Trey was slumped against the wall, still impossibly good-looking even in defeat, his mouth a small *o* and his eyes blank with shock.

I locked my knees and pushed Jason's arm off of me. "I'm not leaving without Trey."

Jason sighed. "Tell her," he said to Trey.

Trey didn't say anything.

"Tell her," Jason said, his volume rising. "Tell her!" he yelled. "Now."

"Go, Carly," Trey said, all the honey evaporated. He turned and sprinted up the stairs, his hair almost iridescent under the fluorescent light.

Jason guided me through the door and then let it slam behind him. "Off we go." He used a doggedly cheerful tone.

He led me through the hotel and into a waiting limousine. "Home," he said to the driver. "As fast as you can."

I curled in a ball on the floor of the limo. "Trey," I whispered over and over. "I want Trey."

The car stopped.

"Here we are," Jason said. "Just a few more steps."

He helped me out of the car and half-carried me into the building. I was still wearing the white ball gown that, just a few hours earlier, had marked me as Trey's bride-to-be. Now streaks of makeup and smudges of dirt grimed the dress. I was a soiled, left-at-the-alter bride because of my blazing incompetence.

In the lobby, Jason spoke to the concierge on duty. "Do not send anybody up to my apartment—I mean anybody—unless you have spoken to me personally. Make sure the doormen know too."

I shivered. Menace chilled Jason's usually warm timbre.

He pulled me into the elevator, which a moment later opened into his apartment. "You're going to stay with me for a few days."

"What about Trey? Where is Trey?" I screamed. "I want Trey." I finished in the pitiful squeak of a mouse caught in a trap.

Jason's nostrils flared. "Trey knows you're with me. He wants you here."

He led me down a hall and opened a door. "This is where you'll be staying."

I trudged into the room, too tired to notice anything except the large bed blanketed with a midnight-blue duvet. I wanted to dive under the covers and never come out.

Jason pointed to another door. "Bathroom is right there."

I sank into the bed. I was still wearing my dance shoes, which were now ruined. With a trembling hand, I pushed the strap through the dainty, rectangular buckle. I lifted the strap from the spoke and then slid it through the buckle. Reaching down, I pulled off the shoe. For the other shoe, I grabbed the heel with the toes of my other foot and wrenched it off.

I fell back onto the bed, weeping. I couldn't manage washing my face, pulling the pins from my hair, taking a shower to cleanse the sweat and failure stinking up my body. As for the ball gown, I didn't have anything else to wear. My crying stopped for a moment as the reality of the situation hit me. I didn't have anything with me. No money, no clothes, no phone, no identification, no nothing. Just my ruined dress, which belonged to the dressmaker.

"You can have whatever you need. Food, a drink of water, pajamas," Jason said. "You're in a delicate emotional state, so I'm staying with you tonight. I have to take care of some urgent business tomorrow, so my assistant will be here then. We'll reassess in a day or so."

"Trey," I said. "I need Trey."

Jason didn't acknowledge me.

I rolled myself to a sitting position and stared at him with wild eyes. "Please, Jason. I have to see Trey."

He pulled back the covers to the bed. "What you need is some sleep."

For the next forty-eight hours, Jason or his assistant sat quietly in a chair and kept a watchful eye turned toward me. He offered me food and made sure there was a glass of water within easy access of the bed. He didn't say anything for which I was grateful.

I burrowed beneath the covers in my destroyed ball gown and bawled. Every time, the tide slowed, I would remember that we'd lost Nationals and I'd lost Trey, and the torrent would recommence.

"Where's Trey?" I asked Jason again and again.

He'd only say, "It's okay now."

Two mornings after Nationals, Jason woke me up. I'd finally drifted off to sleep, my hands clutched to my heart.

He placed a glass of orange juice on the nightstand. "Good morning."

"Where's Trey?" I struggled to a sitting position, fighting my legs free from the dress, which had knotted itself around my body. My hair had loosened from its upsweep, and filthy hanks of it dangled around my face.

Jason sat beside me on the bed. "Trey won't be contacting you."

"He dumped me?" I whispered. I wanted to cry, but I'd used up all my tears.

Jason's eyes brightened as if he was pleased about something. "It's for the best."

I gripped his hand. "You have to help me, Jason. Help me get to him."

Jason removed his hand. "I won't do that."

"Please," I said and then added with a soft, broken plea. "I'll do anything."

He shook his head. "Absolutely not. He was a manipulative, controlling creep, and he was sucking you dry."

Jason passed me the glass of orange juice. "Drink. You'll feel better."

I drank the juice, sweet sunshine with scraps of pulp that clung to my tongue.

Jason was right. I did feel better. Buoyed by the sugar and citrus, my brain kicked into high gear. If Jason wouldn't help me, then I would help myself.

I scanned the room, searching for a phone or a computer, anything that I could use to get in touch with Trey. There was nothing.

Jason followed my eyes. "Let it go, Carly. He's gone."

I won't let him be gone.

"Today you're going to rediscover the pleasures of living." He pushed a bag in my direction. "My assistant picked out some clothes. If they don't fit, tell me and we'll figure something out."

The bag held blue jeans, a red t-shirt, black flats—normal people clothing.

"We'll go for breakfast as soon as you shower and get dressed. We're going to have fun." He smiled at me. "You could use some."

I showered and got dressed. I trailed a finger around the stiff fabric of the denim waistband. I hadn't worn jeans since moving to Charleston. Trey and I always dressed up, even when we traveled.

My heart wobbled. *Trey.* I had to get to him. To apologize, to throw myself at his feet, to beg him to take me back.

Jason led me into the elevator. "Pancakes or eggs?"

"Whatever."

"Your choice. Pancakes or eggs?"

"I don't care."

"Choose, Carly," he said in a steely tone. "Pancakes or eggs?"

"Pancakes?"

We went to a '50s-style diner that specialized in comfort food. To my surprise, I finished a stack of pancakes drizzled with maple syrup. It'd been ages since I'd had eaten anything beyond an omelet for breakfast, and I'd forgotten how good slabs of fluffy carbohydrates could be.

Jason kept up a steady stream of innocuous conversation—the weather, tabloid gossip, the new condo building planned for his block—that required little participation from me beyond a word or two. When he spied my empty plate, his lips curved upward.

"It's been a year since you left New York. Anything you've missed and want to do?" he asked.

"I don't know." I threw my hands up. "Even when I lived here, I never did anything except dance." As soon as I said the word dance, my heart dropped. A few more marks in our favor, and I would be in Charleston, planning my wedding, rather than gallivanting around New York with Jason.

"Then you need to make up for lost time."

We went to the Empire State Building. I thought I would hate it, but the high vantage point made it fun to look down on New York, all the enormous buildings rendered tiny and inconsequential. Then we walked the entirety of the Highline under a sky varnished robin's egg blue. There were people everywhere, chatting on phones, laughing with friends, chasing after children.

The last few months, Trey and I'd followed an inflexible triangle of home, airport, hotel. I'd forgotten how enlivening it was to share space and time with other people in an aimless, amicable way.

Trey.

I had to get to him. If we could take dance position, then I could make things right. I had no money, though, and no way to get to him. Jason had to change his mind. But how could I make him understand?

Jason was a kind companion. At every turn he asked me to choose—chocolate or vanilla, cone or cup, one scoop or two (a single chocolate cone), but he required nothing from me in the way of conversation.

"Burgers or pizza?" he asked.

I knew better at this point than to deflect the question.

"Burgers," I said, and he steered me to a high-end burger joint. Too exhausted to peruse the menu, I ordered the same thing as Jason.

The waiter clanked down a glass of beer in front of me, and I took a sip. I hadn't had alcohol in months. Trey rarely drank due to his father's death from liver disease, which meant I didn't drink since I did whatever Trey wanted. I took another sip of the beer. I'd forgotten what beer tasted like, frothy and bitter.

"Thank you for putting a smile on my face," I said.

"My pleasure." Jason dug into his burger.

I took a bite of mine. Red meat, another thing I hadn't had in ages. I chewed slowly, savoring the fatty, earthy flavor.

Jason put down his burger. "We need to talk about a couple of things."

"Okay," I said uncertainly.

"Do you own things you've bought for yourself? Clothes, books, a phone? Even a magazine or some hair clips?"

I nibbled on my lip. It was a weird question. "I have stuff at my parents' house in Ohio, and I left a box with Nina when I moved to Charleston."

"How about in Charleston? What about your makeup or your dance shoes? Did you buy a postcard from one of the cities you visited?"

"Everything was provided for me. When I ran out of something or it broke, a new one would be delivered."

I'd stopped using Trey's name since Jason got agitated whenever I mentioned him. And since my sole goal was to get back to Trey, a journey that would have to be funded with Jason's money, I wanted to keep Jason in good spirits.

"So nothing in Charleston?"

"I had a phone, but I couldn't get a signal, so I stopped using it." I hesitated, trying to remember where I'd put it. "I'm not sure where it is now."

Jason exhaled. "You don't think that's strange, going an entire year without buying yourself one thing?"

"I guess I'm a minimalist," I said. "I never wanted for anything."

"Do you have a bank account?"

"Maybe . . . I had one in New York, but there weren't any branches in South Carolina. Then my bank merged with another bank, and I sort of lost track of where my account went."

"Did you have any money in there?"

"A little," I said. "I spent everything I made on dancing."

I'd planned to track the account down after Nationals. Use it to help pay for the wedding or the baby.

"So you went an entire year as a working adult not making a single deposit or withdrawal?"

I nodded.

Jason leaned across the table. "Do you know how much money I have?"

I played with a French fry. "Um, a lot?" I took a bite of the fry, twitching with discomfort at Jason's line of questioning. He was trying to get at something, but I couldn't figure out what it was.

"I have more than you can imagine. I have so much that I can't possibly spend it in my lifetime. Even if I lost all my money, I could make it back and then some."

I placed my fry back on the plate. "Okay?" With my finger, I twirled the fry in a circle.

"I'm going to give you some. It will seem like a vast sum to you, but I can assure you, that to me, it's the equivalent of buying a cup of coffee."

"That's generous of you, Jason, but I can't take your money."

"The money is a thank-you present. When my wife died, I died too. Dancing—dancing with you—brought me back to life. It gave me something to look forward to every day. I never was very good, even with all your efforts, but we always had a grand time on our lessons." He paused. "Thank you, Carly."

I opened my mouth to protest.

Jason held up his hand. "I'm giving you the money. I've always had to pay someone else for the lessons, first the Castle and then . . . " He scowled. "Point being, I'm giving you the money. If you feel you need to work for it, that's fine. Give me a lesson, cook dinner, alphabetize my bookshelf, I don't care. Tomorrow we'll open an account for you."

"Thank you." My stomach bounced up and down. As soon as I had cash in hand, I was getting on the first plane to Charleston.

Jason read my thoughts. "There's a caveat."

I cocked my head toward him.

"You must cut off all contact with Trey. You will not see him, you will not call him, you will not write him, you will not even look him up online. If you do any of those things, I will close the account and deny you access to the money."

My shoulders collapsed into my ribs. What was the point of having money if I couldn't use it to get back to Trey?

"Otherwise, you can spend the money any way you see fit. Visit your family in Ohio, go shopping, set yourself up in an apartment." He ate a fry. "You're welcome to stay with me for as long as it takes to get your life in order. You can come and go as you please." He gazed at me, his jaw firm. "The same caveat applies. No Trey. If you try to contact him, I will throw you out on the streets."

Jason's eyes bored into mine. "Do you understand?"

I nodded.

"One last thing. I want you to see a therapist. You've been through a lot this year, so much so that I don't think you understand the magnitude of it."

I tuned him out. Maybe I could get the therapist to talk to Jason and make him understand how I had to get back to Trey. Trey needed me.

"The choice is yours, Carly."

A couple of days later, I went to see a therapist—Louise Gelman. She sported a corporate pantsuit in lipstick red and gold-rimmed glasses that reminded me of the ones Cyrus wore.

I smiled, confident that I could make her see things from my side. "Trey treated me like a princess," I said as my opening argument.

As I talked about happy I'd been with Trey, she scribbled down copious notes. Occasionally, she stopped me to clarify a fact.

"You ate three meals a day alone in your room? And these meals were brought to you on a tray?"

"With a flower in a bud vase!" I said.

"You never went anywhere alone? Not even to walk around the block by yourself?"

"Trey escorted me everywhere. He was the perfect gentleman!" I said.

"You never handled money even though you were earning some from teaching and competing? Not even to buy yourself a cup of coffee?"

"Trey made sure I had everything I could ever want!" I said.

When I got to the end, I made my closing statement. "I was so happy with Trey. The happiest I'd ever been."

I looked at her expectantly, sure I'd convinced her that the best thing for me to do was get on a plane back to Trey.

She peered at me through her glasses and asked, "Have you heard of Stockholm syndrome?"

Chapter 49

NINA: THE CONFESSION

THE SILVER HAIR and three-piece suit disappearing into the elevator were unmistakable.

"Jason!" I yelled.

I was going to be late for my lesson, but the students could wait. Vadim wasn't teaching this hour, so maybe he'd take pity on them and start the lesson.

Jason looked over his shoulder, and his eyes widened. I shoved my hand in the elevator to keep the doors from shutting.

"Don't move," he said. "They'll open in a second."

The doors slid open, and I stepped into the elevator.

"Nina," he said. "It's nice to see you." His tone was polite, but he avoided my eyes. "Going to four, I presume?" He punched the button.

"Later," I said. "I'll ride up with you."

Jason pressed his lips together and crossed his arms.

I smiled at him, baffled by his coldness. Jason had always been friendly.

"Do you know where Carly is?" I asked.

The elevator pinged for four.

"This is you," he said.

I didn't move. "Do you know where Carly is?"

The elevator doors closed.

Jason sighed. "Does this have to do with Trey?"

I blinked. "With Trey?" I paused. "Not really. It's about Nationals."

"Carly doesn't care about that anymore." He turned his eyes toward the numbers lighting up.

So he did know where she was.

"I need to talk to her," I said.

The elevator pinged for twelve. Jason exited, and I followed. Although it was late January, some of the offices still had Christmas wreaths on their doors—last guests who refused to leave a party that had ended long ago.

"Jason, please," I said as he walked ahead, ignoring me. "I have Carly's gold medal."

He stopped and turned. "Her gold medal?"

I nodded. "It was declared a tie the next day."

"Does Trey know this?"

I nodded. "Cyrus brought him the medals when Trey wouldn't pick up the phone. Cyrus said that Carly wasn't with Trey anymore. No one knew where she went or how to get in touch with her, so Cyrus passed her medal onto me. He told me that I had a better chance of giving it to her than Trey or he did."

Jason wrinkled his brow as if he was debating whether to tell me where she was.

"Have you spoken to Trey since Nationals?" His eyes were narrowed, his gaze intent.

"No one has talked to Trey since Nationals except Cyrus. The last time I saw him was after the awards ceremony when he was dragging Carly out the door." I played with the fringe on my scarf. "Is she okay, Jason? I was worried about her last year. Trey kept her on an awfully short leash."

He exhaled. "Carly's fine." A huge smile cracked across his face. "She's better than fine."

"That's great," I said. "Could you put me in touch with her? I'd like to give her the medal and explain a few things."

"She has some news of her own."

"Where is she?"

"She's with me," he said, his eyes starry. "Why don't you swing by this weekend? I have some business to attend to, and she'd enjoy the company."

On Saturday, I stepped off the elevator into Jason's palatial apartment. It was decorated in a modern aesthetic with boxy leather sofas and glass tables.

"Nina," Carly said, appearing from around a corner.

I extended my arms, and we embraced.

"Come. Sit." Carly gestured to a black leather sofa, but I stopped, blinded by the huge twinkle on her left hand.

"Is that . . ."

She held out her hand. A diamond the size and shape of a nickel rested on her fourth finger.

"That's some ring."

Carly giggled. "It's ridiculous, but Jason insisted."

"Congratulations." I gave her another hug.

I plopped down on the sofa. Carly sat down next to me and pulled her legs up.

"Thank you," she said. "That's not my only news."

I tilted my head toward her.

"I'm pregnant. I'm due at the beginning of September." Her cheeks were blooming like roses.

Very pretty, I thought, remembering how I'd debated whether Carly was plain or pretty. The matter had been decided. Carly was lovely.

"You've been busy since Nationals," I said. "So Jason's the one?"

She combed her fingers through her hair. "I was in a bad place after Nationals. Trey needed to win, and I let him down." Her voice was expunged of emotion.

I patted her shoulder.

"Jason was there for me. He gave me a place to stay and helped me get back on my feet," she said. "One night, we were making dinner together, and I thought—something I'd thought before—what a good husband he was going to make some lucky girl. That's when I realized I wanted that lucky girl to be me." She blushed. "So I kissed him."

I lifted my eyebrows. "I gather he returned that kiss."

"He did," she said. "He wanted to take things slow." She threw me a mischievous smile. "I didn't, so I . . . persuaded him." She hesitated. "It'd been a while."

"You and Trey . . . Weren't you together?"

"Trey is complicated," she said as an explanation.

"Were you okay? He really kept you under his thumb."

Her eyes filled with tears. "People broke him a long time ago. Trey didn't know any other way to be." She looked down, but not before I saw her eyes, which were blazing with ferocity, a momma lion that would do anything to protect her cub.

She might be marrying Jason and having his baby, but she was in love with Trey.

I flitted a finger toward her stomach. "Are you excited?"

She inhaled and recomposed her features. "Very."

"Were you trying?"

Her cheeks flamed. "We both knew what could happen although I didn't expect it to happen as quickly as it did," she said. "Jason was overjoyed. He proposed immediately and told me to design the future I wanted." Her eyes shifted to some papers that fanned across a glass end table, and I followed with my gaze.

Living rooms with high ceilings and crown molding, master bathrooms with Jacuzzi tubs, grassy tracts holding swing sets and sandboxes. Real estate listings.

"Are you moving?" I asked.

"To Westchester, so Jason can have an easy commute. I'm figuring out which town."

"I'm impressed with your calm. Especially with all these changes."

"Losing Nationals was the best thing that could have happened to me," she said in a bright, determined tone.

I reached into my purse and pulled out her gold medal. I placed it on the coffee table in front of her. "You didn't lose."

"What?" Carly's lips were parted, her eyes unfocused.

"It was declared a tie the day after. They tried to get in touch with you, but Trey wouldn't pick up his phone and everyone assumed you were with him."

"How did that happen?"

I took a deep breath. "Because of something I did."

"What could you have done?"

I didn't say anything for several long moments, just marinated in my shame and depravity. I took a slow breath.

"Papa had a thing for me," I said. "He'd had one for a long time. He offered to throw the competition in our favor if I would sleep with him."

I looked at my feet. "I was having excruciating arthritis in my knee, and Jorge had a labral tear in his hip. There was no way we could stick it out another year without gravely injuring one or both of ourselves."

Carly wrapped her arms around herself. Her hair hung in her face, a beige curtain obscuring the emotions zipping across her face.

"I wanted to win badly. Jorge and I were doing something different. We were different, kids of immigrants from the outer boroughs, and we wanted to inspire the next generation of dancers." I stopped for a moment. "I thought it was greedy of Trey to come back when he'd won three times. He was already a legend."

Carly lifted her head. "He needed to win, Nina. He wouldn't have come back otherwise." A tear and then another snaked down Carly's cheeks.

"I only knew what I knew, which is that I'd been working for thirteen years to win Nationals and this was my last chance." I gulped. "So I told him I would."

"It must have been close for Papa to throw it." Carly scrubbed the wetness from her face. "So close."

I nodded. "Papa insisted on collecting my side of the bargain immediately." I shuddered as images from that odious seduction tumbled through my head. "Jorge walked in on us," I said in a small, dead voice. "He told the judges."

"Why would he do that?"

"He wanted to win Nationals fair and square." I waited for the lump in my throat to shrink. "He was very ethical."

"Were you and Jorge . . . "

"We were heading in that direction. Everything was easy with him." I laced my fingers together. "During our last pose in Viennese Waltz, he said, 'I love you, Nina.'"

I breathed in and out a few times. I was not going to cry. Crying would not bring Jorge back, and it would not change my actions.

"Where is he now?"

"He went to San Francisco to be with his former partner. She has some mental health issues."

"I don't know what to say," Carly said.

"I do," I said. "Congratulations. You won Nationals."

"How did they prove Papa did it?"

"They couldn't. Papa had shredded the score sheets. Even I don't know if he threw the competition in our favor, or if he just told me he did. The Nationals committee had a meeting the next morning to discuss how to proceed. They considered having the judges resubmit their marks, but who would know if that's how they actually called the competition?" I swallowed. "They could change their marks to punish Jorge and me. So they decided the most principled thing would be to declare the competition a tie."

I came up for air.

"So we did win," Carly said to herself. She picked up the medal and traced the engraved surface with the tip of her pointer finger.

I jiggled my leg and then looked away. The heartbreak strangling Carly's features was causing me intense remorse. By deciding that my dream was more important than anybody else's, my actions had set off ripples far beyond my life.

"They fired Papa, and I got banned from competing, which was no loss since I was retiring anyway. He and Maxine moved to Boca Raton." My stomach sloshed with bile. I'd hurt a lot of people, but Maxine was the one I regretted the most. She'd been a phenomenal coach, and I repaid her by sleeping with her husband. "They're looking for a new Chairman of the Judges. Plus they're finally going to get with the times and invest in a computer, so nothing like this happens again."

"How are you holding up?" Carly asked. "It must have been awful after Jorge told."

I picked at the hem of my sweater. "It was worse than awful. I could barely get out of bed and go to work." I closed my eyes, remembering how terrible those days had been: the whispers from the staff at the Castle, people I knew and people I didn't know calling me a slut on ballroom dance forums, my mother crying, saying it was her fault. "I lost so much by winning."

Carly inched closer to me. She put her arm around me as tears, hot and swollen with regret, surged down my cheeks. "Shh," she crooned. "Shh."

I mopped up my tears. Her niceness made me feel even more guilty and contrite. "I'm sorry, Carly. If I could do it again, I would do it differently."

"Wouldn't we all?" she asked, her lips bowed with sadness.

She passed me a handful of tissues, which I wiped under my eyes, still sniffling.

"Is it better now?" she asked.

I shredded a tissue between my fingers. "Ralph stood up for me. He threatened to fire any staff member who gossiped about it. Then Vadim nominated himself as the enforcer. It helped me get my life back."

"Ralph was the most feminist misogynist I ever met," Carly said.

I laughed, and then we fell silent.

"Are you happy?" I asked. "For real?"

"I am," she said in that same bright, determined tone she'd used when she said losing Nationals was the best thing that could have happened. "Jason is wonderful, and we have so much fun together." She laid a hand on her stomach. "I'm going to be a mother. It's everything I wanted."

Liar, I thought although Carly had sounded convincing. *You wanted Trey Devereux, and this is what settling for second place looks like.*

I shifted my eyes around the apartment, noting the expensive art and the expansive view of Manhattan. Carly tucked a lock of hair behind her ear, the gargantuan diamond flashing from her finger. Really, second place wasn't that bad. Jason was a good man who'd bend over backward to make Carly happy.

I would take second place right now. I would have Jorge and my morality, and at this point, months after the event, I'd probably be happy. Jorge and I would drink tea and make love and discuss the future. I looked at Carly's belly, upon which her hand still rested. Maybe that future would have included a baby.

I shook my head. Gold had cost much more than it was worth. I longed to go back in time, so I could end up with silver.

"How did your parents react to the news?" I asked.

"They weren't happy. It meant I wouldn't ever be coming back to Ohio. But they came around when I told them that Jason wanted to set up a trust for Archer to make sure he gets the care he needs."

"That's promising."

"We're getting married on Valentine's Day. It's tacky, but the timing worked. My parents can't leave Archer, so we're flying out the day after to visit them over the long weekend. Jason is excited to meet Archer." She squeezed my hand. "I'd love it if you'd come to the wedding, Nina."

"I'll be there." And I would.

Carly smiled, her eyes happy.

"May I ask a question?" My curiosity, unrepentant and unchecked, reared up. I wanted to ask something rude.

"Shoot."

"Do you really look like his dead wife?"

Carly tittered. "See for yourself." She got up and walked across the room. She returned with a photo in a silver frame, which she handed to me. "Here you go."

The woman in the picture had the same coloring as Carly with ivory skin, long taupe hair, and brown eyes. But that's where the resemblance started and ended. This woman was short and curvy with a heart-shaped face and full lips. She wore an expression that reminded me of a pit bull.

I handed the picture back to her. "Ralph needs to get his eyes checked."

"Right? We both have light brown hair and dark brown eyes. As do millions of people around the world."

"I'm glad it worked out. Although I regret the role I played in it."

"It's crazy, isn't it? A few marks of the judge's pen in either direction, and we'd both be in different places."

"Who'd think a ballroom dance competition could matter this much?" I asked.

Chapter 50

CARLY: COTILLION

IT WAS NOON ON SUNDAY. Noon on Sunday had a routine. Grace's lunch and then her nap, which I would use for some much-needed studying.

Routines progressed me through space and time. One step in front of the other, each action connected to the hands of a clock. The music played on, my only job to stay with it.

The grief, powerful in its ability to turn trifles into enormities, asserted its presence. I'd been feeling better, but today, no different than yesterday with its blaring sun and unseasonably warm temperatures for March, the routine was proving to be a challenge.

I heaved myself off the sofa and into the kitchen as I went through the routine of making lunch in my head. Two slabs of bread, one disc of turkey, another of ham. A squiggle of mustard and then a streak of mayonnaise. A handful of carrots, an apple sliced in eighths. The plate arranged in a pleasing fashion, a square framed by sticks, a blocky sun.

"Mommy," Grace said, her pigtails swinging. "Look." She pushed a piece of paper festooned with scrawls in red, purple, and green at me. "It's you doing the laundry."

"You got my nose just right," I said, bending down to give her a kiss. She was tall for two and a half. "Shall we put it on the fridge?" She was so much like Jason, easygoing with twinkly eyes. Not for the millionth time, I wished he were around to watch his daughter grow up.

The grief had settled into my legs, now ponderous and ungainly.

Lift and place. Lift and place, I told my feet. Step like a Tango where weight changes are created without the drag of a heel or a toe across the floor.

"Ready for lunch?" I asked Grace as I reached into the cabinet for a plate. She'd run to the window and was staring outside.

"There's a man at the door."

"There is?" A knock—slow, quick, quick, slow—answered my question. Some dormant memory jumped but retreated before I could hold it in my mind.

Probably it was a delivery person with the groceries I'd ordered online. I dried my hands on my jeans and then opened the door with a face meant to be polite but not encourage chattiness.

I gasped. The hand I'd extended in anticipation of a package fell limply to my side.

Light blond hair and silvery eyes. The classical features of a Greek statue. Tall, slender, and impeccably formed. Still the best looking man I'd ever seen.

I sagged against the doorframe. "Trey." I gazed at him, forgetting to blink.

"It's good to see you, Carly."

"Who are you?" Grace had materialized by my side and was looking up at Trey, her eyes windows thrown wide open.

"I'm an old friend of your mama's."

I pushed myself off the doorframe and tried, but failed, to organize my thoughts into coherence. I'd banished Trey to the dusty bin of my memory, someone significant once but no longer, and I was ill equipped to see him on my doorstep.

"This is for you." He handed Grace a doll, an exquisite one with a cascade of golden curls and delicate features. She wore a satin dress of carnation pink with loops of darker pink ribbons.

"Give it back," I said, but Grace turned on her heel and ran off with it.

"Thank you," she called over her shoulder.

"May I come in?"

"I don't know."

"I'd like to talk. Just for a few minutes."

An image of the last time I saw Trey popped in my head. Me, in that bridal ball gown, looking over my shoulder at him, his mouth gaping slightly, his eyes blank, as Jason led me away to a new life.

I shuddered as I rethought all the thoughts from that horrible moment.

How did we lose?

It was all my fault.

And the most insistent, important one: *I'm going to lose Trey.*

He flashed me a dazzling smile, one that didn't reach his eyes, which looked bitter. "Please?"

I stood back to let him pass. "To your left."

He turned into the living room and settled himself on the sofa. I sank into a leather club chair next to him.

Trey pointed his chin at my outfit of jeans, boots, and a tank top. "You look like a college kid."

"That's what I am these days."

"You went back to school?"

"When my husband died . . . " I looked down and then back up at Trey. "I married Jason. I don't know if you knew that."

Trey pressed his lips together. "I heard." A muscle twitched in his cheek. "I'm sorry for your loss," he said in a wooden voice.

"After Jason died, I decided it was high time that I learned to stand on my own two feet instead of flitting from guy to guy only to end up alone. So I told my parents I wasn't ever moving back to Ohio and enrolled in classes to finish my degree."

"What are you majoring in?"

"Psychology. I want to be a counselor specializing in siblings of special needs children."

"I read that Jason donated a fortune to a drunk driving charity and another to autism research. How did he die?"

"He had a brain injury." I swallowed. "It was so unexpected. We went to Disney World for Grace's second birthday. He tripped and hit his head on a park bench. He was fine afterward, joking about all the dance lessons he'd taken and how he was still a klutz. That night, he had a massive headache. I finally talked him into going to the emergency room, but it was too late. He was gone by morning." I stared at my knees, remembering how I'd held Jason's hand, too stunned to cry, as his organs shut down one by one.

"How are you holding up?"

I pushed my fingers into the corners of my eyes. It'd been months, but I was still raw from Jason's death. "I have good days and bad days."

I looked for Grace. She was at the opposite end of the living room, sitting by the dining room table, reverently stroking the doll's hair. "Grace is a big comfort."

"How's Archer?"

"He's in a home, a good one. He got too big for my parents to manage," I said. "They visit him every day. I try to go out every couple of months when I'm on break from school."

He nodded.

"Did you sell the mansion?"

"A Russian oligarch bought it." Trey laughed without humor. "He thought antebellum was my family name."

I threw him a tentative smile.

"You've changed, Carly."

"I had to." I fiddled with a lock of hair. I hadn't cut my hair since Grace had been born save for the occasional trim, and it crested to the pockets of my jeans.

Trey stared at me with hungry eyes and slack cheeks, an expression at odds with the mask he'd worn in the past. I shivered and searched for something to say.

"You haven't," I said.

Trey was wearing his blousy gray pants and white dress shirt with the discreet monogram on the cuff.

"There was no reason."

I nibbled on my lip, uneasy, even more worried. I'd trained myself never, ever to think of Trey. It'd been the only way to move forward. Now, with him here, in my home, I didn't know if I'd be able to keep the memories at bay.

He leaned toward me. "What do you remember from the night of Nationals?"

"I don't want to rehash that."

"Please, Carly. It's important to me. So important that I tracked you down and flew up here."

I pulled my hair over one shoulder. "I don't remember much. We lost. I was devastated. We did the awards presentation with the other competitors. The whole time I was trying to think of how I could make it better."

"What about afterward?"

"You were enraged. You grabbed my wrist and pulled me down the hall." Tears were filling my eyes. I blinked them back to the past where they belonged. "It gets blurry at that point. I was crying so hard I couldn't see straight. I was terrified I was going to lose you."

My heart beat a tattoo against my chest, and all my desperate, twisted love for Trey that I'd I tamped down zoomed back up. "I did lose you," I whispered.

I inhaled and looked over at Grace. She was singing a song to the doll Trey had brought her. "Your name is Princess Pretty. Your name is Princess Pretty."

Trey paled. He was gripping the edge of the sofa. "Do you remember what happened next?"

"We got to the stairwell. Jason was there. You two had words, something about cotillion." I tugged on my earlobe. I'd never understood what that meant. "Then Jason took me to his apartment. That's all."

Trey drew his eyebrows together. "Cotillion?" he said to himself before smiling grimly. "A million."

I cocked my head at him. I had no idea what Trey was talking about.

"What did Jason tell you about me?"

"He said you'd dumped me. That you wouldn't be contacting me again."

"What did you do?"

"I begged him to help me get to you, but he refused." I met Trey's eyes. "He hated you. He thought you were controlling and manipulative."

I rubbed my hands over my jeans. "You were controlling and manipulative. Do you know that I never handled cash during our relationship, not even to buy a tube of lipstick for myself? I never ordered for myself in a restaurant. I never wore an outfit that you hadn't picked out. I drank my coffee the way you did. Everything I did, everything I said, was designed to please you."

Trey's spine rounded. "I thought you were happy, Carly. You said you were happy."

I pushed a hand against my heart, which was threatening to leap out of my chest. "I thought I was. But you treated me like your prisoner. I even ate three meals a day brought to me on a tray." I took a deep breath. "It wasn't normal."

"I'm not normal," he said softly.

"I know."

"Why Jason?"

"I wanted to kill myself after Nationals. Jason brought me back to life. He helped me. He loved me." I glanced over at Grace, who was still crooning to Princess Pretty. "And then he gave me something to live for. He only asked for one thing from me."

"What was that?"

"That I would never, ever contact you."

"And you agreed?"

"What choice did I have? I didn't even own the clothes on my back." My volume rose. "If I'd had enough money for a change of clothes and a bus ticket, I would have come back. Even if I couldn't make it all the way, I would have walked." I took a deep breath. "But you kept me on such a tight leash I didn't even have that." I shook with the effort to restrain my emotion.

He closed his eyes. "Carly," he whispered.

"Jason was good to me. He had me see a therapist." I glared at Trey. "She said I sounded like somebody who had Stockholm syndrome. You kept me so isolated and so dependent on you for everything from food to affection that I didn't realize I'd given you all my power and all my freedom."

In a broken, sad voice, I continued. "I had to be your perfect girl. If I wasn't, you'd cut me off and there'd be nothing I could do, nothing I would have to convince you otherwise. All I wanted was for you to reward me with a smile or a laugh or a few minutes of your time. Anything that would show that I had value to you beyond a means to your ends."

Trey placed his head, eyes still shut, in his hands

I did a quick check on Grace to see if our conversation had disturbed her. She was introducing Princess Pretty to Mr. Bear and Carrot, her favorite stuffed animals.

"Jason was a wonderful husband and a doting father. I miss him every day."

Trey had dropped his hands and opened his eyes, which were glittering. "So he never told you?"

"Told me what?" I sighed. "Let me give Grace her lunch." I ran to the kitchen and slapped together a sandwich and poured a glass of milk.

"Time to eat." I forced a light, cheerful demeanor as I slid the sandwich and milk in front of her.

She put Princess Pretty, Mr. Bear, and Carrot in a line in front of her. "Now we eat lunch."

"Be a good example to Princess Pretty and eat your sandwich."

I walked back to Trey. "I've had enough remembering for one day."

"I'll go once I tell you what I've come to tell you."

I dropped into the chair and brought my knees up to my chest.

"When we lost Nationals, I was not in my right mind. I'd hung all my hopes on winning, and when we lost, I didn't know what to do. I directed my anger at you, but I was angry with myself. I was too old, too tired to come back, but it was the only option I had."

"It's okay, Trey. I don't care anymore."

"Listen to me, Carly. Jason—that ridiculous man with his three-piece suits, corny jokes, and out-sized crush on you—sensed I was weak. He followed us."

He took a deep breath. "It is very hard for me to tell you what I'm about to tell you."

"Worse than training me to be your pretty little puppet in that decaying dollhouse?" I snapped. Then I softened my tone. "It's in the past."

"I only wanted to take care of you. Give you anything you could ever want."

I looked away, swiped at the tears brimming in my eyes, and then shifted my eyes back to Trey.

He pointed at Grace. "You are likely going to get upset when I tell you what happened in that stairwell."

I stood and walked to Grace. "Why don't you go get one of your other dolls to introduce to Princess Pretty?"

"Okay, mommy." She trotted off to her bedroom.

I waited until her pigtails disappeared around the corner. I made my way back to my chair, settled into it, and turned an expectant face toward Trey.

He took a shaky breath as he looked up at the ceiling and then back at me.

My heart lurched. I'd never seen Trey this unsettled.

"I sold you to Jason for a million dollars," he said.

Chapter 51

NINA: HOME

IT WAS 12:30 on a Sunday afternoon in March when I pushed open the glass door to The Vernon and Irene Castle School of Ballroom Dancing, an action I'd made thousands of times over the years. This day, though, it had special significance. The glass of the door, cold at first, warmed quickly in my eager hand.

The Castle had been my home for a decade and a half. Even when my life smashed apart, I'd always had the studio to depend on. But until today, I'd only been a renter. Now I was going to become an owner.

Ralph exited his office carrying a box that brimmed with loose papers, manila folders, and a few dance manuals.

"That's the last of it," he said.

"Do you need help?" I asked.

He shook his head. "There was less stuff than I thought there would be."

I studied Ralph. Red veins laced the whites of his eyes, and his words sounded clogged with sadness. I flicked my eyes to the trashcan. Crumpled tissues were piled high.

Bless his rapacious heart. Ralph had been crying.

"I'm gonna miss this place," he said.

"When do you leave for Florida?"

"Tomorrow." He rubbed his eyes. "Allergies," he said, his voice still stopped up.

"March brings out the worst of them," I said, playing along.

"The worst."

"Thank you for selling the studio to me," I said.

"I was glad to do it. You were the first teacher I hired. And one of the best. I know the Castle's in good hands."

Last year, Ralph had started having health problems. There was a scare with his prostate, and then his blood pressure went through the roof. He'd decided to sell the studio and move to Florida.

I'd approached him about buying it. It took some doing for me to put together the money, but I figured it out. I had savings thanks to Jorge's financial tips as did my mother, and Carly lent me the rest. She'd tried to make it a gift.

"If you hadn't taken me under your wing, I would be in Ohio, teaching special education," she said as she wrote out the check. "Instead, I've had all these incredible adventures."

"Thank you. You know I'll pay you back."

"I know you will." She hesitated. "But you don't have to."

"Stop by for a lesson. It's on the house."

She laughed, and we hugged.

Ralph had other interested parties with deeper pockets than me, but nostalgia won out.

"I got enough money. I'd rather see the Castle go to someone I know and like." He extended his hand for me to shake. I grasped Ralph's hand as internally I raised my eyebrows. His health scares had curbed his greed.

We made it official a few days earlier with the lawyers, and today we were doing the handoff of keys.

I patted Ralph on the shoulder. "We're going to miss you around here." I peeked at Ralph's EEE feet. "I've got some big shoes to fill."

"Lotta memories here," he said under his breath as he passed me the keys.

I clasped my hands around them, feeling their weight. I did have some big shoes to fill. Ralph had been a good boss.

I offered my hand to Ralph, who was looking distinctly teary. "How about a dance?"

We did some social Foxtrot, the kind beginners learn. It wasn't fancy, but it was fun. I'd danced with Ralph many times over the years, but I never stopped being amazed at how good he was even with his blocky body. We looped around the studio, jostling for space on the floor, which was packed with ghosts and memories.

Ralph hugged me. "Good-bye." He sniffled.

Alone but happy, I ambled around the studio. It'd been the backdrop for my entire adult life. Against its cream-colored walls, I'd loved and I'd lost; I'd struggled and I'd won. I'd grown up from an impetuous eighteen-year-old girl from deep Brooklyn to the woman I was now—Nationals champion and studio owner.

It'd been hard, harder than it needed to be, but I was still standing. Alone. I'd been too miserable for a long while to risk my heart again, and when I finally started feeling better, I'd been too busy organizing my finances in anticipation of buying the Castle.

My eyes snagged on the Castle's logo. *Step in to step out.*

It was the truth. Life, like dancing, required participation. Maybe once I got a handle on being the boss, I would step in to the dating pool, so I could step out of single life.

Ping.

It was the elevator. I scrunched up my face in surprise. It was Sunday. The studio was closed as were most of the offices in the building. I shrugged. It was probably Ralph, returning for something he'd forgotten.

I walked to meet him and then halted.

"Hey," Jorge said, pushing through the door with an easy smile.

My lips formed the word *hey*, but no sound came out. I drank him in. Still the same Jorge.

"Let me teach some lessons for you," he said.

I remained mute, unsure of what to say. Because I had so many things I wanted to say, and they were all crowding at the back of the throat, shoving and nudging to be the first thing I said.

Jorge shifted from side to side. "I can come back later if this is a bad time."

I swallowed all the things I wanted to say and said, instead, "Let me put on some tea."

Chapter 52

CARLY: THE RING AGAIN

"WHAT?" I shrieked. "You sold me? As if I was a piece of furniture you didn't want anymore?" I clapped a hand over my mouth, hoping Grace hadn't heard me.

Trey winced. "Technically, I sold the opportunity to contact you for a year."

"Where was I during this?" My hands were trembling as black specks swarmed in front of my eyes. I placed my hands on the armrests.

Breathe, I told myself. *In and out. Then in and out again.* Slowly, the specks receded, and my breath, still jumpy, returned.

"You were there but too undone to understand what was going on."

"And no one asked me what I wanted?"

Trey pinched the bridge of his nose, his eyes shut. "I'm sorry, Carly. I will never forgive myself."

"What did Jason say?"

"He asked how much money it would take for me to get out of your life for a while. I told him a million dollars," Trey paused. "I pulled the number from the sky. The whole thing felt surreal, like it was happening to someone else. In the real world, we'd won Nationals, and I was going to marry you."

An inadvertent laugh escaped. "And Jason agreed?"

"He didn't blink. He said to give him seventy-two hours. He did it in twenty-four," Trey said, his forehead in his hands. "I went upstairs, drank myself silly until I passed out, and then the next day, I caught the first flight to Charleston. The lawyer showed up that night with a cashier's check and a contract, which stated I would cease contact with you for a year."

My heart was clanging against my chest as I processed the information. My worth as a person had been quantified and agreed upon by two men who'd never thought to ask what I wanted. The information felt too enormous, too outrageous to hold in something as small as a body.

Trey pressed his pointer fingers to his temples. "I signed the contract and deposited the check," he said, the honey in his voice coddled.

"Is that even legal?" I half-screamed.

"I don't know. I came to my senses a few days later and contacted a lawyer. I'd already spent some of the money on the most immediate debts, but there was plenty left. I wanted to give it back, get you back."

"What did the lawyer say?'

"He thought the whole thing was hilarious. He told me, 'You've got yourself a million bucks, buddy. Good-looking guy like yourself, the lady will wait,'" Trey said. "I could've fought it, but I didn't have the resources that Jason had." He sighed. "So I waited it out." He gazed at me as my heart hiccuped. "You can't imagine how much I regret that now."

Grace appeared at the bottom of the stairs, clasping a rag doll in a prairie dress.

"Which doll did you get, sweetie?" I asked, striving for my typical mom manner.

"Sally."

She showed me, and I smoothed Sally's yarn hair down.

"Princess Pretty is going to love her," I said as Grace rushed back to Princess Pretty. I waited a moment to make sure nothing had spooked her before turning my attention back to Trey.

"When did you find out about Nationals?" I asked.

"A couple of weeks later. Cyrus phoned me a few times, but I refused to take the calls. He finally drove down to tell me the news in person." Trey swallowed. "Cyrus was livid when I told him what I'd done. He didn't speak to me for over a year."

"Why?" I crinkled my forehead. Cyrus had been so devoted to Trey.

"He thought with you by my side, I had a chance at happiness, at normalcy."

"Did he know? About the . . . "

"He guessed. It happened to him."

I inclined my head.

"His stepfather," Trey replied to my silent question. "He ran away at sixteen. He cleaned the floors at a dance hall and slept in the coat room." He smiled sadly. "The world is lousy with boys like us."

I stared at my feet.

"I fear my hasty decision hastened Mama's decline. She'd gotten attached to the idea of a grandchild, and when she found out that wasn't going to happen, she took a turn for the worse."

"I'm so sorry, Trey," I said, and I was. So, so sorry for all the ways a few marks in a ballroom dance competition had drastically altered this many lives.

"When did you find out about Nationals?" he asked.

"Nina came to see me a couple of months after it happened. She had my medal. She was deeply apologetic about the whole thing."

"Did you think about me?" Trey asked.

"A little, but my life had changed. I was pregnant. Jason and I were engaged. It seemed like something that had happened to someone else." I plucked at a loose thread on my jeans. "I was training myself never to think of you. It was the only way I could move forward."

I shifted my gaze to Grace who'd fallen asleep, Princess Pretty clutched to her chest.

"It was awful and it was my fault, but I hadn't reached rock bottom yet," Trey said. "Because, you see, I still had hope. I had a plan. On the day the contract expired, I was going to track you down, get on a plane, apologize, beg you to come back. I wanted us to get married as soon as possible, so I couldn't lose you again.

He didn't say anything for a minute or so. "It was getting close. Just a few more months, then a few more weeks. Before I knew it, there were only days left. I was excited, like a boy before Christmas. One day before the contract expired, a courier hand-delivered a birth announcement," he said. "The words are engraved in my memory. Jason and Caroline Justus celebrate the birth of their daughter, Grace Martindale Justus."

I remembered the birth announcement. Grace, impossibly tiny in a pink cap on the front, on the back, Jason and I holding her with proud, sleepy grins.

Trey was trembling. "I've had dark days, but that was the darkest."

I reached forward and patted his arm. He grabbed my hand and kissed it. The tingle, familiar and devastating, started in my stomach. I snatched my hand back.

His eyes met mine. "It was going to be a real marriage, Carly. In every way."

"A real marriage? With you in the shower all day and pacing all night? Moldering in that mansion as the walls fell down around us?" I said in a quiet scream. "Never seeing anybody? Never doing anything? That's not a real marriage, Trey."

"I had a plan," he said. "After Nationals, I would take you somewhere beautiful, somewhere romantic. We could walk the streets hand-in-hand, and I would propose to you properly. Then there would be the tour. Different places, fresh memories. By the time we got back to Charleston, I thought things would be better. And we could work on the things that weren't better, like we did our dancing."

I gave up trying to hold the tears in, and they coursed freely. "Do you know what's missing from all your plans? Me. My needs, my wants."

His lips drooped. "You wanted to marry me."

I didn't answer Trey, just let the tears gush down my cheeks.

He gazed around at the house that was not his home, at the woman who was not his wife, at the child who was not his daughter. "I think all the time about the details I could have changed to end up somewhere different. What if I'd begun an inch further back on the floor, so I didn't get that rhinestone stuck under my shoe? What if I'd moved to a new place on the floor when Jorge and Nina set up? What if we'd taken the elevator instead of the stairs? What if I'd just told Jason no?"

I dabbed at my cheeks. "Everyone would act differently if they knew the future."

"The marks were close. Papa couldn't cook them if they weren't. Just a few more in our favor, and everything would be different."

"It doesn't matter anymore, Trey. You won your fourth Nationals. You paid off the debts. Nina told me you're Chairman of the Judges now. You're winning."

"I lost, Carly, because I didn't understand what the competition was about."

The architecture of my bones could no longer hold up my sagging muscles, and I fell back in the chair. I needed Trey gone.

"Please go," I whispered.

Trey reached into his pocket and pulled out a small black jewelry box. "One last thing."

I averted my eyes from the jewelry box. It was the threat that had been veiled as a proposal. I'd been too infatuated with Trey to appreciate the difference at the time, but I understood it now.

"I want you to have this. To thank you, to apologize." He placed it on the coffee table and slid it to me.

I pushed the box back toward him. "I can't."

"Please, Carly. I don't care what you do with it, but take it. I loved you, imperfectly, incompetently, but in the best way I knew how."

I closed my fingers around the box. "Thank you, Trey." The box warmed my hand, a hot coal uncooled by the past.

"I appreciate you seeing me." He stood and turned toward the door. Then he paused and pivoted to me. He offered me his left hand. "A dance? For old times' sake."

I balled up my fists and stuffed them into the back pockets of my jeans. "The music ran out for us a long time ago," I said, my voice pitched in a tiny, tinny key. I was trembling all over, the cells of my body vibrating like electricity. This marked the first time I'd ever told Trey no.

Trey dropped his hand and turned to the door. "Have a good life."

"You too."

He looked over his shoulder. His mask was gone and in its place hung the face of a lonely, regretful forty-year-old man. "A good life? I punch numbers into a computer, and then I drink myself to sleep."

"It doesn't have to be like that."

"I died a long time ago. I'm just helping my body to catch up."

Trey flashed me one last golden smile that didn't reach his eyes before I closed the door behind him.

Chapter 53

NINA: LET ME

JORGE and I sat side by side, cradling our cups of English Breakfast tea. It should have been awkward, but it was Jorge, the person I'd always felt comfortable with. It seemed like we'd just finished practicing and were going over our questions for Maxine, not like we hadn't seen each other in over three years.

"Can I go first?" he asked.

"Of course."

"I was pretty upset after Nationals. I'd been on top of the world, and then that world came crashing down around my feet," he said. "I didn't think. I just did. I told all the judges I could find and then I got on a plane to San Francisco. I figured I could do some good there."

I stared into my teacup. That day had been the best day and then the worst day of my life.

"How's Amber?" I asked.

"She's not great." He sighed. "The doctors keep fiddling with her meds, hoping something will work long term, but nothing has so far."

"I'm sorry to hear that."

"It was a tough couple of years. I didn't feel like I could leave her."

I wanted to hug Jorge, but I resisted.

"We danced together for twelve years and were involved for a lot of it. She's family," he said. "I was twenty-one when I moved to California, and I was blown away by Amber. She was sophisticated and educated and rich, and I was a Latino kid from the Bronx who hadn't been to college much less Europe."

Out of the corner of my eye, I drank in Jorge's profile, lingering over his skin—still warm brown like tea with a dash of milk.

"I was shocked when she liked me back."

I nodded although I didn't know what was so shocking about her liking him back. Jorge might not be rich or educated, but he was kind and smart and a hard worker. That trumped fancy degrees and bulging bank accounts any day of the week.

"But we were too different to make it work. As the years went by, our relationship got worse and worse. We'd break up, make up, and then break up again. All we did was argue. About money, about dancing, about who used all the hot water."

"That sounds rough," I said.

Jorge took a sip of tea. "It was, but I didn't know any better until I started dancing with you," he said. "Amber was jealous. Of you, of me, of our dancing. She had all this money, but she couldn't buy any of the things that she wanted."

Poor little rich girl, I thought.

He put his cup down. "I went back to California knowing I couldn't make it work with Amber. But I felt like I needed to be there for her. She'd paid for our dancing in the beginning when I was getting on my feet, and I wanted to pay her back."

Jorge ran his hands through his hair, shorter and spikier than it had been when we were dancing together. "I planned to stay until she got better, and then I'd figure things out."

"What kinds of thing?"

"You-and-me-type things," he said. "I was pissed at you, Nina. I'd told you that I loved you, and then I walk in to find you with Papa. Plus we didn't win Nationals fair and square."

I swallowed. "I'm sorry." I traced the outline of my teacup, the shame just as potent as it had been the day it happened.

"Why'd you do it?" Jorge asked. He didn't look at me.

"Papa had a thing for me. He'd had one for years. He offered to throw the competition if I would sleep with him." I clasped my hands together. "We weren't going to have a second chance. So I said yes."

Tears were welling up. "He asked me the day before. I was tired and in tremendous pain, and I wanted us to win. I wanted what it would mean for us." I closed my eyes, wishing for the umpteenth time I could go back in time and say no rather than yes. "Instead it got me nothing that I wanted," I whispered.

Jorge slung an arm over my shoulder and pulled me close. His warmth overwhelmed me, and I flung my arms around him. It might have been three-and-a-half years, but I was absolutely, completely, most definitely still in love with Jorge.

He massaged my back. "It's okay."

"Is it?"

"It is," he said. "I had a lot of time to get over it."

I relaxed into him. Jorge had such a comforting chest, broad and landscaped with so many muscles. It was nice to lean against it after all the years of standing on my own.

"I have a confession of my own," he said.

"What's that?" I peeled myself from his chest and turned to face him.

"Even if you hadn't made that deal with Papa, we were never going to win Nationals fair and square."

"Why not?"

"We were never taking Waltz or Foxtrot from Trey and Carly. The only dance we could take beyond Tango was Viennese Waltz."

"True."

He bowed his head. "I started in front of them on purpose," he said. "And then I cut them off for as long as I could."

I remembered the conversation Maxine and Jorge had before the final. "Is that what Maxine told you before the last round?" I asked.

"I don't know for sure if that's what she meant. But that's how I took it."

I placed my hand on his hand. "We wanted it too much."

"We did. And look what it got us." He switched our grip, so that he'd clamped my hand in his warm one.

"I feel terrible about what I did to Maxine. She was my coach for so many years, and look at how I paid her back."

"She understood. None of us were thinking clearly. We were too caught up in the moment." He squeezed my hand. "She's good. I call her every month. She knows I'm here. She told me to come."

"She did?" My surprise blew up the words. Maxine's magnanimity made me feel small indeed. She really was a class act.

"She wanted us to get together since our tryout." He laughed. "She told me, 'Your mother knew immediately.' Our chemistry is what gave her the idea to make each routine a story."

I smiled at the memory of that runaround. Hindsight being what is was, I wished I'd acted on my feelings a lot sooner. So much grief could have been spared.

"Papa, though, he's not doing so good," Jorge said.

"I heard."

I'd stumbled in on Ralph discussing Papa's condition over the phone. Papa had had a massive heart attack, and now he was experiencing problems with his memory. Ralph switched the subject when he saw me, but not before he'd caught sight of my face.

"I don't think he's here for much longer," Jorge said.

"Ralph went to be with them in Florida."

Ralph hadn't come right out and said this to me, but I knew Papa's poor health had accelerated his desire to sell the studio.

"That'll be good for him. All Papa remembers is the past."

We sat for a moment, holding hands, thinking about the year we'd spent dancing together.

"Why did you come now?" I asked.

"I kept waiting for Amber to get better, so I could move on. But she didn't," Jorge said. "She'd be okay for a while, but then she'd fall off a cliff. I couldn't leave her when she was in such bad shape."

I squeezed his hand.

"She's difficult, and over the years, she's lost more friends than she's made. Most of the time, the only thing she had was me, which made it even tougher to leave. Before I knew it, three-and-a-half years had passed." He sighed. "Time I couldn't get back. Time in which I did nothing beyond teach and take care of Amber."

I laid my head on his shoulder. It was a little forward, but it wasn't like Jorge didn't know that I'd been in love with him. Still loved him, if I was being honest.

"I heard through the grapevine that you were buying the Castle from Ralph. I was impressed." He ran his free hand through my hair. "You've taken some hard knocks, and you always get back up on your feet."

"Thank you."

"I still had feelings for you, so I asked around to see if you were single. When I found out that you were, I left. I couldn't do anything more for Amber. So I talked to her shrink and got some tips about how to break the news to her."

"How did she take it?"

"Not great. I didn't think that she would, but . . . " Jorge stopped, and I caressed my cheek against his shoulder. "This sounds mean, but I didn't care anymore. She'd always run hot and cold, but she'd been cold for a long time."

He pulled me away from him, so we were face-to-face. "And there was this other thing."

I waited, my breath caught in the back of my throat.

"I missed you. We never got going romantically, but I felt like it would be as easy as our partnership on the floor."

"I missed you too," I said.

"I got regrets, but my biggest one is telling you that we shouldn't get involved," he said. "I liked you right from the beginning, but I was still burnt from Amber. I wasn't up for doing it that way again. I figured we could always start up after Nationals, when we didn't have the pressure of dancing hanging over us." He squeezed his eyes shut. "I didn't expect all that stuff with Amber to happen."

I didn't care anymore. I swung my legs over Jorge's lap and buried my head against his heart. Having him here reminded me of how much better he'd made everything. The year we'd competed together had been, physically, the most grueling one I'd ever experienced, yet my spirits, until the very end had remained high. Because of Jorge.

"I miss us," I said into one of the many muscles banding his chest.

"On the outside, we're different." He grazed my hair. "Jewish Russian girl from Brooklyn." He tapped his chest. "Catholic Puerto Rican from the Bronx." He grinned at me. "But we're the same on the inside. We work hard and we try hard and we know how to make each other happy."

We gazed at each other for a moment, brown eyes meeting green, and then we erupted at the same time into a salvo of "Let me."

Whoever said let me kiss you won, because that's exactly what we did.

Chapter 54

CARLY: THE HAPPIEST I'D EVER BEEN

AFTER TREY LEFT, I held it together on the outside although my thoughts were whirling.

Did Trey really sell me to Jason?

I woke up Grace from her nap and gave her some grapes for a snack. I helped her into her coat and tied the laces on her favorite purple sneakers.

Did Jason really buy me?

I took her to the park and pushed her on the swings. I brought her home and made pasta for dinner.

Why didn't Jason tell me?

I pulled a bath for her and read a story. I tucked her under the covers and kissed her goodnight.

Once Grace's breathing evened out, I let myself into Jason's study. I'd only been in here once or twice since his death to get this file or that paper for the lawyers. I'd been putting off cleaning it out until I felt more up to the challenge.

Methodically, I flipped through Jason's folders. Mortgage papers, business dealings, our marriage certificate, Grace's birth certificate. Then my hand closed around a manila folder labeled Louis Pierre Devereux, III.

Trey.

Inside was the contract. With trembling hands, I scanned the contents. At the bottom, two signatures, Jason's vigorous scrawl and Trey's copperplate cursive, dated one day after the Nationals that Trey and I had lost and then won.

Trey hadn't lied. I didn't understand all the legalese, but the gist was clear. For a million dollars, Trey would sever all contact with me for one year.

In reality, I'd been bought and sold because no one had asked me what I wanted.

The world jerked and jittered like a plane in a bout of operatic turbulence. I curled into the fetal position, trying to settle my quivering limbs.

For long minutes, I stayed curled up, grasping for a reason, any reason, to explain why Trey and Jason reduced me to an object to be bargained over?

I struggled to my feet and found the album Jason had made me for our first wedding anniversary. There we were on our wedding day, Jason, ginning as if he'd won the lottery, in a black three-piece suit beside me in a long-sleeved white maternity dress I'd picked out myself. Another picture of Jason carrying me over the steps of our Westchester house, my belly poking out. A beach trip, my huge stomach sandwiched between the triangles of a bikini. Grace's birth announcement. Our first Christmas card, Jason and I looking goofy in Santa hats with Grace clutched between us.

Jason had been a wonderful husband, kind and generous. He'd been so easy to make happy with a joke, a kiss, a home-cooked dinner. He enjoyed easy, pleasant things, and he had few to no expectations of me.

"Whatever makes my wife happy," he'd said whenever I broached the subject of going on vacation or replacing some of his horrid black leather living room furniture.

After the year I'd spent with Trey, trying to be enough, and the year before that year, with Sam, thinking I was enough, and then all the years before that year, having to always be enough, it'd been irresistible to be loved in the way Jason loved me—fully and with no expectations of being loved back in the same way.

My blood burned. I'd told Jason how happy I was with Trey, and he'd refused to believe me because my happiness didn't look the way the world thought happiness should look. Without asking me what I wanted, without considering that he might have misunderstood, he'd wrenched Trey and me apart so thoroughly that we could never fit ourselves back together.

I sighed. After losing his first wife, Jason had become over-vigilant and read things into a situation that was too complicated for normal explanations. He'd cut in on my dance with Trey because he thought I was heading for a crash and wanted to save me, the way he couldn't before. He'd worked with what he had—his money.

"I forgive you," I whispered to the man in my wedding picture.

Then I went online until I found the video I was looking for. *Trey & Carly: Beautiful Smooth Dancing*. I gasped after I clicked on the link. The video had hits in the five digits.

I hit play.

My throat tightened. Trey was guiding me onto the dance floor as I beamed at him. We took our opening pose for Waltz, our arms overlapping garlands. By the second bar, my eyes were tearing up, and by the fourth, I was bawling, one of those ugly, honest cries where nothing could staunch the flow.

Through my tears, I saw the truth. We were gorgeous, expansive, connected, and so clean. I was prettier and a much better dancer than I'd ever given myself credit for. As for Trey, he shone, golden and stunning, the sun around which I'd revolved.

And our love. It was everywhere, in every action and each reaction. I'd always deemed our relationship lopsided. My fervor for him, so large and urgent, filled in the deficiencies of his more minor feelings for me.

But the camera didn't lie. Trey loved me, and he'd told me every time we moved together, dance position the sole place he felt safe expressing himself. The manner in which his fingers lingered on my arms, the way he'd directed the brightness of his gaze in my direction, the obvious pride he took in me when he turned me out for introductions, the tenderness in his lead. We were incandescent in our love, and it would live forever on the Internet for anyone to see.

On the video, we took our places for Viennese Waltz. As the opening notes sounded, he pulled me close. I laid my cheek on his shoulder, and he placed his head on top of mine.

"Follow me," his lips were saying. We shifted side to side, any old husband and wife slow dancing at a wedding. Then we segued into an enormous Reverse Turn, his feet crossing and then mine crossing as we engraved the floor with invisible Xs, a string of impassioned kisses.

Our bodies grew up and away from each other, but we stayed connected where it mattered most—our guts. We rotated counterclockwise, a small circle, while traveling counterclockwise around the line of dance, a big circle. Our bodies churned in these nested circles, beautifully determined and determinedly beautiful to turn back time.

Trey lifted his arm, and I whirled under, a tornado of emotion corked by technical motion. I pivoted to face him, and our eyes met. I unfolded my leg, a figure four to a number one, as Trey extended an arm behind him. His face exploded into a smile that reached his eyes where it stayed and stayed.

I buried my face in my knees. "I would have followed you anywhere," I whispered. That was the job he'd trained me to do: to trust, to interpret, to take the seed he'd given me and then nurture it to bloom.

The music swirled to an end, and we melted into our last move. Trey lunged, and I arced over one of his arms, a rose fainting in the sun. Then we bowed and walked off the floor. Trey kissed my hand and pressed it to his chest as I glowed, happy, so happy to be with him. I whispered something funny in his ear, and he laughed. On the video, people were chanting our number, *thirty-four, thirty-four, thirty-four*.

My love for him, undiminished by time, unbroken by space, poured through me and filled me so completely that I couldn't understand why we weren't together, why we hadn't always been together.

I popped open the box with Trey's grandmother's ring.

Just this once, I thought. I placed the ring on the fourth finger of my left hand. Then I answered the question I'd never let myself ask since the therapist told me it sounded like I had Stockholm syndrome.

Yes!

Then, now, forever.

If we'd won Nationals outright, I would have wanted nothing more than to follow Trey back to Charleston where we would have lived out our odd, exquisite fairy tale—a princess and her beautiful, broken prince waltzing through an antebellum castle, our moat a Line of Dance that would keep the rest of the world at bay. In that tiny world, Trey had been enough. He would always have been enough.

I took off the ring and put it into the box.

"I forgive you, too," I whispered and then closed the lid. I placed it in a lockbox next to the enormous engagement ring Jason had given me.

Maybe when Grace got older, I could show her this video and give her the ring. I would tell her about this sliver of the sun that had drifted into a world too cruel and dark for him, and how happy I'd been, the happiest I'd ever been, to bask in his presence.

Then I stamped down on my love for Trey until I'd pushed it into a dusty, far-flung corner of my heart that I wouldn't be visiting again.

When my breathing returned to normal, I wiped my eyes. It was time to study; I had a test tomorrow.

Chapter 55

NINA: THE LAST DANCE

I SMILED, glad for a moment alone. The floor buzzed with couples dancing, the good ones, the bad ones, the mediocre ones who thought they were good.

I smoothed my hair, feeling the weight of my wedding ring, a thick loop encrusted with diamonds on the fourth finger of my left hand.

My eyes sought out Jorge, my husband as of a couple of hours ago, when Nationals ended and the ballroom was restaged into a wedding. He was leading his mother into a Chasse From Promenade.

Kerplunk. He'd landed heel-toe.

He did another Chasse From Promenade.

Kerplunk.

I cringed and then laughed. Jorge might have won a Nationals Smooth title, but he was a Latin dancer at heart. I smiled as an image of him swiveling his hips in a Cucaracha popped into my head.

Jorge escorted his mother back to our table. He pulled out her chair while fussing to make sure her wine glass was full, that the waiter didn't remove her cake plate. He turned his attentions to my mother and performed the same song and dance.

I am one lucky girl, I thought as my heart swelled with love for and pride in my husband.

I touched my neck. On it, hung a slender chain of platinum adorned with a tiny diamond heart. It was from Maxine via Jorge.

"Give it to Nina," she'd said to Jorge. "You two are perfect for each other."

He did, and I'd cried.

Papa was in bad shape, so Maxine couldn't make it to the wedding.

"I'm there in spirit," she told us over the phone.

And she was. I might have lost a father as had Jorge, but we'd both gained a mother who cared for our happiness and forgiven us when we'd messed up.

From that March day when he'd surprised me at The Castle, Jorge hadn't left my side. Not that I wanted him to. Three years and change might have passed since that fateful Nationals, but when we were together, it felt like no more than a few minutes.

He'd been back in New York for a couple of months when I broached the topic of adding him as co-owner to the Castle. I was doing fine as a boss, but I was well versed in the benefits of sharing responsibility with Jorge.

I handed him the paperwork. "Let's help ourselves by helping each other."

Jorge signed it with a flourish. "The Castle now has a king and queen."

Plus there was the other reason. If Jorge and I shared business duties, then that would allow us to spend more time together outside of the studio, namely in bed, where we were making up for lost time.

It proved to be a great decision. Our business partnership worked the same as our dance partnership. We had each other's backs.

"We're in it together," he said. "Let's never forget that."

I snuggled into his warm chest. "I don't ever want to forget that."

"Nina." Carly, my maid of honor, was walking toward me with outstretched arms. She was wearing a halter-necked dress of black chiffon that floated around her slender frame. "I haven't had a chance to congratulate you properly," she said. "We were so busy with pictures and the ceremony. And since then, you've been mobbed by well-wishers."

I hugged her as I counted back time through my head. It'd been over six years since Carly had started at the Castle, but I couldn't imagine my life without her. She'd been my student and then my competitor and now she was my closest friend.

"Happy?" Carly asked.

I beamed. "We're going to start a family. Jorge wants a boy and a girl. Vernon and Irene."

"Vernon and Irene Gonzalez. The next amazing dance couple of the 21st century."

"Watch out world." I peeked through the couples on the dance floor. "I want to meet your date. What's his name again?" I'd been so busy with wedding planning that I was behind on Carly's love life beyond the fact there was a promising candidate on the horizon. Once Jorge and I got back from our honeymoon, I'd invite her into the city for some girl time.

"Dr. Joshua Goldblatt."

I raised my eyebrows. "A Jewish doctor. Mazel tov."

"I do live in Westchester, and I am pursuing a master's degree in psychology. Jewish doctors are everywhere," she said. "He's very nice, and he adores Grace." She pointed to a burly man with dark hair and a beard dancing with Grace. "He, sadly, is a terrible dancer."

The doctor, blissfully, obliviously, led Grace, poised for her age, through a clunky box.

"It's a bold choice, a Waltz to the Cha Cha."

"It took him forever to get that down. Now, it's the only thing he'll do." She smiled ruefully. "He's so proud of his box."

"How does it feel being back at Nationals?"

"Better than I thought. It's nice catching up with everyone."

"Did you see Sam?"

Carly's lips tweaked. "He hasn't changed at all. Still looking for his second wife to marry first," she said. "We did our Foxtrot from the Rising Star." She giggled. "Both of us still remembered it."

I nodded, remembering that summer when I'd introduced Sam, Carly, and myself to Smooth and all the ways it'd played out since then.

"I danced with Cyrus," Carly said. "A Mambo of all things. He's as spry as ever. And a Rumba with Ralph."

Trey's name hung heavy between us.

"Trey wanted to come. In all the years I've known him, it's the first time he's asked me for something."

Carly kept her face composed, but her eyes flashed with longing. "I wondered if I'd see him here."

"I told him no. He understood."

She bobbed her head in thanks. "How is he?" She didn't meet my eyes.

"Same old Trey. Charming, so good-looking it hurts to look at him. He's terrific as Chairman of the Judges. Every season, one of the newbies gets a huge crush on him, which he politely but adamantly deflects." I paused. "Last year, one of them sneaked into his hotel room with the intention of seducing him. Trey was livid when he found her. He wanted to ban her from competition."

Carly's face stiffened into a death mask. "He's very private."

The girl had quit, but not before she told everybody what she'd found—pictures of Carly ringing a nearly empty bottle of bourbon.

"He drinks himself to sleep every night while staring at pictures of his former dance partner." Her eyes had been wide with disbelief at the sad state of Trey's personal life.

"He's still in love with you," I said, telling her what everyone already knew.

The death mask slackened, and Carly's eyes pooled with tears. "He's in love with someone who doesn't exist anymore." She hugged herself and blinked away the tears. Then she pasted a resolute smile on her face.

And you're still in love with him, I thought. One of these days I was going to get the story of what happened between Trey and her.

Carly squared her shoulders and gave me a bright smile. "I'm so happy for you and Jorge."

She turned as Grace ran to her. "Mommy," Grace said as Carly scooped her up. The doctor appeared and draped an arm around Carly's shoulder. We exchanged introductions, and he was just as nice as Carly said he was. The doctor kissed the top of Carly's head and then led her to the dance floor.

Jorge appeared beside me. "My wife." He pulled me close, and I sank into him, still amazed to have this man as my partner.

I kissed him, a sloppy real one that ignored my lipstick and dress. "My husband."

"This is the best Nationals yet," he said once we pulled away, minutes later.

"Couldn't ask for a better one."

"Let me take you out for the last dance."

I accepted his hand, and we walked to the center. A Waltz swirled around us, the melody of the cello instructing our hearts in happiness and in sadness. Everyone found partners, some the partner, while others a partner, and we danced joyfully, sentimentally.

It wasn't proper etiquette, but I rested my head on Jorge's shoulder.

The door to the ballroom opened, and Trey slipped in, still wearing his Chairman of the Judges tuxedo. He met my eyes and inclined his head, his face betraying nothing. His eyes sought out Carly, who was valiantly trying to keep the doctor on time. The doctor whispered something in her ear. Carly threw back her head and laughed. Beside them, Grace was standing tall as she danced with Oleg's five-year-old son, Dmitri, who had Oleg's blue eyes and Ksenia's blonde hair.

Trey's face crumpled, like a little boy fighting back tears. Then he recomposed his features into their normal arrangement of indifference. He opened the door and backed out of the ballroom, his eyes still fixed on Carly before closing the door behind him.

As easy as one, two, three.

As hard as one, two, three.

Down, up, up.

Down, up, up.

All of life's peaks and valleys captured in one bar of music, a progressive wheel of fortune that only halted when the music ran out.

We moved as a mass, toward no destination, because life, like Line of Dance, is a circle. We wound around it with hearts turned toward our partner, each time filled with hope founded on prior experience. We danced our best and we tried our hardest, but it was the doing and the being rather than the winning that mattered because life, like dance, required saying yes to the invitation.

Step in to step out.

THE END

Author's Notes

OR WHY I WROTE IT LIKE THIS

The Structure of *The Winner*

I employed dual narrators to underscore the setting of ballroom dance. Ballroom dance unfolds on two floors: the social and the competitive. My hope is that two narrators would allow the reader to "dance" with more than protagonist plus act as a judge to decide who, exactly, is the winner of *The Winner*.

Siblings of Individuals with Autism

At the time of writing, most scientific research has been directed toward the individual with autism rather than his or her siblings. My inspiration for Carly stemmed from Dr. Ranit Mishori's article in The Washington Post about growing up with an autistic brother. In fashioning Carly's story, I also leaned on Andrew Solomon's *Far from the Tree* and many first-person narratives gleaned from the Internet.

As Dr. Stephen Shore says, "If you've met one person with autism, you've met one person with autism." I feel families are much the same way. My depiction of Carly and her family is not meant to be interpreted as universal. Instead, I hoped to suggest that siblings of autistic individuals might benefit from more research and resources.

Fact versus Fiction in *The Winner*

It proved untenable to accurately reflect the complexity and liveliness of ballroom dancing due to the constraints of the narrative form—specifically word count. As such, my goal was to evoke but not represent the world of competitive ballroom dancing. I stayed as true as I could to the physical experience of dancing, mine as well as those alongside whom I danced, with the caveat that words can never capture nor reveal embodied sensation. I hope ballroom dance practitioners will understand and forgive the changes I made in service of the story.

~The countrywide ballroom event is called United States Dance Championships, more commonly referred to as USDC. I dubbed it Nationals to avoid the clumsiness of an acronym and to stress the opportunity to be the best in the United States. I moved the event to New York, its original location, from Florida, its current location, for simplicity in the narrative.

~It is impossible to overstate the influence that Eastern European individuals have exercised over ballroom dancing in the United States. A cursory glance at any professional final reveals the plethora of Eastern European competitors. As for timing, *The Winner* is set in what's called the "eternal present" in storytelling parlance; however, the Russian Invasion occurred in the late '90s and early aughts.

~I removed the word International before Standard and Latin and the word American before Smooth—the official names—to avoid slowing down the prose with an unnecessary modifier. Since writing, Standard has been renamed Ballroom (as in International Ballroom).

~It takes years to become a proficient ballroom dancer, much less a champion. The idea that a dancer could go from training class, even one with a dance background like Carly's, to Open Professional champion in a little over two years is unlikely. The progress of Jorge and Nina from new partners to top contenders in a year is also unlikely although more possible since they're seasoned competitors. I sped up all the timelines to increase the dramatic tension.

~The Castle is made up, but Vernon and Irene Castle were real people. Turn-of-the-century dance icons, their story was made into a movie featuring Fred Astaire and Ginger Rogers.

~The judging system of ballroom dance is different and significantly more transparent than I portray here with all judges' marks posted after competitive events. The Chairman of the Judges is the individual who oversees the judging panel; I folded into it the job of the Scrutineer, which is the person who uses the judges marks to come up with the final placings. Usually, each competition has different Chairman of the Judges and Scrutineers. I combined the jobs and made it a singular position for the sake of intrigue.

~Although I clearly delineated judges from coaches, in the world of competitive ballroom dancing, coaches judge and judges coach. I made this distinction to avoid a lengthy discussion on these dubious ethics.

~Rule Eleven is commonly invoked to arbitrate a tie. In it, all the placed marks from the tied couples are processed as a single dance. It is common in American Smooth, the only division with four dances.

~Trey's perfection is an exaggeration, architected by me for several reasons. First, I didn't want to overburden the text with more dance terminology. Second, I hoped to highlight Carly's naivety when it came to Trey. Lastly, I wanted to emphasize the dissonance between Trey's flawless outer demeanor and inner turmoil.

~I strove to align all steps and techniques with the Imperial Society of Teachers of Dancing syllabus. All choreography is mine although anyone familiar with the ethos of American Smooth will recognize the elements as common in competitive routines.

~To my knowledge, no one approaches ballroom dance routines as a narrative unless it's for a show dance. Most Smooth couples put together routines that combine open and closed work to show off the couple's technical prowess and personal style. To create contrast, both between the dancing and the love interests, I borrowed an idea from the visual and performing arts—the Apollonian and the Dionysian, based on features of Greek mythology. The Apollonian is light, reasoned, structured, and controlled while the Dionysian is emotional, enthusiastic, dramatic, and sensual. To help the reader visualize the dancing, I expanded this notion. Trey and Carly's ethos leaned toward an abstract distillation of a dance, which is more typical in the ballroom dance field, while Jorge and Nina's routines were a narrative, something more associated with concert dance.

~No one goes into competitive ballroom dancing for the money although many individuals have successfully monetized their wins after the fact. At the time of writing, winning a Professional Open division in the United States nets a couple in the low four figures. This is minus the considerable expense it takes to get to that level. I invented the enormous financial gain to give Trey a plausible reason for returning to the dance floor.

Thanks!

Thank you, thank you, thank you for reading *The Winner: A Ballroom Dance Novel.* Words only quicken to life when read, and I am so grateful to you for reading. If you found the book to be a four- or five-star reading experience, then I would be delighted by and deeply appreciative of a review and/or rating on the website at which you purchased the novel. A recommendation to a reader whom you think would enjoy the book would also be welcomed. If you have a critique or would like to offer suggestions for improvement, I hope you'll contact me at erin@erinbomboy.com with them; I'm constantly trying to improve my craft and create a meaningful, enjoyable experience for readers.

If you would like to read more of my writing, my acutely dark, brutal, and provocative book, *The Piece: A Contemporary Ballet Novel,* is available for purchase. A short excerpt of it immediately follows this. My next novel, tentatively titled *The Pas de Deux: A Classical Ballet Novel,* will explore the relationship between a ballerina at the end of her career and the much-younger dancer with whom she falls in love. Taking the shape of a traditional pas de deux, it will premiere in 2018.

Please visit me at erinbomboy.com to learn more.

About the Author

A native of Richmond, Virginia, Erin Bomboy trained as a classical ballet dancer before spending a decade as a professional competitive ballroom dancer. She holds an MFA in Dance Performance and Choreography from New York University Tisch School of the Arts. She lives in New York City with her husband and daughter where she works as a writer, editor, and teacher in the dance field. In her free time, Erin enjoys bacon, books, cats, and wine.

She is the author of *The Piece: A Contemporary Ballet Novel* and *The Winner: A Ballroom Dance Novel*. Her next novel, tentatively titled *The Pas de Deux: A Classical Ballet Novel,* will explore the relationship between a ballerina at the end of her career and the much-younger dancer with whom she falls in love. Taking the shape of a traditional pas de deux, it will premiere in 2018.

www.erinbomboy.com/
erin@erinbomboy.com

Also by Erin Bomboy

The Piece: A Contemporary Ballet Novel

Their eyes met through the heat and glare as their hearts crisscrossed from stage to pit. Only good things could happen. Right?

Against the pitched backdrop of pointe shoes and bloody blisters, Elinor Roth confronts her decaying dream. She is unlikely to become a leading ballerina. Longing for affection, she leaps into the arms of Jon Hansen, a seemingly nice music conductor. When the fling ends, Elinor abandons her stalling ballet career and moves to New York.

The city's contemporary dance scene stirs her imagination, and she enters into a showcase that will launch her as a visionary choreographer. Unable to forget Elinor, Jon joins her and struggles to become a composer. Soon, he grows dependent on Elinor for inspiration and alarmed by her dwindling affection.

Determined to keep Elinor as his muse, Jon devises a plan to take her far away from dance. When she uncovers his deceit, Elinor must decide how far she will blur the line between life and art.

Acutely dark, brutal, and provocative, *The Piece* explores the manipulation of honesty, the perpetuation of trauma, and artistic obsession. Designed for readers who appreciate moral complexity, it combines the dance setting of *Black Swan* with the domestic noir of *The Girl on the Train* and *Gone Girl*.

"A compellingly vivid story highly recommended for romance readers seeking more depth from their stories than most romance genre novels offer"

Midwest Book Review

Available for purchase

The Pas de Deux: A Classical Ballet Novel

Set among the palm trees and glam metal scene of '80s Hollywood, a ballet company fights for its survival: its superstar Robert Winslow is dying of AIDS, aging ballerina Peridot "Peri" Jones has lost her glitter, and Armenian artistic director Mr. D hasn't had a hit in years, leading the company into financial ruin.

Mr. D casts whiz-kid Mark Maroulis Jr, a baseball player's son, as the lead in a new ballet. A chance dance between Mark and Peri ignites an intense chemistry that she, the lover and muse of Mr. D, can't ignore. Against better reason, Mark and Peri fall in love, even as Mr. D plots to tear them apart.

Coming in 2018

Made in the USA
San Bernardino, CA
12 December 2017